THE LIFE OF ROSIE

Somebody is watching me. I can sen[se?]
it is. My movements are becoming sti[ff as it creeps?]
into my consciousness. As I am in a c[rowded?]
department store, move towards the s[helves and?]
pretend to study the racks of clothing [as somebody?]
enters behind me. Nobody appears to be suspicious so after a few minutes I move cautiously along the perimeter intending to exit through another doorway. I linger in the store longer than necessary trying to look nonchalant but reluctant to leave the security of the store.

At the opposite end of the store is a second exit, I cautiously go outside and continue my business. As my lunch break is nearly over I return to work and try to dismiss the incident from my mind. In the afternoon I accompany a colleague to a meeting out of town. She gave me a lift home so I did not leave at the usual time. As it gets dark early in winter I drew the blinds and settled down for the evening. In the morning I dashed to the bus stop because I slept a bit longer than usual. As I boarded the bus I felt a sense of being observed again.

I wondered why anybody would want to watch me. There was nothing remarkable about my appearance, I dressed plainly and had no claim to fame or fortune. Nobody would mistake me for a dolly bird so what was the attraction? Perhaps I had inadvertently attracted the attention of a stalker. Why me? Why anybody? Did the observer not have a life to conduct? If this continued to happen I would have to report the situation although I lacked proof or identity. There was no doubt in my mind that this was happening deliberately.

When I was asked to go to the cinema with friends I worried about returning home alone in the dark so asked someone to accompany me and stay over. I rarely went out at night and ensured I returned from work while people were about. For a few days I had peace and thought my imagination had been in overdrive. However, when I went to do my weekly shop at the supermarket the sensation returned. Stopping with my trolley on a highly stacked aisle I waited but nobody suspicious came. The stalker waited so I decided to wait too until one of my neighbours came by so we walked around together.

After feeling watched intermittently over a few days I thought about reporting it but lacked evidence or substance. I wanted a friend to observe me when possible but before I could make arrangements the feeling stopped and life continued in its usual format for about a month. This made me question my previous inkling, perhaps I had been imagining the sensation. There was no reason to take an interest in me, no broken romance or unacknowledged pledges. When I went out I viewed my surroundings with caution but saw nothing suspicious. A feeling of unease permeated my consciousness, but after some time I resumed my life trying to change my routines to avoid predictability when possible.

A local gym offered self-defence classes so I joined. My reflexes were slow and clumsy but I persevered. The teacher had patience and told me to practice at home. We dealt with possible forms of attack provided I didn't freeze with fear. To prevent this we drilled various positions and remedies until it became second nature. My instructor told me to keep a record of dates and times I felt watched. It was also essential I varied my routine as much as possible. I researched online for surveillance miniature cameras that could be attached discreetly to view behind me. Before I could investigate further the surveillance feeling stopped for a while.

During the summer when the days were long I enjoyed outings and adventures usually with friends. As winter approached and days drew shorter, I felt uneasy venturing out alone at night and had a doorbell installed showing who was ringing. It was during the short days that I felt I was being watched again. This alarmed me because it was difficult to see who the perpetrator was. Sometimes I stopped and tried to view from shop windows who was around me. The temptation was to stop and look around me but I did not want to encourage the watcher by revealing I knew.

THE LIFE OF ROSIE

There was no pattern or consistency to the surveillance so I had to rely on my sixth sense whenever I went out. Alarmed and uncomfortable I kept a record and felt relieved to arrive home safely. In the news there were constant violent incidents of stabbings and attacks which was not reassuring. I was also wary of potential attacks by close contact such as injections or knock out masks so kept my distance from strangers. I thought about moving but my mortgage was affordable plus the route was convenient for work. A surveillance guy came to check out my home security and I followed his recommendations.

This situation affected my life and confidence. Instead of being carefree and enjoying myself, I was always anxious about background interest. I hoped in time my stalker would lose interest in me and move away. Whilst I did not wish somebody else to suffer, I fervently hoped that the stalker would find my life boring and stop. My cousin visited me for a long weekend and when we emerged one afternoon, she also became aware of being watched. Unlike me she turned around gazing in all directions and thought she may have glimpsed somebody in another building watching. Perhaps he had binoculars but before she could check he vanished and she was not sure which window it was.

We scanned the surrounding buildings and tried to ascertain where she had seen somebody briefly. It did not occur again during her stay but she wrote an affirmation on my record sheet with the date and time. Each time I emerged or came home I scanned the building but did not see anyone. There was less surveillance for a short time but it did not go away. I decided to make a statement at my local police station to open a file for the record. Taking with me the sheet containing my experiences, I explained that although I had no evidence, I wanted them to open a file in case the situation deteriorated.

They noted that my cousin had also experienced the sensation of being observed but told me there was not much they could do as they were understaffed and had heavy workloads tackling serious crime. They sympathised with my plight and gave me sound advice and tips plus an emergency number to ring if required. One of their suggestions was to wear an emergency phone device to press if anything happened. I thought those phones were used for people with disabilities but agreed to sign on to feel secure. Much of their advice I was doing already.

On my way home I felt better but as I drew near my place the feeling of being watched began. I ordered the emergency phone as soon as I got in. Leaning out of my window I scrutinised the road taking photos but there was nobody suspicious and nobody at the windows opposite. Instinctively I felt the perpetrator was still out there waiting silently in the shadows. Although I longed to shout or scream abuse to release my inner tension, I restrained myself and had a brandy. I seriously considered getting somebody to share my house but preferred my privacy. If I had a live in partner, my life may be a bit easier. I locked myself in each day, closed the blinds and tried to distract myself with Netflix.

I bought some binoculars and scanned my area discreetly through my blinds before venturing out. For a while nothing seemed to happen as I tried to vary my movements to change my timetables. My annual two week holiday enabled me to escape for a while. By the time I returned rested and refreshed I had forgotten my precautions and resumed my lifestyle. It was a shock to feel I was being watched again. Standing still leaning on a wall I pulled out my mobile and pretended to be listening to a call while I scanned my surroundings. Apart from a hint of slight movement from one of the buildings, I could not see anybody. The feeling of surveillance continued.

Wondering what I could do about the situation I scrolled on the internet to check out other experiences to seek a solution. I also contacted my trainer to book in more defence lessons. There were some organisations to contact for help and advice. It also suggested that: "Some people become stalkers because they feel like they've been mistreated in some way. These stalkers often have some form of mental illness, experience feelings of paranoia or persecution, and can be self-righteous and self-pitying. Stalking the victim can be a way to get revenge for their perceived mistreatment." Some stalkers were described as ex suitors or known people." This did not seem to fit my case but I could not be certain.

I read that some stalkers use technology, like hidden cameras or global positioning systems (GPS), to track where you go Therefore I checked all my shoes, clothing and devices but could not find anything. As I used mainly public transport I could not be traced via my car which was parked at my parents' house. My dad checked it over for me but said it was sound. Surveillance around my house was restricted to the new camera system I had installed which recorded anyone approaching. It seemed that laws do not stop most stalkers. Studies of stalkers indicate that they stop when their target is no longer available to them, or they find someone else to harass. Once I contacted the various help sites online I felt more comfortable as people were aware of my situation.

Wondering if I had inadvertently upset anyone I knew, I failed to come up with anybody. My neighbours were on nodding terms, we greeted each other cordially but were not intimate. Working full time meant little free time to socialise locally. As my friends lived in different areas, we tended to meet in central locations. Online I had a list of contacts and friends but did not post constantly. If any strangers contacted me I generally ignored them or responded briefly. Phishing media got blocked. Therefore, I could not think who could be watching me or why. Perhaps somebody housebound watched me going out but that would not account for surveillance outside.

While I had some free time to think I considered potential stalker situations.

- Perhaps it was somebody housebound in the neighbourhood who watched people. This had to be discounted because I had been watched in several locations so made a note to write down the location next to the date and timing.

- A secret admirer

THE LIFE OF ROSIE

This had to be discounted because I had no indication or logical prospect of that.

- Perhaps I resembled somebody else, we are all supposed to have a double
Why not tell me then?

- It could be somebody crazy hopefully with no harm intended

Each time I left my home I felt uneasy and wary until I felt safe again somewhere. It became part of my persona. If strangers approached me or made small talk I scrutinised them to check out their intentions. At this rate I had no chance of meeting someone special. Asking "why me?" did not provide me with any answers. My hope was that somebody liked watching people and I had somehow come into their line of vision. Perhaps the stalker was busy watching others too. Whoever was doing this must have a life to lead, somewhere to go or be, so thankfully was unable to devote much time to this. My fervent hope was that no contact would be made as I did not wish to be kidnapped or murdered.

Life was challenging and rarely ran smoothly. I had to work from home to have repairs done. The workman had to show me his credentials before I let him in. When I explained my situation he said he would look around outside for me whenever he came and departed. Of course while the workman was there nothing happened. However, I could not relax my guard. The chat help line people maintained regular contact and reassured me by their caring attitude. To be honest I did not see anybody unusual or unknown who took any interest in me. As I sort of blended in rather than attracting attention, it did not surprise me that I normally passed by unnoticed. As I had taken all the precautions I could and maintained contact with the helpline, I thought I needed somebody to shadow me when I felt watched.

For a time I felt easy and hoped the stalker had lost interest. Going about my life felt comfortable but I still remained vigilant. Although I wanted a relationship I was wary about making contact with strangers. My friends met in a flexible group. When somebody was dating that person could join in or the couple went elsewhere together. Sometimes friends of the group joined us so we had a wide circle to share drinks with or have a laugh. One of the group called Ed who was a friend of a friend lived in my neighbourhood so offered to accompany me home. This was reassuring and felt unthreatening so when we were both present Ed took me home. We chatted easily en route and became friends.

I told Ed about my stalker experience and he was alarmed and protective telling me to call him at any time if I felt threatened. This was comforting and reassuring. Ed was a builder handyman working for himself successfully. He had more work than he could manage so employed some contractors when the need arose. At present Ed was into property and hoped to establish a portfolio in time. Purchasing properties to renovate then sell on, he could turn his hand to most trades impressively. He was confident and good company but there was no romance. Apparently Ed's former girlfriend had broken his heart so he was wary of relationships and unwilling to try again. Instead he rang me sometimes to go to the movies or out for a drink. We had casual dates when although I tried to look my best there was no response from Ed. It made for a relaxing companionship and he always took me home. I never felt watched when Ed accompanied me.

Inadvertently Ed's former girlfriend saw him with me and felt jealous so they got back together. It must have worked out because they got engaged. I was unable to sweep a guy off his feet yet. Perhaps somebody out there would fall for me one day but I did not know how to meet him. In my mum's day there were clubs and dances. These days there were dating sites which I did not trust. Getting chatted up in a bar was risky because drinks could be spiked and you could not let a stranger take you home. Some couples met through work or activities. My best bet would be through some regular activity to get to know the person, or perhaps an introduction. There was no easy way. As far as I could tell there were no suitable eligible bachelors in my neighbourhood.

Casual sex and drugs seemed to abound as normal. I hated drunken men looking for an easy woman. My defence lessons surfaced on any such occasions and I ensured my practice continued at the gym. Although my stalker seemed to have given up perhaps because of the dark winter evenings, I remained vigilant. These days if my eyes met a stranger's across the room, I would worry if he turned out to be my stalker. I blame the movies and romantic stories giving false expectations. Was there somebody special for everybody? Naturally I had my dream list of specifications detailing appearance, personality etc. How to find him was the hard part. Did he even exist? If he did would he be attracted to me? Day dreaming sessions created ideal imaginary scenarios.

At work my male colleagues were either too young or spoken for. We got on well together but that was it. Except for team occasions we did not socialise. My friends had boyfriends that came and went, a couple were serious and would probably marry. It was hard to meet someone because since the Covid lockdowns, people were going out less. With the cost of living rising constantly it was cheaper to drink indoors. Pubs were closing and town centre hotspots attracted the students and youngsters. On previous occasions town had been buzzing with excitement. I rarely went unless my destination was centred there. Drunken revellers were unappealing, perhaps I was getting too old for these things.

My friend Sue had been living with her partner Graham for a few years. When they decided to marry, I was invited to the wedding. At the reception I sat next to Lee who asked me where I had bought my dress.

"Why do you want to know?" I asked surprised.

THE LIFE OF ROSIE

"I'm in the business and you are wearing one of our stock dresses so I am curious to know whether you bought it online or from a department store," he told me.

"Well that's an original way to start a conversation! Are you with a fashion company?" I asked.

"I run a wholesale outlet selling to fashion companies. You still haven't told me."

"I bought it from Kenton's and thought it would be suitable for special occasions."

"Good, it suits you. I noticed you immediately when you came in."

"Were you at the service?" I asked.

"Yes, at the back because I got stuck in traffic road works."

"It all went well for them."

"So far yes, this is the easy bit."

"They have lived together for a few years so should know what they are getting into."

"Marriage is not easy."

"Are you speaking from experience?"

"Yes, unfortunately. I was married briefly to a woman who changed from an angel to a demanding shrew."

"Not all women are like that."

"I should hope not so I have put it down to experience. Have you been married?"

"Not yet, I haven't found my Mr Right."

"I hope you are not seeking perfection," he smiled cynically.

"Of course not, that would be boring. Everybody has pluses and minuses."

"So what are yours?"

"That's personal."

"Ok is that because I am a stranger?"

"Only partly, I have been troubled by a stalker so am reluctant to reveal information about myself."

"Really? How terrible. Do you know who the stalker is?"

"Not yet but I am extra cautious these days."

"Have you reported it?"

"Of course and I am online with helpful sites. I keep a record of incidents."

"Does that frighten you?"

"Of course, I do self-defence classes."

"Goodness, I can accompany you when you go home if that helps."

"It's ok thanks, tonight I am staying over at a friend's place."

We chatted and danced spending a pleasant evening together. There was no chemistry but he was good company. I enjoyed the evening and slept in my friend Ava's spare room. It was a warm evening so I opened the window and lay listening to the street noises taking a long time to fall asleep. Perhaps it was too much excitement from the wedding or the unaccustomed wine and champagne, but I found it hard to relax although I felt tired. The bed was comfortable and I felt safe as I slowly drifted off.

Footsteps were following me. I could hear somebody getting closer and I felt afraid. It was dark on an empty road. There were no houses just closed shops. I felt hot then cold with fear penetrating my ability to think. Telling myself to remember my defence classes did not help as I felt almost paralysed with fear. Should I turn around? Instead I crossed over. The footsteps crossed over too and sounded loud. As they seemed to approach panic set in. Unable to run or move faster I took out my mobile to call for help. My breathing increased, I felt hot and wondered whether my end was nigh. As I tried to control myself I woke up sweating. At first I did not know where I was. The relief to find myself safe in bed was amazing. Switching the light on I drank some water from the bedside glass then lay still until I dozed off again.

In the morning I slept later than usual probably due to my nightmare. After a late breakfast I headed home making plans to meet Ava during the week. My social life was flexible and usually evolved spontaneously. Apart from holidays I rarely planned in advance. Most of the time was taken up by work and catching up on chores. There was not much time nor energy for adventures. There was time to devote to personal choices but I seemed to be stuck in a rut unable to figure out what appealed to me. Ambition, finance or advancement were alien to me. While I earned enough to support myself, I lacked all inclination to push myself to achieve more or work overtime to grow my role. At home time I was off and always tried to be punctual.

While shopping in my local supermarket after work one evening I noticed a crowd of shoppers surrounding the fish counter. A cookery demonstration was just ending and the shoppers surged to get special offer salmon packs. Thinking that would make a tasty meal I moved forwards and as the area cleared leaned forward to pick up the last pack just as a hand reached out to grab it pushing me onto the edge of the counter. Indignantly I pushed back still holding onto the packet and confronted a tall man who was also holding the packet.

"What shall we do?" he asked me holding tight.

"Do you always push people out of the way?"

"Sorry about that, are you ok?" he asked smiling.
"What if I am not?" I argued.

We were both holding onto the last pack awkwardly.

"Shall we share it?" he asked me.

"How do you propose to do that?"

"I'll ask the fishmonger to cut it in half."

"There are two slices in there."

"Well he can separate them. If you want I will cook it for you."

"No thanks, I am not dining with strange men."

"Ok I am Tony Jenson, pleased to meet you."

Sighing with annoyance I told him to get the pack divided. He dutifully went over to the fishmonger to explain. Instead the fishmonger made a second package with two slices which Tony handed to me.

"Thank you," I said sarcastically, rubbing my shoulder.

"Did I hurt you?" he asked apologetically.

"Never mind," I said turning away.

"Will you not tell me your name before you go? I told you mine."

Tutting I said Rosie Jones," before turning away.

"Can I buy you a coffee to make amends Rosie Jones?" he said following me.

At that moment I felt dry and needed a drink so as the instore café was public and handy, I reluctantly agreed. We wheeled our trolleys over then I sat down while he ordered. From behind he looked tall and fit, I had not studied his face or overall appearance. When he returned with two coffees I noticed that he was attractive rather than handsome with a clear complexion and a warm smile. We paused while we sipped. I waited for questions or polite conversation but none was forthcoming. This was fine with me and I relaxed when a colleague at work greeted me and asked to be introduced to my boyfriend. Tony winked at me so I introduced them and sighed when she moved on.

"Now I'll get an inquisition at work," I grumbled.

"So what, there's nothing wrong with dating and you could do worse!"

"I have only just met you and we are not dating."

"Not yet I agree but we could get to know each other to see if it would be suitable."

"Do you always pick up women in supermarkets? Once you have overwhelmed them you probably hope for a submission?"

"It depends on the supermarket. Only joking, I went to investigate the scene and leaned forward too much. We both had the same idea."

"I think I got there before you."

"Only marginally, I was right behind you."

"See behind is the issue. Anyway we have both got salmon now so it doesn't matter."

"How will you cook yours?" he asked.

"Grilled with lemon juice."

"What will you make with it?"

"Are you into cooking?" I stalled.

"I enjoy good food, my salmon will be delicious and very special."

"Why?"

"Stick around and I will show you."

"I will just take your word for it."

"Do you shop here every week?"

"More or less because it is convenient."

"On the same day?"

"Not always but more or less after work if I am free."

"Ok then let's meet up again same time next week. Your turn to get the coffee next time. I've got to go now lots to do. See you here then," he said rising abruptly and he was off to the checkout.

Surprised by the experience I was unable to respond thinking there was a whole week to decide whether or not I would appear. It had made my shopping experience interesting and Tony seemed unconventional but pleasant enough. We knew nothing about each other except that we would both be eating salmon for dinner. There were far worse first meetings in my past. Amused I joined another checkout queue and watched Tony disappear. He loaded his shopping into a range rover car and drove off. At home I cooked some new potatoes and peas to accompany my salmon and wondered what Tony's special version contained. The salmon tasted fresh and it was delicious. I treated myself to a fancy dessert cake to finish off. It made a pleasant end to the day and upon reflection I laughed at my diversion. We must have looked ridiculous both latched onto one tray of salmon.

Owing to the mundane routine lifestyle I was leading, when the shopping date came round I found myself attending with enthusiasm. Trying to look nonchalant I got there a bit earlier armed with a shopping list so that I would not look desperate. Heading around the deli counter I bumped into Tony who had stocked his trolley already.

"Couldn't you wait to see me?" he asked grinning.

"You are early and this is not the café," I huffed.

"Have you tried this and this?" he asked putting two pots into my trolley.

"Hold on, not so fast, I may not like this."

"Yes you will, they are delicious. It's your turn to get the coffee."

"I haven't finished my shopping yet," I protested as he headed towards the café pulling my trolley along as well.

This man took big strides and I found myself following him rapidly to keep my shopping in view. He parked the trolleys outside the café then chose a table. I asked about his coffee choice. While I queued he read the free newspaper. I had to admit this man was different from guys that hung out in bars. When I returned with the coffees he read part of an article out to me indignantly about some political correctness issue.

"The world has gone mad with all this nonsense," he remarked.

"Everything is upside down," I agreed.

We then discussed ethics, moral guidance, lack of religious education and belief systems in general. Before our discussion became too heated we remembered we still needed to do our shopping. As we regained our trolleys I asked him if his salmon meal had been delicious.

"Absolutely, you will have to try my recipe some time. I won't see you next week, I've got something on," he said heading away before I could answer.

The rest of my shopping did not take long and when I reached my checkout Tony was just finishing further along. He waved to me and left before I was ready. We had still not exchanged any personal details. I only knew his name and when he shopped. Perhaps it was more interesting that way. It was certainly a different experience and made shopping fun. Perhaps he lived locally too which would be handy if anything developed. If he was already married or with someone I doubted whether he would be having coffee with me. In any event I felt safe in the supermarket. It also took my mind off my stalker.

On my way to the supermarket the following week, I parked my car then cut through the park behind to post a birthday card. As I was returning I heard footsteps behind me making a distinctive sound. I quickened my pace noticing there was nobody around and the light was fading. Suddenly I felt afraid because nobody knew where I was. Tony would not be in the supermarket either just when he could have been handy. Not daring to run or turn around I walked briskly then as I approached the car park the footsteps stopped abruptly. When I turned around nobody was there. It was disconcerting. Looking around the trees and bushes I could not see anybody hiding. In the safety of the supermarket I shopped quickly without stopping for coffee and hurried home.

With no arrangement for the following week I decided to go at the usual time to see if Tony showed up. There was no sign of him so I shopped and went home. It occurred to me that I had become a creature of habit doing the same routines each week. My life had become mundane and predictable which eased pressure but was not stimulating. I really needed to get a grip on myself and be more adventurous. Maybe the stalker would get bored watching me. If I didn't vary my patterns I would be an easy target. Deciding to go to the supermarket one more time as usual, I was pleased to see Tony shopping. He waved and came over asking if I had missed him.

"Maybe a bit," I said shrugging but grinning.

"Let's catch up over coffee, my turn, see you when you finish at the café," he said striding away.

Over coffee I discovered he lived locally, he had been to Cornwall to visit his mother for her birthday, he was a planning officer contributing to the development of our city by balancing land demand with community needs. When questioned he told me his job involved determining whether a housing project was suitable for a particular location. Also he had to ensure environmental conservation during industrial development. His degree accredited by the Royal Town Planning Institute (RTPI). included: planning, environment and development, city and regional planning. To counteract his work he was into music and played the guitar.

"I used to be in a group and we got gigs before we split up to go our separate ways," he told me proudly.

THE LIFE OF ROSIE

"What were you called?"

"The Best."

"Really?"

"These days I enjoy cooking what about you?"

"What about me?"

"Now I have answered your inquisition it's your turn."

"I live locally too, work for the tax office and write poems when I feel creative."
"Why do you charge so much tax?"

"First, I don't set the tax codes, second not enough people pay."

"Do you enjoy your work?"

"No, but it pays my way and is steady."

"Is there something else you could find to achieve your potential?"

"I am still working out what my potential might be. Meanwhile I have set hours and don't do overtime. My colleagues are ok and I can handle the workload."

"Is that enough for you?"

"Life is expensive these days and getting worse. Jobs are scarce and it is hard to change. There is too much competition."

"Well if you are satisfied with it then carry on."

"I am not satisfied personally but sensibly it is a means to keep me afloat."

"Can you advance?"

"With more responsibility and pressure plus extra red tape you mean."

"Ok I get it, you will stay there until a better opportunity presents itself."

"I don't plan on staying there until retirement but the economy is in a mess so right now I need stability."

"Fine."

"Do you like your job?"

"Most of the time, I get to go out and about sometimes and meet people."

We finished our coffee so he stood up and asked: "same time next week?"

"I suppose it's my turn then," I said wondering what he did the rest of the week.

We had not discussed any personal matters such as partners or obligations, families or interests. Perhaps these coffee breaks would reveal more in time. Ignorance was bliss so the saying goes. If we became more friendly I could tell him about my stalker because I did not think it was him. He could maybe accompany me to my car after shopping when the dark nights kicked in. By now he had become a familiar acquaintance rather than a stranger so I felt more relaxed around him. Tony gave no indication he was interested in me. Some people liked talking to strangers so I was probably unthreatening and handy. Even without any advancement it felt better than being chatted up in a bar.

THE LIFE OF ROSIE

The following week we met in the café and Tony asked me if I liked movies.

"Yes if suitable."

"Somebody at my work is raising money for Children in Need charity by showing 'Star Wars' at the Odeon cinema."

"I don't know if I saw that," I told him.

"Really! I thought everybody had seen it."

"Perhaps I saw clips of it but I can't remember."

"Would you like to go?"

"If it's for charity I could but I would need you to accompany me home afterwards."

"I can do. Are you afraid of the dark?"

"No but I am being followed by a stalker at times."

"How long has this been going on?"

"For months now on and off."

"Have you reported it to the police?"

"Yes and I am in touch with various helplines."

"Do you know who the stalker is?"

"No, I have only heard footsteps and felt myself being watched but I haven't seen anyone yet."

"Right well if you want to go I will certainly take you home. Do you work in town?"

"Yes, I could meet you after work if you want."

"We could get something to eat then go to see the film," Tony suggested.

"Fine."

"So do you consider me to be a stranger?"

"A bit strange yes, but I am getting used to you."

I enquired about his marital status to ensure he was single. We did not discuss family situations at this stage. It was more an outing between friends rather than a date so I did not feel pressurised. On the day I applied fresh makeup and sprayed perfume before leaving work. We strolled around the city centre and went to a café for food. There was just time to go for a pub drink before the cinema. During the time before the movie we tried to put the world to rights. Our conversation flowed easily and there were no awkward moments. Walking next to Tony felt pleasing because he was so tall, I felt safe. Nobody followed us to the cinema when we queued to enter. I offered to pay for my ticket but Tony refused telling me to put something into the charity box instead. He nodded to a few people in the entrance and we sat in the back stalls. The cinema filled up quickly and we settled down to watch. It was not really my type of movie but I enjoyed the ambience and the excitement of the younger members of the audience.

Tony drove me home and asked whether we should car share going to work in the mornings. One car would be easier to park than two. I thought it was a good idea but it wouldn't work as we both finished at different times so needed to get back. After thanking him for taking me, Tony said he would wait to see me go inside. He looked around the neighbourhood but we couldn't see much as it was cold, quiet and dark. We arranged to meet at the supermarket again. It seemed to have become routine with turns at buying the coffee. I parked on the supermarket car park and nipped round the shops to do a few errands. Walking back I was conscious of loud footsteps following me. A lady was sweeping her front step and garden path.

"Hi," I said walking down her path then whispered softly to her. "Pretend that you know me please, I think I am being followed."

The lady took my arm to pretend to greet me and looked over my shoulder. We heard the footsteps cross over the road. When we both looked a man was walking down the street with a walking stick. He entered one of the houses. Nobody else was visible. I explained that I had a problem with a stalker. She told me Mr Jones was the old gentleman with the stick who was not fit enough to be a stalker. We both studied the landscape which was turning dusk but there was nobody suspicious. I thanked her for her courtesy and headed back to the supermarket. The lady stood guard at her gate to watch me go. When I arrived at the car park I waved. Tony was angry when I told him what had happened offering to accompany me in future.

"This stalker has great disappearing skills. I hear him but don't see him."

"You should get a camera hidden in the back of your coat, we should see what can be arranged. One of my mates is good with technology, I will ask him."

"Could it be effective if it was small and inconspicuous?"

"Let's see," he said offering to buy me a cake to get over the shock.

We chatted casually and Tony made me laugh accompanying me to my car when we parted. It was not possible to get together for the following two weeks as I had a drinks birthday session after work for one of my colleagues. Tony had something on the following week. Although we could have met

on another day, it did not occur to us. I was walking through the city centre when I became aware of running footsteps at a distance behind me. Suddenly I felt alarmed as they continued to approach so I stood in a shop doorway waiting. Eventually I saw a young man run past the window to catch a bus. The driver stopped for him and off they went to my relief.
On a bright clear day I went for a local walk in my area around lunch time. I went through a small park then as I was about to return I felt watched. Wondering whether to turn around I slowed my pace. The road was quiet with occasional cars passing. At the newsagent I turned around. Whilst the footsteps had been loud they suddenly stopped and there was nobody to be seen. This incident really spooked me. My whistle alarm was primed and I had my emergency telephone number ready but I could not report an invisible perpetrator. If somebody was playing games with me, it was not funny. Perhaps I was become neurotic getting startled at noises. I seriously considered moving but could not afford to.

I had an engraved name disc with a contact telephone number worn on a chain inside my clothing in case somebody attacked me. Every day I practised my self-defence exercises even when I didn't feel like. As I had a sit down job, I tried to keep fit. Fear made me stiff so I had to keep flexible not rigid. It was a nuisance and I really disliked it but my safety was more important. At work one of the girls was getting married and invited me and partner to her wedding. I wondered if Tony would accompany me. So far we had remained just friends which worked well. Neither of us had made any indication of taking things further. For my part I was ambivalent. While I found Tony attractive and good company, I did not want to risk losing his friendship.

When I saw him again I showed him the invitation and asked if he wanted to join me. He studied the invitation and said he would check his diary when he got home. This gave us both space to consider the situation. If he declined I would not be disappointed because it would not be appropriate to go alone. To my surprise Tony agreed and we made arrangements for

THE LIFE OF ROSIE

him to pick me up. He came wearing a suit looking smart. I felt proud to be seen with him. My best dress felt suitable and I made an effort with my hair and makeup. At work we had made a collection for a suitable present. The wedding venue was in a big old stately home with illuminated grounds. Everything was tastefully arranged inside where it felt warm and welcoming. We handed in our coats and were handed champagne glasses.

"You do realise that if I get a similar invite, you will have to come with me," Tony said.

"Of course, I owe you," I agreed.

We went over to congratulate the radiant bride and glowing bridegroom then found somewhere to sit. After the first dance by the newlyweds, Tony and I danced for a while to popular tunes before tucking into the evening buffet with drinks. A few of my colleagues invited us to join them. We had a pleasant time and I enjoyed having a partner to smooch with at the end. Time seemed to fly by and all too soon it was over. As we drove home silently I felt disappointed that we had to part. Tony said he had enjoyed the evening and thanked me for the invitation. I told him that if he wanted to get together sometime we could meet up apart from shopping.

"I thought you would never ask," he told me leaning over and kissing me briefly.

Shocked and pleased I hardly responded as I was planning to get out of the car.

"Off you go, that's enough for now," Tony said leaning over me to open the car door.

Flustered I climbed out awkwardly and waved him off.

Nothing more happened we continued to meet at the supermarket which became a habit. I decided that in future if I heard footsteps behind me or felt as if I was being watched, I would turn around and try to catch the culprit provided I was amongst other people. As soon as I made that decision nobody disturbed my presence. Life returned to regular routines and although mentally prepared for action, nothing occurred. Perhaps my life was so mundane the stalker had got bored with me. The experience had been frightening. Every time I left my house I carefully viewed my surroundings. Sometimes runners passed me while I was out but they generally did not make much noise being light on their feet.

Winter arrived suddenly with arctic winds making our faces burn with cold, at night the temperatures dropped to freezing with heavy frosts and icy patches. It was enough to make people hibernate. Only the young people seemed to cope well barely wrapped up. Most of us felt reluctant to go out unless essential or during the day. With rising prices and industrial strikes taking place, spending was curtailed and council funds severely restrained. Cuts had to be made so people were considering heating or eating. Charities appealed, hospitality venues were closing due to lack of trade plus cuts during the festive period due to a lack of public transport from strikes. The country struggled but it seemed to affect countries globally since Russia attacked Ukraine causing oil and gas prices to rocket.

Tony invited me to his firm's Christmas party to be held in a city centre hotel with a meal followed by a disco and some entertainment. I had my hair done and wore my best dress covered by a warm cardigan which I could be discarded. He collected me and introduced me to his colleagues who made room for us. They assumed we were dating and I said nothing to dispel the idea. Once we had a few drinks it became easier to converse and we popped crackers reading out the silly jokes which became funnier as the drinks flowed. A lady comedian entertained us after the meal who was moderately amusing, not really my type but she did her best. This was followed by dancing. I enjoyed joining in all the popular routines which were played this time of year finishing with New York New York.

We took a taxi home sharing the expense because we had been drinking. I felt a bit tipsy but happy. Tony escorted me to my door waiting until I went inside. At the last minute he pecked my cheek before disappearing. My legs felt a bit wobbly from the drink. Could this be the start of a relationship I wondered? Did I want a relationship with Tony? The idea was okay because he did not seem to be a demanding or controlling type. I wondered what had happened to his previous relationships. At the supermarket the following week I asked him:

"Why did you speak to me at the supermarket the first time?"

"Because we both reached for the single piece of salmon at the same time."

"So why did you offer me coffee?"

"Because you looked upset about the salmon."

"I was because I fancied it for my evening meal."

"Likewise so I could have given you the salmon if I was a gentleman."

"But you never offered."

"Because I also wanted salmon for my dinner. Anyway we both got some in the end."

"Yes due to your intervention."

"So you should thank me."

"I did at the time. So how come we keep meeting at the supermarket like this?"

"It breaks up the shopping. Why? Don't you want to?"

"I do but after going out a few times I wondered if we are going to remain just friends or start dating?" I said boldly.

"Do you want to date?" Tony asked surprised.

"I don't know. How come you are single?"

"We have never discussed our personal business, I could ask you the same."

"I asked first. You are a presentable bloke, good company, employed, tall, probably a good catch."

"Thank you madam. I was engaged and it fell through when she went off with someone else. That does tend to put a person off dating."

"It would do, more fool her. Not all women are the same."

"They start off sweet enough and obliging then start giving orders, making demands, expecting compliance to suit their wishes."

"That's very cynical. What happened to your ex?"

"She married the other man, they have a family now."

"So this happened some time ago. Are you still carrying a torch for her."

"Good grief no, I had a lucky escape. Her husband is welcome to her."

"Did you date since?"

"Never you mind, it's your turn now. What's your history?"

"Nothing dramatic, I have dated but it never lasts long. One of us gets fed up or is keener than the other. Although it is good in the beginning, I have never felt truly committed. The guys I fancied liked other girls. Those that liked me irritated me because they tried to please me. I like my independence but it would be good to have somebody special to share life with."

"Do you want to get married?"

"Are you proposing?" I joked than seeing his face drop added: "Only joking, the answer is that I like the concept but in reality I cannot imagine it."

"Do you want to date me?"

"I don't know, not if you are not interested. We seem to have enjoyed ourselves on the three occasions we have been out together."

"As friends."

"Ok leave it at that then. I would rather we remain friends than lose our connection if romance fails."

"I need to think about it."

"Don't bother if you are not interested, I won't be offended."

"What do you expect from me?"

"Nothing much just good company now and again, conversations .."

"Do you find me attractive?"

"Yes, I have got used to you but I won't be jumping into bed with you right away."

THE LIFE OF ROSIE

"Why not?" he asked smiling.

"Because I am not a woman of easy virtue. We would need to spend time together to develop any intimacy. The best things in life are worth waiting for."

"So you will play hard to get then?"

"I don't wish to be got, I need to be swept off my feet like in the movies! Only joking, let's remain friends it's easier."

"Leave it with me while I think about it."

"I feel embarrassed now that I mentioned it, just forget it. This is my cue to exit swiftly."

Tony laughed heartily as I felt my cheeks burn. Before he could say more I collected my trolley and headed swiftly to the checkout. He later sent me a text telling me to let him know when I wanted to go out. That was unsatisfactory leaving the onus on me to make a move. I decided to leave it for the supermarket for now. Before I could consider the matter I received a call from my local police station telling me that they had apprehended my stalker. If I wanted to discuss the situation I should call in and ask for Detective Riley. I rang to make an appointment and was told to go next morning at 1015 am. After texting Tony to advise him about it I was unable to sleep all night worrying.

I got to the station just after 10am and sat waiting. Detective Riley invited me in and offered me a drink which I refused.

"How do you know this is my stalker?" I asked impatiently.

It seemed the police had been called to a block of flats near my house owing to a loud party going on with drugs flowing. During a routine inspection of the building, the officer making enquiries noticed a display board in the bedroom as the door was open. The stalker tried to close the door but the officer moved forward for a closer look and recognised one of the girls and me pictured there. When questioned the stalker became agitated and disturbed. There were several girls pictured in various locations. Aged 22, the stalker reluctantly admitted that he had no confidence with women but he liked looking at them. His ideal situation would be to take one to his house to play with. The constable took him to the station where he was confined temporarily to await legal action.

As the stalker had not physically approached any of the girls or done anything untoward apart from frightening us all, I wondered what that meant. Detective Riley explained that stalking is defined as a course of conduct directed at a specific person that involves repeated (two or more occasions) of visual or physical proximity, non- consensual communication, or verbal, written, or implied threats, or a combination thereof, that would cause a reasonable person fear. Stalkers are often obsessive in multiple areas of their life including their romantic inclinations. They usually have repetitive thought patterns that play like a broken record, so they gradually become so preoccupied with their target, they're unable to sleep, forget to eat, and let their jobs go to the wayside. Sometimes they use technology, like hidden cameras or global positioning systems (GPS), to track where the target goes.

For the offence without violence, the basic offence of harassment, up to six months imprisonment can be imposed. If the offence is harassment (putting people in fear of violence) or stalking (involving fear of violence or serious alarm or distress): the maximum sentence is 10 years' custody. If racially or religiously aggravated, the maximum sentence is 14 years' custody. Victims of stalking experience a number of disruptive psychological consequences of stalking, including significant fear and safety concerns, as well as symptoms of depression, anxiety and posttraumatic stress disorder. Most stalking victims do not seek mental health services. In this case the perpetrator had stalked at least five women causing fear and anxiety so would not be released without trial. It would take some time for him to appear on trial.

"If he serves time while waiting will that be deducted from his sentence?" I asked.

"Yes."
"What about these other women have you told them?"

"They have been informed and feel relieved. You are my first case interview."

"If he is released within six months what if he repeats the crime? Will we be safe?"

"Let's wait and see what happens first. Don't jump the gun."

"Easy for you to say, but I bet the other girls are going to say the same."

"Incidentally, a tv researcher is planning to do a documentary on Stalking. Would you be interested in taking part if she contacts you?"

"Possibly if I could do so anonymously. I don't want to encourage anyone else to Stalk me."

"Can I put your name forward then? You can always decline if she asks."

"Ok. Did the perpetrator say how he chose his victims? Like why me?"

"He said he looked at the girls bodies and imagined them naked."

I pulled my coat around me and wrapped my arms together involuntarily gasping.
Detective Riley was sympathetic and told me that the perp was safely contained so not to worry.

THE LIFE OF ROSIE

"Yes but for how long?" I asked.

"I will keep you informed of the progress but it may take a while."

Feeling worried I left the station musing on the way to work about possible consequences. I gathered the perp was some kind of loser with women. He had read horror stories of women locked in a room and being messed with. This was frightening information and I decided to up my defensive lessons. Practice should centre around being attacked unexpectedly. While he was in custody I had the chance to get more lessons and fitter. My curiosity about the other women made me wonder if we were all a similar type with long dark hair. The detective would not reveal the other victims without their consent. In a way I was grateful that I was not the only victim, but I also understood their concerns. One apparently had been oblivious.

Tony was very supportive when we discussed the situation. We both wanted to hear what would happen. During the dark cold winter nights we did not go out much but maintained our regular supermarket routine which had become a habit. When it came to dating I had always imagined the man doing the chasing. Whilst Tony was amiable and always pleasant company, there were no awkward pauses, the spark leading to romance seemed absent. I felt ambivalent about it not wanting to ruin our friendship. If Tony ever made a move he would not be rejected. It seemed easier to maintain our friendship. Perhaps we were both afraid to spoil things. Therefore when he suggested booking a holiday in the sun together I was surprised and pleased.

We booked a Spring break to Puerto Rico de Gran Canaria, a holiday resort situated on the south-west coast of Gran Canaria. Temperatures in the winter remain around 20-25 °C so we thought by the end of March we should be okay. Having packed some mixed clothing in case it got cold at night, we set off arriving early evening. Our hotel was located on a steep hillside. When we opened the door to our room there was a strong smell of smoking. Tony immediately closed the door and went back to reception to complain telling them to change our accommodation. We waited in reception but nothing happened. When we tried to contact the tour representative nobody answered. Despite all protests we had to sit unaccompanied the whole night.

In the morning we were moved to another place further along the hill. This was a one bedroomed apartment clean and spacious. We were both exhausted so had a meal plus brief walk around the local area which overlooked the coast far below. To recover from our ordeal and aggravation we had an early night in our twin beds. Next morning showered and recovered we went exploring. Once we walked down winding paths to the town centre we viewed the shops, bars and restaurants where we ate. Nobody wished us good morning or spoke to us to thank us when we bought anything. It also seemed strange not to be offered a bag for any purchases. The centre was clean and attractive but not very large.

As the beaches were in different locations we explored both sides individually to find out where to go to suit us. We also wandered around the shopping centre. It was pleasant with surrounding hillsides clad in white buildings. The weather was warm enough for comfort which felt good after leaving home. Our day was spent walking, sitting in the sun, eating when it suited us. Getting back to the apartment we took a taxi. Neither of us had the stamina to climb up the hillside. This meant that when we got back and rested we would need to get another taxi if we wanted to return to the centre. During the week we took everything we needed with us so that we could stay out. At night we heard music from the clubs playing loud until late. We did not go to any preferring to be outside during the day.

I wondered whether Tony would become amorous now we were far from home. He didn't and when I once tried to hug him, he froze and turned away. This offended me so I turned in my direction and did not try again. We dressed in the bathroom. In the movies romance bloomed when a man and woman went away. It made me realise that Tony was not interested, I was probably not his type. Instead we remained on a friendly companion basis. When we went home I decided to try to meet a boyfriend. Tony apologised for rejecting me claiming I took him by surprise. I shrugged and said: "Never mind, I am still waiting for my prince to come to sweep me off my feet."

At first I liked the resort but after a few days it did not excite me and I knew I would not return. Although it had all the ingredients, for me it was lacking that special enticing element. It did not seem friendly unless punters were seeking business. There seemed to be indifference from the locals and a lack of good communication skills. Apart from the weather and the beach with blue sea, I was ready to go home. Fortunately, the journey was efficient and we got back in time for tea. As I needed to go shopping I indulged in fish and chips from my local noticing the price increase since my last time. Tony went home and we arranged to meet after shopping. I made a replenishment list.
All summer we met at the supermarket and went out together occasionally. Most of my social life was spent with my friends going on day trips or outings together. We had fun and enjoyed fooling around. Sometimes we flirted or even dated but not seriously. Life was for living and we enjoyed ourselves when we could. At work I plodded on and was offered a promotion unexpectedly when someone left. A colleague was jealous as she wanted the post. Being a zealot at work she tried to overtake me but the powers above chose me so I performed well. Truthfully, I was not ambitious about work but performed conscientiously. Life continued uneventfully until the trial occurred of the stalker.

Tony came to court with me. My stalker report had been given in as evidence and somebody from the support group came along. I had prepared a statement about my situation and said I would appear only if essential. Looking around I saw a few girls who could have been the other victims but as everyone was accompanied, I was not sure. Perhaps it was better that way. The perpetrator had an abusive upbringing, abandoned by his mother, brought up in a Council home until 18. He looked like a big overgrown puny kid. His whole demeanour suggested he was a nobody. If I had turned around I don't know if I would have thought it was him. For most of the proceedings he kept his head down but when he stood up for sentencing he looked around the court and I saw malice in his gaze.

He was given a six month sentence with the time served deducted. With good behaviour he could be out in four months. This alarmed me and I noticed a stir amongst the other women. There seemed to be nothing to prevent him repeating his behaviour or even do worse for spite. Noticing our fear the judge concluded that at the termination of his sentence the perpetrator planned to move away to make a new start so we had nothing to fear. In fact it seemed he was planning to go to Ireland where his brother lived so that felt a relief. There were five victims including me. We shook hands and went for a drink together in a neighbourhood pub. All the companions came with. Four of us had long dark hair, the fifth was small with curly red hair, she was the one who had been unaware.

When I asked the others if they had seen the perp before the trial? Four said they had not. One of them had filmed him following her but had not been able to track him down. We all agreed how efficient he was at disappearing. I told them I had taken self-defence lessons but the thought of being stalked filled with me fear of the unknown. Hopefully, we could get on with our lives peacefully now. Before we left we exchanged names and phone numbers so that we could make contact if required. We all hoped not to meet again. Two of us were local the others lived in different areas. My legs felt wobbly going back as if the shock and reaction had been delayed. It had been an ordeal and I appreciated Tony's support taking me home. I had taken the day off work.

THE LIFE OF ROSIE

Once our regular routines resumed I imagined Tony and I would continue to meet indefinitely as we were very comfortable together. Therefore I was astonished when he announced that he had met a very special lady at work. It seemed a consultant had attended an executive meeting with a view to joining Tony's team on secondment, to develop new strategies to cope with current legislation. There was a shortage of housing developments, new builds were too expensive for many to get on the property ladder and rental prices were constantly rising.
"How long will she be with you?" I asked.

"For my part she can stay forever but I think at least nine months."

"So time for you to make a baby," I teased. "Is she pretty?"

"She's regal, a classy lady, very smart."

"Will you ask her out?"

Tony blushed saying he only just met her. It would take time to get to know her to find out if she was single and if she liked him. He didn't know her age or background yet but would find out. At first I thought he had a crush on her but as time went on his conversation was all about Victoria, what she had said or done. It became boring and irritated me because he could not change the subject for long.

"Doesn't she go by the name of Vicky?" I asked saying: "Victoria sounded old fashioned.

"As in Victoria Beckham?" he responded.

"If you are obviously so obsessed with this woman why don't you invite her out and show her around."

At some point he took my advice and they started dated sporadically at first.

"Am I allowed to meet her? Can I see if she suits you?" I asked.

Reluctantly Tony thought about it and suggested I attended the Town Planning Open Day meeting coming up. Taking half a day's leave I went along wearing my work clothing to look more professional in case Tony introduced me. He did not but pointed out Victoria to me. She was with the hierarchy busy networking. At first glance I disliked her. Even from a distance I could tell she was a strident, arrogant career woman who would control poor Tony into submission. Henpecked came to mind. Victoria was hard faced with hair virtually glued into place, nothing moved, she was dressed conservatively in an old fashioned style, neither slim nor plump, plain rather than attractive. I honestly could not understand what Tony saw in her.

"She's so powerful and dynamic," he told me at the coffee table.

"Is that a good thing?" I asked cynically.

"Oh yes, I know you are not career orientated but Victoria could conquer the world," he said proudly.

"Be careful what you wish for, she could make mincemeat out of you."

"She can do whatever she wants with me," Tony said dreamily.

I departed soon after drinking my coffee before he accused me of jealousy. Not long after we stopped meeting at the supermarket as Victoria expected Tony to be at her beck and call. Still besotted Tony did not want to be seen with another woman. In turn, I did not want to hear any more about her nor express my opinion. Apart from occasional text messages, it seemed to be the end of a beautiful friendship. In a sense it was a relief because I was free to go shopping whenever I wanted. Since Victoria had arrived Tony had changed from an interesting guy to a soppy bore so I felt like a weight had been lifted. He had previously been a good friend to me. Being alone again was a relief and I took control of my life and interests.

One morning I was making myself a drink in the staff kitchen at work when a man came in behind me saying:

"Make mine white with no sugar please. Mark here likes tea with two sugars."

"Who are you?" I asked startled.

"I'm Pete Lawson here to sort out your plumbing problem," he said.

"The problem is in the men's toilet as I understand not the kitchen," I told him.

"We know that but need to check all your facilities while we are here."

"If you want drinks help yourselves, mugs are in the cupboard," I said turning to go.

"Drinks always taste better when somebody else makes them," he said smiling.

"Nice try. It's also good manners to wait to be asked," I said.

Linda, one of our receptionists came in offering both men a drink. Mark the younger one looked embarrassed. I raised my eyebrows and walked out holding my drink leaving them to it. The rest of the morning I got stuck into my work. Around lunch time Pete the plumber somehow found my desk to ask me where I recommended to eat locally. My colleagues around me looked surprised.

"Are you not familiar with the city centre?" I asked.

"Perhaps you can show me somewhere good," he smiled.

"Why are you asking me?"

"You are the only person I know."

"We don't know each other. I don't know how you found my desk but please go away and disturb somebody else."

Pete leaned over close to my face whispering that he liked me. Close too I noticed he was masculine and confident. Although he was attractive he was far too pushy to appeal to me. Hopefully he would finish his task and disappear. I did not see him again that day but found him waiting outside a few days later with a bunch of flowers. Attempting to ignore him I was trying to evade him when he stood in front of me handing me the flowers.

"What are you doing here?" I asked annoyed, trying to return the bouquet.

"I'm waiting for you of course. Can I invite you to dine with me?"

"No you cannot. Take these flowers back. I'm seeing someone and he won't approve."

"No you are not, I checked."

"Go away, I don't want to be with you."

"Why not? You don't know me yet, I can be good fun."

"Leave me alone, find somebody else to annoy," I told him heading for my car.

Undeterred Pete showed up at various times after work had finished. I tried varying my timings as we could work flexibly, but he left messages on my car windscreen. When I was on the verge of borrowing Tony or a male cousin to escort me, I decided to put a stop to this nonsense.

"Why do you keep appearing here?" I asked him.

"I told you I like you and want to get to know you."

"The feeling is not mutual and is causing me harassment."

"I'm sorry about that," he said sincerely looking forlorn. "Take my card then and if you change your mind I would be happy to take you out. Don't worry, I am not a pervert or dangerous, you would be safe with me."

His business card revealed that he ran a building and maintenance company with contractors in plumbing, electrical and building works. I put the card in my pocket and watched him walk away. He had dressed smartly, was clean and looked attractive. Wondering why he seemed to be chasing me, I felt uncomfortable. In all my past history I had not attracted much attention. Was I being too hasty by throwing an opportunity away? Realistically, I knew nothing about this man. Deciding to leave the situation as it stood meant more lonely weekends or empty evenings now the Spring was here. If I had met Pete in a public place when I was accompanied by friends, perhaps it would have felt safer. Instead his overt attention felt alarming.

If I hadn't sprung a leak in my bedroom roof following some stormy weather, I would not have called him. I hesitated before doing so but the other firms I tried were all too busy to attend for weeks. He answered the phone and when he heard it was me, he said he would come out later that day to check out the problem. I invited my elderly neighbour in for a cup of tea to stay with me when Pete came. The fact that he would know my address was concerning. In the event he came dressed casually, found the fault and promised to send someone round the next morning at about 8 am. Once the repair was rectified he would invoice me. Before he left he asked how I was, if the work situation was resolved now. As we were both busy we cut short the conversation. Before I closed the front door he winked at me saying his offer still stood if I was interested. Without giving me chance to reply Pete was gone.

"What a nice fellow," my neighbour said. "You are lucky to get somebody decent to do the work so fast. These days you can wait ages."

The repair was done quickly and efficiently so I was able to go to work afterwards. Pete sent me an invoice online stating official rate and charging me "Mates rate". I did a bank transfer saying my name and thank you as a reference. He rang me a few days later to see if I was satisfied with the work. Once again I expressed my gratitude.

"So perhaps you can join me for a drink now we have become acquainted," Pete suggested.

I didn't know what to say so hesitated. Filling in the gap Pete told me he would pick me up at 8pm on Friday and hung up before I could refuse. Wondering why the man was so persistent I knew that if I avoided him it would only encourage him to return. On Friday I dressed casually but made myself look presentable and was ready when he arrived punctually. He looked good and opened the car door for me.

"I like your perfume," he told me.

"Thank you," I said.

"I didn't know if you would come."

"Well I don't know why you are so persistent so I decided to find out."

He drove us to a bar on the outskirts which was modern and spacious. Telling Pete that I did not drink except on special occasions led him to say:

"This is a special occasion, it's our first date."

"I think it is just a chance to get acquainted," I hedged.

Pete laughed, brought drinks and entertained me with a wide range of topics including some amusing anecdotes from his business. It seemed he ran the company and had contractors working for him. The business had expanded with specialists in all fields. Word of mouth clients brought him more so he provided a quality service. When he enquired about my experience, I complimented his staff especially when they cleaned up after themselves.

"We always respond to all our calls even if we can't take on the task immediately."

"That's very reassuring these days."

"Yes, there's plenty of cowboys out there just out to take your money. We pride ourselves on getting the job done professionally."

He asked about my work and if I enjoyed it.

"Not really but it pays my way. I recently got promoted over someone who tries hard and wants to succeed. When I work I do so conscientiously but have no ambition to advance into management. If I could earn the same doing something interesting I would leave."

"That's a shame when you spend so many hours there."

"True but I work regular hours then go home. There are worse jobs."

"What would you choose to do if you could?"

"I don't know perhaps something creative."

"Like art, music or writing?"

"Creating something unique must be satisfying. I haven't tried my skills for a long time."

"You could try something as a hobby then develop it if it is worthy."

"Time constraints make me tired and when I get home I can't be bothered."

"If you want to do something you find time."

We then discussed the economic climate and world situation. Before I realised it the evening passed quickly and Pete took me home. He had been interesting and informative on a variety of subjects so when he suggested another meeting I agreed. Opening the car door for me again outside my place he said he would call me then drove away. I waved him off and went inside pleased with the way it had gone. Gradually we started dating mostly during the weekends as we were busy during the week. Pete invited me to interesting places and treated me like a perfect gentleman, opening the car door for me, buying me flowers at times or chocolates. We talked and I felt comfortable with him rather than excited. In fact I was not concerned whether we met or not but had a pleasant time when he did.

Therefore when Pete proposed to me I was shocked. He told me to take my time to think about it.

"I am not ready to get married yet," I told him.

"Well we don't have to rush it, when you feel ready."

"But I don't feel the same."

"Maybe your love will grow in time."
"We haven't known each other for long," I protested.

"I knew the moment I saw you in the office kitchen."

"Well it didn't happen to me. Why do you want to marry me?"

"We can make a good life together, I can support us so you can give up work if you want or I will finance you if you want to study. You can do whatever you want I will not stand in your way. In time maybe we can have a couple of kids and raise a family together. At the end of the day we can share our experiences, take interesting holidays and live comfortably. I will be faithful and generous."

"Well that sounds a wonderful proposition, most girls would be happy with that."

"But not you?" he asked sadly.

"I like my independence and am still immature enough to need space to grow up."

"Ok fair enough, let's carry on as we are for now. All I'm asking is that you think about it."

We did not speak about it again but it stayed in my mind. Around the same time Tony told me that Victoria was moving in with him as it would save rental. I said I hope she would be sharing expenses as I sensed she would take advantage of his good nature. He said they would sort everything out and he was excited. I wondered whether Pete wanted to move in together but dismissed the thought. If we moved in I would have to give up my apartment. Pete was a good kisser but we had not been intimate. While the prospect did not dismay me, I was not ready. If we married I would not have any financial worries and I knew Pete would be a good husband. Was that enough? Where was the spark, the chemistry? Perhaps in all relationships one partner cared more than the other. In this case he would care more than me.

At my age most of my friends were settling down. Whilst I did not want to grow old alone, I did not want to marry for convenience. Perhaps romance was over rated in movies and books. Harmony and friendship was good but predictable. When I had a bad day or struggled, I was sorely tempted to say yes. There were no queue of suitors lined up ready to take me on. Pete was caring, attractive and sincere. Was I expecting too much? These questions occupied my free moments and were creating a barrier between us. I decided to visit my mum for advice. She wanted to meet him and told me that marriage was not a game, it was serious, I could not just end it when I got fed up. Pete's mother was kind and gentle, obviously proud of her son and made me welcome. I decided to take him to meet my parents for dinner.

Pete brought flowers and a bottle of wine and looked smart. He was courteous to my parents speaking about his business and aspirations frankly and concisely. My father thought he was a decent straight forward man. Mum encouraged him to eat well. I didn't have much to say. Obviously he made a good impression. It would be my decision whether to consider marriage or move on. On the plus side Pete and I got on well, he cared about me, I would be secure and he would be a faithful husband. If I had a marriage of convenience it would save me a great deal of soul searching, loneliness and heartache. Passionate love stories could be media projections. Reality was daily experience in the real world. I felt I could manage comfortably if I married Pete, my only decision was whether I wanted to marry him. Indecision reigned for several months until I hit a low period where nothing seemed to flow well. Pete was very supportive and sympathetic so I accepted his proposal. My parents and his mother were happy and met for a congratulatory meal.

We wanted a low key wedding, Pete offered to pay for everything but came to an arrangement with my father. A friend of my mother's was a dressmaker so made my gown as a present. I wanted it kept plain and simple in decent smooth material. The service went well, we posed for photos, fortunately it was a clear day. Afterwards we had a chicken meal followed by live music from friends of Pete then a disco. Our wedding night was spent in a hotel before heading off to Bali, Indonesia for our honeymoon. Described as "Land of pirates, and dragons, of a million islands, misty, mythical mountainous stacks," it had some of the most beautiful places to stay in the world with heavenly hotels. There were deep-green infinity pools, jungle-cloaked and inviting.
Bali is a magical, spiritual place which retains its authenticity and culture, with unspoilt beaches and green tropical landscapes. Resorts are known for pulling out all the stops for honeymooners. There were private island picnics, intimate snorkelling excursions and elaborate spa packages. Bora Bora is surrounded by sand-fringed islets and a turquoise lagoon protected by a coral reef, making it a prime spot for scuba diving. There are no direct flights to Bora Bora, but, we chose the most popular stopover en route Los Angeles. It was an opportunity to tack some Hollywood glamour onto our trip. We did a city bus tour around LA due to time constraints, but it was a relief to arrive at our holiday destination enchantment. As well as being loved by travellers the world over for its unrivalled collection of overwater bungalow suites, beachfront villas and fine dining options, it has been used as the backdrop for several movies over the past few decades. It was a beautiful relaxing experience. With plunge pools and the sea surrounding us, paradise came to mind. We did something every day but mostly chilled and enjoyed the experience. Pete was a considerate husband and we bonded well. This escape from reality passed too quickly and was probably the best time in our relationship. Everything was perfect including the meals

and the temperature with plenty of shade on offer if required. Unfortunately, we had to return to reality.

I moved into Pete's house renting out my apartment. He gave me free reign to style it to suit my taste. From a bachelor house I softened the décor to feel cosy. It had been extended with bi fold doors and an eat in kitchen diner. My work was going smoothly since marriage. We both had after work regular activities and friends to catch up with so kept our own spaces. At weekends we went out together, sometimes shopped together or visited joint friends/family. It worked well and eventually I became pregnant with our son Martin. People told us a baby would change our lives forever. From the middle of the night birth onwards Martin ruled the house. He had colic, could not distinguish day from night and I felt exhausted.

Pete worked long hours and sometimes had meetings after work so most of the childcare was my responsibility. When any visitors came especially the two mothers, I would dump Martin into their arms and try to get some rest. Once Martin was bottle fed he settled down more into a routine. When Pete was home he admired his son, held him and occasionally changed his nappy. Most of the time Pete was content to leave the child rearing and house maintenance to me. We hired a cleaner who came twice a week. Both mothers tried to help by bringing us home cooked meals or delicacies and were besotted by Martin. Thank goodness I was on maternity leave as I could barely cope with the endless feeding, changing and home chores.

Fortunately, I was able to work from home when the time came to resume my work but it was a strain and I was constantly tired. Martin seemed to wait for me to work then become demanding. Pete recommended that I give up work for the time being. If I wanted to do something he could bring work from his company for me to tackle. His view was that he was happy to provide for his family. I had a whole lifetime to work if I wanted to. Meanwhile I should just stay home and enjoy the baby who would grow quickly. I think in his mind I just sat around coddling Martin and playing with him. Pete should spend one day at home alone with his son. He would soon run back to work. When the weather was good I wheeled Martin outside for fresh air.

Life was busy and our social life declined. The parents babysat or we left Martin overnight occasionally but mostly we stayed in or Pete went out to the pub with his friends. When Martin was 18 months old I was pregnant again. This was not planned but I decided that two children were enough. Martin was walking and needed potty training before he could go to the nursery. Pete took Martin out when he could so that I could have some time to catch up on things. We hoped for a girl this time but as long as the baby was healthy, we would be happy. I felt tired most of the time and sometimes my legs ached. We got through the pregnancy and our daughter Sadie was born in the early hours. Pete took Martin to the nursery and helped with potty training while I nursed Sadie who was a placid contended baby rarely crying.

Like most families we were proud of our children attending their nursery then school functions, applauded their performances and tried to give them adventures or learning experiences during the holidays. They grew quickly so I was always buying the next size clothes. Martin was a bright boy among the top few in his class, sporty playing football on the school team. Sadie was a quieter girl, caring, sharing, diligent, among the top stream towards the middle. They learned to swim and had religious instruction from school so knew about the festivals. At school they were taught about environmental issues to save the world. We taught them not to throw their rubbish outside and good manners. Martin was a more handsome version of his father, Sadie was slightly more my side but somewhere in between with delicate features.

Once the kids matured and were ready for high school I became restless and irritated by the fact that Pete left everything to me. He worked and maintained the family and felt that was his role. When I consulted him about household or family matters he would tell me to do as I felt fit. Everything was "Whatever you want" whether it was a question of meals or projects. Pete was so laid back he was almost horizontal. This was annoying as I wanted him to make some family decisions. Our lives also became predictable. This drove me mad, there was no excitement, anticipation or even passion. I needed stimulation or more attention, there had to be more to life than washing, cooking, cleaning and running things. Everyone expected me to support them without considering I had needs too.

Everybody took me for granted expecting me to do everything for them. Pete and I were not close any more. We rarely made love, he was either working or snoozing in his chair. Socially he saw his friends, I joined mine when he babysat. Sometimes we barely spoke to each other. Feeling aggrieved by the situation I decided to speak to him about it.

"What's wrong?" Pete asked me. "Most couples are the same once the first flush is over."

"We are living together that's all, we don't have common interests or do anything as a couple anymore."

"You are living comfortably, I provide all your needs, most women would be pleased."

"We don't spend time together or even talk much."

"That's because we have done all that, we are not still dating."

"I know that but we are drifting apart and I am not happy."

"Why aren't you happy?"

"I feel that you don't even see me as a woman anymore."

"Well that's because you have let yourself go, always in old clothes, no makeup or grooming. When I first saw you at work you were exciting and enticing. These days you don't make any effort unless we are going somewhere then you scrub up well."

"Thank you, I don't need to dress up to do housework speaking of which you and the kids need to contribute more to the running of this household."

"That's your job."

"No it isn't, where does it say that?"

"The man brings home the bacon, the woman rules the house."

"That is so old fashioned, these days there is equality in roles."

"Ok so you provide for us all, go to work full time then we will share the jobs."

"You live here but leave all the decisions to me. Whenever I ask you about anything you don't ever make any decisions."

"That's because I let you have your own way. It's to please you. Happy wife, happy life."
"Well I am not a happy wife."
"So do something to make you happy. You shouldn't rely on me all the time."
We argued until the kids came home then indignantly I went out for a walk to cool my temper. To try to improve things we booked a family holiday to Italy. Leaving the family around the hotel pool one afternoon, I walked along the coastal path as the sun was heading for dusk with the promise of a glowing sunset. Along the way I stopped to lean against a barrier gazing at the setting sun. Further along a man was also leaning watching. It looked so beautiful I gasped with pleasure and found myself turning to him saying:
"Isn't this beautiful."
He agreed and smiled at me. I noticed his accented English and asked where he was from.
"South Korea," he told me.
We gazed at the beautiful scene in front of us reluctant to move. The sea glowed and the air felt balmy. I noticed the man was immaculately groomed, he had good features and seemed relaxed. He was tall, slim and had a charismatic presence. A few people passed by but we remained apart in unison so we exchanged a bit of small talk. This was his first visit to Italy and mine to this resort so we agreed it had been a good choice. I asked what he did in Korea, he told me he was an actor.
"Are you famous?" I asked innocently.
"Yes," he told me confidently.
"Do you enjoy it?"
"Most of the time when I have good scripts."
"Do you have all the women after you?"
"I have a huge fan base yes, but they go after my image or the roles I play."
"What are the downsides?"
"I have to live up to the image in public, people don't want to know the real me."
"Your English is very good."

THE LIFE OF ROSIE

"My father was widowed young so married an American the second time so we spoke English at home."

"I see, don't you think that most people take each other for granted. They grow accustomed to the familiar image and stop seeing the individual?" I asked.

We then had a long discussion about life expectations, the roles between the genders and anticipations. Suddenly talking to him I felt stimulated and alive, as if my opinions counted. The contrast between my home communication and this conversation with a stranger made me realise that I had to make changes in my life to survive. Putting up was no longer an option. It would not be easy but it was necessary for my future sanity. If Pete thought I could do everything myself, why did I need him? If it was a question of finance I could work to provide. The children were both in high school so could manage to come home themselves. They were accustomed to doing their homework before going out so I would be home in time.

This Korean man spoke to me as a person, he was courteous and although I would not see him again, revived my intellect and confidence. We spoke for a while then parted amicably. It was a special moment in shared time that stayed with me. In fact it was the turning point in my life. The contrast between the way my husband mostly ignored me and the way this attentive stranger spoke intelligently and politely to me shocked me. A thought occurred to me that if I never saw Pete again it would not bother me. Even the prospect of Pete seeing another woman would be a relief. This was not right. I had no feelings left for the man I married who had once been fairly attractive and attentive.

As Pete grew his business he had a team of contractors to do the grafting while he sought out business and was growing a property portfolio. His only exercise was going to the pub where he sometimes played darts or pool. His religion was football but as a critical spectator. As a result his girth had expanded and he had signs of a beer belly. We spent hardly any time together as when he stayed home I went out. My future was too important to waste in this situation. Instead of growing closer we had drifted too far. For my part I was not

interested in any reconciliation so I decided to talk to him. Pete was taken aback.
"What do you mean?" he asked. "Did you just wake up and decide this is it?"
"Not at all, neither of us are happy nor close any more. We have given it our best shot but it is not working."
"What do you want me to do?"
"Let's separate and get on with our lives."
"What about the kids?" he asked alarmed.
"They will be better off with two happy parents."
"I am happy enough here as a family. You do what you want. If this isn't good enough for you, get out."
"Ok then, you look after the family and the house and I will leave. When you want to talk sensibly, let me know," I said pulling down a travel bag and opening the wardrobe.
Pete got up pulling me back.
"What are doing now?" he asked angrily.
"You said I should get out …"
"Where will you go?"
"I will find somewhere."
"Don't bother," he snarled grabbing his jacket. "I'm off until you calm down and come to your senses."
"I have come to my senses which is why I am doing this," I told him.
Pete came close to me sniffing: "Have you been drinking or are you on something?"
"Not at all. I just don't want to remain in this marriage."
"What have I done that is so terrible? I work hard, give you a generous allowance, let you have your own way. Other husbands are unfaithful, gamble or beat their wives. I don't do any of that."
"No you don't do anything to sustain any interest or excitement in this relationship. I feel taken for granted like a paid housekeeper."
"Do you expect me to go back to courting days again after all this time?"
"No, I expect you to let me go."
"You bitch I'm going out before I do something bad," he said storming out slamming the front door.

Pete stayed out all night and did not return the next day. The kids were used to his absenteeism and occupied themselves with homework and studies for exams. I checked the job situation in the area but there was nothing appealing. It seemed that Pete came back to the house at odd times removing anything he fancied. As the house was in both names I could not prevent him access. Making a note of the date we unofficially separated, I started checking the kids clothing plus my own. We could not live with the uncertainty. One day I came home to find a drunken snoring Pete sprawled across the living room. He had drool on his chin and smelled of stale beer.

As it was almost school holidays, I had an idea. My mum's sister Clare lived in Somerset running a bed and breakfast. She always spoiled me growing up. I rang to ask her if I could stay with her bringing the kids. As it was winter she was delighted. I told her not to mention it to my parents in case they expected me to go to them. Before the kids could go to bed, I went to their rooms and told them to be very quiet. They each packed their favourite things plus a case of mixed clothing. We sneaked out through the back leaving their father snoring oblivious. I drove my car around the back and we loaded up the luggage then drove off to Somerset. The kids wanted to know what was going on.

I told them we were going on an adventure. Their dad was staying home as he had work. They wanted to know what was going on with their father.

"Well dad and mum both love you equally but we are not getting along together these days. It is not easy living with someone else. Rather than make each other unhappy any more, I asked your dad if we could separate for a while to see how we fare."

"Are you getting a divorce?" Martin asked anxiously.

"Not yet but I would like to," I said truthfully.

"Don't you love daddy anymore?" Sadie asked me earnestly.

"I don't love daddy but he is a good person."

"So what about us? You didn't ask our opinion. Are we running away?" Martin asked angrily.

"At the moment it is school holidays ....."

"Not until tomorrow," Sadie told me.
"Well the atmosphere at home will not be pleasant for a while so I thought we could have an adventure away from home for now."
"Daddy won't know where we are," Martin said.
"Good, don't tell him yet. He keeps going somewhere then coming in taking things from the house when we are not around," I said.
"It's his house too," Martin protested.
"Yes, so let him enjoy it on his own."
"Did daddy do something bad?" Sadie asked me.
"It's not so much bad, it's just like you go to school. Some people are your friends and there are some who don't do anything but you dislike. Well daddy and I have different interests and ideas. We are like strangers living in the same house," I explained.
"So why did you marry him?" Martin asked.
"At the time he was different and desperate to marry me."
"So you said yes," Sadie said.
"We have both changed and the situation is not working now. Life is short and too important to spend being unhappy."
"What does dad say?" Martin asked.
"He thinks he is a perfect husband and I should be pleased with him."
"He's not perfect even I know that. He's hardly around and doesn't do much when he is," Martin said.
"Will he see us?" Sadie asked.
"Of course, whenever he wants but we haven't reached that stage yet. It may take a long time."
"So what will you do to support us? You don't work," Martin asked.
"Not yet but I will. You will go to school, study and I will find a job. We will share the housework between us fairly. I think we can manage together if we all pitch in. There won't be much money for extras but we can eat and get clothes etc."
"Will daddy want to keep us?" Sadie asked anxiously.
"If he has free access or arranged times I am sure we can work something out. I am the one who looks after you now so that shouldn't change."

"How long are we staying at aunty Clare's?" Martin asked.
"We can sort it out when we get there. I just wanted somewhere distant so that dad can't find us easily. If we went to grandma's he would go straight there."
"He may worry," Sadie said.
"I left him a note saying we are spending the school holiday on a trip,"
Both children were subdued and played with their mobiles until they fell asleep in the car. I felt shattered myself and thought about stopping for coffee but left them sleeping. We arrived very late in the early hours disturbing aunt Clare who let us in and allocated rooms for us saying we would catch up in the morning. I had a hot drink and went to bed. Exhaustion hit me and I woke up late when everyone had eaten breakfast. Apparently the kids had been telling Clare about our car conversation. Shrewdly she said nothing to me until they went outside to explore.
"What's going on?" she asked me over coffee and toast.
"I'm trapped in a loveless marriage and I want to break free."
"Do you want a divorce?" she asked surprised.
"Yes."
"I thought Pete was a decent guy. Has he changed or done something bad to you?"
"We have no common interests, barely speak to each other, I am taken for granted as housekeeper, we don't have sex and he repulses me. Everything is left to me to control, he never makes decisions so if I am in charge of it all, I don't need him."
"But he looks after your finances, you don't work. How will you manage?"
"I will find a job."
"They are not easy to come by these days if you want to earn a decent wage."
"I will find something or more than one job. When the kids are older they can get Saturday jobs."
"What does Pete say about this?"
"He called me a bitch and was upset that his comfortable lifestyle was under threat."
"Have you thought about Counselling to see if you can reconcile?"

"Out of the question, I don't want to see him unless I have to."
"What about your home and possessions?"
"It's in both names but I want to live in another place. Lately he's been staying elsewhere but coming in and taking things from the house."
"What kind of things?"
"Various including some of the kids' stuff. I can't live like that. One night he came in drunk and snoring on the armchair drooling. That was when I packed up and came here."
"But you have to go back."
"I need to investigate my options while I am sufficiently distant without interference."
"Have you told your parents?"
"No, not yet. I want to have a plan in place first. Pete would go there first looking for us. Don't mention us if you speak to them."
"How do the children feel?"
"Confused but I think accepting, they don't see much of their dad anyway."
"They have to go to school."
"Yes, I have all our documentation with me. They can enrol at a new school when we get settled."
"Where do you want to go? Housing is not cheap you know."
"I want to be far away enough so that Pete cannot bother us easily. We need somewhere to live, a decent school and near amenities in case I can't run my car."
"That's going to be difficult without support. I will check out my connections to see if anyone can help. Do you have a specific destination in mind?"
"Not anywhere too remote or isolated that's all."
Clare made an appointment for me to see a lawyer friend of hers for advice on divorce procedures. Meanwhile I kept my mobile turned off. When I switched it on briefly it was full of missed calls from Pete. In the movies they seemed to be able to track locations so I left it off again. I kept the children's mobiles with me to their dismay telling them they could use them when I sorted myself out. Interestingly they were more upset about losing the use of their mobiles than the absence of their father. They did not mention Pete at all but asked me

what we were going to do. I had two weeks to try to form a plan. The lawyer told me that I can get divorced in England or Wales if I've been married for over a year, my relationship has permanently broken down, and. My marriage is legally recognised in the UK.

1. As I answered affirmative the lawyer gave me some information to take with me on how to apply
2. What happens when you apply
3. Apply for a conditional order or decree nisi
4. Finalise your divorce

She told me to read everything carefully then if I wanted professional guidance, I could make an appointment. I also needed to consult with Pete to see if we could agree on the process to save time and money moving forwards. This felt like progress so I made a to do list waiting until my mind cleared before reading. I then went online to check on rental price indications throughout the country. The cheapest areas were not the best for education and future employment possibilities. If I went back to my parents we would be squashed but I had care for the children. It was too convenient for Pete to find us. I checked out job situations in Somerset but the rental situation was too expensive to contemplate. Clare made many enquiries on my behalf. The kids found local friends and kept themselves happily occupied.
I was still doing research when it was time to go back home. We needed to return to sort out our affairs although I had no plans to remain in the family home. If we sold it I would have funds as my savings were meagre. We drove during the day stopping off to eat along the way. It was dark when we got home, the lights were on in the house. Inside Pete was in bed with another woman. I told the children to go to their rooms and wait there. A shocked embarrassed silence occurred before Pete said I should have told him I was returning. "Why so you could send your trollop home?" I said scathingly. "Who are you calling a trollop you bitch," the woman shouted in a Cornish accent.

I waited downstairs, the house was a mess, everywhere lay discarded take away trays, clutter and items of clothing. Making myself a cup of tea after washing a mug, I knew this was truly the end. Eventually I heard the front door slam, Pete came into the living room looking aggressive and ashamed simultaneously. There was nothing to say except to tell him I would be sending him divorce papers.
"Where have you been? Where will you go? Do you have money?" Pete asked in a rush.
"I will go to my parents for now."
"I'm sorry you had to see that but it's your own fault for not telling me."
"It's my fault you are with another woman?"
"At least she finds me desirable."
"She's welcome to you then."
"Aren't you jealous?"
"Not at all, make a new life with her."
"What about the kids?"
"You can see them when you want."
"How will you manage?"
"I will get a job. You can support the kids. If we sell this place I will have funds to find somewhere else."
"You can rent one of my properties."
"No thanks, I want to be independent."
"This house is a family home. Do you want to stay here?" he asked me.
"Not any longer. Let's split the proceeds from this place and go our separate ways. If you want to keep this place just provide me with half the price. We can get a few estate agents to do valuations."
"You've got this all figured out," Pete said sarcastically. "What about my feelings?"
"What feelings, you are already with someone else."
"She's a good woman, warm not like you."
"Lucky you," I said rising to call the children.
Pete came towards me with a menacing expression and a clenched fist so I ran upstairs telling the children to take anything they wanted from their rooms. I rang my parents saying we were going to see them and would explain on

arrival. As I carried stuff downstairs we found Pete barring the front door.

"You are not taking the kids," he said.

"Children do you want to stay here with your father or come to grandma's with me?" I asked calmly.

The children looked frightened and came close to me. Martin told Pete that we should visit grandma for now.

"What about me?" Pete asked pathetically.

"We will see you soon," Martin assured him. "Grandma hasn't seen us since Christmas."

Smelling of beer Pete moved aside, Martin opened the door, we filed out carrying stuff and I drove away feeling exhausted and wanting to cry. Martin told me the woman was a barmaid from the local pub.

"How do you know?" I asked him astonished.

"I have seen her outside there when passing going to school or coming back sometimes."

"As long as you have not been pub crawling," I said attempting some humour.

"Not yet."

"She's fat," giggled Sadie.

"So's your dad these days."

We all giggled and the tension eased. From then the children were in agreement about moving on. Their respect for their father had gone but they still retained a sense of loyalty. We did not speak about him. My parents house had two bedrooms so the kids occupied one, I slept on the sofa which was not very comfortable. In the middle of the night my parents often went to the toilet so there were noises of doors slamming, lights on. Sometimes they made a brew in the kitchen disturbing my sleep. I found a job working for the local Council and applied for housing. As there was a massive waiting list I did not hold out much hope. We needed to find a place of our own. Meanwhile the divorce paper had been issued.

There was a £593 fee to apply for a divorce. The fee would not be refunded once the notice that your divorce application had been issued. We had to make arrangements concerning the children, to divide money and property, plus the family home situation. Pete had to respond to the acknowledgement of service notification within 14 days saying whether he:

- agreed with the divorce
- intended to dispute the divorce

If Pete did not respond, the court what advise what I needed to do. I would not need to go to court.
Pete agreed so we continued with the divorce by applying for a conditional order. We had to wait 20 weeks before applying for a conditional order or decree nisi. A conditional order and decree nisi are documents that say that the court does not see any reason why you cannot divorce. I also needed to fill in a statement confirming what I said in my divorce application was true. There were 5 statement forms to cover the reasons I'd given for my divorce. A copy of Pete's response to the divorce application had to be attached. He wrote the bare minimum grudgingly. We had to wait 43 days (6 weeks and 1 day) before we could apply to finalise the divorce and end the marriage.
All these procedures took much longer than stated owing to a backlog in the system, administration overloads plus various strikes that interfered. It was nerve wracking because I was dependent upon Pete not changing his mind. Our arrangement for the children was that Pete would pay maintenance for them monthly. In return he would be granted access to see them provided he notified me in advance. He would not pay me any maintenance but agreed to pay for the home rent until the marital home had been sold when we would divide the sale price. To get a legally binding arrangement for dividing money and property, I had to apply to the court for this before applying for a final order or decree absolute. At times I despaired that the divorce would ever be finalised.
When the divorce was finalised I felt a great sadness rather than relief and was despondent for a while. The marital home had been sold for a good price so I felt secure. There was no sense of relief rather I felt failure. We were renting a terraced

house near my parents temporarily where a neighbour had died. As my parents had been friends, the rent was a special low rate to help us to get on our feet. My parents were close by which was good for the children. Pete initially saw them for a few weekend trips out but these dwindled in time.
Eventually, he did not remember their birthdays. The children lost interest in him and his lifestyle. They did not like his new woman who was not used to children so disliked them too. The three of us made rotas for the housework sharing the responsibilities.
Once the sale of the house went through I was able to put a deposit on a small ex Council house which had three bedrooms, high ceilings in a quiet area. It needed some decoration and modernisation but was fit to move into. Our furniture was basic and my parents helped to kit it out. Over time we made improvements but the location was close to shops, bus stops, a library and there was a public park nearby with a boating lake. It suited us and the neighbours were helpful. In time when the children were old enough they got part time supermarket shifts to earn money to purchase the luxury items other kids received as presents for doing well. It taught them the value of money. They kept their earnings and spent them carefully. I earned enough to feed/cloth us and pay the bills.
In their teens the kids preferred to do weekend activities with their friends. Pete did not see them often but they sent text messages. Sometimes he invited them out for pizza or meals. They did not want to go but I encouraged them. Apparently Pete was still living with the barmaid in our old house which was decorated differently in grey and red. Sadie said Pete had a fat tummy. I declined any invitations from him. My social life was mainly with my friends. Occasionally I dated but not seriously and it never lasted. Once bitten twice shy was my philosophy. Life functioned solo proving that a man was not essential. Sometimes I felt the lack of a partner when couples smooched at a function or paired off. Despite that I enjoyed choosing my television programmes, when or what to eat, doing or ignoring tasks. There was nobody to interfere because the children had their own televisions in their rooms

plus computers to play games on. They ate what I made, Martin emptied the fridge snacking, Sadie was easy going and remained dainty so did not eat much. As a family we bonded well. I only nagged about homework and studying for exams. I decided to get fit so attended local classes. Once toned and more flexible I noticed an improvement in my shape so my clothes fit better. Regular hair dyes kept my colour and I tried to walk regularly for fresh air. Changes at work meant less staff expecting the same impact so we were constantly busy. Legislation changes meant new procedures and wordy updates which were too boring to read. People came and went but my colleagues became friends quickly. We shared the tasks. Time moved on swiftly as we led busy lives. During school holidays the children sometimes visited their grandparents or occasionally saw Pete briefly so I was surprised when he offered to take them to Disneyland Florida during the next vacation.

To my mind teenagers were a bit old for cartoon characters but they both wanted to go so I let them. Apparently the barmaid's mother had cancer so she was headed to Cornwall to relieve her sister for a few weeks to take over care duties. Pete felt it was an ideal opportunity to bond with the kids. While they were away, a friend invited me to join her on a Spanish retreat holistic break. Located in a Cortijo not far from Granada, it was a whitewashed Andalusian little settlement. I was meeting my friend Kelly there as she was travelling from London. We shared a twin bedded chalet. Other participants came from all over England, Scotland and Wales, but also from abroad.

As an ice breaker we were told to bring our favourite book then explain why. Meals were taken outdoors under a trellis with home cooking vegetarian style. Everything tasted fresh and delicious. In the mornings there was yoga on the roof terrace, we went on organised walks, there was meditation, spiritual dancing, individual therapies on offer, a chance to relax and swim in the pool. It was laid back, friendly but not pushy. We quickly made friends and enjoyed the ambience, the wild flowers and the scenery. Excursions were made into the scenic surrounding villages, there was a day trip to

THE LIFE OF ROSIE

Granada to explore Alhambra Palace, plus picnics and local amenities. Adjacent to the property was an open bar with an honesty box.

I had told the kids just to text if they wanted as phone calls were expensive. They seemed to be enjoying themselves. Pete texted to say all was going well. For most of my holiday duration I forgot about the family and tried to emerge as a person again. It was interesting to hear about other people's stories and anecdotes. One person had gone into Hanley's toy store to buy a present and accidentally knocked over a whole display. When he asked if he could help the assistant to pick it all up she replied: "No thanks, you have done enough!"

There was just one room upstairs on the roof part and of course the only person with disabilities on the trip was allocated that space! He swapped with someone else. Several people had travelled alone. Emphasis was made on self-improvement and holistic life styles. One session everyone had to write positive things about each person then read them out. This was difficult to hear as normally people were used to being criticised or negativity. The time flew by and reluctantly we were transferred to the airport. My plane was delayed by several hours which was unpleasant in the heat. Everyone else got away. We had exchanged addresses and contact details but apart from three participants, I never saw anyone again. At least I arrived home before the kids so prepared everything for their return and school in peace.

One of our friends on my holiday was John who lived in Scotland. We always ate together along with a couple called Carl and Molly. His brother lived a few miles from me. When the holiday snaps were developed John offered to visit me while seeing his brother. We would be able to view each other's snaps. I offered him accommodation if required. The children did not mind a guest coming. At first John drove across the bottom of our road by mistake then eventually came back. John was still eating vegetarian holistic food so made the mistake of putting his special breakfast food in our cupboard. Next morning I was horrified to discover the kids had nearly emptied the packet! It was embarrassing.

THE LIFE OF ROSIE

John was slim so I tried to feed him up. When placing the meal before him John asked me if that was for him or the whole family. It became our joke. As we all got along harmoniously, we arranged to go on holiday to Northumberland with Carl and Molly from the holiday. We met at the apartment we had rented in Seahouses. While there we travelled around to Holy Island, Bamburgh, Alnwick admiring the scenery, history, castles and sense of adventure. It had special vibes and a fascinating history. It almost felt like time had stood still. The coast was scenic and almost deserted. Elsewhere it would have been popular. We cooked, walked and had fun. When we parted to go home we drove to Berwick upon Tweed and home slowly exploring places along the route. After that John went back home and we communicated by phone and letters.

The kids were growing up fast in their teens with long slim arms and legs. I had to keep buying Martin new trousers. Apparently he had been flirting with a girl during the American trip. Sadie told me she had been trying to help him even though she was only 13. They both studied for exams with Martin always coming top or close to. He seemed to be talented in Maths and the sciences. My daughter was steady just above midway and liked History, English and enjoyed helping people. Sadie was good at gymnastics, netball and could bake well. Both had plenty of friends who often came round. I saw my friends when I could but preferred to be home in the evenings to make sure the kids came in at a reasonable time. Sometimes I socialised with work colleagues on special occasions.

We were away on a summer day trip when mum rang to tell me that dad had been diagnosed with early symptoms of Parkinson's disease, a condition that affects the brain. It causes problems like shaking and stiffness that get worse over time. It is caused by a loss of nerve cells in part of the brain. Currently there's no cure for Parkinson's disease, but treatments are available to help relieve the symptoms and maintain quality of life including:

- supportive therapies like physiotherapy
- medication
- surgery for some people

During the early stages patients may not need any treatment as symptoms are usually mild. However, dad would need regular appointments to monitor his condition. Mum was advised to give him a healthy diet. When his symptoms developed a care plan should be agreed with his healthcare team and family. We were all upset and dad was shocked. He took medication and walked for exercise and fresh air. We all went on line to read up on advice. It did not sound promising so we tried to enable him to enjoy life as much as possible while he could. There was no family history of the disease. It made me aware that opportunities should be taken when they came along instead of putting things off.

I bumped into Tony one lunch time in town. He looked a bit strained and seemed to lack his previous vigour. We had not kept in touch except to wish each other well during Christmas. Living with Victoria had aged him, I asked about them.

"At first I enjoyed being bossed around it felt like I was being cared for. Now it seems that Victoria thinks she has taken over my life," he said sadly.

"Well why do you let her? Assert yourself," I told him.

"I still care about her."

"That's fine but you should tell her how you are feeling inside. It's your place after all."

"We moved and have bought a house together."

"Did she contribute or was it bought from selling your place?"

"She did contribute but it was mainly the sale."

"Therefore you need to speak up, she will respect you for your honesty."

Tony sighed saying: "It is difficult sometimes but we manage."

"If you excuse me saying so, you don't look so good, before you had an energy. Don't let her subdue the real you."

"Thank you for your concern. How about you?"

We spoke briefly about the kids and my divorce and reminisced about the supermarket coffee days fondly then we both had to return to work. I felt sad to see Tony so downhearted but it was his business and I could not intervene. In my case Pete had told Martin that I had been a bit stand offish. His new lady had a kind heart, she made proper meals instead of that healthy eating lark that I insisted on. Both of them were now very plump and did not exercise. When I enquired about the barmaid's mother's health in Cornwall, Martin said that her sister who lived there took care of her. Martin said Pete had been more like a friend than a parent when they went away. In fact Martin had felt more in charge than Pete who was not very sensible. I was pleased they had got along and enjoyed themselves. Sadie said Pete treated her like she was still a little girl but she didn't mind.

A text arrived informing me that my stalker had been released early for good behaviour. It was sent via one of the other victims so at first I panicked then I realised we lived in a different area. Wondering if the prison sentence had reformed the stalker in any way, it seemed a short time to have made much difference. Perhaps the impact may deter him from stalking us again. I hoped he would not seek new victims. Once again the fear struck a cold terror inside me. For weeks I checked the areas surrounding me when I left the house. Both kids were told not to speak to strangers. I found news cuttings to show them his picture in order to keep them distant if he turned up. Fear of the unknown is threatening and very real, some victims suffer violence or even death so it necessitates caution.

We all visited my parents weekly to check on my dad, taking him treats and encouraging him. In the summer they managed a holiday in a convalescent home seaside location when my dad started to deteriorate. They managed coastal walks and made a few new friends. It was their last holiday together which they enjoyed. From then my dad's health declined despite medication and regular supervision. He had always been a proud independent man and hated his loss of control. When we visited he seemed depressed in low spirits. When it became too much for my mother to manage, he was reluctantly taken to a care home. We hoped it would be temporary but he stopped eating and cooperating until he passed away. All the staff lined up outside for the funeral cortege.

My mother was distraught as dad had always taken care of the finances and home management. I took the children to move into her house as she needed us. My plan was to remain there indefinitely while decorating my place, emptying it of personal things then offering it furnished for rental. The kids and I collected our belongings and I got a decorator to paint it cream and white throughout. When it was done and decluttered, I called three estate agents to value it for sale and rental. For the time being I chose the highest rental and handed over the keys. It was worth paying management fees to have everything taken care of. At mum's I slept in the same bedroom as Sadie while Martin occupied the box room cum office. It suited him as he was studying for his GCSE's in earnest.

Pete had attended dad's funeral and offered his condolences. He asked if he could take the children away during the summer holidays again. I agreed and was pleased to hear him encourage Martin to study well for his exams. Sadie was also told to do her best so she would have a good future. We greeted each other cordially and I sometimes glimpsed traces of the former Pete I married hidden inside the overweight man he had become. The barmaid avoided us all but remained with Pete steadfastly. With the children taken care of for the first part of the school holidays, I found an advert for a Journey into Turkey holiday, specially designed for those who want something different from the standard package trip. It was an opportunity to have a special Turkish experience. I booked in solo as nobody could accompany me.

The holiday was based in Kas, a village on Turkey's Mediterranean coast, site of the ancient Lycian city of Antiphellos. We stayed in a small family owned hotel on the sea shore with scenic views including the Greek island of Meis. An English lady married to a Turkish husband arranged the trip taking us sightseeing exploring the region. We visited the blue lagoon at Olu Deniz, the amazing deserted peace village of Kaya Koy where residents had to leaves their homes to evacuate. Previously Turks and Greeks had lived together but the law changed and Greeks had to cross to the Greek island whilst Turks from there came to live in Turkey. Their house remain unlived in with trees growing inside the toilets and open apertures.

We had breakfast in the roof top restaurant but ate our evening meals in various local restaurants. One of the highlights was a group visit to a traditional Turkish bath establishment where we nervously awaited our turns hearing slapping sounds. We were served apple tea everywhere. The experience of the bath and massage was exhausting. Another time we saw a wedding procession led by a cart carrying a red ribboned goat. Locally the shops stayed open until late in the evening. Colourful balconied streets offered rich patterned traditional carpets, spice stalls and crafts. Everywhere we went we were offered tea and invited to sit. On our travels we visited an old ruined amphitheatre comparing styles with the Greek.

THE LIFE OF ROSIE

We visited the market town of Fethiye with few women about. On a trip to the scenic mountains we had a competition to see who could maintain their bare feet in a glacial river for the longest. A boat memorable trip took us across the water to the Greek village Kekova and Sunken City, with appropriate flag on the boat. We spent a day there which was interesting if small. On an overnight trip to Mount Olympus to see a volcano, a beautiful beach and some ruins, we climbed up a mountain with vents spouting flames intermittently all the way up. Travelling on a bus up the local mountain we stopped at a traditional tea house where a massive bronze kettle hung in the fireplace. They offered herbal tea remedies for all ailments and cures to aid good health.

Our area was spacious, bright, mellow with picturesque countryside villages. There were no high rise buildings. Many old buildings had archways, curved windows, balconies and were well kept. Every village had a mosque. On the markets there were exquisite leather wares with prevalent silk. The language was difficult to pick up as it was so different from the European tones. It was warm but being coastal there was a breeze. Women wore traditional attire. The currency was in millions which was confusing. The food was freshly cooked made to order. There were no sandwiches or cakes. Juice flavours include peach, apricots and cherry. School started at 6, girls wore peacock blue dresses with long sleeves, white colours. Boys were short shirt jackets like half an overall.

It was a really fascinating holiday and I was sorry to leave. Although I was tanned, my kids returned from their holiday without noticing. My new car was waiting for me to collect as the original one had needed replacing. It was a pale blue Corsa which was easy to drive. Alongside the hotel in Kas each day there had been the equivalent blue Corsa parked although it traded under a different name. We all settled down again and the kids agreed to see Pete spasmodically. Life continued for a while although nothing stayed the same indefinitely. Changes occur whether welcome or not. I think life revolves in cycles so that everybody experiences the ups and downs eventually. As my life revolved around the family aspect, it was always important to be a sound provider. Pete offered to assist if needed but I had my pride and did not ask. He was my child allowance provider which I used for their school and clothing needs. I saved it up so that they could use it when expenses occurred. My money ran the household and kept us fed and me clothed.

At work there was a new structure imposed which meant downsizing the departments with everybody interviewing for the new limited roles. Despite being in the job for years, I had to have my turn answering questions. There were jobs allocated to two of my colleagues, but apparently my answers were not as good so I was offered redundancy or going to a regional office to work. This regional vacancy had been offered to all the department. It turned out that nobody wanted it because of the location which was convenient to me. This meant that I could avoid the city centre traffic and even walk if need be. I agreed and left my office to its new procedures.

In my new role I had to open and copy files for new cases, research and follow up investigations and make telephone calls to clients. This meant familiarising myself with current legislations and procedures which were constantly evolving and being updated. The role was varied enough to suit but the red tape was frustrating. In all my career I hated reading long winded documentation that held no interest to me. It is why I never pursued an academic career or became a top scholar. Quickly bored and impatient, I got frustrated when forced to succumb. When something interested me I was oblivious of time or appetite. I had to store information in my head before calling clients. Sometimes I had to ask managers for advice who expected me to know it by heart. One was supercilious saying: "I told you last week!"

Another upsetting change occurred in my social life. Since the Cortijo holiday I had maintained good relations with John who came over at regular intervals to see his brother. He always stayed with us, we went travelling around the UK in his car and developed a close relationship. The kids and John got on well and we had some fun experiences. This continued for a few years, I went over to stay with him one time. Suddenly without explanation John stopped calling or answering any texts or emails. This was hurtful and I could not understand whether I had said or done anything untoward. Nothing happened to change the situation so I had to accept this was the end and he could not bring himself to tell me we were over. Without any proper closure I was upset but powerless. Perhaps I was not suited to lasting relationships.

Martin got excellent GCSE results and chose the sciences and General Studies for A-levels. Sadie was in her first preparation year for her GCSE which would take place the following year. Whatever future choices they made for careers, I told them to choose something they were interested in because they would spend a long time working. If they enjoyed what they did it would be so much better. Many people remained long term in jobs they did not like for security. Once committed to mortgages or family life, security meant affordability. Interesting caring work or being creative was the best but often paid the least. Practicality held sway over choices. Being a highly competitive world meant enthusiasm and a good CV was essential. I encouraged the children to record new experiences and achievements.

I had encouraged my mother to join in senior social groups where she reunited with some of her old friends. When she saw one little old lady with a grey perm and glasses mum cried out: "Oh Gertie, you have not changed a bit." They had gone to school together. This got my mother going out and mixing. They had meals, entertainment and festival celebrations. Volunteers manned the action with enthusiasm and a good time was had by all. I was roped in to help when there was a staff shortage. It was a good experience so I made myself available when required. As I worked full time my help was mainly during weekend functions or early evening. Older people preferred day time activities. There were many characters and individuals with interesting life stories to tell.

In time Martin applied to universities before taking his A-levels. He was interested in Leeds University where the programme said: "Within the School of Science we have exciting areas of study for undergraduate students covering Chemistry, Computer Science, Mathematics and Physics, while our Natural Sciences course gives students the option to gain interdisciplinary skills. We also offer Chemistry with

THE LIFE OF ROSIE

Computing and Physics with Computing - enabling you to pursue your preferred science alongside computing. Our courses are designed to grow your skills and knowledge, but also to challenge and inspire you. Your experience will be enhanced by the insights of academics. There will be opportunities to get involved in exciting research projects that address today's global challenges. Take a look at some of the projects our students have made vital contributions towards and start exploring your own future in science today!"

Sadie proved herself to be adept at computer programming, something she was not interested in. The ability came naturally to her but despite being lucrative, she did not want to pursue it. However, it served her well finding temporary work as a student to keep her afloat. Martin had worked in a supermarket on a part time basis to support himself. Whereas Martin wanted to go away to University, Sadie wanted to save money and continue to live at home while pursuing a caring professional qualification. Both children had work experience while at school. Whilst still uncertain about her future direction, Sadie looked up Physiotherapy as she enjoyed helping people She was informed about a possible career path.

Amongst a team of skilled healthcare professionals, physiotherapists independently identify, assess and analyse physical problems and treat them by taking a holistic approach. Courses incorporate the core values of the NHS to help prepare for the challenges of working in contemporary healthcare. Practice skills in simulation labs provided a safe space to develop expertise in a supportive environment. Time was spent on clinical placements in every year of studies to help apply learning and skills in a real world setting. After graduation as a chartered physiotherapist, there would be work in the NHS or the private sector, in community and care homes, or schools.

If that did not materialise, Sadie checked out a number of social work options. A community support worker visits people in their own homes, to help them live their lives as independently as possible plus ensure they were safe and healthy. Community support worker duties included supporting and encouraging people to manage their own domestic responsibilities also assisting with their personal care. Sadie wanted to help people. Another description of the role stated that community development workers help marginalised people to tackle the problems they face in their local area. They sometimes work with communities as a whole, but they may also focus on specific groups, such as women or refugees. She fancied a career in social work and was contend to plod on with her exams until she could achieve a plan.

Sadie felt that Social work was a challenging, rewarding and diverse profession offering opportunities across a wide range of specialisms. The degree programme prepared for the demands of the role by offering a balance of theoretical, practical and practice experience. I told her to research carefully and choose something that motivated her. People could be difficult to handle and her task would not be easy nor straight forward. If that was her choice then I would stand by her. It could be stressful seeing people struggling to cope. My daughter told me that was why she wanted to help them. We both knew but did not mention that she could always fall back upon her computer skills if needed for support. I was proud of both of my children. It had not been easy raising them by myself but they came out well balanced and mannered.

My mother started to decline in stages. She fell asleep easily, developed aches and pains from arthritis, sometimes became absent minded or repeated things being uncertain whether she had said them or merely thought them. Although she retained her faculties, she lacked the energy and stamina to do much. We arranged for lifts to take her to and from the social centre or places she needed to go. Our doctor told me it was a mixture of old age plus wear and tear. We bought a new bed and turned the front room into mum's new bedroom for convenience. It had easy access to the downstairs toilet.

Upstairs the bathroom had been converted into a wet room so we purchased a stair lift to get her there.

Throughout her decline mother rarely complained except to say she felt stiff or weary. The kids adored her and willingly helped to make her comfortable. They would confide in her. In turn my mother listened to them and gave them secret spending money or any treats people had given her. Sometimes mother had visitors but often benefitted from her outings. There were good days and bad. I knew we were going to lose her, but it still came as a shock. She just went to bed and never woke up. Mothers were supposed to last forever so we were all distraught and felt her absence keenly. At the funeral her friends, neighbours and relatives paid their respects. For me the sense of loss came and went affecting me unexpectedly for a long time.

The house had been left to me so when I managed to pull myself together I used some money I had accrued to make some improvements. I knocked through the wall between the kitchen and living room to install a new modern kitchen/dining room. New double glazed windows were installed throughout plus a modern new front door. A patio area was paved behind the kitchen window with French doors leading out. The house was decorated in a plain light shade throughout with the bathroom which was tiled in a modern style. I left the toilet separate for convenience but had it tiled like the bathroom. All this took time to be carried out but by then both children were living away studying so there was only me to accommodate.

Martin had decided to get a science degree with a view to doing research later. He had gone from being a big cheese at school to one of many bright students at university. Once he settled down he made friends easily and after spending the first year in halls of residence then lived in a rented flat with some friends. After that he never lived at home again but visited and rang fairly regularly. As he was bright and determined he did well but had to make an effort to stay on top. Pete helped him financially as I was unable. Our son made us both proud and all we asked was that he should keep in regular contact. We used his old box room mainly as an office with his bed to sit on. It was also good for storage but I tried to keep it tidy.

Sadie had taken a social study degree course intending to remain at home. Her best friend Ellie came from a wealthy family. Ellie's dad purchased a small terraced house near the university on the condition that Ellie did not live alone. They arranged for Sadie to live with her rent free. Both girls shared living expenses which taught them to manage on a budget. Although Ellie was studying economics, they were good company together and shared adventures. Again Pete helped Sadie financially. She kept in regular contact and visited. Ellie was a pleasant girl who was like an extra daughter so we were all happy with this arrangement. I warned both girls to be cautious when out plus not to leave their drinks unattended.

My work had changed again with more streamlined measures, cuts and new legislation. It was hard for me to absorb all the constant nit picking changes plus the work pile never diminished. As soon as it went down slightly more piled up on top. I was too young to retire and lacked confidence to apply for other roles. When I did manage to get an interview elsewhere I was never chosen, perhaps it was my age. Young people worked cheaper. Telling myself each day brought me nearer to closure felt good. Socially I saw my friends mainly at weekend or I did voluntary duties at the Community Centre which catered for a wide range of interests and services.

Familiarity with the regulars at the Community Centre brought me on greeting terms with many people who attended routinely. There was a food bank, computer courses, a disability group, pensioners, quizzes, art, financial advice, a walking group and many other activities. Therefore I was surprised one evening to receive a phone call from a man called Jeff who was on the management team. Expecting him to ask for my assistance, he invited me out to go for a drink. Astonished I agreed then rang Sadie for advice on what to wear. I was so out of practice dating, it made me nervous.

THE LIFE OF ROSIE

Martin popped home on the evening of my date to give Jeff the onceover. They shook hands before we left.

He took me to a hotel bar fairly local where we relaxed and chatted about our backgrounds and interests. I found him easy to talk to and attractive in a masculine way. Jeff did not have film star looks but he was well groomed, confident and appealing to my taste. At the end of the evening he dropped me off outside my house and waved goodbye. I wondered whether he would ask me out again but for a fortnight nothing happened. When I had just relaxed into my usual routine Jeff rang again inviting me to a country hotel that hosted dinner dances on Saturday evenings. We would skip the meal but enjoy the entertainment. I agreed and enjoyed myself.

This was the beginning of a spasmodic series of outings with no physical relationship developments. At times I wondered why but left well alone. I enjoyed the outings and conversations. Jeff made me laugh and was always well equipped for any occasion or emergencies. Without bulging pockets he had solutions for all types of mishaps contained in his jacket. We became a platonic dating couple which felt good. Here was a man who could take charge, I liked that. He had been divorced for many years with two grown up children but was estranged from his wife and children. At the time Jeff was living in his deceased parental home but had plans to move to Cyprus. The English climate did not suit him.

We went on holiday together remaining platonic which I found annoying but when I tried to move closer to him, he turned away rejecting my advance. I did not try again. Before me he had been involved long term with someone but that had ended. He seemed solvent, affable and was obviously intelligent with a professional career behind him so I did not understand why he was still single. He asked me if I was interested in going to Cyprus with him. Whilst the idea of a coastal continental place was appealing, I was reluctant to leave my children, friends and home behind permanently. We discussed it regularly but I remained hesitant. When I had a bad day it seemed like a good idea.

Eventually, Jeff put his house for sale and planned to go abroad. In the interim I invited him to move in with me until everything was finalised. Living together had its ups and downs. Always a picky eater Jeff told me he objected to additives in his food despite eating takeaways that used stock etc. He was also allergic to fragrances so even the most minor smells upset his system. While I worked Jeff had taken early retirement as he had invested wisely providing for himself. When I came home he expected conversation and attention. If I started reading a book to relax he complained. During the day he made friends with my neighbours. I also found him furtive about his plans as he was rarely forthcoming.

Although generous towards me, he was always researching on the computer and was especially health conscious. At times he seemed to be a hypochondriac. There were times when there was tension in the house and he retreated to his bedroom with the door closed. We had formed an intimate relationship but he always retreated to his room afterwards, we never spent the night together. On the other hand if I went out late somewhere, he always waited up for me to return safely. Initially I was always pleased to see him but towards the end I was anxious about the mood he would be in. Jeff was good in many ways but difficult to live with. In the end he told me one evening that he would be leaving the next day for Cyprus and would arrange for his belongings to be collected.

Early next morning a taxi arrived for him and off he went without leaving a forwarding address. His room was a mess, cluttered, dusty, stuff everywhere. I did not know what to do with everything or where to start. Sadie came to help me. As Jeff had left discourteously, she bundled everything up and eventually Martin came by and took it all to the tip. Jeff never made contact again to enquire about his possessions and nobody came to collect anything. Despite my best sincere efforts I was dumped once again. My conclusion was that I was not suited to long term relationships. Men were either controllers, gropers, losers or cheaters. I decided to abstain for the future from mankind. Once my house was adjusted back to its original state, I was able to relax. There was a quiet satisfaction of choosing which programmes to watch, buying food and drink to suit my taste, undertaking chores as and when I chose.

Pete was still with the barmaid who seemed to suit him. He texted the kids mainly who were too busy to visit much. Martin graduated and we proudly attended the ceremony clapping loudly when his name was announced. His ambition was to do research so he stayed in Leeds and entered the Milk Round race to find a post. There was much competition but he eventually found a job In South London. We went down there to find him a place to stay. He stuck it out there until he was accepted in a large firm which offered graduate training schemes in our home town. Martin shared a house with two friends.

Sadie was enjoying her course which offered hands on experience in segments. She made friends and was equally happy at home or living with Ellie. I felt sure that she would be beneficial to all the people she helped as her nature was warm and caring. Ellie told me that a guy called Ian adored Sadie and hung around hoping she would notice him. Sadie told me he was too soppy and she had no interest in him. It seemed often to be the case that when one longs to belong, the other had other aspirations. At this stage Sadie just wanted to have fun with her friends, get on with her studies and was too busy to date. Martin never told me about any romances so when I asked he ignored me.

Through my volunteering at the Community Centre I discovered that a respected elderly gentleman who lived in my locality had suffered a stroke. When he was sent home in a wheelchair, I took him homemade soup or cooking sometimes dropping by for a chat. He was a learned man full of interesting anecdotes and stories. At his house he had a team of carers consisting of family and friends to supervise him. It was always good to visit him and update him about the Centre. I also managed an occasional stint at the Food Bank where many employed people struggled to manage financially so depended on extra help. To my surprise they collected together to buy me a Christmas present for helping them.

Whereas it was easy to be judgemental about circumstances, dependents on benefits or the homeless, it was wrong. Everybody started off as similar sized babies, they did not all grow up having equal opportunities. Sometimes incidents happened unexpectedly that destroyed their regular life patterns. Once on a downward spiral it was very difficult to escape. Whilst there were charities that helped, soup kitchens, Food Banks, the Salvation Army etc., it seems that Westminster was the capital place for Homeless people sleeping rough. Most people ignored them as if they were invisible. It was a frightening struggle, the Community Centre did their best to accommodate everyone and offer advice or assistance.

When I was caught up in married family life I never considered outreach facilities or much else. I donated to some charity appeals and passed on outgrown clothing to charity, but my life was too busy running my own affairs. Many of the less fortunate people I now encountered were pleasant, kind and genuinely suffering hardship through no fault of their own. Their modest incomes did not meet the ever rising outgoings. Of course some people were belligerent or grumbled negatively, but they were the exception. Donations freely given by the better off were gratefully received and even life savers during the winter months. We took for granted all our luxuries and comforts imagining they would last forever. Unexpected events could happen any moment like the invasion of Ukraine. One day the inhabitants were living their lives then suddenly war invaded them destroying all their homes and infrastructure. It could happen anywhere as the world was in a precarious state.

My soup was no longer required as my old gentleman friend died. His funeral was well attended because he has been a familiar figure in society. Initially I felt sad at his loss then I realised that the funeral was a celebration of his life. The gathering meant that he had been appreciated and contributed to those around him. His life had not been in vain. Although he had not achieved fame or fortune, he had been loved and appreciated. His family gave him a dignified send off. Nobody knows what follows the departure. I imagined an enormous bale of material or ether and that the soul gets absorbed back into its origin. We enter and leave this world alone despite how numerous the people are who surround us.

The priest indicated that we would all eventually receive an invitation to depart from this world. This meant that we must seize all opportunities that came along, not put off things for an unknown future date. I read once that when we failed to take opportunities, our bodies lost their form and our momentum. Many people take the easy option of giving up instead of making the effort of creating a meaningful life. Often it is only when adversity strikes that they consider their vulnerability and seek a more spiritual path. Moral codes or religious guidance have survived throughout the world for generations because they channel a route offering a sense of belonging. In secular modern society this has been lost as people confuse scientific developments as a substitute believing that only their world exists.

If nothing is sacred, belief is scorned and replaced by anything goes. Liberty and selfishness prevail leading to a constant emptiness which no desires for new experiences can fill. Possessions and styles are frequently changing in order to part with our money. Keeping up with the fads is empty because there is no substance. Being a trendsetter or instigator of something new or original that is widely copied means great expectations for ever more. Fame and fortune are temporary and illusionary. Whilst the celebrities are young and attractive it is their image or the parts they express that are worshipped. When they age or new competition arrives on the scene they tend to disappear overnight. Few survive for the duration spending fortunes to try to prolong their images.

I was in the prime of my life approaching middle age as an independent woman. Although I did not like my work, it enabled me to meet my commitments. My home was mortgage free which was a blessing. Both children were leading independent lives. My life was flexible enough to be able to make my own decisions without conforming to others. The only issue I had was a lack of direction. Time was passing by swiftly and I did not know how I wanted to proceed with the rest of my life. At times I felt alone but not lonely. I had adjusted to being solo and the only time it bothered me was at public functions when people were in pairs or during slow dances. By keeping busy and trying to remain fit, I had enough to occupy myself. When I was tired or unwell I felt low. My glass was half full rather than empty most of the time.

Hackers and scammers were increasing their attacks on innocent users of Facebook and media platforms. Scams wanted security details in order to steal money from the unsuspecting targets. Attacks ranged from telling somebody about fraudulent usage of credit or debit cards; to implying the target was listed on a benefactor pay out of funds. These people pretended to send their wicked messages impersonating somebody listed as a friend on the target's contacts. Older people or victims not media savvy lost their money if they were not careful. Vigilance was called for. If these people were bright enough to be able to infiltrate other accounts, I wondered why they didn't find gainful employment using their ability.

Martin brought home his girlfriend Mia, a petite girl who scampered behind him each time he moved and tried to avoid me. They went out for a while before she headed off to America for a year as part of her studies. Sad for a while Martin also transferred to Watford where he found a placement position. I accompanied him to find a place to rent. He stayed there for under a year and brought home a snooty girl who sat stiffly on the edge of my sofa, I disliked her on sight. Fortunately, Martin caught her cheating on him when he went back unexpectedly so that ended his relationship. His job was not suitable for his ambitions and took over all his time as he was on call all hours, so he returned home to take up a new roll. Back home he moved in with his friends and just visited me occasionally.

As Martin's friends were personable young graduates who led a busy social life, they attracted female attention. One of the girls called Maisie was purported to like Martin so he asked her out. Unfortunately, Maisie got flu just before the big event so it was a while until they got together. By then most of the friends were pairing off and Martin joined suit. He was settled in his new job and looking to buy a house. Maisie planned to move in with him. I thought this was a big step so went along to meet her parents to make sure they were comfortable with the arrangement. Her father told me that with many divorces these days, it made sense to see if they were suited. They moved in together then went on holiday where Martin proposed. I liked Maisie who was a pretty warm hearted girl, stylish with a pleasant personality.

At their engagement party I invited some friends and former neighbours who had two sons. I told them to bring their sons if they were home so they brought Nathan, the youngest boy who was at university. Growing up my parents and the neighbours had been friends so we had known each other for many years. Seeing Nathan I introduced him to Sadie. Over the years from when my children were babies in prams, I had bumped into our neighbours at school functions or out walking. To Sadie's embarrassment other people introduced Nathan as well. They chatted for a while and with encouragement from his parents, Nathan invited Sadie out. She told me he was too quiet, but I said he could have been nervous so she should give him a chance.

Much later when both were qualified and working they got engaged. At their wedding a pregnant Maisie was bridesmaid. Sadie became pregnant months after her wedding so that in a short time I became a grandma twice to Martin's son Isaac and Sadie's daughter Abby. It was such a thrill for me to have babies to play with and indulge as they grew older. In time they were joined by a second son to Martin called Zak and a son to Sadie called Mark. The children grew up and played together, went to the same school and visited me during the holidays when we had fun times and learning sessions together. My greatest pleasure was seeing my grandchildren who were so innocent and affectionate. In my eyes they were all beautiful with individual personalities and traits. I bought treats for them to keep for visits. Maisie bought me a fridge magnet saying: "Grandchildren spoilt here".

Both couples started off in small modern houses, later on they moved into bigger properties in more convenient areas. Thankfully they moved before mortgage rates went sky high and slowly they made some improvements. Sadie's house had a garden in several parts with screening by overhanging trees to make it private. I found both houses modern and comfortable. Returning to my place sometimes disappointed me as I would prefer to live near my family, but I counted my blessings and felt lucky to have my own secure place. As a family we were close and both Maisie and Nathan were delightful. My good fortune lay that they were all within reach, not abroad or long distance.

A volunteer called Lawrence in the Community Centre used to go for rides in the country at weekends. He often took me and another lady called Gloria or others if we were not available. Sometimes I went with him alone. We would drive around scenic villages, stop for afternoon tea, walk about then come home. There was never any attraction between us because we were on different wavelengths. He was very right wing and quite intolerant but somehow we muddled on and had good afternoon adventures. Coming back he liked to play games of 'Dead or Alive' or similar. I suppose it kept his mind alert while driving. Lawrence was divorced and seeking a new wife who would cook him tasty meals, she had to be petite as he was not very tall. On our travels we discovered areas of outstanding beauty.

Another new friend I made was part of the security at work. We went for coffee a few times during the year to discuss putting the world to rights. He was a creative person with interesting hobbies. We were on the same wavelength but I was much older so we were just good friends. My friends were married most raising families. As time evolved there were a couple of divorces and one widow. Nobody I knew was seeking a second spouse. Only unmarried women still looked for men. It was hard to meet someone trustworthy because since the pandemic all the mixing had been sparse. Younger punters and students occupied the bars. Dating sites were suspect because there was no verification on who you may be meeting. Gone were the dances and discos of the past in the main. Most people were paired off by their mid-twenties.

During the summer I went on holiday with some of my girlfriends. We always enjoyed ourselves and relished blue seas and sunshine. Over time we grew more adventurous and had an amazing holiday touring the Rockies in Canada. Breath taking scenery, amazing wildlife and vistas made it our holiday of a lifetime. Day trips also kept us going. We pleased and amused ourselves making our own adventures. In relationships it seemed that one person always had to please the other for the sake of harmony. If we annoyed each other we grumbled but put up with occasional bad behaviour because we were familiar. In addition, we supported each other through trials and tribulations. The years seemed to pass quicker every year as we grew older. Our children grew up, married, some of us became grandmas and we all admired everyone's offspring equally. Without blood ties we intrinsically became one family.

I reflected upon incidents during my lost youth. When I was a little girl an older girl pinned me against a wall demanding to know if I believed in Jesus. She intimidated me because I did not know anyone called Jesus or why she was bothering me. I felt alarmed and confused until she released me. Religion was not something I was familiar with then apart from labelling Catholics as Tom Cats, Protestants as Proddie Dogs and Jews as Jew Drops. That seemed to cover the community then where we all lived together harmoniously. All the neighbours knew each other and told parents about any misbehaviour.

THE LIFE OF ROSIE

In our street there was a small corner shop stocked with basics. The shop keeper's daughter, Moira, used to stage dramas in their back yard with a few costume accessories. Although Moira always took the main parts herself, she called upon me and other kids to support her. Sometimes I sat on the pavement chalking hopscotch or making my own designs. The green lamp posts at the end of the street were good for swinging on, but hanging off them made your arms hurt. Playing two ball rhymes against walls or skipping rope games in the street also passed the time. Boys made gliders to wheel along.

On Bonfire Night we had our own bonfires and fireworks. There were noisy bangers like mini radiators called Ripraps that scared the girls, pinwheels, gentle Snowdrops and rainbow fountain fireworks plus the sparklers. Teenagers congregated around a few houses so I was familiar with the fashions, trends and music of the era while still young. Life was simple and mainly routine. Few people were well off, there were hardly any cars, telephones were contained in red public boxes, facilities were basic, storage minimal entailing daily shopping to cook freshly made meals. Readymade meals were years away. We ate what we were given and played out freely until bed time when we hid at call in time.

Because my birthday was in the summer I could not go to school at Easter, but went in September aged 5, sitting two to a desk in rows. There were play areas and turns to enjoy the facilities. I remember picture cards with printed words to learn from. Boys and girls sat together. We had morning assembly with singing and learnt prayers. Some friends made in those days remained with me until the present, others disappeared from my life as time moved on. Crepe paper in two shades wrapped bundles of sweets at Christmas party time. Dinner ladies assisted. We were thrilled to receive simple pleasures with no expectations of major presents.

As I moved along to junior school the 11+ public examination loomed. Together with other low achievers I attended extra maths lessons. We had to sit the examination in another school a bus ride away. It never occurred to me that I would one day live in the vicinity of that other school. Life is full of surprises and I did not expect my mature destination to end up there. I passed the examination and was invited to choose my future school. My friends chose one so I followed suit although my mother felt I was not a studious child and queried whether grammar school was the best choice. True to form I was good at the subjects I enjoyed and mediocre at the rest.

Getting my initial uniform thrilled me and I rushed to try it on to display to visitors. Later when I returned from school I immediately changed out of it. We had a hat to wear, failure to do so meant detention. I had to write repeated lines saying useless phrases like "I will wear my hat." Wearing a blazer eliminated the hat so we froze for as long as possible until we had to wear our gabardine raincoats. Homework was completed as quickly as possible. I usually featured midway in the class lacking ambition to achieve. In art and English, even domestic science I fared well, other topics had occasional highs but mainly lows. Truthfully, I did not care. Life meant outdoor activities, pop music, pin ups, social events. Applying myself to serious studies or aiming for a career was alien to me. My reports said: "could try harder."

One night I saw on the news that the new group sensation The Beatles were coming to a local nightclub so I rushed round there standing outside vainly waiting for hours until my curfew time without seeing them. Another time I was at the cinema watching "Mutiny on the Bounty" when the film broke down and we were given tickets to go again. There was a dancing school locally, the ice skating palace and a bowling alley, plus two cinemas. We also had big empty fields to play on and build dens or plait flower chains. Mid way up our street was a big fenced area where the boys played football. Many of us had bikes to ride around on safely with limited traffic.

In those days it was possible to leave school at 15 or 16. At 16 I left school and found a temporary job at a warehouse but struggled to complete orders in the long rows of stock because I could not locate the goods. My memory lacked the coordination required so I went to college to do a commercial course including shorthand, typing, accounts and commerce. School had been girls only so it was exciting to be in a mixed community.

As we were the first entrants in the new college, we had to unpack the furniture. Making friends there was easy, there were cliques of established groups plus the leftovers. I was a leftover but not for long. Without trying hard I was successful on the course and left with distinctions. I also won my first and only race on the Grand National by backing a horse named after a book I had read. We had male teachers who told us to write what we heard. Therefore my friend and I wrote down the punctuation dialogue as well. Typing was done on manual and electric typewriters, we swapped periodically. Speed was taught to the accompaniment of The William Tell Overture.

We had nicknames for the boys we saw in the canteen or around the place. Without knowing their real names there was Green Jumper, Strong Man who couldn't push open the door, Blue Jacket etc. I expect we were given nicknames in turn but it was not important. After the course ended I found work and continued at night school to upgrade my qualifications. In those days it was easy to find work or change jobs. There was scope to educate or expand one's horizons without incurring debt. Although the wages were low compared to today's expectations, we managed to enjoy life, go to clubs, shop and treat ourselves. We had fun without getting drunk or taking drugs.

My father's firm had set holiday times in the summer so we usually took a week's holiday then. They also tended to give him presents of cigarettes for Christmas although he did not smoke. Our trips were taken in England, the furthest we got was Torquay where it rained all week. Other more successful venues were Scarborough, Llandudno, Rhyl. My best friend accompanied us sometimes which was fun.

In college I felt ready to go abroad for the first time with my friend. We had our first adventure blown away by blue skies, constant sunshine, blue seas and fit handsome foreign men. It made me dissatisfied coming home to grey Britain, so I adopted a policy of working to save for more foreign trips to escape. This was possible because I still lived at home and had no responsibilities. I paid some money to my parents for my keep, but the rest was mine.

Abroad I met interesting people and learned different ways of life. It was exciting exploring new places, customs and food. In those days I felt safe. My friend and I had some interesting experiences mainly because we were naïve and trusting. No harm came to us and we always returned home eventually. Travelling abroad was exciting, interesting and I made new friends and saw scenic locations. When the sun shone it just felt better to be alive compared to the inevitable drizzle and grey skies back home. I found work a few times abroad entering information onto a spreadsheet and translating into English various texts.

Back home I had a group of friends to socialise with. At weekends we met in the city centre going to clubs and events to suit ourselves. If anyone had a date they could join us or go privately. We went to concerts to see our favourite groups rushing to catch the all night bus back. Live music events at student venues attracted the leading artistes of the day. Pop newspapers and magazines kept us updated with our pinups and events. There was also a magazine offering alternative sessions and happenings around the area. It was good to be young with fashion, music and safe times to enjoy our expeditions. Coming home late alone in miniskirts was a regular occurrence which would not feel safe these days.

My work was varied, I had no desire to aim higher or do overtime. At home time I was one of the first to leave. Although I was punctual and worked hard, it was never my intention to reach to the top. Sometimes it was annoying when higher ups nit-picked or were scathing. My ethos was to do everything as quickly as possible so that I could finish and go. Twice I was made redundant from big companies who were downsizing. The first time I cried all day involuntarily, wondering how to support my children. By the second time I was resigned to plod on and keep trying. Eventually I found work with the Council until that folded when they moved me to another role. I always worked full time and looked forward to paying off my mortgage and eventual retirement. There was no alternative.

When I finally achieved my goal of owning my house outright I felt a huge sense of achievement. Without the monthly payments my income felt secure. Retiring a year early due to aggravation and lack of motivation in my role, meant a sense of holiday time. Immediately I filled my time with volunteering at a Food Bank, keep fit, swimming and house duties. One day per week was kept free for appointments or commitments. The weeks passed swiftly, I met new people and kept busy. My life was active and inspiring. Freedom meant that when the weather was good, I could enjoy outdoor activities. It was wonderful to manage my time to suit myself. At work I was trapped inside for the best hours of the day, endlessly.

The world around me kept changing and deteriorating. People became aware of the effects of climate changes with Save the Planet campaigns. War broke out when Russia invaded Ukraine. We had three prime ministers elected in a short time from the same party. Prices and inflation kept rising and the worse part was the dramatic increase in energy supplies. People were afraid to turn on their heating because of the astronomical increases. Food shortages were blamed on the war and also diseases on poultry. Eggs were in short supply and also turkeys. Cooking oil became very expensive. Shopping bills kept rising each visit. This became a global problem not only affecting us.

As the world kept changing some things remained the same. Most babies are born within a similar size range. As they grow their clothing ranges reflect the size usually associated with their age. When they learn to walk they rush to run to discover life around them. Young children run everywhere with excitement. At school they do physical exercise to use their energy and keep their bodies fit. It is when they discover the

THE LIFE OF ROSIE

joys of food, drink and sloth that their sizes expand. Their energy levels disintegrate unless nurtured constantly. This accounts for the overweight bodies and feeble energy supplies. Once they were lean, fit and active but some decline rapidly from over indulgence. Sizes of population members vary considerably.

Bodies are expected to perform indefinitely according to the wishes and commands of their owners. When wear and tear occurs or some mishap, their owners are surprised and disappointed. They spend fortunes buying advertised miracle cures that fail to deliver. If it's herbal remedies or drugs, a larger dose is indicated to help. Equipment offers healing but fails to deliver indefinitely. Pain killers keep the pharmaceutical industry thriving but tend to make patients drowsy. Addiction can follow but after some time the body is familiar with the remedy so a stronger dose is required to be effective. Alternatively, sometimes surgery is offered which is alarming. Some patients prefer to suffer indefinitely.

I, Rosie Jones, am a fit active person leading a hectic busy life. At school I played netball, rounders, was good at sports day specialising in hurdles. When my weight stabilised I did regular exercises, charity walks and participated in events to raise funds. After school I studied then found a job in social work. I quickly discovered why there were so many vacancies in the field. Long unsociable hours and huge caseload demands ensured stress and mental fatigue. For a few years I persevered but then searched for an alternative income. There was a limit to expectations from one overloaded case worker and I struggled to maintain a balance between home and work life.

There was no chance of ever catching up but I managed to find a Care in the Community role with regular hours intensive enough to keep motivated but not overwhelmed. Eventually I had to find alternative employment to earn enough to support the family then myself which is how I joined the tax office. It needed some training and studying along the route until my income level was sufficient. So life was full and active with my family leading busy social lives as they grew older.

All was going well until I began to suffer with knee arthritis problems. After spending a small fortune to try all the suitable remedies I could find, I consulted my doctor. Initially the consultant recommended having a one day surgery to clean out my right knee area called liposuction. Early in the morning I went to hospital for the procedure and surprised myself by walking about in the afternoon before Martin collected me to take me home. Although it took several months to completely subside, it had been worthwhile. I was walking pain free for a time until the other knee started to ache. When this became unbearable I thought the second knee needed doing too.

The second knee was too badly deteriorated for cleaning. Surgery was an option to have a replacement knee. This was shocking to hear and I needed time to digest the idea. When I reached the stage of constant sit down interruptions to my routines, I decided to go ahead. After consultations I was put on the hospital waiting list where it could take up to a year to hear. Resigned to waiting, I was surprised to be offered an early slot due to a cancellation. Everything was straight forward so with arrangements in place, I left early in the morning to check in at the hospital.

In a ward consisting of six beds with modern fabricated blue curtains that worked like blinds horizontally, I had the corner bed and made friends with Jean, the lady in the next bed. Various surgeons and the anaesthetists came round to discuss the procedure. We were told we would be able to get up after the operation and walk around. Instead of taking a general anaesthetic, the consultant recommended IV sedation which meant injections at the base of the back. It was suggested that patients enjoyed pain relief for longer after this procedure. Obediently I leaned forward on the bed and complied but did not feel the benefit after the operation. I did not go into theatre until the afternoon after Jean.

THE LIFE OF ROSIE

When we both came round from the surgery we were told to remain in bed. As we could not go to the toilet, bed pans were brought although difficult to manoeuvre. Next morning after breakfast they told us to get out of bed and handed us crutches. It proved difficult to get our operated legs off the bed onto the floor, but we persevered and were helped onto the crutches, accompanied around the floor to the toilet and surrounds. There was no physio assistance apart from the accompaniment. A flight of three stairs with a small central platform stood in the centre of the ward. Instructions followed to go up and down the stairs watched by staff. During the afternoon a bag of medicine was produced and we were both allowed to go home.

In the ward one patient could not get out of bed, another needed a blood transfusion. Upon discharge Jean and I were not allowed to go out together so I went first. Martin agreed to stay with me overnight to supervise for 24 hours. It was very difficult to lift the operated leg to get it into the car. On the journey home I felt light headed and lethargic. At home assisted into the house I lay on the sofa covered over feeling hot and cold. The children and Martin went to bed leaving me asleep. During the night I needed the toilet so managed to sit up, grabbed the crutches and hoist myself up. Staggering to the toilet near the front door, I struggled in the doorway with the crutches, my attire and the need to turn around to reach the toilet. Suddenly the crutches parted, I fell heavily on my left side wetting herself with shock.

I remained jammed in the doorway half in and out, unable to get up. Helplessly, I banged on the toilet door but nobody heard me as they were all sleeping on the other side of the house. I took off my wet nightie and dumped it into the sink, pulling down a long winter coat in the cloakroom to wrap around me. For five hours I half sat in the doorway with the operated leg at a bent angle waiting for the family to rise. Martin was alarmed when he found me there and immediately called for an ambulance only to be told there would be a minimum five hour delay.

THE LIFE OF ROSIE

Unable to move me or wait, Martin found an emergency charity ambulance who came within half an hour. It took two men an hour to remove me from the doorway because I could not move my operated leg which protruded at an awkward angle. The ambulance drove back to the hospital but no out patients were being admitted so they went to a large teaching hospital in a different location who admitted me to Accident and Emergency. Immobile and in pain I saw a warren of desks and cubicles staffed by a large team of young doctors and nurses. After taking an X-ray it was discovered that I had broken my hip in the fall so I was moved to a ward. The consultant told me that I needed an operation swiftly to straighten the leg and repair the hip. Otherwise it may impact on the knee operation and impair flexible future movement.

During that weekend there were sixty urgent admissions that needed priority surgery so it was not until three days later that my second operation took place late in the afternoon. Meanwhile I was given morphine pain relief, a naked bed bath by two fit young men, various X-rays and I could not move from the bed. Lying helplessly drugged I reflected on the meaning of life. In good health I had taken for granted the luxury of movement, activity, productivity and abilities. Wondering if I could recover and resume my routine lifestyle, I tried to consider alternatives. Deciding I was not ready to give up, I decided to fight for recovery. I still had responsibilities and payments to meet so would try my hardest to get well again.

Life seemed to mean different things at various stages. In the beginning babies are fascinated by their surroundings, young children run everywhere to discover the world around them. By school age many want to conform to the styles and trends of their contemporaries. Teens are filled with angst about examinations, fashion, trends, music trends. There's stress about achievements, the future, the planet and expectations for future careers. After school they must decide which route to take if they have suitable options. Life is not easy with additional worries of skin outbreaks, stress, social media inputs, crushes, romances, being considered cool. Each age faces dilemmas and dramas of unexpected circumstances to deal with. It is not easy for any especially when 'X' fancies 'Y' who likes someone else.

In the ward only one elderly lady was able to walk assisted by her Zimmer frame. Elsie was in the next bed to me. Every day we would have the same repetitive conversation. It seemed Elsie lived locally and told everybody where she lived. She claimed to have felt better before she came into the hospital mainly because she refused to have any procedures at her age. When the doctors offered to assist her with treatment, Elsie refused and agreed only to have her medicine adjusted. She claimed to have no appetite whilst tucking into two Weetabix and toast for breakfast. When the dietary team brought some flavoured milkshakes to offer her to boost her appetite, she was disgusted by them and did not use them. However, when a young handsome male consultant came to ask Elsie how she found them, she said they were ok. As a result he arranged for some to be sent to her home for use.

Elsie had a loud voice and noticed a young patient brought in after a rock climbing accident who had an attentive boyfriend. Each time he came visiting Elsie asked when they were getting married! She also noticed a handsome doctor discussing cases with the Ward Sister and told the entire Ward how handsome he was. The conversation then moved outside the Ward. At home Elsie enjoyed smoking and a regular tipple to her daughter's dismay. In hospital Elsie was visited by a stop smoking adviser who left her with samples and literature. They would send more to her house. Elsie's greatest annoyance was the fact that at 91 she was the oldest person on the Ward, the lady opposite was a mere 90!

Each patient had a noticeboard above the bed with their names on. The 90 year old was listed as Laura Edith so everybody addressed her as Laura. After some time it was discovered that she was known as Edith. This poor patient could barely see or hear which meant she needed feeding. If the tray was left out of reach Edith could not find it. When she tried to put her dishes back onto the tray they crashed and broke onto the floor. Twice her raised bed collapsed after the cleaning staff had pushed it too close to the wall. She was frail but determined to go home so had to be watched. At one stage she was on 24 hour watch to prevent her escaping when she was unable to stand up alone.

Poor Edith was suffering mentally and would fall asleep with her mouth open. Elsie watched to see if flies would enter Edith's mouth. Often Edith would wake up confused shouting that she had been left on the bus or asking for help to go home. Sometimes she saw invisible people and carried on conversations with them. Her son was upset one visit to discover she had been arguing with him before he even arrived so she did not want to speak to him. Edith had a daughter and son who visited in turn. At times Edith confused the patient in the bed next to her with her absent daughter. She also claimed to see doors and windows in the Ward ceiling. It was difficult to keep covers on Edith to conserve her modesty without underwear.

A patient arrived next to Edith who had been attacked by five people wearing knuckle dusters who had beaten her and left her for dead. After a four hour head surgery, this patient returned to the Ward, removed her turban bandages and surgical socks then proceeded to walk about. Despite the nursing staff asking her to refrain from movement for recovery, she dismissed herself and went off to a centre for rehabilitation. It seems she was prosecuting the culprits for a large sum plus suing some care facility. Another patient at the end of the Ward lived in an apartment on the fourth floor which had caught fire. This patient had to jump out of her bedroom window breaking her leg and losing all her possessions.

The patient at the end of Edith's side of the Ward was very irritable and argued with staff. When they wanted to take her for an X-ray she refused to go unless they could guarantee to return her in time for lunch. When after midnight a new patient was brought into the Ward following emergency surgery, she complained about the disturbance saying: "Just what I need and thank you very much." She was loud and complained expecting immediate attention despite the Ward being full. Patients came and went but most appreciated the care they received. A young American lady stayed overnight after an under arm surgery. Everybody had their own story and wanted to go home. Physios came round each day to encourage patients to become more mobile.

Every day the doctors, anaesthetists and operational staff had an early morning meeting to plan the operations taking place that day. Afterwards the consultants and student attendants would do their rounds visiting their patients to explain the procedures. Often a computer on a pole would be wheeled around to collate the information. It was a procession of Men in Blue instead of Black like the movie. Physios came around at various times. They insisted and encouraged patients to try new manoeuvres however alarming to the nervous patients. Gradually, patients were able to rise in a limited fashion. It was a source of dread and anticipation to cope with their expectations. My ambition was to go to the toilet unaided as I hated the bedpans.

Part of the daily routine was the medicine round, another was to discuss the menu offer for the three meals a day. Making a choice did not signify that the desired dish would appear. Some patients were startled to find different choices had been made for them as a result of limited delivery supplies. It was warm in the Ward and being confined to bed did not bestow much appetite. Anybody considered for operation was not fed during the day. If the operation was cancelled then the person could eat later on. My operation was delayed for three days so I got used to not eating. As I was afraid to drink too much resulting in more bedpans, my skin became flaky and peeling. The morphine I was taking made me constipated.

During a mega heatwave ice pops were handed out to the patients. Visitors complained about the heat outdoors. A sympathetic Italian doctor told me that the hospital ethos was to heal the whole patient before discharge. Once the medical side was completed satisfactorily, the patient was handed over to the physio team who would design a routine for mobility. Nobody would be discharged until they felt able to cope. He also offered me the opportunity to go to a rehabilitation centre where I would be able to regain my mobility on a more personal basis. Once my 24 knee stitches were removed painfully as they had sunk into my skin, I was eager to try the rehabilitation scheme. I waved goodbye to everyone and left in an ambulance to venture forth into a new modern rehabilitation centre uncertain what to expect.

Whilst I lay dormant in hospital with limited movement, I was able to move my bed into varied positions. I could raise the head or foot part or create a V formation sitting up. There were distractions watching staff and visitors entering the ward, routines, conversations or views of passing personnel along the corridor. Meal times and medicine taking were the main parameters of each day. This left me with plenty of time to contemplate my life to date. Whilst I wondered whether I would be able to resume my previous life routine, there was ample time to remember my past. Modern life moved swiftly along at an alarming pace but the past remained clear in my memory as if it happened recently.

Many people pass through our lives. We meet, greet and sometimes exchange conversations with strangers briefly interacting then never seeing them again. Often we seemed to take to some people while instinctively avoiding others. After school, college or university, we tend to lose touch with most of our former buddies. Similarly, when we change jobs or move away we gradually lose our previous friends in order to create new ones. Life is too busy and pressurised to be able to maintain all our relationships. When a romance ends it is painful because we become individuals again instead of sharing our lives with a partner and everyone knows. It is hard to rebuild our social lives as a single again. Some people take sides although it takes two to tango.

At one point in my life two friends and I went searching for the meaning of life. We went to a Buddhist Meditation, a Catholic retreat, a Jewish spiritual event and various lectures. The

Buddhist meditation took place in a suburban house front room. I found it impossible to still my mind and meditate. While I wriggled and struggled, I could not focus my mind at all. It was a relief to escape and I have avoided meditation since then although I understood how beneficial it seemed to be. The Catholic retreat fared better and was philosophically uplifting. We emerged on a high only crashing down when reality kicked in. Positive thinking played an important part, combined with looking outside the box for solutions.

The Jewish event was held over a weekend in the city centre university with renowned speakers. One Rabbi who looked like Rip Van Winkle spoke softly without repeating his punch lines. There was complete silence from the captivated audience with an overspill section outside and screened viewings. This Rabbi had written many books and his speciality was rehabilitation for addicts. His talk was riveting and moving. I thought that there had to be more to religion than just rhetoric and traditions because a man of such integrity could place so much value on it. We all left impressed planning to try self-improvement. Once again regular routines took over with life's ups and downs competing with good intentions.

Life rarely ran smoothly for anyone. At times all was going well then everything went wrong or unexpected mishaps occurred. Appliances like bodies were supposed to keep working. Parents were expected to live indefinitely. Other people were suffering ailments or breakdowns. We thought we would be able to continue our lives as active mobile participants until old age when we understood we would slow down. Just like parts wear out, we deteriorate from middle age onwards. Therefore, when something lets us down, we feel aggrieved and disappointed. How we tackle the issues is food for thought. Do we sit down and sulk or work towards overcoming the mishap in order to rise again? Can we overcome our difficulties?

There was a film called "Alfie" where the song words "Is it just for the moment we live?" rang out. Do we live momentarily or plan ahead? Some people believe in fate, are we in charge of our own destiny? Despite our best intentions sometimes we cannot proceed with our aims. Other times we fly ahead unintentionally. Bad people sometimes seem to be rewarded for their ill deeds whilst the poor honest types get trodden on. On the radio it spoke about kindness often being seen as weakness. However, it stated that kindness spreads and creates more positivity in the world so is actually a strength because it influences others to do the same. Is anything really absolute? There is good and bad in every sphere. The bad hits the headlines whilst the good mainly gets ignored. Does the shock of wickedness generate more attention?

Despite modern advancements and technology where global influences prevail, there are still dictators, destroyers and cruel leaders determined to drain their communities of financial resources, opportunities and a decent way of life. By cruel means they dictate policies to keep the majority downtrodden. Any resistance is met by death or prison. There has also been a worldwide rise in refugees many for economic reasons unable to make a living in their own country, expecting the West in particular to accommodate and take care of them. Many local populations have internal members who also expect to be taken care of from the cradle to the grave without contributing themselves.

Most countries are struggling with dwindling resources and high price increases. Something has to give and it is usually the poorest who suffer. Illegal migrants were invading the West in search of a better life. People smugglers were making fortunes loading migrants into overcrowded dinghies to be picked up or drowned in the sea. Countries already struggling with financial difficulties were being forced to accept thousands of unwanted people desperately trying to climb on board. Tax payers money was being spent in billions to deal with the crisis while regular inhabitants struggled to eat and heat. There were no easy solutions. Taxes and bills kept rising whilst incomes got squashed behind.

I arrived in an ambulance at the Rehabilitation Centre where nobody answered the front door buzzer for a long time. They took me to the Blue wing down in the lift where I was greeted by medical checks, numerous forms, my operation dressings were opened, various physical tactics and then a sandwich meal was brought. The room was spacious with an en suite shower room, a wall mounted television, modern fittings and furnishings resembling a luxury hotel room rather than a hospital. It had a wardrobe, chest of drawers and bedside cabinet, a buzzer to call for assistance 24 hours and a window with a small side enclosed window adjoining it. The bed was comfortable and adjustable. It was quiet inside the facility so I felt as if I was alone there after the bustle of the hospital ward.

All the staff were friendly and helpful although I could not remember all the names as they kept changing according to day and night shift patterns. In addition there were cleaners, people offering refreshments, people bringing the meals, physios, the doctor when required, plus various personnel from different departments. Every week the entire crew including social workers met to discuss each case. The patients were invited to join in to represent themselves. They had a set format enquiring what the patient was aiming to achieve. I told them that I wanted initially to be able to go to the toilet independently. Ultimately, I wanted to be able to walk again.

At the time I needed assistance lifting my operated leg on/off the bed. I was also struggling to lift my bad leg off the floor. Going to the toilet required assistance to get onto the Zimmer frame plus initially pulling down my underwear. Gradually, I managed the Zimmer frame, doing my own underwear and could shower myself sitting on a chair. The showers were not adjustable and had a tendency to flood the floor in the bathroom. However, each morning I felt refreshed to use them. All the staff went out of their way to be helpful. Always busy they found time to exchange friendly dialogue, find suitable meals to cater for all tastes and go out of their way to make the stay comfortable. Nothing was too much trouble even though they worked 12 hour shifts. Most of the patients were elderly and many infirm.

THE LIFE OF ROSIE

Conversations held during meal times in the communal dining area were sometimes strained as some patients were hard of hearing. One poor man had digestive problems and could not help making unappetising noises. There were various devices for lifting and manoeuvring patients around. The physio team visited daily encouraging patients to extend their capabilities trying new exercises. It was not easy but I tried my best and practised in between sessions. Some patients gave up or did the minimum when their turn came. However, I was determined to make progress so persevered although it hurt. I could not turn over in bed so still took a morphine tablet at night which enabled me to sleep in one position.

One of the highlights of the communal meals at the table was the conversations and banter between the caring staff and patients. It was fun and interesting to find out about social activities in the outside world, a handsome doctor who was getting married, meals, treats and outings. Homemade lasagne was brought by a dedicated member of staff on huge trays for the staff serving both shifts. In the extreme heat another member left me a small fan by my bedside to cool down. A caring mother and two daughter teams worked tirelessly providing care and comfort to all. As a treat we all enjoyed small cartons of orange or apple juice at meal times taken from the fridge.

A balance of patients was carried out between the blue, yellow and orange coloured sections of the unit. Allocations were decided by how many patients needed constant care and who had limited independence. As a result I was moved to the yellow wing where I had a prime view of the private landscaped garden with fruit trees and abandoned herbal plots. Similarly, the staff rotated between the three units so many were familiar. Each unit had big communal wall mounted television screens with armchairs. One patient mistook the blue area for a cruise ship. Each wing had ample paperback books, snacks, tea and coffee facilities plus limited games. Sitting around too much led to sore bottoms as some of the seats felt hard.

THE LIFE OF ROSIE

In contemplative mood, I wondered if love made the world go round. When contact was made with somebody special and it was reciprocated, the world sparkled. There was physical attraction, family love, the love of caring, sharing, kindness in general. Most parents experienced everlasting love for their children, those deprived of that bond tended to suffer later. Love freely given was the ultimate prize but often bad elements slipped in like jealousy, controlling influences, domineering or even taking it for granted. If the love was not nurtured sometimes boredom destroyed the passion. Many people stayed together from habit rather than desire.

Life in Rehab consisted of too much sitting creating sore bottoms, three meals, physio, visiting hour, watching television and having time to think. Initially, I wondered if I would ever walk again. Each slow improvement stage spurred me on. My biggest achievement was being able to go to the toilet alone. For a long time I still needed assistance lifting my leg on/off the bed. I graduated from three stairs with a central landing to climbing up and down 25 stairs supervised. The Zimmer frame was replaced by two walking sticks. Standing exercises using the corridor banister completed my training. When I felt like some melon one day, one of the staff donated a fruit salad selection from her lunch box. These staff went all out to please their patients.

I distracted herself by remembering my first kiss which had taken me by surprise. During the evening I had been to the fair with my friend and two boys. On the way home my escort John had turned me around and kissed me. The affection had not been reciprocated and that was the end of the friendship. I hung around with a crowd of local youth on the streets, but it was a long time before I had a regular boyfriend. Going to university dances with top groups performing led to romance with a Cornish chemistry student called Maurice. His father died during term so Maurice returned to Cornwall. When he returned he did contact me again. I was heartbroken for the first time.

THE LIFE OF ROSIE

Around that time there were advertisements on the noticeboard about foreign trips sharing travelling expenses. My friend and I had £10 each to go to Bath to meet up with the van driver who was going to Europe dropping people off and returning at various times. We stayed overnight at his parents' house then made the journey across Belgium, Austria, former Yugoslavia, Greece and had adventures along the way. The journey back was less exciting but the experience broadened their horizons and made me long to escape back to sunshine and blue seas. Families used to promenade in the evening along the seafront. England seemed grey and dull in comparison.

When I made sufficient progress I was discharged and visited at home by a home carer and physio to ensure progress and safety. In time I found mobility easier because the house was much smaller than the centre had been. It was short distances to everything. Gradually I progressed from two sticks to one stick, to walking unaided with a tendency to a small limp when tired. This meant practising walking increased distances. Although I was walking it was limited amounts. Every morning I practised the physio exercises before breakfast and increased aerobic exercises a few times a week. Sometimes the cold and damp created aches. Heat seemed to be the best solution although pain killers were at hand if needed.

This now left the option for me to think about the future. My kids were married and led independent lives. I wanted to take early retirement. I had been transferred to a department that did not suit me. It kept changing the legislation and had ever increasing workloads so it was impossible to catch up. When I queried responses to relay to the public before calling them, one of the hierarchy made snidey remarks claiming to have told me the week before!

None of the windows in the building opened so when it became stuffy people complained if a fan was switched on or a heater in the winter. I wanted to leave because I had never been able to absorb by rote subjects that held no interest to me. By manipulating my finances, I could manage as the house was paid for. At work I was given a good send off. It felt fantastic to plan each day to suit myself.

Due to my operations the whole summer had passed by. While I recuperated at home, I thought about the following Spring plus future activities. Previously, I had enjoyed aerobics, swimming, art classes, rambles and volunteering at a Food Bank. While my progress was increasing, I felt unable to commit to many activities. I wanted to go on holiday the following year plus on many day trips using the local coach company. The best policy seemed to be moderation in all aspects. Everything was possible with perseverance and determination. Motivation and positive thinking enabled ordinary people to win the Bake Off competition or other events. Knowing what was suitable or where talent lay was the main criteria.

Recovery was a slow painful process with good and bad days. I wanted to stop taking medication but had the security of pain relief if required. For a while I was unable to drive. My car was not automatic so I could not put pressure on my operated leg to conduct an emergency stop. Walking was limited from Zimmer frame to two sticks, one stick and finally a limping independent walk. Eventually I progressed to walking unaided but not for long distances. Gradually I managed to walk further but always welcomed a sit down when available. Family and friends drove me places. This situation limited my activities for several months and I enjoyed the services of a home help and cleaner. I could not take my dustbins out, bring down the washing basket, plus other mundane tasks.

With determination and perseverance I felt the future was open to live in as I saw fit. As long as I could pay my way without debt or being a burden to anyone, I felt ready to explore my next adventure. Creativity seemed to open up new opportunities. Music, art, writing and watching home improvement programmes appealed to me as I now had the time to indulge in projects for enjoyment rather than necessity. I had always indulged in scribbles of poetry and short stories but had never pursued them. Often people would tell me they were good. During the Christmas holidays when all was quiet I was having a house clear out when I came across some written items from the past. Uncertainly I read them again and told my family.

For a while I wondered whether to try my luck at finding a publisher. Looking online there were advertisements seeking new writers. As I was speculating whether to try my luck, Maisie's father recommended consulting a publisher in their area. He would give me an honest opinion without an exorbitant fee. This would be advantageous but embarrassing if he said I was no good. Thinking nothing tried nothing gained led me to send a note introducing myself and asking whether the publisher would be interested. The publisher replied asking me to send some samples online stating what criteria he wanted. As my efforts were ancient typed documents, I had to type everything onto the computer before sending.

When a positive reply came back I was thrilled. Before a contract could be exchanged I agreed to contribute towards the publication cost. An editor sent me amendments and I had to approve the final layout and in the case of stories, the cover. The publisher was not interested in short stories but suggested I combined a whole series into a book. Poetry was a specialised field and entrants had various publications and opportunities. I studied media group outlets, formats and continued writing. After my first publication I was thrilled and excited until I realised that hundreds if not thousands of other people published every day. The difficulty lay in being recognised among the crowds.

Meanwhile I made friends with an artist, a musician and a photographer, all of whom were vying with the multitudes to get noticed. It was not enough to have talent or be good, standing out from the crowd was very difficult. Constant efforts needed to be made for even mediocre recognition. It was not easy to stand out from the crowd. The publisher told me not to spend money on advertisements because they were often presented by others as a form of shopping list. I would be the latest on a list until the next one came along. Local promotions and marketing were key plus podcasts, videos and other chatting stations discussing various topics not just mentioning my work which could lead to breakthroughs. It was hard to maintain staying power. My readers enjoyed my work but they were few in number.

Every morning I dutifully did my short physio exercises before my shower and breakfast. Three times a week I gradually introduced aerobic exercises in addition from my old routine, although not all of them were suitable. When I remained at home I usually incorporated some writing into my schedule. It became as natural as breathing. When I ran out of inspiration or grew tired, I went outside for a walk. This did not detract from my chores, classes or appointments. In this way life passed quickly especially during the short days of winter. It was a welcome luxury to plan my activities each day. Life was uncertain so my aim was to be productive while I could be. There was always the opportunity to take an afternoon short nap if needed.

Many single people were lonely or found it difficult to meet others safely. Not everybody was looking for a partner but wanted to socialise. At the Community Centre I helped to launch a moral maze discussion group on topical issues. Dilemma were discussed like whether to protect the environment or build a factory on a countryside field which would create many jobs locally. The audience split into groups lengthwise so that people could talk to others not just their accompanying person. After a set time one person from each group announced their verdict which was written on a board. The spokesperson then gave the official view according to law which usually had a twist. Afterwards there followed refreshments and chat.

This attracted a regular audience. For some it was their only social interaction all week, especially if they lived alone. Sometimes the caretaker had to flick the lights to clear the room at home time. From this group there were even a few marriages. It was possible to find topics of interest to discuss because the world was constantly changing, generally not improving. We had one session where we spoke about what we would do if we ruled the world. Often there was good humour and banter amongst the audiences. I stayed helping as receptionist with the organisation until my life changed and I had to go away. Once again it reminded me that nothing lasted forever. The wheel kept turning.

Meanwhile life had been eventful for my girlfriends too. There had been a divorce, one was widowed young, one lost her husband to alcohol abuse, one had to wait for her husband to divorce his first wife, one married later in life after raising her son as a single parent. As a result we tended to socialise together without seeking partners. If anything was happening locally we arranged to go. Sometimes we visited and made meals or celebrated special occasions together. It worked out well for booking holidays and having adventures. Familiarity meant comfort and ease or support for all occasions. Life was not perfect but when it was shared it felt cared for. We all had offspring so we watched them grow up and felt equally proud of their achievements. I felt I had a great extended family.

Charles Henderson entered my personal life unexpectedly when he obtained my telephone number and invited me to go for a drink. He was the accountant for the community centre and I greeted him when I saw him occasionally. Always smartly dressed and groomed, he looked exactly like the professional business man he had become. Confident, intelligent and competent to deal with all situations he encountered, Charles was not somebody I had ever considered on a personal level. Allegedly he was divorced but that was all I knew about him. Surprised I arranged for him to pick me up. I rang Sadie to ask what to wear for the date. Martin said he would come down to meet this date before I went to check him out.

At the appointed time Charles came into the house to shake hands with Martin then we drove to a hotel bar in the suburbs where we chatted generally to get to know each other. The evening passed comfortably, Charles drove me home and wished me goodnight. Nothing happened afterwards for three weeks when Charles rang again to invite me to the entertainment part of a rural hotel dinner dance. The guy playing the organ sounded like Neil Diamond so it was a pleasant evening. Couples danced and during the intermission records were played. At the end of the evening Charles took me home without making any further arrangement. I decided to go with the flow and was not perturbed about the lack of romance. It was pleasant while it lasted.

Initially all went well, conversation, activities and communication flowed. We even went on a platonic holiday abroad together in a twin bedded apartment. I began to wonder whether this relationship would progress or diminish. Everything was open to interpretation. When eventually a relationship started slow changes were introduced that affected the outcome. At first when Charles wanted to know what I was doing I did not object. When he asked who I was with, how long I would be or when I would return, I felt uneasy. He said he was worried about me being out alone in these uncertain times. I let it pass but avoided some calls. This annoyed Charles who began to try to control me. I did not feel obliged to account for my movements.

Charles got the message but increased his ardour and efforts to make me more committed to the relationship. He told me I could depend on him, he would always be around for me. Implicit in his courtship was the idea that with him around I did not need anyone else. In fact he discouraged all my social engagements or activities with other people. When it came to family occasions or visits Charles was polite but maintained his distance when he could not avoid engagement. He actually told me that he would never be part of my family. On the positive side Chares made me laugh, he had a good sense of humour and was always supportive and encouraging.

Whilst I had filled my retirement with various activities and interests, Charles occupied himself on the computer, with private projects and at the end of the day was ready to socialise. I liked to read or watch television to relax in the evenings. If I did when Charles was around he grew angry saying he had waited all day to talk to me. Charles chose the films or activities for us to watch. He was also a very picky eater which made him difficult to cater to. I brought my children up to try all types of food, Charles had an aversion to additives although he sometimes bought takeaway meals. He also never stayed with me overnight. Sometimes Charles was disagreeable and we argued, he was adept at belittling me and putting me down.

In time my confidence diminished and I changed from a lady who had a "can do" attitude to one of avoidance. I saw few people and seemed to be treading on egg shells with Charles who had no contact with his former wife or two daughters. In the early days I wondered why his marriage had failed as he seemed a personable generous man. In his marriage he had lived in a big house with all mod cons and been close to his daughters. After the divorce the ex-wife got the house and Charles went back to live in his parents place. Since their demise he had inherited that small semi. It seemed he did not attend his daughter's marriage either and had not met his grandchildren. One daughter was still single travelling the world.

Something was definitely wrong I realised having seen the negative side of Charles. He could be scathing, sarcastic and unpleasant towards me but I hesitated to end the relationship. In fact I felt so disturbed I no longer knew what I wanted. Somehow I had lost myself in this relationship. Charles instigated the relations between us. Whatever I did or said, my moves were not acceptable or conducive to good relations. This was soul destroying and undermining my abilities. He made me feel second class, inferior and unhappy. Ultimately, Charles decided to move home and as I was not inclined to accompany him, he told me no details and went away one day. As I had no idea where he went, I kept some belongings he left at my house for a while before donating them to charity.

My children were annoyed with Charles and wanted to find him to tell him off about the way he had treated their mother. When they could not find him I felt relieved and put it all down to a bad experience. If there was only limited amounts of love to go round, I wanted it reserved for my children. They were happily married. It made me reflect on my own failed marriage. I decided that I had married Pete for the wrong reasons. Without love to cement the relationship, it had no substance to sustain it. Years ago during his midlife crisis Pete and his barmaid had sold up and moved to Murcia, Spain where they bought a small terraced house near the coast. In the school holidays the children often went for their summer holidays. In between they exchanged text messages with Pete. As there were no young people their age near the house, their interest fizzled out as they matured although they were always welcome.

Pete had supported the children right through university and told me that he would help me if required. Fortunately, I had maintained my independence and remained on civil terms with Pete during occasional contacts. I had not seen him for many years apart from photos the children showed me. He remained a rotund figure with a beer belly. Pictured alongside the barmaid I thought of the weather vane typical couple, two rotund figures. As the barmaid had stuck with Pete and they seemed happy enough together, I had no hard feelings. Instead I was pleased that Pete had found a life partner. I harboured no resentment nor the need to seek a replacement for him.

Late one Sunday afternoon I received an unexpected telephone call from Spain police department. An officer told me in English that he had some bad news and asked me to sit down. Following a festival event it seemed that Pete and the barmaid were driving home when there was a car crash. An English drunk driver had crossed the red light and smashed into them. Pete and his barmaid both died. The drunk driver had been unconscious but had gone to the hospital. As I was listed as next of kin, I would need to go to Murcia to sort out their affairs. The officer said he was sorry for my loss. I needed to sit down and dreaded telling the children. It was such a shock, it was too soon for them to die.

I rang Martin and Sadie asking them to call round urgently as I needed to talk to them. Alarmed at my voice they came quickly, Martin's family were in the car as they had been out. Sending them outside when Sadie arrived, I related the news. Both were shocked and upset.

"What's going to happen now?" Martin asked.

"Well I will have to go out there obviously," I replied.

"Do you want me to come with you?" Martin asked.

"I could join you if I could bring the children," Sadie offered.

"No Sadie love, you take charge here and keep an eye on things. I don't know how long I will have to be out there or what will be required."

"What will happen to the villa?" Martin asked.

"I don't know we will have to see," I said frowning.

"You had better take all your paperwork with you in case you need identity stuff," Sadie suggested.

"Take all our birth certificates etc," Martin said.

"I suppose I will have to book a flight and find somewhere to stay," I said helplessly.

"No problem, I will see to that. We can stay at the villa," Martin told her.

"But I have never been, I don't have access," I said.

"It's not a problem, he gave me a spare key," Martin told her. "When shall we go?"

"You will have to tell your work," I said.

"Maisie will explain for me. I think we should go soonest," Martin said.

"The policeman asked me to go over as quickly as possible," I said.

"Yes, dead bodies will not keep in the heat," Sadie remarked.

Martin gave her a dirty look saying: "That is not reassuring."

Sadie started to cry as the impact of her loss set in. "He may not have been the perfect husband but he was a good dad to us," she wailed. "He did his best when he saw us. I'm sorry we didn't go more often."

Martin looked emotional but went to the computer to check flights asking for my passport. Sadie signed a piece of paper with her details saying she gave permission for us to act on her behalf. In a rush I found myself packed and sitting next to Martin on the plane. It felt reassuring to be accompanied by Martin who was practical and competent I felt a mixture of sadness, guilt and uncertainty about the prospect of sorting Pete's former life and attachments. It had never been my dream to live in Spain, but if the villa was paid for we could perhaps use it or rent it out. Martin said they would deal with each issue as it occurred, speculation was arbitrary.

It was hot when we arrived so we took an air conditioned taxi to the villa. Martin paid the driver and led me to the terraced house with small patio area in front. Inside it was tidy and obviously lived in. The living room had a wrap slung over the sofa, a pint pot on a coffee table, the kitchen had dishes stacked in the rack, there were slipper flip flops behind the back door. Upstairs in the main bedroom we found their nightwear, cosmetics and perfume on the dressing table, various toiletries in the bathroom. Everything reflected a regular lifestyle, the fridge and freezer were stocked, clothes were divided in the wardrobes and apart from a kitten that kept miaowing outside, the place awaited the return of its inhabitants.

I sat down while Martin made tea. We brought English tea bags with. As we had left early we made some food for ourselves from the fridge. A wave of exhaustion hit me combined with the shock of being there so we decided to go to the police station the next day. Martin gave the kitten a saucer of milk and some tuna feeling uncertain whether it belonged to

THE LIFE OF ROSIE

Pete. He showed me the two bedrooms he and Sadie used when they visited. I took the larger of the two, Martin used the office bedsit. Both avoided the master bedroom which had an en suite. We took towels from the cupboard and used the main bathroom. It had been a traumatic day so we both had an early night. The house felt humid so I opened the windows to bring in some air. I felt uncomfortable being there. A swimming pool looked inviting at the back.

Next morning we took a taxi to the police station address I had been given. We could have walked but were uncertain where it was located. We took a folder containing all our documents. After waiting in reception for a while we were shown into an English speaking policeman's office. He offered us condolences and checked our identification. A drunken Englishman had left the festival weaving and crashed into Pete's car at a junction when the lights were on red, there was no place to manoeuvre too. The culprit was now in custody awaiting trial. He had been driving alone whilst under the influence and there were witnesses.

I felt stunned and speechless so Martin took charge enquiring about funeral arrangements, getting power of attorney and any official notifications they would need to comply with. The officer was patient and sympathetic handing Martin information in English, advising him to get legal assistance and explaining what would be involved. There was a list of practising English speaking lawyers and advice centres. At the end of the meeting I shook hands with the officer feeling near to tears. I felt grateful Martin had taken charge as I could not have managed without him. Martin thanked the officer and led me outside where we had a coffee at a nearby café.

Instead of going back to the house Martin suggested showing me around the centre and the coast to get my bearings. I felt numb and realised Martin was given me space to adjust. We walked around the tourist spots and shopping centres. Everywhere seemed clean and cheerful with many English speakers in evidence. I suggested we should make a To Do list including informing people that the couple knew. The officer had handed Martin a bag containing the personal belongings of the couple found at the scene. It would contain their money and probably mobiles or personal artefacts which would reveal their contacts. Martin offered to inform their contacts while he was around.

Our first priority was to make funeral arrangements so we headed to the company the officer had recommended. Unfortunately, it was closed for a siesta so we planned to return mid-afternoon. Martin slipped a note through the door explaining we would be returning concerning the recent demise of the couple. Back at the villa we decided to find suitable funeral outfits and any paperwork that may be relevant. On the way back to the villa we stopped at the supermarket to buy more milk and items we fancied for future meals. I seemed to have lost my appetite and felt upset even though I had not been in contact with Pete for a long time.

In the master bedroom I went through the wardrobe and drawers feeling upset to see their personal belongings waiting for their return. All the time Pete had been with his partner, I had always called her "the barmaid" never referring to her real name Mel short for Melanie. This upset me as the woman had very little personal belongings and had stuck by Pete for many years. He had made a will which was with his lawyer. Martin rang the man's office to make an appointment. Mel seemed to have friends but not much family, unless she was not in regular contact with them. Further revelations included a short first marriage but no offspring. I felt sad for her. Mel had left everything to move to Spain with Pete. She had welcomed his children for holidays and never made any demands on me. As far as we knew the couple never married. There was little to show for Mel's short life.

A knock on the door revealed a middle aged lady called Frances, a neighbour originally from Liverpool. She offered her sincere condolences and said she was willing to help in any way. I invited her in and over a cup of tea asked if Frances knew any of the couple's friends and acquaintances who needed to be told. Frances said the couple had been a popular part of the English speakers group who enjoyed functions and activities together. They all met regularly and were really upset about this terrible tragedy.

"Dave was an alcoholic but he should never have been driving. He's gone too far this time and will spend years in prison. He's already lost his family, now he will lose everything but nothing will bring back Mel and Pete," Frances said emotionally.

"So you know the culprit," I said.

"Everyone knows him, he is a disgrace to the community, totally wasted," Frances said wiping her eyes.

Frances said Mel had been a kind warm hearted friend who would help anybody in need. She had never said a bad word about me or the children and enjoyed having them stay in the holidays. I felt bad that I had not been more open minded and encouraged the children to go regularly.

"We have an appointment this afternoon to see the funeral company. When I find out the arrangements will you tell everyone for me?" I asked Frances.

"Of course I will. I can help you sort out all the clothes and things if you want," Frances volunteered.

"Oh thank you. This has been a big shock and I don't know where to start or what to do with anything," I said.

"Do you need help to pick out an outfit for Mel?" Frances asked.

"Yes please, I was going to take along an outfit for each of them, although I am not sure if they need it."

Frances pulled out a blue dress and a bolero saying it had been one of Mel's favourite outfits. She also offered to return later to find out the funeral details so she could pass them on.

"Everybody is upset and will be very supportive," Frances said as she left.

Martin had spent time texting contacts on Mel's mobile and had begun on Pete's. They agreed to make a list of all the bill suppliers and household expenditure when they could analyse the finances. Banks needed to be informed and Martin said the lawyer would advise them about taking over the accounts. I agreed with everything but seemed to lack the ability to take charge. While Martin was around I would leave it to him. When he had to return home I hoped I would be able to gather my wits.

Everything seemed surreal and distressing. I felt reluctant to touch or use the couple's possessions as if I was intruding. Matin had no hesitation in sifting through all the drawers trying to put together all the relevant information he could find. At times I cried with weakness and fatigue for the loss of the couple in their prime. Pete had been a decent man who deserved much better. As next of kin the children and I inherited the villa and all their belongings. His partner did not have any known family.

Once the funeral was arranged Sadie and family flew out to be there. Their boys were happy to play on the beach or go out with their father while Sadie helped me sort out the home. Sadie slept in the master bedroom with the boys sleeping in the spare bedroom. Martin's family came out and booked into a hotel. I slept on the sofa. Many people attended the funeral and the media attended as it seemed the couple had been popular. Others came because one of their own had suffered a tragedy. Amongst the most surprising attendees was Tony Jenson, the Planning Officer who had booked a week's holiday and flown out with Martin's family. I was pleased to see him but did not have chance to talk to him much with so many wanting to greet me.

Sadie and Martin flew back together because they had work commitments and the children had school and nursery. I remained behind to sort out the house and think about the future. Frances remained on hand to assist and support me. We were becoming close allies. Although the house was dated, it was comfortable enough to live in. The whole place would benefit from modernising right through. Frances knew an English decorator who could give me a quote. All the furniture needed updating and there was money to do it but I felt uncertain about my future intentions. This would be my only opportunity to have a holiday home for all the family to enjoy. Martin transferred the financial operations to a new bank account which he and I could access.

In time Frances helped me to donate the clothing and unwanted goods to a charity shop. We also found somewhere who would accept furniture donations for future reference. Frances took me around furniture outlets where I chose two new sofas, six new dining chairs and had a carpenter fit modern wardrobes in the two main bedrooms. The small third bedroom was kitted out as an office so I left it but bought a smart sofa bed to replace the old bed which was uncomfortable. During shopping expeditions I chose new bed linen disposing of the old plus new towels. Anything looking used and worn was discarded. The house retained some original pieces but looked refreshed.

While the renovation work was being carried out I decided to explore the area to familiarise myself with all it offered. I had read that the Region of Murcia is an autonomous community of Spain located in the south eastern part of the Iberian Peninsula, on the Mediterranean coast. I took a trip to Murcia, the capital, a university city. Plaza Cardenal Belluga is the city's architectural showpiece, with the ornate cathedral. The colourful 18th-century Palacio Episcopal contrasted with the modern 1990s Ayuntamiento City Hall. With picturesque parks and numerous plazas, Murcia felt lively, vibrant, full of culture, history and amazing food. I enjoyed my visit but felt hot and tired so was relieved to go back to the house.

There were seven magnificent beaches and coves in the areas of La Manga and Cartegena. Some football stars went to an exclusive resort to train and chill. Costa Calida was home to a selection of stunning seaside towns and residential developments, so Pete had chosen wisely. As I explored the region it grew on me and I felt reluctant to return home where

THE LIFE OF ROSIE

Sadie was keeping an eye on things. If I transferred my finances over it occurred to me that I could avoid English winter and perhaps try living there. The house was paid for and only had living expenses. Perhaps my English home could be rented. It was something to think about. I had nothing urgent to return to.

Frances invited me to join the English speaker group activities. Whilst I was not interested in the night life consisting of boozing, cabaret, drag shows, games and quizzes, I made an effort to go to a morning coffee session to thank everyone for their support. Mainly a bunch of middle aged plus women with a few brave husbands, they took coffee with brandy, gossiped and wanted to question me about my life. Pleading restraint because I was still in mourning, I avoided personal issues and made my escape. Another lady called Tracey also visited me at home telling me she would accompany me anywhere or help if needed.

I told Frances and Tracey that although I appreciated their kind offers, it was too soon for me to participate and that I needed space to recover. They told me they were always available for me and would push the programme through my door each week. While the decorator called Freddie after Freddie Mercury was busy, he told me about a walking group which sounded promising. Each Sunday there was at least one walk varying in length and ability as the month progressed. He also mentioned a few other groups that sounded appealing. The decorator was a young, blonde with blue eyes so bore no resemblance to the legendary Freddie. His mother adored the original and was satisfied to have named her son after him.

While the house was being done, I decided to explore on my own. Murcia had over 170 km of coastline. With time on my hands I enjoyed exploring the coastline or sitting on the beach daydreaming. My English friends took turns to visit asking if I wanted things bringing from home. Surprisingly, apart from some extra clothes I missed nothing and found everything I wanted locally. They brought English tea bags and treats.

THE LIFE OF ROSIE

While I had visitors I did not seek other company. People generally were friendly and I conversed with them when they stopped for coffee or meals. When there were tribute shows or easy walks I took my visitors. Everyone found the experience there relaxing.

Impressive mountain landscapes, fine sandy beaches and small, hidden bays made the beaches on the Costa Cálida an often overlooked holiday potential of a special kind. A mild climate all year round made beach holidays possible until the autumn months. As time progressed I felt increasingly reluctant to return to England. Realising that if I planned to stay something needed to be done with my English home and my passport. It would necessitate a return trip to sort things out. The idea of renting my English home when it was decluttered and personal artefacts were removed seemed like a potential solution. When the temperature rose in Murcia in the summer, I gave Frances a key for emergencies and went home to England to sort myself out.

I felty so happy to reunite with my grandchildren, family and friends. I decided to learn Spanish online and investigate the financial aspects of moving there. At home I blitzed the house of unwanted items, clothing that was no longer worn plus non-essential items. A local decorator came to paint over the rooms to freshen up. After a deep clean throughout the house looked pristine. Back home the weather varied considerably with too much rain. I checked on line about the viability of becoming a resident in Spain after Brexit. My main advantage was that the house there was paid for so I would only incur living costs.

All non-EEA nationals including British who wished to stay in Spain for longer than 90 days, need a visa. To apply for a suitable visa, I would have to contact the Spanish Consulate in England. I would be able to stay in Spain for a maximum of 6 months without becoming a resident. If I spent an extra day (184 days and onwards), I would be regarded as a resident, then have to pay resident taxes in the country. After 5 years of living in Spain legally and continuously, I could apply for long-term residency (previously called permanent residency). Spain does not accept dual citizenship, but nationals of those countries won't have to forfeit their citizenship.

To be eligible for the retirement visa, I would need to have an income four times the yearly IPREM. This therefore meant a yearly income of €27,936.96. Spain charges a non-refundable fee to process citizenship application. The price varies and can range from €60-€100, even if they say my application was rejected. Fees may also apply to issue certificates and documents required for my application. If I retired abroad, I could continue to receive my UK State Pension and get pension increases yearly in an EU country.

Spain was really as affordable as everyone said. Living solo meant I could live on €1000 per month in Spain. This included room rent, groceries, health insurance, rare use of public transport, eating out a few times a month and shopping moderately. I would not need to pay rental so would be able to live comfortably. Although financially sound at home, the fact that I had inherited all Pete's financial affairs split with the children meant that I could meet all the expenses incurred if I decided to stay. Alternatively, the house could be used as a holiday home or rental property.

Before making any decisions I invited three estate agents to value the house and access it for rental. I asked each agent to advise me on managing the rental side. Valuations were similar with little difference between them. Services offered included finding tenants, let and rent collect or fully managed with six month inspections, with maintenance and repair reporting. There were short versus long term rental agreements, price comparison sites for various agents charges, plus various legislation compliance issues. I would have to conduct an inventory, provide an Energy Performance Certificate and reference potential tenants. Martin would check everything out for me if I decided.

There was too much information so I put the idea on hold. Also the prospect of being abroad alone without any friends or family was daunting. Living independently in England was familiar with no shortage of company when required. Although I found it easy to communicate with strangers, it would take time and effort to discover like minds abroad. Frances and the English speakers were friendly and welcoming but had little in common with me. I understood how Pete and Mel had enjoyed that social scene but it had never appealed to me. I rarely drank or applauded vulgar humour. Ideally, I wanted to spend the winter months and autumn in Spain, returning to England for the summer months and December. Perhaps I could find a Spanish agent to rent out the property there too.

Bearing in mind that the Spanish house would be used by Martin, Sadie and close family and friends as well, I realised that it belonged to all the family so the rental periods would be restricted. It also meant that personal belongings would need to be stored locked away. Somebody could be found to manage the rentals and maintain the place when it was vacant. Nothing was straight forward in either location. Unless somebody suitable or familiar came along, I decided to proceed with caution and use the following year to experiment in both locations to see what worked well. I could stay for up to six months continually so decided to try it.

In the middle of September I left for Spain accompanied by my friend Mandy. We had worked together for several years. Mandy had divorced unpleasantly the previous year so I hoped Spain would provide therapeutic experiences for my friend. At first we enjoyed being on holiday marvelling at the constant blue skies and sunshine. After a couple of months Mandy became restless saying every day was the same. Mandy missed the variety of the English climate, the department stores and shops. Despite the smart Spanish shops and variety of food providers, Mandy went back to England saying that one could have too much of a good thing.

By that time I had made some new friends of varied ages who enjoyed walks, talks, adventures and artistic endeavours. Sometimes I joined small groups at other times booked for trips and expanded my circle. I even entertained at times when we held the Book Club or other activities. Some people had moved to Spain because they had suffered various ailments and felt the warm climate was more beneficial for them. Others came because they had lost a loved one and felt lonely stuck indoors at home. A few women of a certain age came hoping to meet a Spanish lover. English speakers came from all over the world so it was interesting to learn about other countries. Everyone brought their own traditions and habits.

Wondering whether I could afford to run two households led to Martin and Sadie setting up a family budget to cover costs. In addition, they sometimes found temporary tenants for the two houses when one was unoccupied. Through connections Sadie and Martin assisted people in need of short term accommodation who were visiting or studying temporarily. It was not always possible but by charging a reasonable amount it kept the budget flowing. Energy was the biggest expense for heating the English home. Between the family they managed to stay afloat. In the summer months they had people queuing to rent the Spanish house. I disliked extreme heat and was delighted to return to England in the summer months.

Although nearly everyone spoke some English, I continued to learn Spanish and attended classes there. When I returned to England I found myself practising what I wanted to say in Spanish in my head. Most of the time when I spoke Spanish people replied in English. They wanted to practice their English. When they did not speak English well, they quoted the names of sports personalities or football teams. Famous celebrity football managers were often recited to show how universal they were. I was not into sports so just smiled and nodded. If any Spanish people knew anybody in England they always asked me if I knew them too!

Many people over indulged in the food and drink available in Spain. As a consequence of this plus lack of regular exercise meant there were oversized lethargic bodies of all shapes and sizes. A warm climate meant an outdoor lifestyle but apart from walking to and from the favoured places that was their only exercise. Keeping fit regularly was offered but required effort and determination to stick with it. Sunbathing was also something to take care with. I had visitors who were so happy to see the beautiful weather they basked for too long and caught sunstroke. In extreme cases some women had baked skin like leather. Moderation was the key in all aspects. Some people spent their winters abroad but as Spring approached waves of tourists started appearing. They were noticeable by their pale complexions.

I liked to people watch when I stopped for coffee or to eat out. In time I established my favourite walks and routines so grew familiar with the regulars and recognised the tourists. Whilst I got to know the familiar faces there were some I found disagreeable. There were ladies of a certain age who dressed too young, plastered the makeup on in search of a new conquest. They did not realise that most Spanish men worked long hours, were usually married or with partners and just chatted to the foreign women to increase business. Older men were just as bad thinking they were still able to appeal to young women. Even well-heeled men were not sought after when they had let themselves go. Womanizers were always seeking vulnerable naïve targets.

Many people in the older age group had health problems. There were hypochondriacs who insisted on divulging every minor detail of their experiences. People with early dementia repeated their conversations endlessly. In addition, there were some lonely people who had lost loved ones after many years together. They all enjoyed a good gossip and news from home. With Sky television and Netflix they were able to keep abreast of home happenings. I tried to mingle and keep my personal information private. Once the sympathy had finished from Pete's demise, I blended into the background as I only made contact occasionally. If I recognised anyone for coffee I made small talk before moving on. I could not sit idly around all day.

Whilst I enjoyed the relaxing lifestyle in Spain, I felt unsettled both there and in England, as though my life was on hold temporarily in both places. I made enquiries about letting the property in Spain. Frances offered to help me find suitable tenants for a fee when I was ready. Meanwhile I received an upsetting message from Sadie telling me that my grandson Mark had suffered a severe asthma attack and was in hospital. Immediately, I packed up, told Frances to use up my food and rushed onto the first flight available.

Mark was in the new children's hospital looking pale but alert. There were toys and games with other children to talk to. He was over the worst but still had oxygen handy and equipment around him. It had been a worrying time and they had nearly lost him. I visited regularly and offered to stay with Mark when he went home so that his parents could work and get respite. The attack had frightened them all as Mark had always been a bit delicate rather than robust but had not suffered from asthma before. Nathan blamed pollution and bought a clean air ventilation unit for the home.

So I found myself back home. Fortunately, the tenants in my place also had an emergency and had to vacate unexpectedly. I declined further bookings for the time being and felt strange being back during the English summer. It took time to adjust to the climate. There were some new buildings going up, roadworks and various neighbourhood renovations. Noticing the changes I felt adrift as if I was waiting for something to happen. Realising that life was how we made it did not motivate me to action. Something was missing in my life but I was unable to figure out a solution. Meanwhile I decided to start writing my memoirs for something to do. Once started I engaged quickly being engrossed in forgotten memories as I recalled past experiences and adventures.

In England I enjoyed spending time with my grandchildren and engaged on the nursery then later school pick up rota or caring for them during school holidays. I indulged them, played with them, taught them games and took them to parks and play areas, bought them treats. It was a mutual love story and made them close. They were growing up so fast I knew that this phase would not last long so I abandoned plans to return to Spain, in order to be with them. All the family were close and enjoyed planning activities together. When time and weather permitted they went on walks or days out together and took turns to host dinner parties in each house.

On my return to the UK, I noticed important changes. I heard the term "woke" being bandied about and discovered there was a whole new range of politically correct vocabulary. People found it difficult to get an appointment to see the doctor. Ambulances were queuing for hours to try to get patients into hospitals where there was a shortage of beds due to a lack of social care to discharge fit patients. Strikes were springing up everywhere with unions taking turns. Due to rising fuel prices workers wanted higher wages at rates the economy could not afford. Choices had to be made between heating and eating. Food Banks were being inundated. Shopping prices kept rising with everything increasing in price at each visit. People on the lowest incomes could not manage.

I caught up with friends, former colleagues and neighbours. Although I had not been away for long, it seemed that many people were dissatisfied with the Government policies. There had been three Prime Ministers in a short time with no improvement in daily lives. Even people with no interest in politics felt aggrieved at the increasing costs and lack of reform to social and medical care. Leaders were out of touch with the reality of struggling finances on limited budgets.

Listening to the World News it did not seem to be faring any better in other countries. Russia was blamed for invading Ukraine and being violent, cruel and destructive. This needless war had caused the fuel crisis and upset world harmony. As it dragged on endlessly, the West tried to help Ukraine to prevent Russia from destroying more. Their inhumanity extended to their own poor soldiers who were forced into the military. Those who could escaped from their country rather than fight. Many were killed and their corpses were trampled on by their own soldiers.

THE LIFE OF ROSIE

In the news there seemed to be a spate of stabbings, gang violence crimes and antisocial behaviour which made me nervous about going out at night alone. Apart from babysitting or special occasions, I planned my activities during day time. In the winter when it got dark in the afternoons, I was returning from a trip to a shopping centre with my friend. A young man with a rucksack stood up to offer his seat on a crowded bus so I thanked him and sat down. When my stop arrived the man got off the bus with me saying: "I like older women."

I was staying over at Lynne's house so we both walked quickly onwards. When we heard him following we hid behind a high hedge in somebody's garden crouching down until he went passed. We waited for a short time before going to Lynne's place. Ever since I was stalked I felt nervous of unexplained footsteps following behind me. Women were vulnerable out at night and there had been murders committed of lone women making journeys. Despite protests about safety for women, it was an issue many women felt nervous about. Drinks were sometimes spiked in bars or clubs and most women would not agree to a lift home from a stranger or someone she had just met.

Lynne and I went to the newly refurbished cinema to see a Tom Hanks film. In comfy recliner seats with drinks trays that swivelled around, we were startled to hear loud music emanating from the adjacent screen. Throughout their showing whenever a quiet moment occurred we could hear very loud music from next door. The lifts and escalators were not all working and the surrounding outside mall was draped in scaffolding and work processes. It was not inviting. Most of the trailers shown were unsuitable for our taste. We appreciated being able to go to the cinema in the afternoon instead of working. It was dark when we emerged but only tea time.

On my first independent trip abroad in my late teens accompanied by Lynne, we took a cheap student trip seeking sun sand and adventures. During the course of our Spanish escape we met a group of teenagers who attended an evening dance club. A tall dark handsome boy asked me to dance. His name was Sebastian but he did not speak much English so had to ask a friend to interpretate. When I looked at him my heart fluttered and my knees went weak. He was special and the language difficulties did not matter. The interpreter said that Sebastian had to go away somewhere so I did not see him again until the last night of our holiday when we exchanged contact details.

At Christmas Sebastian sent me a card with the greeting words obviously copied from another card. I was thrilled to receive it and wanted to return to Spain to see him again. When I arrived I discovered that Sebastian had gone to England to his aunt's house to study. While I was in Spain, Sebastian was in Sheffield. We lost touch until I was married then resumed sending Christmas cards and a few occasional telephone calls. When Sebastian was getting married he had to complete some paperwork in my domain so we met up for coffee. We talked like old friends, Sebastian had grown his hair as it was fashionable. After that we did not meet again until I invited them to both my children's weddings. In return, Sebastian invited me when his children married.

On my first trip abroad with two girlfriends to Rome for a working holiday, I was walking down Via Veneto after accompanying a fourth girl to the Excelsior hotel where she had a job, when I was stopped by a handsome man saying to me: "I know you, is your name Elizabeth?" Astonished, I engaged in a short conversation with him. The man introduced himself as Giuseppe who then rejoined his two companions before setting off. Next morning at the hotel the handsome man turned up at our hotel to invite us three girls to go on a sightseeing tour. The girls had to collect some luggage first but afterwards we all went on a driven tour around the city. This led to a romance for me with Guiseppe. I had intuitively known in advance this would happen. He sang love songs aloud to me in the street and was a character.

Looking in the mirror for signs of ageing I felt certain that nobody would notice me now. I was therefore surprised to be stopped in the town centre by a slim man wearing a hoodie with a cap pulled over his face:

"You are Rosie Jones right?" the man asked me.

"Yes, do I know you?" I asked.

"Huh I wouldn't want to know you now," he said sloping off.

"Hey, who are you?" I called to no avail as he melted away.

I racked my brain to try to recall who he could be. As I had not seen his face clearly I wondered whether he could be my old stalker. The encounter made me nervous so I recalled my previous safety exercises and carried an alarm with me. Looking up old news cuttings about the stalker did not help either because the man had been covered up and it was hard to judge his height and build from old photos. None of the other victims had any encounters when I checked. They all became wary and uncomfortable. It took time before I went to town again. At night I checked everywhere was locked and remained inside mostly. The family checked on me regularly.

Unexpectedly I began to get statements, contract receipts and notifications regarding contracts made by A. Hunter, an unknown person who was using my address. This began occurring with frequent regularity which meant time and trouble for me to expose these transactions as fake. I nearly got my utility and energy supplies cut off. Apart from the irritation caused by holding on in a queue trying to get through to my suppliers, I was also passed around the Bank and other institutions trying to sort things out. My credit and debit cards were secure. Whilst I was alert to online scams, it was the first time my address had been compromised. Although it happened quickly, it took a long time to sort and rectify.

Why couldn't these criminals use their brains for something productive and constructive I wondered. I dreaded getting post as I rarely received more than advertisements or jargon. The Government seemed to be no better as cases arose where Ministers avoided paying their taxes, secured illicit loans, or failed to comply with their own legislation. There seemed to be no prime examples of moral behaviour in the world leaders to use as an example. Globally everywhere was scrutinised constantly. Anybody famous had to be scrupulous regarding their behaviour each time they left home plus appear groomed. News was broadcast around the clock so everyone knew what was happening instantly.

Lynne and I discussed the world situation.

"Do you remember when the news used to be broadcast at 6 pm and 10 pm?" I asked.

"Yes and tv shut down at 11 pm so you got a little girl on a static on screen card the rest of the time," Lynne agreed.

"That was so that tv engineers could check sets."

"Life seemed much simpler when we had less choices, relied on paper and pen receipts, had bank account books, accounts had ledgers, you could keep records of everything at your fingertips."

"People would say you can do all that online."

"Until the system fails then what? How is life better now that so many banks, post offices and other institutions have closed down?"

"You can still pay by cheque but people dislike the inconvenience of it."

"What gets me is how difficult it is to speak to an actual person these days."

"Yes, you get pushed from pillar to post, press this or that. They say, "your call is important to us" before they cut you off."

"The Internet has been good and useful for many things and Facebook links you with people all over the world, however it has its downside."

"True, some people put absolute garbage on it. Why do they think anyone is interested in 50 photos they took or what they had for dinner? I don't need to know what people are doing all the time. There are regulars who seem to spend all day putting pictures on or useless information."

"Some put guessing games on that are trite. Like who cares what your personal preferences are. Maybe some are just attention seekers. The bright ones have more sense."

"Mobiles kill the art of conversation."

"They should be banned at mealtimes."

"And family get togethers."

"Time is flying by so quickly."

"Yes, it's hard to know what day it is and whether I have achieved my objectives."

"I have to write down a To Do list."

"Me too, I keep a post it on the table to write down groceries as I run out hoping I remember to take it with me."

"Do you go upstairs get side tracked then come down forgetting what you went up for?"

"Don't ask!"

"I suppose we are lucky we are able to keep going."

"Yes, make sure you keep moving while you can."

While I was living an active life I hit a sudden negative patch. My assumption was akin to a big wheel in the ether which rotated into positive and negative portions. Everybody had their turns of good and bad situations. Suddenly I needed roof repairs, my washing machine ended its service, I had the remains of a cough and cold which lingered and made me tired. My friends fared no better. Jackie had been divorced and taken in a lodger who helped her with the housework and kept her company on trips out. He developed cancer which spread so had to endure constant painful therapy at the hospital on the other side of town. Another friend lost her husband to alcoholism. Lynne's mother died. Two neighbours died within a short period of time. There was no positive news from anyone. The weather was also dismal so did not help mood swings.

Despite an abundance of social outlets for diverse activities, many people were lonely and felt isolated from society. Some were too shy or reticent to attend a new venture alone. Others were sceptical about making new friends later in life. I formed a new discussion group designed to discuss topical issues and socialise. There were more women than men initially but I ensured everybody mixed and talked. People came for various reasons, some ladies hoped to find a new mate, a few men confessed that they hoped to find a lady friend to cook them delicious meals. A few were loners venturing out to see if they would be accepted. It became the highlight of the calendar for some and they were reluctant to leave. Apparently, it was hard to meet new people in the modern world except online with social media.

Most people getting together enjoyed a good moan about rising prices. Everything from fuel to groceries kept increasing in price. Businesses struggled to obtain stock, parts and bills to keep afloat. A large part of the community were striking to get income rises despite a massive debt on Government funding. Ministers said the strikers needed to liaise with their owners or management to sort it out. This Government was not negotiating with the Unions which annoyed the strikers. Wages were not keeping up with the cost of living. Investment and growth were shrinking. The country was in a mess with no obvious solution. Even worse were allegations of corruption and sleaze in some quarters. There were no dynamic potential leaders.

Scammers were prolific on social media platforms, telephone calls and any way they could trick punters into parting with their cash. From dating sites to imitating national resource offices these criminals were prolific. Money Saving schemes and opportunities were also flooding the media offering expert advice to find solutions to staying afloat. Food Banks were

THE LIFE OF ROSIE

overwhelmed to keep supplies flowing. It seemed that while the rich got richer, the middle class struggled and the poorest suffered. Poor people tried hard to manipulate their limited income and even when they worked, their efforts were undervalued and they could not rise above their situation easily. In a really cold winter decisions had to be made about eating or heating.

The property in Spain was being managed by Frances with occasional visits by the family. Frances rang to tell me that she did not want to continue the arrangement. I flew out to see what I could arrange instead. It felt good to see bright skies and sunshine again. Having felt the cold continually in England, I basked outdoors. I looked up rental agencies in the area and went to see them to discuss their terms and opportunities. Inside the house I hired a decorator to paint the living room but the remainder of the place was clean and looked good. With an extra clean and tidy up the place would be ready to let. Meanwhile I enjoyed being out in the warmth.

When I had the opportunity I walked along the seafront to sit somewhere with a book and a picnic. Often strangers would approach me to chat. People asked what I was reading, if I was on holiday, plus enquired whether I had been sightseeing. Although I made new acquaintances, I did not manage much reading as I frequently found myself day dreaming looking at the sea. One of the regular walkers, a tall fit looking man with a good head of grey hair, asked if he could join me one morning. We sat quietly for a while both acutely aware of each other. I told him I had seen him walking along the front regularly.

"That's right, I like to go along a few times during the day," he told her.

"It is very pleasant," I agreed.

"Are you on holiday?" he asked.

"I have a house here which was being rented for me until now. The person managing it has decided to terminate so I came to find new management."

"Perhaps I can help you as I had a good experience with the company I used to find my place."

"Thanks that would be marvellous, I will certainly look into it."

"I have a card at home with their contact details on plus a brochure. If you meet me here again later, I can let you have it."

"That would be great. I am Rosie by the way."

"I'm Chris Langton," he said offering his hand to shake.

"Do you live here?" I asked.

"I do now. My wife and I dreamed of having a place in Spain so we saved and found our ideal place. Once we purchased it, furnished it and got everything the way we wanted, we discovered that she had incurable cancer so I lost her very quickly. As we had sold our home in England, there was nothing to go back to."

"Oh I'm sorry, that is so sad."

"Yes, it is a lesson not to waste opportunities in life because you never know what can happen. Have you had your house long?"

"Well, I was divorced a long time ago. My former husband bought the house with his new partner. They were both killed in a road accident returning from a fiesta. As the house was in his name, it passed along to me and my children."

"Another sad story, what a tragedy."

"Yes, it was an English drunken driver that killed them."

"How awful, was he killed too?"

"No, he was sentenced."

"How old are your children?"

"They are both married, I have a daughter and a son, with four grandchildren now. Do you have any children?"

"I have a daughter, a musician who lives in Vienna but travels around the world with the orchestra. Her husband is also in the orchestra but no grandchildren yet. I think they both enjoy their roles too much to settle. She visits me when she can."

"That's good. Have you made friends here?"

"You know what it's like, people always talk and try to be friendly. When they discover my circumstances they try to matchmake me."

"I expect they mean well, probably think you are lonely and need looking after."

"Is that the impression I give? I can assure you I am an adequate cook and learnt household maintenance taking care of my wife."

"Was she a dainty feminine person?"

"She was actually, why do you ask?"

"Tall men usually pick small slight ladies whereas short men aspire to tall ladies in general."

Chris showed me a photo of a pretty brunette with delicate features. I admired the photo and asked if his daughter took after her mother.

"Not at all, she is tall like me but slim, she doesn't eat much and she has my colouring," he said revealing a photo of a model type light brown haired young woman.

"Do you ever go back to the UK?"

"I haven't wanted to, people visit me and I can get online shopping if I need anything. How long will you be staying?"

"I'm not sure yet, I only arrived a few days ago. Once I get the house situation sorted, I can plan ahead. It feels too good to rush right now. It was cold, grey and damp back home. At present I have the decorator in my house here."

"So you don't have to rush back, no deadline?"

"No, I am retired now thank goodness."

"Are you enjoying your retirement?"

"Loving it, the flexibility and freedom to choose my actions can't be beaten. I also get involved in various activities so time passes swiftly. Sometimes I don't know how I found time to go to work."

"What did you do?"

"Inland Revenue adviser how about you?"

"I am an architect still working part time to suit myself."

"Are you designing here or do you have to go out to various locations?"

"Both really, with modern technology I can work anywhere."

"Well it's very pleasant sitting in the sunshine but it is getting a bit hot now so I had better make a move," I said.

"Which way are you going?"

I indicated to her right, Chris said he was going in the opposite direction but asked her if she wanted to meet him again to get the agency information. We agreed to meet late afternoon when it cooled down a bit. As I walked away I reflected on the conversation and thought perhaps I had made a new friend or contact. I did not feel ready yet to make any decision about the Spanish house because it was too soon. First I needed to enjoy the warmth and freedom, there was no pressure to make a new contract. However, it was not feasible to maintain two households on a pension so a decision would have to be made. There was no rush to return to an English winter so I decided to make the most of my break.

THE LIFE OF ROSIE

It seemed Chris lived in an affluent suburb that I had heard mentioned but never visited. I walked along the coast in both directions but favoured the central part of town plus seaside promenades. I had not bothered to explore the suburbs so had an awareness of their existence but no connection. Pete had chosen the house on the outskirts of town within easy walking distance. Apparently more housing locations had sprung up since his purchase. If I had been buying a place I probably would have chosen another location but felt grateful for the chance to live there. The house was spacious, low maintenance within reach of shops and facilities. It was furnished comfortably but I would need to modernise it if I planned to stay. For a rental it was adequate but for a permanent home it needed an upgrade.

Picking up a pizza on her way home I ate it then felt tired so enjoyed a siesta. Waking up I showered and put on a sundress. With newly washed hair, a touch of makeup and spraying perfume I set off to meet Chris pretending it was a date. It was still warm but pleasant as I strolled along. En route I greeted a few familiar people and arrived at the bench first which was occupied. Sitting at the next bench along I saw Chris approaching. Tall, tanned and smartly dressed in a casual style, he looked like an advert from a catalogue. I could not tell how old he was or if I fancied him but felt pleased to see him. As he came near I stood up to greet him explaining that the earlier bench was occupied.

Chris suggested they went for a drink so they headed off to a bar he recommended.

"They have live music sometimes and it gets busy later on," he told me.

"Is this your local?"

"One of them, I vary my outings according to my mood."

"Do you go out with friends or prefer to spend time alone?"

"There are people I can hang out with. The trouble with being a close couple is that you get used to being together so it feels strange to go it alone."

"Life goes on though regardless. Would she want you to be alone?"

"Not at all, she told me to find a good woman when she was gone."

"Well you don't have to, it's not compulsory but mixing with other people is good for you. A certain amount of social contact is ok. You don't have to marry again if you don't want to."

"At present I have no interest in anyone else, I would feel guilty."

"Fine but you can have friends without romance."

"Do you think so? Women say that but after some time they have expectations."

"Not all women are the same, don't generalise. It's like me saying that all men try to get women into bed."

"Don't they?"

"Of course not, look around you, however attractive or desirable a few may be, most people you meet do not excite you."

"I'm out of touch. My wife and I were childhood sweethearts and she is the only woman I needed."

"Well lucky you, treasure the experience you enjoyed. Few people have such good fortune. Now she's gone are you going to switch off and send the rest of your life living on memories? Time whizzes by, you are still fit and active, try new things while you can. Nobody knows how long we have so make the most of it."

"Do you apply your advice to your own life?"

THE LIFE OF ROSIE

I blushed guiltily saying: "Well I try to volunteer, I went to a pottery group at home, did keep fit exercises, swimming, plus the usual stuff. At home I had friends to hang out with."

"Are you involved romantically?"

"No, I haven't done too well on that front so decided to enjoy my freedom now."

"Well perhaps we can be company for each other while you are here if you want to."

"I am not sure how long I will be staying but as long as you have no expectations, let's see. This place is making me unwind and relax, I even had a siesta this afternoon. My motivation has been diminishing so I am not ready to make decisions yet."

"That's good you must need it. Living back home is busy compared to here. That reminds me, here's the brochure for the agency. You can use it when you are ready or I could take you."

"Do you have a car?"

"Yes, a villa with a swimming pool, all mod cons plus a car. I could take you for a drive to explore places around here if you are interested."

"Thank you. I would love to go exploring, I have used the bus service slightly but I usually walk. It sounds like you are living the dream."

"In theory I have all the trimmings but nobody to share it with."

"Nobody has everything. However, life is what you make it. Nothing will change unless you make it happen. Instead of feeling sorry for yourself, you need to take action if you want to have company or change. I blame the movies and books for unrealistic stories where magic comes to your door etc."

"Are you a cynic or a therapist?"

"Perhaps a bit cynical but no therapist. I have just learned to move on. Life has its misfortunes and joys for everyone. You have to take opportunities when they occur."

"Well you are certainly interesting company. I probably need a kick in the proverbial."

We sat quietly drinking and listening to a guitarist playing some Spanish music. I relaxed and watched the sun going down slowly over the horizon. The drink was making me dreamy. Chris ordered more drinks and slowly I felt a bit tipsy. When Chris asked me if I was hungry, I was surprised and thought about it. He ordered some food saying it was specialities of the place and he wanted to know what I thought about it. I was contemplating how to get home in my tipsy drowsiness so hoped the food would help me sober up. Perhaps I could get a taxi. We ate tasty food then moved on as the place was filling up.

Walking along the front we sat people watching near the town centre chatting easily about likes and dislikes. Conversation flowed easily and I was surprised to see that it was getting late. Suddenly I felt a bit tired so decided to go home. Chris offered to accompany me. I felt awkward so asked him to find me a taxi. He put me in the taxi saying he would drop me off then take it back to his place. I sat in the back while Chris sat with the driver. I gave the driver my address, got out first then waved him off. He refused to take any money for the fare and had paid for the drinks and food. I decided to treat him in future. We had not exchanged contact details so I would leave it to fate whether we met again or not. Yawning and giggling I drank some cold water then went to bed.

Next morning I woke up early and went out for breakfast before visiting some local estate agents to discuss rental terms. I wanted to get everything done before it became too hot. My plan was to go for a swim when I finished then pick up some shopping on the way home. When I returned I found a note in my mail box from Chris giving me his number telling me to contact him when I wanted to go out. I stored his number on my mobile but decided not to contact him because next day I had a walking trip booked with a group. Another early start meant that I was out all day then joined the group for a meal at the end plus a few drinks to unwind. Feeling pleasantly tired and relaxed I planned a lie in next day so was annoyed to hear the doorbell ring early.

Trying to ignore it proved to be impossible so pushing my hair back and rinsing my mouth, I grabbed my dressing gown and asked who it as before opening it.

"Chris," came the reply.

Surprised I told him to wait a minute while I brushed my teeth and hair before fastening my dressing gown. When I opened the door Chris stood looking immaculate.

"Sorry, have I disturbed you?" he ask anxiously.

"Yes, I was planning to have a lie in this morning but as you are here come in and I will put the coffee on. What brings you here?"

"Did you get my message?" he asked following me into the kitchen.

"Yes, have a seat."

"I was worried when I didn't hear from you."

"Why? We only met for a few hours on one day. Surely you can't worry about strangers you meet."

"Well as you are on your own I hoped you were ok so thought I should check. I came yesterday as well."

"There's no need to worry. Yesterday I went on a walking tour."

"I nearly went on that trip but came to check on you instead. Where did you go the day before?"

"Really, do I have to account for my movements?" I asked irritably.

"Sorry, you don't. I just enjoyed your company the other day and wanted to take you out to show you different places."

"Well that's kind of you. I actually had some business to attend to with various agencies to discuss terms for this place plus other stuff to see to. As it gets too hot and busy later in the day, I made an early start. So after two early starts I was planning to have a lie in this morning."

Chris laughed saying: "Sorry I ruined it. How did you get on?"

"I am writing everything in a notebook keeping a file for when I am ready."

"Do you want me to take you to my agent?"

"Not yet, I need some space."

"How many bedrooms do you have?"

"Three although one is more like an office. The place is spacious but I realise it would benefit from updating. It's clean and has let well so far. I need to decide whether to invest in it or just tidy up and let it as is. None of it is my taste."

"Ah so your ex-husband furnished it."

"With his partner."

"Ok so now you are up what are your plans today?"

"I haven't made any apart from considering cleaning the place right through."

"It looks ok, why not do that another day and come out to play."

"What are you thinking of playing?" I asked cynically.

"A bit of exploring down the other end of the coast perhaps, lunch, a swim perhaps. How does that sound?"

"Well it's the best offer I have had so far. You will have to wait while I have a shower and get dressed."

"Fine, do you mind if I look around in case I know any potential tenants?"

"Go ahead, ignore any mess or clutter I am in the process of clearing stuff."

"Fine enjoy your shower."

I showered and wondered why this man had been so persistent in contacting me again. He was very presentable, amiable and it would be easy to get used to his company. Chris seemed dependable and well mannered. Perhaps he was not used to women who did not fawn over him or chase him. As I was not planning to stay, I thought I might as well enjoy myself while I could. It was not as if I had a line of suitors queuing up for my attention.

Realistically, I knew that I was no beauty, I was not ugly or noticeable but had learned to live with myself. At present I had no desire to get involved so assumed Chris felt the same. With a tan plus heat from the shower, I was flushed when I presented myself ready to go. Chris nodded and led the way out saying the house was a good asset. If I smartened up the offer by modernising, he reckoned I would get a good income.

I told him I had not decided yet plus had no idea where to find furniture or workmen. Chris assured me he knew suppliers, workmen, everything I would need from having gone through the whole process himself. He decided to stop off at his place to show me on the way. We headed through town and out the other side to a smart area new to me. When he opened the gates remotely and drove into a smart detached villa with a dream swimming pool, I gasped saying:

"Wowzer, this is the dream place, no wonder you have all the women after you. It's like A Place in the Sun house. You even have bi fold doors. I always wanted them."

Chris smiled saying: "I'm glad you like it. Would you like a tour?"

"Yes please," I said dropping my bag on a recliner.

Inside the house was immaculate, stylish and tasteful.

"Do you actually live here?" I asked him looking for signs of life.

"Ah it's like this because the cleaner has been today."

"Is she a local?"

"She's an ex pat who does several properties in this neighbourhood."

"It looks like a show home."

"There's only me to use it and I tend to spend most time outdoors."

"The swimming pool looks amazing."

"It's lovely, would you like to have a swim?"

"Not if we are going out but another time I would love to."

"Ok I'll just get a few things and be with you."

I sank onto the recliner feeling totally inadequate, out of my depth. My house looked like a dump compared to this luxury. While there was no need to feel ashamed of my house, this place made me aware of the need to improve it. Chris obviously lived well and was comfortable. He had good qualities and was attractive, but I did not feel the spark or chemistry for involvement. Perhaps it was because he was so openly still attached to the departed perfect wife. Who could play second fiddle to perfection? I did not want to compete but recognised that between them they had excellent taste. Once again I wondered why Chris had pursued me. Could he be lonely and seeking some safe company?

Chris put a picnic bag into the boot of his car and whisked me away along the coast stopping alongside little villages for refreshments, showing me beauty spots and secluded beaches. Some were sparse and unoccupied. We stopped for a swim and picnic sitting on a big blanket. Talking about retro trends and styles led to music tastes, old advertisements and popular television programmes. We chatted ceaselessly until feeling tired then sunbathed spreading lotion on each other. It was easy and soothing without any tension. I actually snoozed and woke up guiltily hoping I had not been snoring. Chris told me I had snored and it amused him.

"That's because you woke me up too early," I told him.

Chris smiled without responding. We disliked similar things and neither joined in the boozing cabaret crowd. It seemed to be the start of a promising friendship. I warned myself not to get accustomed to enjoying his attention. He told me that his daughter was visiting him the next week for a vacation so he would not be available all week. I told him I was pleased for him and hoped he would enjoy it. His daughter and husband would arrived in two days, Chris would collect them at the airport and was obviously very excited.

"So that's why your house looks so perfect," I teased him.

"No, it's always like that. I try to keep it tidy because I hate looking for things or viewing a big mess."

"Houses need to be lived in to turn into homes," I told him.

"In moderation yes," Chris agreed.

Internally I felt relieved as I would not be able to live up to such high standards. Although I was a tidy person, at times it was comfortable to spread out. The prospect of not seeing Chris for a week or more did not disturb me either. I had managed well before and could get on with things without him. Perhaps I could check out some furniture places online to see prices and styles for ideas.

When I returned home Sadie rang to say she wanted to come out with the boys for half term week. It would be the week after Chris's daughter's visit. I felt happy and told her to bring some mixed clothing in case it rained. Perhaps Sadie could help me with refurbishing the house. The boys would be happy at the beach and in the pool so it would work well.

I did not hear from Chris all week so decided to ring him to tell him Sadie would be visiting me the following week. It turned out that Sadie's plane arrived lunch time the day Chris's daughter departed.

"Perhaps I will see you at the airport then, I hope your daughter and husband have enjoyed their trip."

"Certainly, we have been busy. How are you getting to the airport?"

"Either a taxi or bus, not sure yet."

"Well if you don't mind an early start you can come with us, I can give you a lift."

"Really, that's very kind of you."

"I will text you what time to be ready. Can you wait outside so we can take off?"

"Sure, I will fit in with you. Thank you once again."

I decided to take a book to read at the airport plus some drinks and snacks for my family when they arrived. Airports were always expensive to buy refreshments. I had a freezer bag for the drinks. It would certainly be worthwhile going early even if it was boring waiting. Whilst getting sorted I packed a short story, some cologne and a few tempting chocolates with some small wipes for Chris's daughter's journey. It would be interesting to meet her so I dressed smartly in a summer dress instead of my usual shorts and tops. Chris arrived punctually with his son in law next to him. I sat next to his daughter in the back introducing myself and handing over her journey package.

Sonia, Chris's daughter was very slender with delicate features, an air of supreme confidence and spoke well. Immediately I felt enormous and at a disadvantage knowing that I was being mentally compared to the late wife and mother. Her husband had a good head of dark hair and a short beard. He was also a musician and composer who adored his wife. The two men talked while I sat uncomfortably being scrutinised.

"Have you known my father long?" Sonia asked in her upper crust accent.

"Not really, I only came out here a few weeks ago."

"How did you meet?"

"I was sitting on a bench watching the sea when your father asked if he could join me."

Sonia raised her eyebrows in surprise as apparently Chris was a reserved man.

"Are you a resident here?"

"Not really, my late husband bought a house here which passed on to my family when he died. It is a good size but in need of modernising. I am just wondering whether to renovate it and your father has been helpful regarding tradesmen, furniture suppliers etc. He seems to have many contacts."

"That's because he and my mother built their house from scratch plus his profession also helped."

"Yes, they did a good job, it looks like a film setting."

"I believe your daughter is arriving today."

"Yes with my two grandchildren, I can't wait. What a shame you will miss each other. My daughter Sadie is a very positive personality."

"Do you just have a daughter?"

"No I have a married son Martin who has two sons."

"Will they be coming over too?"

"Probably next school holiday."

Before Sonia could enquire further the airport was in view in the distance so the conversation filtered around last minute enquiries and instructions from and to father and daughter. At the airport Chris handed the luggage to Sonia's husband then went to park the car. The others walked slowly into the air conditioned airport terminal and waited for Chris. I decided to give them privacy when he joined them and would tell Chris I would take a seat in a café to wait. I felt ready for a coffee. Chris nodded when I told him. Shaking hands with the visitors, I wished them a safe journey and waved goodbye. Their flight would not depart for another couple of hours then it would be a further two hours until Sadie landed.

Eventually Chris found me and invited me for another drink with something to eat.

"No thanks, I brought some sandwiches. Would you like one?" I offered.

"I rather fancy a pastry for a change, a sweet indulgence would do me good."

"Are you upset now they are going?"

"A little, it's only natural."

"She will come back again."

"I know but it will be quiet at home without her."

"She has your colouring, lovely eyes."

"Yes, she takes after her mother but is much taller."

"Are you going back now?"

"No, why?"

"It's going to be a long wait and I don't expect you to stay."

"I have nothing else to do."

"Let me pay for the petrol."

"I wouldn't hear of it. Even if you weren't here I would have used the same amount coming and going."

"Can I at least pay for the parking then?"

"It's all done and dusted."

"Can I buy you a meal?"

"Maybe later, let's take a walk around the airport shops then find somewhere to sit and read. I'll get the paper and I brought a book to read. Did you?"

"Yes, ok sounds like a good idea."

"It's getting busy now, I'm glad I am not travelling."

"Me too, the queues and checks, waiting around, very boring."

We trawled the shops amazed at the high prices then found a sheltered spot to sit, people watch and read in peace. I felt too excited to concentrate so made notes on things to do, watched people, visited the toilet, then waited restlessly. Chris asked me about my family to take my mind off the anxiety. Whilst time sped by normally, the clock seemed to move very slowly while waiting. When the plane finally touched down we headed to arrivals where there was a long wait until the luggage was released and claimed. I leaned over the barrier scanning all the new arrivals. Suddenly a small girl and boy came rushing over to hug me, each pulling a small vanity case behind them.

Introductions followed while Chris handled the luggage and led them to the car park. Sadie's eyebrows rose questioning me silently behind Chris. I shook my head negatively preparing myself mentally for an inquisition when we got home. I sat next to Chris in the car asking my daughter about the English weather plus for news from home. Sadie told me they had left a mild cloudy day behind.

"We have plenty of time to catch up, you tell me about here," Sadie told me.

"Have you been here before?" Chris asked Sadie.

"Oh yes, a few times, my brother and I used to visit our father during the school hols."

"Do you have plans for this trip?" he asked her.

"Not really, I need a rest and the kids will enjoy the beach. There are a few favourite places to visit."

"A week soon passes it's not long enough really. If you need a lift perhaps I can help."

"Thank you, we have got school the following week so although I agree it's not long enough, it's our best option at present."

"Chris please stay for dinner, I have made a delicious casserole and special dessert. There's plenty," I said.

"Thank you Rosie, I look forward to it. My daughter flew out this morning with her husband so I am not rushing to return to an empty house."

"So we just missed each other then," Sadie said.

"Yes, it was kind of Chris to wait for your flight," I said.

"Thank you," Sadie told Chris.

"Has your daughter flown back to England?" Sadie asked.

"No, Austria. She is a musician in an orchestra with her husband so they travel all over. Currently, they are based in Austria but don't spend much time there," Chris said.

Before they could talk more Chris was absorbed in traffic with roadwork restrictions.

"This reminds me of home," Sadie said: "They seem to be doing roadworks everywhere you go."

"True but at least they do them a lot faster over here," Chris told her slowing down.

"At home they take forever and you rarely see men at work," Sadie said.

THE LIFE OF ROSIE

The children were busy on their game consuls. Eventually they hit traffic around the town before getting home. While Chris dealt with the luggage, the children pulled their cases behind them, I put the oven on and everybody piled into the cool house. All the blinds had been drawn so it was pleasant after the burning heat outside. While the meal warmed up, Chris and I discussed potential refurbishment plans. I wanted to open up the kitchen area then put an oblong table and six chairs as a room divider, two sofas in the living room, plus open up the room with bifold doors overlooking the pool area. Chris suggested a new wider kitchen window plus a few tweaks to save space in a few places.

Sadie came in to join the discussion saying we needed new furniture too. I told them both it would all depend upon the cost. While the ideas were good, I was uncertain about the investment. Did we want to rent it or use it more? Would I like to stay there? At present all was speculation but Chris had contacts with trades people and suggested we get a few quotes to help with the decision. If we wanted he could drive us to a furniture sales area to check out prices and stock. He seemed to know where to go for everything because he had experienced it all making his own home. Sadie was impressed and asked if Chris would take us while she was here.

"The kids won't be interested," I said.

"You can put them in the play centre until we get back. It's supervised and kids love it," Chris suggested.

"Is it safe leaving them with strangers?" I asked hesitantly.

"It's well supervised and has lots of safe climbing and adventure equipment," Chris said. "I can ask my neighbour's teenage daughter to take them if you want. She's very good with kids."

"As long as someone is there for them I think it should be ok. We can get them ice cream and beach time when we return," Sadie said enthusiastically.

My meal was succulent and I made a tropical fruit flan for dessert so everyone made clean plates. We planned to go the next day. Sadie explained to the children that they could accompany us to furniture shops or go to a play centre with Chris's neighbour. Both opted for the centre unreservedly. We got up early next morning before it was too hot. Chris arrived with Libby, an ex-pat 16 year old neighbour of his. The kids went happily off into the centre without looking back. She seemed a cheerful girl and was happy to earn some money. We drove to an out of town industrial area with several furniture outlets. It was interesting viewing the styles and comparing prices. There was a plethora of grey furnishings.

Before we returned we visited another place off track which was cheaper because it stocked ex storeroom and display wares. It was like a permanent sales offer. Inside there I found plenty to choose from. When and if the time came I would definitely go there first. Currently we had no measurements or means to start buying. If the kitchen wall came down and work commenced it would be dusty.

"What would I do with the old furniture?" I asked Chris.

"Get the charity people to collect it," he told me.

"It's quite worn, they were big people!" I said.

Sadie giggled saying: "They were both plump but happy."

We collected the kids, paid Libby and headed for lunch and the beach. Chris took Libby back and did his own thing. It was a lovely afternoon so we monitored the suncream, insisted on some shade time, then sauntered home towards tea time.

"I could get used to this life," Sadie sighed contentedly. "Are you sure you don't want to marry Chris, live in his big house then we can all enjoy it."

"Don't be silly," I replied tutting. "We have a house and you can use it whenever."

"Chris is a decent man, knowledgeable, attractive, prosperous, how old is he?" Sadie asked.

"I haven't asked him. Anyway there is no chemistry between us. He is still mourning the demise of his wife. Theirs was a big love story from their teens, he is not looking to replace her. Besides although he is a good catch I don't feel that type of connection. My life suits me the way it is. Men can complicate life. I don't want to look after anyone or fit in with them."

"You are an independent woman mum, but I understand," Sadie said. "You should pamper yourself and make more of your appearance. When you make an effort you clean up well. For your age you can look decent!"

"Cheeky monkey, wait until you get older. Leave me alone, there's nobody to dress up for. Chris is a valuable friend but I don't need to impress him. His wife was small and dainty, his daughter is very slender and delicate. I don't think he goes for big women."

"You are not that big these days but you should take care of your skin in this climate. Keep using moisturiser etc …" Sadie's lecture was interrupted by the children arguing.

At the end of their trip I booked a local taxi to drive Sadie and children to the airport. I was just stripping the beds ready to clean the house when the bell rang. On the doorstep stood Chris with a casually dressed man wearing sunglasses.

"Hi Rosie, this is Bob the Builder …" Chris began.

"Hey watch your lip, Bob," the man said introducing himself.

"Sorry, couldn't resist it. He did my place and can do everything. As he is very busy with a waiting list of clients, I persuaded him to check out your house and give you a quote," Chris said enthusiastically.

"Well you could have told me first," I said put out. "My daughter and family just left for the airport and I getting the house sorted."

"That's fine, you carry on," Chris said oblivious to my annoyance. "I can show him what you want done."

I stood back flabbergasted at his affrontery. This was my house and would be my decision. Bob took his sunglasses off noticing my discomfort. As our eyes met I felt an impact like a collision of senses. Without saying a word Bob and I exchanged a glance which made my heart flutter, my knees felt weak and the world disappeared. Without knowing Bob, I instinctively connected soul wise and felt unable to move or speak. Meanwhile Chris was telling Bob about my potential plans. Bob looked as shocked as Rosie felt and allowed himself to be led away. He measured a few places and made notes. Unable to cope I went to the bathroom to wash my face, brush my hair and regretted wearing my old cleaning outfit but could not change.

Chris was still in command when I emerged. He told me that Bob was top quality and would not fleece me. In the meantime I should get another couple of quotes for comparison purposes. I stood at the front door to see them out, thanked Bob for coming. Bob said he would prepare a quotation for me. I told him it was not urgent. He smiled, shook my hand and followed Chris out. Closing the door I had to sit down, I felt weak with shock. What had happened? This was real life not a movie. At my age I thought I had more sense but nobody in my life had ever aroused such passionate feelings in me. How could I manage any home renovations with such a man in the house? At the same time I longed to see him again to check out whether the magic still worked.

As I hesitated before starting my cleaning again the doorbell rang. Nervously I walked over wondering if Bob had returned. Libby stood on the doorstep.

"Hi," she greeted me.

"Hi Libby how are you?"

"Great have the family gone now?"

"Yes they left this morning, their flight leaves soon. What can I do for you?"

"I forgot to tell you when I was here that I do cleaning jobs as well as babysitting. It is all going towards my studies. I passed Chris down the road and he mentioned you were busy."

"You clean houses?" I asked surprised.

"Shops, houses, anywhere reasonable. I'm good, no complaints so far."

"What do you charge?"

"I charge hourly are you interested?"

"Well we can give it a go. My family just left so I have stripped the beds and put the washing on. All the floors need cleaning plus the surfaces needed wiping down and anywhere little fingers have been touching. Do you want to do it?"

"Ok I have space now but you will have to book me if you want it doing again," Libby said handing me a contact card.

"Are you ok if I pop out to get some cash and stock up on a bit of shopping? They cleaned me out."

"Sure, take as long as you need, it will give me space to crack on."

I headed to the supermarket and cash machine, my head was reeling with the impression Bob had left behind. He must be married and was probably a family man, I reckoned. Knowing nothing about him I had nothing to focus on. Unable to rationalise the impact he had made upon me, I decided to concentrate on my duties to try to calm down. With the housework being done for me, I planned to take a big coastal walk later to burn up some energy and agitation. If Libby did a good job, I would hire her regularly. After years of housework it felt good to have somebody take over. Life was for living not dreary chores. Feeling rather pleased with myself I shopped smiling.

THE LIFE OF ROSIE

I arranged for Libby to do another clean and sort out while I was out. Upon my return I was surprised to be told that Bob had visited to hand over a quotation for my building work. After lunch when Libby had gone and the house was sorted, I sat down with a coffee to read the quotation enclosed in an envelope. One was for the work discussed, there was a second slightly different quotation where Bob designed to open up the existing layout into a more spacious light filled environment. Two prices were indicated accordingly. This made the project seem real. Uncertain how to proceed I photographed the quotes and sent them over to my family asking for their opinion.

The prices quoted were within the family budget range excluding furniture which could be bought at the wholesale place. I had not sought other quotes yet because I was still uncertain whether to go ahead and modernise or leave the house untouched. It looked old fashioned and dull so a good paint job would improve it. Decorating was pointless if any work would take place. As the property was now a family inheritance, I waited for the family opinion before taking any action. I had not asked for any more quotations. Chris had been doing something out of town so he had not been around. Leaving a thank you message on Bob's mobile, I felt relieved not to speak to him and said I was consulting my family and would get back to him.

Apart from the disruption and mess that would entail if the project went ahead, I felt a mixture of nervousness and excitement at the prospect of seeing Bob again. I had planned to ask other builders for quotations to compare should I decide to go ahead. Most tradesmen were busy and had waiting lists. If the family approved the plan, it would probably take some time to come to fruition. Martin gave me the family verdict saying I should go ahead with the more open version that Bob had devised. It was within the family budget and met with their approval.

Martin wanted to come over when the project commenced to learn a few new techniques and said he would help with the decoration of the place. Everyone was excited and Sadie had told them about the wholesale furniture place. With family approval I sought two other contractors for quotes but despite one being cheaper, it was a forgone conclusion that Bob would be chosen especially with Chris recommending him. When the decision was made I rang Bob who was pleased and said he would call round after he finished work to show me what the scheme would entail.

I bought some beer, showered and did my hair, waiting nervously for Bob's arrival. He came from work affecting my equilibrium again. I handed him a cold beer from the fridge and followed him into the kitchen listening to his plans whilst keeping a safe distance. The atmosphere between us felt electric especially when Bob stopped talking. He explained he was doing a project at present and said he would advise me when he could start my work. A holding deposit would be required to purchase all the materials he would need for the work. I thanked him for coming and was escorting him to the door when he invited me to join him for a drink later in the evening. Bob told me which bar he would be in from 9 pm, then said he would be there if I wanted to discuss any aspects of the job or just socialise. There was no pressure or commitment.

When he left I felt flushed and excited uncertain whether to go to the bar or not. I could not resist although it was foolish to think of it as anything more than a business invitation. Nevertheless, I tried to look casually smart smudging my mascara and eye liner with nervous tension. Feeling foolish I set off at 9 pm taking a leisurely stroll to the bar where Bob waved and went to get me a drink.

"Have you been here before?" he asked.

"I'm not sure but I don't think so."

"The beer here is good and the prices are fair. Sometimes they have live entertainment and its usually top quality. Where do you usually go?" he asked.

"I don't go out much at night unless it's for a stroll around or special occasion."

"Why not?"

"It's not something I do on my own much. I think it's a hangover from home, I would hate people to think I was seeking attention."

"People are not like that here. This is a holiday place. Are you single then?"

I blushed and explained that my ex-husband had owned the house and been killed in a road accident with his partner.

"That's how I inherited the house with my children of course," I finished.

"Ah yes, I remember that. How many children have you got?" Bob asked.

"A son and daughter both married, you met my daughter and her two. My son wants to come out to work with you on the project and help with the decorating. He has two sons. Where are you from?"

"Middlesex originally. Are your family all in England?"

"Yes but we own the house jointly."

"Will you rent it out when you are not here?"

"Probably but not permanently, we want to use it for holidays."

"Don't you want to live out here?"

"At present I don't know what I want. My place at home could be rented out but I am not sure whether to move here permanently on my own."

"People are very friendly here, everyone talks to each other even when you don't want them to. In fact it can be difficult to be private."

"I have noticed, everyone talks to strangers. Do you have family here?"

"I have two daughters but not here. One is travelling the world with her work, the other is married to a Dutch man and they live in Holland."

"What work does the travelling daughter do?"

"She works with the United Nations so travels around."

"Impressive, so do you manage to see them often?"

"Not often but fairly regularly. We keep in touch."

"Do you have any grandchildren?"

"Not yet but perhaps in the future, it's being considered. These days they are too busy earning a living and getting ahead in their careers."

"As long as they are well and safe."

"That's the main thing and they know where I am when they want something."

"What does your wife say?"

"My wife remarried years ago and has a second family now."

"Sorry, I didn't mean to pry."

"That's fine, we are on good terms now because we only communicate when we need to. I live here with my partner, an Asian lady I met here. She's away at the moment due back next week. Do you have a partner then?"

For a moment I felt breathless then composed myself saying that I was an independent woman at present. As I was living in between two homes it had been difficult to sustain a relationship. One side always wanted to impose or take centre stage so I was single at present, finding my way forward."

"Do you want to stay?" Bob asked shrewdly.

"Sometimes it seems the best option but I am not ready to give up my English home yet."

"You could rent it out with a contract."

"Is that what you've done?"

"Not exactly, I have been here for years now, my English place is part of a portfolio of properties I share with my brother."

"Where are you from originally?"

"Middlesex."

"Is that where your properties lie?"

"No, they are scattered about. My brother takes advantage of auctions and deals. I am the sleeping partner but lend him a hand when I go over there. We share the profits and invest wisely."

"Homes Under the Hammer" type arrangement," I said.

"Ah the television programme, I have seen a few episodes. Something like that," Bob agreed. "Have you asked for any other quotes?"

"Not yet, I am still deciding whether to go ahead. My family think I should as they have a vested interest in the property. We own it jointly."

"So if I do a complete makeover to turn your house into a modern comfortable home would you stay?"

"Maybe or at least for some time to enjoy it. We would need new furniture and fittings to compliment it."

"I could help you with that as I have connections."

"To tell you the truth I have hit an impasse in my life. I used to be decisive and dynamic, active and energetic. Now I look for easy options and lack motivation."

"You are too young to give up, perhaps if you get involved in the renovation project you will have a new lease of life."

I looked at him directly and something inside me fluttered. Bob raised his eyebrows and looked at me speculatively so I looked away saying:

"Tell me about your life here."

"Well I am very busy as my reputation succeeds me, everyone needs my services at some time. I work hard and perform well. The climate and pace of life suits me. When I am free I like swimming and hiking. My home has impressive views. Many people consider me as their friend so my social life is as active as I choose it to be."

"Do you live with your family??"

"No, I live with Mahalia, she's Filipino but has lived here for four years now."

"Does she work?"

"Yes she's a therapist and beautician. She does all types of work when things are quiet."

"So you met her here then?"

"Yes on a group hike. She's away at the moment visiting her folk but comes back next week."

I digested the information with mixed feelings. Mahalia, I imagined would be good looking, younger than me and probably have a perfect figure. There was no way I could compete. I did not feel that a partnership with me would prove to be better than his existing one. Having mentally made that decision, I felt relieved and more relaxed.

"What are you thinking about?" Bob asked shrewdly.

Flushing I replied: "I am wondering when you are expecting my decision about the house."

"Take your time I couldn't start straight away. Are you sure you weren't thinking about my relationship with Mahalia?"

"That's your private business," I replied indignantly wanting to leave.

At that moment the musicians started playing so we sat back to listen and sing along to some of the golden oldies and latest hits. It eased the tension and made conversation hard to hear. When it ended I decided to go so Bob said he would walk me home.

"It's not far, I'll be ok," I told him.

"Maybe but I have to protect my interests," Bob said smiling.

"Interests?"

"You are a potential client and until I get the business I need to make a good impression in case you change your mind," he quipped.

They walked along quietly, I felt acutely aware of his presence beside me. I avoided looking at him again because my heart was thumping. Hoping I was not betraying my feelings, I felt torn between wanting to get home quickly and not wanting the journey to end. When we arrived outside my house Bob asked if he would be invited in for coffee. I declined saying it was late really meaning the prospect of being alone with him was too dangerous. Bob smiled and waited for me to go inside. I leaned behind the front door unable to move. Telling myself to get a grip made no difference. When Bob was around my common sense disappeared. Despite my age and appearance, he was like a magnet to my senses. There was a powerful connection between us.

Chris had been working on a project so I had not seen him for a while. He rang one morning to ask if I had made enquiries concerning other quotations for the work.

"Not yet, I am still deciding whether to proceed," I told him.

"Well here's another couple for you to contact. Get a pen and paper and I'll give you the numbers."

I dutifully wrote the phone numbers down plus another contact number of an Ex pat who used to service the area. When I rang the third one he told me he had retired and referred me to one of the other two numbers. The second one was on holiday and left a message stating he would return in a month. Maybe it would be the third time lucky I thought dialling the third number. He answered and said he would be occupied for the next month or so but would call round to see what I wanted. It seemed that these tradesmen were in great demand so nothing would be done quickly. In my heart I knew that Bob would be my choice if I proceeded.

When the third contact came round after work, I showed him around the house indicating what I had in mind. He was from Sheffield originally and was a pleasant good humoured man. Telling me he would quote when he had time so we shook hands and he departed. There was no news from Bob so I decided to keep my distance as his partner was due to return. Bob also had a disconcerting gaze and a tendency to stand too close to me so he represented danger. I felt attracted but would not interfere with a man who was already committed. When Chris rang to suggest we went for a drink to catch up, I agreed. He took me to the bar where I had met Bob who was there with Mahalia so Chris went over to join them.

Mahalia was a surprise to me. Instead of a young beauty, Mahalia was a bit older than Bob, attractive rather than pretty and looked fit. She was friendly and told them about her trip saying how good it was to see her family and friends again. Talk between the men centred around sport and business so we women chatted about my impressions of the area.
Although Mahalia enjoyed living in Spain, she hoped to save money to return home when she had enough to buy a house. There was entertainment so we listened to a comedian and a singer before parting company. Bob approached me asking if I had made a decision yet.

"I am getting there, Chris gave me some other numbers to ring so I am waiting for another quote," I told him.

"I'm the best you know," Bob said leaning over me.

I was pleased to see the others return from the toilet and said my goodbyes. Instead of driving back, I wanted to walk so Chris accompanied me telling me about his latest project. He talked for most of the way with me distracted, trying to calm down. Eventually, Chris asked me what I thought about Bob.

"What do you mean?" I asked startled.

"Well he is the best in the area, he would do a good job."

"Oh I see, I'll just wait to see what the other quotation is like before deciding."

"Don't leave it too long, you need to grab Bob when he is available."

I thanked Chris for his help and advice and went into my house to calm down. If I used Bob's services, I decided to distance myself. To my surprise Martin rang asking when the work would start. He wanted to join in to learn some tricks of the trade. This meant that Bob would work and Martin would be around so that gave me confidence to go ahead once the other quote came in. It would be interesting to see the interpretation the other man would quote for. When the second quotation arrived I thanked the man then texted Bob asking when could he begin. Bob required a holding deposit for materials so I arranged a bank transfer.

Before work began I had to blitz the place and clear out as much as possible to generate space. Martin would arrive solo, he would bring the family for a holiday when the work was done. I used the bedrooms for storage and the house was mostly cleared. Sheets covered the furniture when work started. Bob arrived and greeted Martin. The two men talked while I made coffee and Martin became Bob's assistant. When the preparation was completed, Bob said he would return the next day with some crew to start. Martin would be welcome to watch and learn. When Bob departed Martin was enthusiastic about Bob saying he was a good role model. I refrained from comment feeling relieved to have my son around.

Martin asked Bob to be his mentor saying he would like to get into the property business but had no experience. His dad had no DIY skills and had not been around to teach him anything. All he knew was painting and simple repairs. Overhearing the conversation whilst in the kitchen washing up after lunch, I felt upset that Martin had lacked a male role to learn from. Bob showed Martin techniques and procedures explaining how to do something the correct way. The two men bonded well and even went out for a drink after work. I made lunch for them each day according to the numbers present. I did not socialise in the evenings preferring to sweep up the dust and mop around. It was an endless task but it needed doing.

When Martin had to return home reluctantly, he instructed me to send him photos of the completion. He shook hands with Bob thanking him for his help and saying he knew it would look terrific. As I accompanied Martin to the taxi taking him to the airport, he hugged me and said: "It's ok mum, he likes you too."

"What do you mean?" I asked flustered.

"I haven't been your son all these years without being able to read you mother. This time you picked well, he is a decent bloke and I approve."

"But he's living with someone," I protested.

"Don't rush him, let nature take its course and look after yourself. You look ok when you smarten up and wear makeup," Martin said winking and hugging me before getting into the taxi and waving goodbye.

I went back into the house flushed deciding to go down to the beach to cool off.

"He's a good boy and your daughter is fine too," Bob said coming to check if I was upset.

I sighed saying I was going for a swim.

"They will be back to visit you when the work is done. That reminds me, what do you have in mind for the furniture?" he asked.

"Chris showed me a few furniture places. I want two sofas in here, a big oblong dining table and six chairs as a room divider from the kitchen …"

"Well come with me when the plasterer is working. I will take you to an auction where you can get everything you need really inexpensive."

"What will we do with the furniture here?"

"Either put it in a skip, donate it to charity or sell it on."

"I don't know how to deal with these things."

"I will help you when the time comes."

Suddenly I felt deflated and upset. Martin had gone, I felt alone and incompetent near to tears. When I slumped Bob came over and gave me a hug, patting my back to comfort me.

"It's okay, you are not alone, I am here for you," he said.

After a few silent minutes Bob moved away giving me a shove telling me to let him get on with his work. I collected my beach bag, changed into my swimsuit and set off for the beach with a bottle of water. I did not return until the work had finished for the day. In the evening I cleaned the house as best as I could and sat outside reading enjoying the cooler air. Next morning Bob arrived with his crew and told me we were going furniture hunting.

"But we are not ready yet," I protested.

"We are making progress, bring your money in case," Bob told me.

"Chris took me to some places."

"I doubt he took you where we are going. This is a trade organised auction and off cut price for end of ranges or unwanted stock. Leave the bargaining to me."

"Ok but I haven't got rid of the old stuff yet."

"That's no problem, I will shift it for you. Do you know what you want?"

"Well modern sofas tend to have low backs. I want a comfy sofa I can fall asleep on and rest my head at the back. For a table I want an oblong six seater with simple chairs. My taste is modern simplicity nothing ornate or fancy."

"What else do you need?"

"I haven't considered anything else yet."

"Ok let's see what we can find today, we can come back again if necessary."

I felt comfortable in the van with Bob, as if we were a married couple.

"Do you usually help your clients so much?" I asked him.

"No, I just give advice if asked."

"I am honoured then!" I said smiling.

"You certainly are and you know why."

"Why?"

"Because we have a connection between us. The question is whether we take any action."

I remained silent and wanted to wriggle with discomfort. Fortunately, we arrived at a big car park. We walked slowly inside viewing various displays and appliances. There was a variety of furniture some slightly damaged, others looking perfect but unusual colours or patterns. In the good as new section there was ample space. Bob pointed out the merits of several large sofas but I did not want leather, I wanted fabric.

"Leather is too hot in this climate," I said.

We found two sofas which suited and had removable covers available as an option. If I bought the sofas with the side tables, I could purchases a set of covers. There were coordinating lamp displays. Bob wrote down the details on a pad and we moved to the tables and chairs. He found a suitable table almost immediately but I didn't like the chairs so we walked around until we found some that would match better. I liked wooden chairs in old fashioned styles. Adding the details to the notepad, Bob led me through the bedroom range to head to the till. I gasped as I saw a classical simple white bed design with side cabinets and a mirrored dressing table.

"I thought you weren't interested in bedroom furniture," Bob said noticing my admiration.

"That is exactly my style and I would be happy to keep the wardrobes and get rid of the bed etc. Is it expensive?" I asked anxiously.

"I can probably get a deal for you if you want it," Bob said.

"Do you like it?"

"Yes, if I was buying a new bed that's the style I would go for too."

Bob added the details to his notepad then they walked over to the cashier where I left everything to Bob. He showed me the price for all the items with a tradesman's discount. It fell within my allocated budget from the family account so I paid hoping the family would approve. Bob arranged for delivery the following week. Sold stickers would go onto the purchases. He told me that work would be completed soon then the old furniture could go into the garage awaiting collection. Bob would make arrangements for it to be collected. His team would remove the bedroom furniture for me plus the rest. I would not be able to move it alone. I thanked him sincerely.

"So if you are grateful buy me lunch I am starving."

"Sure, where can we go?"

"There's a café at the back here for all the staff and visitors, generous portions let's eat before we go."

They queued up the self-service place which reminded me of Costco then sat at a basic table eating well.

"Thanks for bringing me here, it's been an amazing morning. I can't believe I just bought all that."

"You did well, it would cost double on the open market."

"I could never have found that place without you."

"Trade secrets. Didn't Chris take you furniture hunting?"

"He showed me places but I was not sure whether I was even going ahead with the project then."

"Do you see him regularly?"

"I haven't seen him lately as he seems to be busy with work. He's doing an architectural project which absorbs him. It's good when you enjoy your work."

"My work is enjoyable when it turns out well. I like the variety and the freedom to deliver it to my standards. If a job is worth doing … etc."

"Are you a perfectionist?"

"Wait and see."

"Is your home like a magazine advert?"

Bob laughed: "Not at all, it's lived in, comfortable and eclectic with Mahalia's arts and crafts pieces dotted around."

"So you seem well settled. Do you ever go back to England?"

"What for? I have everything I need here."

"When I am here I don't miss England but my family are all there."

"They can come to visit you. Are you looking for a partner? Do you want someone to share life with you?"

"I am used to being an independent woman now, plus I am older so am probably passed the age of attraction. It is not something I have thought about. When I had partners in the past it never worked out beyond the honeymoon period."

"Why not?"

"Perhaps it is my fault but I don't want to be taken for granted as a housekeeper, cook or convenience. That may sound selfish plus I don't need to be told what I should or should not be doing. I realise that there should be give and take in a relationship but I think it should be both ways."

"Points noted."

"Sorry, I got a bit carried away."

"A relationship needs ongoing nurturing and building with trust and care."

"Yes when two people get together they merge but still retain their individual personalities. Often the woman is relegated to the kitchen and substitute mother figure."

"I don't treat women like that."

"Then Mahalia is very lucky."

"While she is here, I get the feeling she will leave one day because her roots are back home."

"Just take one day at a time then and do your best."

"I do."

They returned to the house after the meal then Bob departed after noting where the furniture would go. When all the work was completed Bob came round with the invoice carrying a big plant as a present.

"Thank you," I said flushed with pleasure.

"I will keep the key a bit longer in case you find any snagging issues then return it to you. Are you having a house warming party?"

"Not likely."

"Why not?"

"After all the disruption I need a bit of peace and quiet to get used to my new splendour!"

"Ah and I was thinking about showing off my handiwork as a promotion."

"I don't want to invite anybody yet, I am still getting organised."

"Are you pleased with the work?"

"More than pleased, who wouldn't want to live in such a fancy house?"

"So you will recommend me?"

"Of course, I am lucky you found time for me as I understand how busy you are."

Before they could continue Chris rang the bell bringing me flowers so Bob departed after exchanging greetings. Admiring the house Chris invited me for a celebratory meal. I told him I had loads of work to do getting straight again so would not be able to stay out long. Chris wanted to wax lyrical about his latest work commission so I let him sound off. Fortunately, a lady I knew from the walking group came to the restaurant. Introducing Chris to Wendy, I beat a hasty retreat and left them talking.

At home I was engrossed in sorting out my bedroom when the phone rang. Nathan told me that my grandson Mark had suffered a bad asthma attack and been taken to hospital where Sadie was staying with him. As he was only three, he could not be left. I was alarmed and said I would return immediately. Mark would recover but he needed to stay in hospital for tests and was currently receiving oxygen. Upset

THE LIFE OF ROSIE

and worried I told him I would text my flight details and put the phone down. I would be able to stay with Mark while Nathan worked and Sadie took care of Abby. After informing Frances what was happening and leaving a spare key with her, I departed next morning for an early flight. I rang Chris to tell him I was leaving.

I caught a taxi home and aired the house which felt dull after Spain. Deciding to go to the hospital in the morning, I unpacked and did some shopping for provisions. Although familiar the house felt neglected. It needed some tender loving care. I rang a cleaning agency to ask them to do a thorough refreshing clean. I had used them before so was on their books. While they were cleaning I would go to the hospital to stay with Mark. Having rung Sadie and Martin to tell them I had arrived, I felt exhausted so had an early night. I was not pleased to be back and needed a period of adjustment. After breakfast next morning I let the cleaner in and told her to throw the key through the letter box when she had finished.

I caught two buses to the hospital which was located on the other side of town. It seemed easier than trying to locate a parking space at the hospital which was part of a complex medical centre so permanently busy. At the ward Mark was sitting up in bed with an oxygen mask on his face. He was pleased to see me. I brought him some picture books and favourite toys from my house. Sadie was there having slept over. While the doctor did his rounds he removed the mask and said Mark was making good progress but was not ready to go home yet. I told Sadie that I would stay so Sadie should go home and rest for now. Sadie agreed but told me that it was too expensive running two homes, I should think about renting one and deciding where to live.

It seemed sensible advice to me too. Already I was missing the Spanish sunshine coast. Breaking into my thoughts Nathan rang to thank me for staying. He mentioned that his cousin was going to commence studying from September at the local university. Would I be agreeable to renting my house perhaps. His cousin was a sensible girl and would look after the place. She could perhaps share the rent with another girl and cover the bills. Perhaps I could think about it. I was surprised but realised it would be a good solution with no management fees. Nathan then went on to say that when Mark was better, the family would go to the Spanish house for a couple of weeks to help him recuperate. The sunshine would do Mark good. This meant that I would not be able to return to Spain then to give them privacy.

When I spoke to Martin later he told me the house photos looked amazing and he couldn't wait to return to show the family.

"When were you thinking of going?" I asked.

"When's Sadie's crew return it should be around half term time so we will go then for the duration. You better tell her to leave it shipshape."

"I'm sure she will," I said my heart sinking knowing I would stay in England for the foreseeable future.

Chris, Bob, Frances and all my friends seemed a world away. For the first time I felt lonely and abandoned. In England everyone was busy running their own lives and routines. The weather varied during the day so it was not always possible to go out or make plans. I felt cold even though the temperatures were fairly mild. It was annoying that I had not had chance to enjoy the Spanish house development. Apart from spending time at the hospital and visiting Martin's family, I decided to blitz the English house ready for rental. I made three piles: keeping, charity and throwing telling myself to use it or lose it.

When I caught up with my English friends we had little in common. They all envied my opportunity to enjoy life in sunny Spain. I invited them to join me when I returned. They caught up with gossip, drank a bit and gradually I adjusted. I went back to keep fit classes, art and volunteered at the Food Bank. Keeping myself busy passed the time. Mark came home and the family left for Spain where they admired the new look house and assured me all was well. Meanwhile Martin booked for his family to go for the half term break. This meant that I would be able to go in time for the students to move in. I made a contract listing the responsibilities for the rental, details regarding the maintenance and wanted a holding deposit in case of damage which would be returned if all went well.

"Please ensure that these girls keep the place hygienic. Cleanliness is important. Also they should keep the noise down at night after 9pm. Students often leave food out all over the place, I don't want any vermin," I told Nathan.

"Don't worry mother," Nathan said reassuringly, "I will make sure they comply."

Nathan always called me mother although his own mother was thriving. His family were always welcoming and gracious to me, including me in any hospitable occasions. Abby and Mark adored both grandmas and their remaining grandpa. It was a happy family unit. Martin's in laws lived further out but were also very considerate and friendly. Close family ties meant caring and sharing so I knew they would take care of my interests.

In Spain I had missed my family now at home I missed Spain with the walks along the coast and casual lifestyle. In England I had to consider what to wear, whether I needed an umbrella, etc. Also apart from city centres and parks, it was more built up and not as exciting to go for walks. At night I stayed in unless asked to babysit.

Sadie had met Bob who asked about me. It seemed Chris had latched on to my friend from the walking group and they were often seen together. Frances sent her regards but nobody else missed me. When I returned there I would have to renew all my acquaintances. Sometimes I felt adrift as if I did not belong anywhere. Normally I enjoyed my independence but suddenly I felt vulnerable and lonely. Feeling sorry for myself was depressing so I made an effort to be more outgoing and active until it passed. Keeping busy to tire myself meant the days and weeks passed quickly.

THE LIFE OF ROSIE

While I was settling down in England, my family took turns to stay in the Spanish house. I told them to leave it spotless ready for renting. Both families wanted to use it during the long school holidays so I would not be able to return until September when the English house would start renting. Disliking intense heat I was happy to wait for temperatures to cool slightly in Spain. Meanwhile I was decorating and clearing my English house to a more minimal content. With my girlfriends I was able to enjoy a few social activities plus partake in local classes for aerobics and art. During the summer months I enjoyed day coach trips and made some new friends.

When the time came to return to Spain, I was accompanied by my friends Sandra and Claire. At the last minute Claire had to cancel to look after her mother. Sandra loved the house, the ambience, the pool and everything about the area. She told me we should start a business and remain there forever. I told Sandra to come up with an innovative idea first then I would consider it. Once we had settled in I rang Chris who was pleased to hear from me.

"When did you get back?" he asked.

"Yesterday, how are you faring?" I enquired.

"Thank you for introducing me to Wendy, we get on well together. In fact she has moved in with me and rented her place out."

For a moment I could not remember who Wendy was then realised she was from the rambling group. It hadn't taken long for Chris to relinquish his bachelor status. I was surprised at the unexpected change. When I enquired about his daughter, I asked about Bob.

"He's not here at the moment. They went to visit Mahalia's family to avoid August here and will probably stay there until the Autumn."

"I see, so any other news to report?"

THE LIFE OF ROSIE

"It's been very busy and hot here so we have not been out as much. Come round to the bar one evening and we can meet up."

"My friend Sandra came over with me this time."

"Fine so let's make it on Friday when there's entertainment then."

"Ok," I said disappointed because that was four days away. Once Chris would have wanted to get together immediately. Obviously, Chris did not need me now.

Living in the house was comfortable, airy and spacious. I enjoyed it but realised that I would have to socialise to make new friends. Whilst the older ex pat crowd still monopolised their cafes and bars, I did not want to get involved with them. When I showed Sandra the weekly activity sheet we chose a few ventures for fun. Walking was always well attended with friendly people so Sandra and I met many regulars and were welcomed. As it as the first walk in the month it was not too long or strenuous which made it pleasant admiring the scenery. As it was a mixed age group I felt comfortable. Sandra made a new female friend who had many common interests with her.

I settled into the house enjoying the improvements. Sometime I spoke to Dave, the neighbourhood watch guy who helped out with any odd jobs, garden work or problems. Originally from Newcastle, Dave was a reliable handyman who was good natured, chatty and an ex policeman so kept watch on his Spanish community. Everybody knew him and respected him. While I was adjusting to my return, Dave was a source of comfort and nurturing when I met him. His son was the community gardener. A widower, Dave knew everything that was happening and was always willing to lend a hand or contribute to worthy causes. Meanwhile Sandra was constantly seeking ideas to be able to remain in Spain.

"How about English cakes?" Sandra asked.

"What about them?"

THE LIFE OF ROSIE

"Well we could have a theme for English afternoon tea perhaps."

"Look around the seafront it has already been done."

"What if we had themed cake days like Lemon meringue or Victoria sponge?"

"And what would you do with them?"

"Sell them to bakers or cafes as part of a special event?"

"There are already bakers plus you would need to sell an enormous amount. Think again."

"Clothes and accessories?" Sandra suggested.

"Do you see any shortage of boutiques and shops?"

"Ok but it's hard."

"That's why everybody is not doing it."

"What do people miss from home?" Sandra mused.

"Think about it and let me know."

"British food and drink."

"There's at least one place selling British baked beans etc. plus costings."

"Ok I am working on it."

I had a bad day with everything going wrong. It started when a problem occurred with my drains. I would have called Bob but he was still away. When I tried to ask Frances I got no reply on her mobile and the house was empty. Next I had to sort out some red tape which was infuriating as the online site cut off at the strategic moment plus there was a long phone queue. Next I heard of a cancer death, and an alcoholic partner problem. Tempted to ignore further texts and emails I decided to go for a walk before remembering Chris had some contractor contacts. I rang him but he was out and told me he would text over some numbers when he returned home.

THE LIFE OF ROSIE

Locking my front door I set off with a bottle of water, towel and headed for the beach to cool off. Sometimes it was good to live alone because I felt too agitated to accommodate any more aggravation. Telling myself to wait until it passed was easier said than done. It was my turn for aggravation in the evolution cycle. Usually active I had noticed a tendency to nod off during siesta time recently. In the mornings I did my chores and tasks methodically and felt energised and lively. After lunch in the heat I found myself snoozing unexpectedly then waking up startled. I missed the endings of several programmes on television in the process. It also seemed necessary to leave myself notes on the kitchen table as reminders or shopping list items. Names sometimes eluded me but people usually knew what I meant.

Discussing the situation with some friends in the café one afternoon they smiled saying it was my age. These traits occurred as we got older. I protested saying that I was not ready to be old yet. They told me to continue to moisturise and keep active mentally and physically. Someone described it as having too many books on the shelf. Sometimes some fall off. Despite the fact that both my children were married with young families, inside I felt perhaps middle aged, only old when tired. Once I used to clean the house, go shopping and cook meals. Now only one task sufficed before I felt tired. It was a stark revelation but I was determined to make the most of any opportunities that came my way while I still felt able.

However fit and able women were in their middle years they often became invisible to most males for dating. Men seemed to either age better than women or were still eligible despite their appearance. Whether they had beer bellies, thinning hair or other handicaps, women seemed to still be attracted to them. Traditional women enjoyed nurturing so put up with a great deal. Independent career women were more choosey and often ended up having relationships with toy boys. I was not expecting to find more romance. Only Bob had excited me and he was taken. I would not interfere with any relationship. Nobody else had floated my boat for years. Chris seemed

THE LIFE OF ROSIE

content with Wendy. He was an eligible guy but I had never felt physically attracted to him. I would miss his friendship though having taken him for granted.

Life never ran entirely smoothly. When it flowed well it never lasted. Changes occurred often unexpectedly. A contractor sorted out the drains. Returning to Spain had meant the loss of Chris and Bob, two friendships I had expected to maintain. At school I remembered everybody fancied Gary Simons because he looked like George Harrison from the Beatles. As I attended a girls school, Gary was only found at the local youth club where many girls admired him. He once spoke to me once about a table tennis game but I was too surprised and shy to respond well. Another girl called Denise vowed she would marry Gary one day. I did not know if she had succeeded. However, Gary seemed to fancy Lynne who was oblivious to his charms being smitten by another boy. Life seemed to be a mixture of desire and fulfilment not always synchronised.

Perhaps it was normal for one party to care more than the other. Sayings like "the grass is always greener" or "forbidden fruit" etc. had some truth because familiarity often did bring contempt. It was not easy living with somebody. When dating or often mating, the parties tried their best so why did they stop trying once the union was finalised I wondered. They were still two individuals who chose to be together. Compromise seemed to be a common solution. Ideally, each partner should try to please the other one putting their needs first. Often people were too self-centred to do that and were determined to have their own way or say causing conflicts of interests. Was it possible to live happily ever after I pondered.

Human beings were frail and on earth for such a short time in the scheme of things so why could they not live harmoniously? Watching the news headlines I often asked why different factions exposed the differences between people rather than the common elements like raising a family, eating, drinking and trying to improve their circumstances. When disasters occurred many people of all nations and belief systems often came forward to offer help either financially or physically. Why could they not help each other all the time? When there was a surplus of food in the world why were poor countries faced with famine and disease caused by starvation? It was difficult to comprehend when caring and sharing seemed to be viewed as weakness.

Late one afternoon I took a coastal walk then sat on a bench reading and watching the sun going down. A man with his leg in a cast holding two sticks sat beside me. We watched the horizon admiring the colour scheme with the man making small talk occasionally. Unable to concentrate further I stood up to go home when the man asked me for assistance. Would I accompany him to his car he asked. I enquired if he would be able to drive in his condition. He assured me that the vehicle was adapted for disability and was automatic. Introducing himself as Arthur, we walked slowly to a white van. Arthur opened the door and asked me to pass him something from the back. As I leaned forward to accede to his request, he pressed something against my face and everything went black.

When I came round I found herself lying on a camp bed in a concrete room. Confused and thirsty I tried to make sense of the situation but couldn't. When my dizziness passed I staggered to the door finding it locked. Frightened I banged on the door asking for help. Nobody came so I sat back on the bed suddenly needing the toilet and desperate for a drink. I tried to make sense of what had happened and worried about how to get out. Eventually, the door opened and Arthur appeared minus the cast and his disguise. He was in fact an agile able bodied middle aged male. I asked him for a drink and toilet, he pointed to a side room no bigger than a pantry with a toilet and shower.

"What's going on?" I asked as I emerged.

"You are hired to keep house for me. Your duties will be to cook, clean, do the laundry and keep everything spotless," he told me.

"Do I have any choice?" I asked trying to contain my anger.

"Oh yes, you do as you are told. I have high standards. Should you desist I will rape you and take all your clothes away so you will remain naked."

"Why are you doing this to me?" I asked frightened.

"Because you are a lonely middle aged woman so nobody will miss you."

"Wrong, I am the mother of two children with friends and family connections who will certainly miss me."

"That's too bad, any unwanted attention will die down eventually."

"Where are we?"

"We are in a spiritual community away from civilisation."

"What's it called?"

"We are the Promised Pioneers and have duties to perform to pave the way for humanity to follow."

"Do you kidnap all your members?"

"Not at all, they come willingly."

"Are you the leader?"

"I am the Chief Disciple."

"Tell me what I have to do in order to return home."

"You will stay here, this is now your home."

"Will you show me around?"

"I will get Miriam to tell you your duties and get you changed. If you obey your instructions you will not be harmed."

Arthur left the room locking the door. Shortly afterwards a plump middle aged woman entered called Miriam. She handed me a long robe with a tie belt and told me to get changed and to remove all my underwear.

"Why can't I keep my underwear on?" I asked.

Miriam glared at me saying: "Your body belongs to us now and it makes it easier to punish you without underwear."

I shuddered and prayed silently for inspiration to escape from these mad people. Studying my reaction Miriam told me gleefully that there would be no escape.

"Am I a prisoner here then held against my will?"

"You are being given the opportunity to become a disciple which is a great honour."

"I have a family who need me."

"We are your family now and you better learn to fit in quickly."

Miriam handcuffed me and led me around a dreary complex pointing out my duties which ranged from kitchen cleaning, preparing meals, serving, washing dishes or alternatively, in a primitive laundry room which would be a full time job in itself. If I behaved and proved worthy, I could be assigned garden cultivation duties. When I asked what happened if I did not prove to be worthy enough, Miriam smiled and told me I would be publicly raped and go around naked. It felt as if I had fallen into a nightmare. I wanted to wake back to normality. I felt frightened and the best I could hope for was the garden. Watching me Miriam said the garden was fenced off and located in an isolated spot with nothing for miles around.

When the tour was finished I was told to wash my hands which were uncuffed. I should watch how the meal was served then do washing up duty afterwards. The dining room filled up with men and women who sat separately. Many men had shaved heads or very short hair. The women tied their hair back and looked tired and hard faced. While the meal was plain and basic, I ate as I suddenly felt hungry and could not be sure when the next meal would come. After a short prayer everyone ate silently. There was water to drink. When I finished I was told to start doing the dishes. Monitors collected the used plates and cutlery dumping them all alongside the sink. I found some old rubber gloves and set to washing up. Nobody spoke to me.

When everything was washed and surfaces wiped down, I was taken to a meeting room and given a place to sit. Apparently there was an evening meeting to discuss the issues of the day. Arthur came to sit near me and told the congregation that I had been assigned as a new housekeeper. Everyone should inform me of my duties to ensure I performed well. If there were any complaints about me, Arthur should be informed. He publicly asked me if I had any questions.

"If you are in an isolated place how do you get your supplies?" I asked bravely.

"We grow our own fruit and veg but get deliveries of items we cannot provide. Our men drive a truck to the nearest town periodically. Clothing and most household provisions are made by ourselves. Anything else?" Arthur challenged looking irritated.

I shook my head intimidated. Arthur pontificated for some time before rising. The group sang a few hymns then I was led back to my cell and left to sleep on the camp bed. Cold, frightened and very anxious, I decided to appear docile while studying the set up to find a way to escape. I hoped that back home someone would miss me or the children would worry when I did not answer the phone. If I was in an isolated place then it meant nobody came around so I knew I would not be found easily. My mobile, book and clothes had been confiscated. On my feet were some simple pumps which would not be suitable for escaping. Trapped and afraid I prayed for divine intervention having no intention of joining these crazy people.

In the night it occurred to me that perhaps the water was drugged as I had a headache. If something was dissolved in the water it would explain why the congregation appeared to be so docile and even lethargic in some cases. The bland expressions and lack of emotion would be explained. I decided to only drink from the tap when I was in the kitchen. Initially, I was assigned to the kitchen where I made porridge, peeled vegetables, cooked, cleaned and washed dishes. A woman called Irene supervised and gave me instructions. Although Irene worked hard, the bulk of the produce was assigned to me to see what I was capable of.

At the end of the day I felt weary and exhausted. I sat through the evening meeting almost falling asleep. At night I cried myself to sleep through exhaustion and cold. While washing up a cup had fallen from a slippery pile and broken. It was reported to Arthur who asked for an explanation.

"The dishes were piled up and as I moved the pile towards the sink one cup slipped off onto the floor and broke," I told him. "It was an accident."

"Will this happen again?" Arthur asked me disapprovingly.

"No, I will be more careful," I assured him.

"Then exercise more care and attention," Arthur said pulling down my robe to expose my breasts to the entire congregation.

Mortified I hung my head down while Arthur explained to everyone how important it was to take pride in doing their duty to the best and highest standards. I let my head hang low until the meeting was over when I was accompanied back to my cell after pulling up my robe. A bunch of leaflets were handed to me to study as I was locked in. I read them until the light faded but none of them made sense. It seemed the egoistic Arthur had founded a movement to glorify his outrageous ideas and concepts. I wondered how the recruited congregation had arrived there. Were they all conscripted by force? Nobody seemed to show any inclination or initiative to escape.

Deciding not to remain any longer than absolutely necessary, I vowed to study intently how things functioned by gaining their trust which would take time. I needed to understand when the truck went to the nearest town for stock. If I could hide inside the truck I could escape. How I would manage to get into the truck without my absence being noticed was the main obstacle. Failure was not an option. There did not seem to be any other viable way to get out of there. Nobody visited or came near the place.

Everyone appeared to be subdued and sometimes edgy before drinking. I felt certain everyone was drugged into a compliant state so avoided all liquids apart from the tap water. It was vital to stay alert whilst appearing to be subdued. Arthur monitored me constantly so I kept my eyes lowered in his presence. I sensed he was waiting for some misdemeanour so that he could stage a public rape and humiliation which I was determined to avoid.

Each night I was locked in my concrete windowless cell and escorted out to perform my duties. I ate breakfast after serving everyone else and was always the last to eat meals. Although fresh vegetables and salad were provided, the food was sprinkled with "salt" which I sniffed and tasted surreptitiously and decided it was a chemical content. I made certain to put my own meals aside minus the salt. Something was sprinkled into the water jugs to purify it so I stuck to the tap. By eating and drinking after everyone else, I was able to remain drug free. Everyone there finished what was placed in front of them.

There were questions I wanted to ask so I made a list on a sheet taken from the order pad. When I noticed dwindling supplies I was instructed to check in the storeroom for fillers. If not available I should write the item on the pad for the next order. Labourers brought sacks of provisions into the storeroom. Making a list of questions I wanted to ask Arthur, I secretly kept adding to it as time went by including:

- Explain what this commune is all about
- What do you believe in
- Why are there no children
- Why do you believe you are entitled to kidnap people

THE LIFE OF ROSIE

- Can people leave if they want to

Waiting for an opportunity to question Arthur or anybody else, I complied with my instructions and fell into bed exhausted. I wondered whether my absence had been noticed. My children would ring my friends when their calls were not answered. Frances had been away, Chris was busy with his lady friend. Sandra would surely notice. Fortunately, I had locked my house and not left anything cooking when I went out. Perhaps Dave might notice my absence. Nobody would find me in this remote location. Each time I left my room I studied the layout. At harvest time all hands were busy picking and storing including me. I wore some old gloves found in a cupboard and as I worked well, I was transferred from the cell to a female dormitory with six beds.

The other females ignored me but one called Jessie was instructed to supervise me so we communicated. Slowly a friendship grew. Jessie had arrived at the commune with her parents and grown up in the children's house which was across the complex behind the fields. Her dad had been an alcoholic unemployed drifter who gave her mum a hard time. In the commune the couple had adjusted and found a new path. It seemed Jessie's brother drove the truck to market. I stored the information in my head. Explaining to Jessie that Arthur had tricked, drugged and kidnapped me by force, I told Jessie that I had two children and four grandchildren who would be very worried about my disappearance.

After some time had passed Arthur called me for an interview in his office. Making me stand he asked me how I found life in the commune. Nervously, I enquired whether I could ask him some questions. Leaning back in his comfortable chair, Arthur's eyes narrowed suspiciously then told me to go ahead. When I asked him to explain what the commune was about, Arthur was in his element and pontificated endlessly. It seemed like he was an egocentric maniac convinced of his own supremacy. When he finally trailed off, I asked why there were no children about. I already knew about the Children's house but listened to him explain that pregnant ladies moved

THE LIFE OF ROSIE

there prior to birth and remained until they had nurtured the babies.

"What happens then?" I asked encouragingly.

"The mothers return here to work and go on organised timed visits to see the children."

"So the children remain there?" I asked.

"Until they reach 12 for girls and 13 for boys."

"Then what happens?"

"They get trained to be useful and learn specialist skills."

"Can people leave if they want to get further training or choose to?"

"They have all their needs provided for here so why should they leave?" Arthur asked looking confused.

"Well, why do you think you are entitled to kidnap me and force me to be here when I live a decent family life elsewhere?"

Arthur huffed and puffed looking angry: "You are a non-believer, an outsider, you are privileged to be chosen to serve here. I thought you were adjusting but I can see I was wrong."

"Tell me what I should believe in."

"You heathen savage …"

"Arthur, I am a G-d fearing woman."

He then lectured me about believing absolute nonsense which was so bizarre that I could not understand whether that Arthur was serious, or that anybody would make sense of it, let alone go along with it.

Finally, my legs were aching and duties were waiting so I politely told Arthur: "Thank you for your time Arthur, I will think about what you have told me. It is too much to take in now. I have to go to do my duties."

I gave Arthur a half bow then fled to the kitchen where I immersed myself doing my duties not meeting anyone's eyes in case they viewed my contempt. Gradually, I adjusted to my new routine although I had no intention to settle. Asking Jessie confidentially for escape suggestions we talked about being carried out in a shroud but I did not fancy being buried alive. Medical conditions were treated on site not taken to hospital. The perimeter fences and borders were security screened. Waste was recycled. Only Jesse's brother and another guy drove away to pick up and drop off supplies. On market days some of the senior women were accompanied to sell the best produce. Internally the dormitories were inspected and there was limited storage space with no hiding places. It was decided that I would have to be smuggled on board the truck in the night before it left in the early hours.

"I can't go like this," I told Jessie indicating my robe and lack of footwear.

"Leave it to me, I know where the clothing store is, I can smuggle you something, what size footwear do you take?" Jessie asked.

"Size 6 but where would you hide it?" I asked anxiously.

"I will take it just before you go, you can put it on last minute."

"Are you coming with me?"

"I would love to but I won't."

"But they will know it's you and do terrible things to you."

"No, you will give me a sedative to take before you leave and I will be out of it."

"What if I get caught?"

"No, I will get my brother to hide you at the back. You need to listen to his instructions and keep still and quiet. Don't move until he tells you. He usually drives and is accompanied by Dan who is his supervisor. My brother does the lifting and unloading while Dan negotiates with the suppliers dealing with the paperwork. It is imperative you take no action until instructed then run out of sight."

"When do you think it will be?"

"I will find out and let you know."

"Shame I can't get my mobile back."

"That will be locked in the office safe."

"How will we get me out?"

"You will go to bed as usual and be around for the two inspections pretending to sleep. Then we will get up silently, you will sneak out behind me. We will go out through the kitchen, get you dressed and onto the lorry before daylight."

"But they will see my empty bed."

"We will wrap a pillow up and drape the blanket round with some dark scarf showing as if it's your hair."

"I hope you don't get into trouble."

"I will be drugged unconscious as I will only take the sedative when you are gone. Your robe will be sticking out from your cover and your slippers will be under the bed. When they rouse me I will be genuinely startled and confused."

"How will you explain me being able to get out of the building?"

"The kitchen will be locked again with everything in place and our bedroom window will be slightly open so I will assume you jumped down."

"What if they ring the lorry to check?"

"My brother will drop you off somewhere safe so will agree to check at the next stop."

I felt trepidation but hopeful I could carry it off. Knowing it would be a short notice endeavour, a one off chance made me determined to carry it off. There would be no second chances.

"I have no money to make a phone call or get help."

"My brother can slip you a bit."

"Do you know the address here where we are?"

"Not exactly, perhaps my brother can give you something, I will ask him."

"You are relying on your brother so much, perhaps he won't want to help me."

"He will in return for you making contact with our gran and his ex-girlfriend."

"Of course I will. How do you know that they are still around?"

"That's for you to find out and then leave a message where my brother tells you."

"Do you want me to do anything for you?"

"Just don't forget me and hopefully, you can bring some justice to this place. Living here is like a prison. If you get help to free the inmates come and get me."

"I promise I will Jessie. You are risking so much I feel guilty."

"Don't be, you are the only one with the strength and courage, the rest of us are turning into zombies with all the chemicals. I know you are trying to avoid taking them. Do your best."

"You bet I will."

Time passed slowly while I tried to hide my nerves and restlessness. When all hope was gone, Jessie told me her brother was leaving the next day. Everything was arranged. We went to bed and remained still for the two nightly inspections. After a quiet interval Jessie signalled to me. We tiptoed down to the kitchen where I pulled on some jeans and a loose sweatshirt with sneakers. There was a pair of knickers but no bra or socks. Jessie had oiled the kitchen door and it opened silently. Pulling on a dark cap to conceal my hair, I followed Jessie to the lorry which was parked on the drive. We hugged silently. Jessie's brother helped me aboard and accompanied me to the back of the lorry behind the driver's seat. I lay down and was covered by supplies and produce.

After a long wait while I froze and desperately tried not to fidget despite feeling itchy and cramped, I heard voices, the door slammed and we drove off after checking the lorry was secured all round. I found myself dozing until the lorry door slammed and I awoke startled. Some supplies were removed and there was a delay until the lorry drove off again. After two more stops Jessie's brother came to shake me motioning me to be silent. He assisted me down from the lorry and gave me a note motioning me to run off to the right and gave me a thumbs up. I motioned a thank you then flew as fast as my cramped legs could move out of sight behind some trees.

I found herself outside a town which was quiet with a few early risers about. Not wanting to draw attention to myself or get caught there, I headed right through the place noting its name. In case this town was in cahoots with the commune, I decided to continue my journey until I found a police station or another location where I could make a report. Lacking a mobile phone was very inconvenient. Pausing to catch my breath I opened the envelope Jessie's brother had given me. Beside a note with some contact requests, also inside I found some money and a coins. Realising I could buy some water and make a phone call gave me courage and gratitude.

Afraid to make contact so soon, I struggled on until I found an isolated public telephone. Wondering who to call for help, I thought Chris would be useful but could not remember his number. Likewise all the telephone numbers I used were stored on my confiscated mobile. Feeling uncertain I called my own house number and let it ring out for a long time. At the last minute Sandra answered sounding sleepy. I urgently explained what had happened to me and told her the name of the market town I had just passed through. Asking Sandra to get the police to rescue me and find the commune meant the call was running out. I told Sandra to send help urgently saying I would wait in the outskirts then the call ran out.

THE LIFE OF ROSIE

Afterwards I sat back exhausted drinking water wondering if anything I had told Sandra made sense. In the commune the days flowed together monotonously so I was uncertain how long I had actually been there. Did Sandra comprehend my message? Would she do anything? Unaware whether anyone had reported me missing, would the police cooperate? Where should I wait or hide? Perhaps I should move on to the next place then call again. It would take time for any action to take place. Afraid of capture and uncertain how to proceed, I prayed then looked for a hiding place to rest in before continuing my journey later on. Reluctantly I crawled into a hollow covering myself with branches behind a hedge and dozed. I awoke to the sound of police sirens. Uncertain whether they were seeking to return me to the commune or save me, I remained rigid with fright.

Standing in the shade behind the hedge I saw police officers around the public phone in the distance. Risking life and limb I felt too drained and hungry to resist. Staggering towards the phone I waved both arms when an officer noticed me. Feeling light headed and dizzy, I fell into a policeman's arms and was taken away in a police car. At the station I was given a meal and plenty of water to drink. They found an English speaking officer who wanted to take my statement.

My urgent request was that they go quickly to rescue to imprisoned members of the commune. I handed a letterheaded invoice to the officer saying that this commune was being drugged and used as slave labour. Telling them that Arthur was running the place, he was cruel and crazy but dangerous. The officer gave instructions and directions to the staff then returned to me. Asking for a computer I preferred to type my statement in detail apart from my escape. Telling them I would not compromise the safety of anyone who helped me until they were rescued, I agreed to complete that part later.

Suddenly I became newsworthy so the media came with cameras and the police station was besieged. Needing to rest I was allowed to lie down in a cell to have a siesta. Afterwards while waiting to be collected to return home, I had a shower at the station and was handed some clean clothing. The clothes I arrived in would be taken as evidence. I washed my hair and appreciated the sports bra and clean knickers. There was even hand cream which I smothered on. It felt luxurious.

To my surprise Chris arrived with Sandra, I burst into tears when I saw them. We group hugged and they swore to protect me in future. Apparently there had been a campaign to find me for months. Although unsuccessful with speculation rife and online rumours, the campaign had attracted attention in England and around Europe. My family were frantic, my friends deeply concerned and now that I had been found I would be subjected to media attention for a while. Thanking the police for rescuing me, I posed for photos and promised to send the clothing back but they told me to keep it. In Chris's large comfortable car, I reclined along the back seat crying all the journey home. Sandra and Chris said little and let me cry to release my tension.

Back home there were balloons and banners decorating the front of my house. A crowd gathered to welcome me home. I had become a celebrity and felt overwhelmed by it all. Chris took my arm and led me inside telling everyone that I was too exhausted to speak at present but grateful to be back. The news had a field day with shots of Arthur and the commune being infiltrated and investigated. The residents were led away for questioning, access remained open and guarded. There was a frenzy as discoveries were found with drugs, passports, mobiles, cash, clothing and articles belonging to members past and present. Arthur had also been dealing and smuggling illicit goods. He was also charged with indecent assault, kidnapping, rape and intimidation.

I sent word via the police that Jessie and her brother had a home with me if they wanted to join me. Jessie rang to say they would be going to their gran and thanked me for saving them. We agreed to meet up later on when things calmed down. After the call I cried again with relief to be safe and stress from the memories. My ordeal was over but the other members would have to find a new way of life poorly equipped after the trauma plus unused to thinking for themselves. Counselling would be available. Once investigations finished the commune would be sold for development. The cultivated estate would attract interest after the controversy.

When making calls at the police station I asked Chris to buy me a new mobile, nothing fancy, easy to use. He should programme in his number, mine and any relevant numbers I may need. My children were relieved to hear I was safe and were making plans to fly over as soon as possible. Eventually I got my old mobile back which was used as part of the evidence found at the site.

When I entered my house Sandra was there with another lady introduced as Molly.

"Molly has been staying with me while you have been away," Sandra told me.

I stiffened saying: "Well Molly, I am here now so you can leave. In fact Sandra, thank you for your help but you will have to leave too. My children are flying over soon and will need the rooms. Please strip your beds and take all your belongings with you."

Sandra gasped with shock: "You mean leave right now?"

"Don't you think you have been here long enough? This was a temporary arrangement. This house is owned by my children and myself. You have no right or permission to allow other people to stay in it. Please find your own accommodation from now on."

Sandra stared unbelieving at me saying: "I thought we were friends and you liked sharing the house."

"There is a time and place for guests, you have exceeded that by far so please go."

"Where do you expect me to go with no notice?" Sandra asked.

"There are hotels and apartments to rent or stay with one of your business friends, that is not my concern," I said turning away.

"After all my help, you are not even grateful… "began Sandra.

Chris escorted both women to their rooms stripping the bedding, opening the windows and ringing for my cleaner to come by urgently. I sank down onto a recliner by the pool overcome with exhaustion after effects of my ordeal. After bringing me a cup of English tea, Chris escorted the two angry women off the premises and drove them into the town centre. He returned with the cleaner who promptly undertook to blitz the entire house for a lucrative payment. Meanwhile I dozed on the recliner. While I slept Chris kept callers at bay and read a newspaper. Eventually, Chris fell asleep beside me with the newspaper on the floor.

The house was clean from top to bottom but provisions were low so Chris improvised and began making a supermarket order for delivery when I awoke. We shared cold juice then added to the list which Chris rang through for delivery.

"If your family are coming you need to be stocked up, especially with cold drinks," he said.

"Chris I can't thank you enough, I don't know what I would have done without you," I said gratefully.

"My pleasure, I am sorry that I have neglected you since Wendy and I got together. I was too immersed in my new relationship."

"That's how it should be. I am sorry to keep you from her."

"That's fine we are more settled now, she wishes you well."

"Do you think I was unfair to Sandra?"

"It's your house not hers so you can do as you see fit. Was she a paying guest?"

"She contributed initially but not enough and it had become more irregular. I was so angry to see that she had moved in her acquaintance without permission using my bedroom apparently. How dare she do that? Did that person contribute? They were sponging off my generosity but no longer."

"Well you did the right thing, if I was you I would get the locks changed so they can't come back. If they are skint they may return to steal."

"Do you know any locksmiths then?"

"I can get you one, let me see," Chris said looking up online.

Chris arranged for a locksmith to come out urgently and said he would require six sets of keys for the front and back doors. A special lock barrier was fitted across the patio door opening. While the work was carried out Chris ordered a takeaway meal for the two of them. Wendy was invited to join them but declined as she had a keep fit class but told me she would call round the next day to see how I was. I thanked her but said not to bother as I was expecting my family to arrive. I lit a candle at the dinner table and Chris ate with me like old times. It felt serene and comforting to see him there. We did not speak much apart from enquiries about local people and situations.

"Bob asked about you," Chris said unexpectedly.

"Oh that's good of him, did he know about my drama?"

"Not at first as he was away but when he returned he was concerned about you."

"Word will soon spread that I am back."

"Yes well everybody will know who you are now, you have become quite a celebrity. When you go out people will greet you and be sympathetic while awaiting the grisly details."

"Thanks. How is Bob anyway? Is he keeping busy?"

"He's always in demand."

"Well he's a good worker look at this place."

"He came back without Mahalia."

"Why what's happened?"

"She decided to remain at home and take a good job offer with benefits too good to resist."

"Is she coming back eventually?"

"I don't know, Bob didn't say but he's living alone now not that he's home much."

I digested that information but decided to think about it later moving the conversation onto the local news. Chris informed me of new legislation and proposed planning permission concerning various properties. We shared a bottle of wine which made me sleepy so Chris departed after checking that all the doors, windows and areas around the house were secure. He offered to stay but I told him to get some rest and thanked him again. He told me he would return in the morning and to call him if I needed anything. We hugged and he left. Yawning I found a clean nightdress and went to bed but was too tired to sleep easily.

Chris left a note with a list of callers including Frances but I didn't feel like seeing anybody. When I looked out of my window I saw reporters outside congregating and some photographers looking towards my pool area which was private. I rang Chris and asked for a fence to be erected soonest to protect my privacy. He sent Bob around who came with a Bonsai plant for me to nurture. Having ascertained I was coping, he set to work erecting the new fence quickly and telling the assembled crowd they would be arrested for trespassing if they approached nearer. To enforce security he called a policeman friend who drove over in a police car to disperse the crowd backwards. The policeman called on me to check I was ok before sitting in his car outside the entrance blocking it.

I felt embarrassed to be the centre of attention. Fortunately, Sadie and Martin arrived. Chris collected them at the airport and I arranged a buffet lunch to eat on the patio in the shade. After hugs and explanations they settled down on recliners. After lunch Chris departed advising me not to go out for a few days until the story lost interest. If I needed anything I should call him. Martin thanked Chris for all his help. Bob joined them for lunch then carried on securing the property. He installed viewing monitors from the doorbell so I could see who was there. When he finished he spoke to Martin privately assuring him of my security and told him that he would keep a discreet eye on me. I felt disappointed to see Bob depart but too tired to make conversation. I nodded off on the chair.

To end the media bombardment I agreed to hold a press conference the next day to conclude the situation. Flanked by Sadie and Martin, I smartened my appearance and prepared a rehearsed speech. Nervously I told them how Arthur had misled and kidnapped me. Explaining how the cult was run in detail and the culture it proposed to lead, I refused to tell the media details of my escape saying only that with the help and support of a couple of good friends, I managed to escape. Telling everybody how frightening it had been, how desperate I had felt. Now I was home again it felt miraculous so I needed some time to adjust and get my confidence back.

Answering questions many of which were repeated, I remained until I began to sag. Martin stood up and brought the proceedings to a close then we all went home. I was on all the evening news channels and in the press. Therefore I felt obliged to keep a low profile for a while. While Sadie and Martin were around I let them do most of the chores while I lazed around. After they departed melancholy set in. Conscious of my solitary state I brooded near the pool or in it.

Normally the house was rented during the hot summer months while I returned to England as I did not like the heat. My English home was rented out so I remained mainly indoors, shopped online and only went out walking during quiet times when I would not be recognised wearing hats. Very quickly new stories occupied the media and I returned to being ignored. Some people pointed or nudged when I passed but these became fewer. I always wore a sunhat and sunglasses. The tourists were oblivious to me.

Chris kept in regular contact. Frances always checked to see if I wanted anything or to join in with social activities. One evening Bob came round to invite me for a change of scene. His brother had a villa down the coast in Muranos and would be willing to invite me to stay there provided that I left it clean ready for him when I left. Since my trauma I had not had chance to speak to Bob privately as there were always people around.

"That's very kind of you and him," I told him.

"Well it's there if you want it. I thought you may be ready for some escapism," Bob said.

"It has been a bit stifling. How are you getting along? I heard Mahalia stayed behind.

"Yes, she got offered her dream job so could not resist plus all her family are there."

"Will she come back here?"

"Maybe who knows? Perhaps for a holiday."

"You must miss her. Are you lonely?"

"Not really, we always had our own interests anyway. I'm busy working then don't have much time or energy for socialising especially in this heat."

"I don't like it so hot so I spend my time in the pool or near it. Is there a pool at your brother's place?"

"Yes, it's a good one."

"Are you thinking of going there too?"

"Maybe do you want me to?"

"Let's just think about it. Is your brother planning on coming over?"

"During the school holidays with the family."

"Ah so we would clean it and get it ready for them?"

"He has a cleaner who does all that so we would probably have to change the bedding and wipe around after ourselves if we went."

Conversation moved over to local topics and news before Bob departed with no decision made regarding the escape to the other villa. I suffered a drop in confidence and self-esteem. Previously, I used to make spontaneous decisions and be assertive. My current inclination was to hibernate and keep a low profile. After some consideration I accepted the offer to go to his brother's villa the following week. Bob picked me up and we did a supermarket shop before setting off as there would be no provisions. The villa was located overlooking the coast but set back in a quiet location with a few scattered neighbours but no signs of any facilities.

Bob switched on the electricity and appliances explaining how to operate everything while I unpacked and made tea. I put some beer in the fridge for Bob who surprised me by saying that he had to go back owing to work commitments.

"Do you think you will manage here alone?" he asked.

"Yes, I think so but where are the shops if I need anything?"

Bob led me outside and pointed to a curve down the coast telling me to follow the road and to find a Spa and a café with a small shop.

"That's why we shopped before we left," he said. "I wish I could stay but needs must. Call me if you need anything day or night."

"Ok when will you return?"

THE LIFE OF ROSIE

"Friday after work, we can eat out to celebrate. I hope this change of scene does you good. You can't hide forever. Life goes on and you have to get your confidence back. Be strong and think about what you want to do in the future."

I felt emotional so Bob gave me a hug then departed. Left alone I wandered around the outside of the villa and stood watching the coast trying to get used to the peace and quiet. Around my place there were always residents and tourists flocking to the beach and along the promenade. Making myself another cuppa, I looked briefly around the villa studying the photographs displayed. I could see a family resemblance although slight. Bob was the most attractive perhaps because he was always active. I felt proud that he trusted me and would make sure to keep the place clean.

It was very quiet outside and I did not see anybody which felt strange. Perhaps the surrounding properties were holiday homes and the season had not started yet. Maybe in the morning I may see dog walkers or other people. I decided to find the café in the morning and investigate the area. Nobody would recognise me here so I felt eager to explore and enjoy the serenity. Nothing appealed on the television and I did not understand how to get the Netflix working, so I had an early night waking up to a sunny morning feeling confused. Once I showered and had breakfast I carefully locked up and set off carrying a bottle of water and sunscreen plus a towel. It was time to have a new adventure.

When Chris made his morning call to ascertain I was okay, I told him that I was staying in a villa down the coast for the week so he was not to worry. I was perfectly fine and just taking time to relax and get myself together. For some reason I did not tell Chris about Bob's offer feeling instinctively that it was a private matter. Chris was pleased for me and told me not to worry about the past. He suggested that I should make plans for my future. Somehow I found it easier to know what I didn't want rather than find aspirations. I took a pad and pen with me to write lists as thoughts evolved. Deciding to find the café first I walked along the beach and noticed a man gardening at one of the villas. In the distance was somebody walking a dog. Otherwise it was very quiet and peaceful.

As the road curved round I followed it until I came to a small row of shops which turned out to be the cafe connected to a small convenience shop, a closed shop was shuttered and a bakery cum food takeaway outlet. Entering the café I ordered a coffee then sat down near the window. A middle aged lady came in and exchanged conversation with the serving lady. Another lady was cleaning the windows and spoke to me in English.

"Are you here on holiday?" the cleaner asked.

"I'm just here for the week for a break," I replied.

"It's a bit early yet the season starts next month that's why it's so quiet."

"Does it get very busy then?"

"Oh yes, this area is known for its peace and quiet but even when it gets busy there is room for everyone to spread out."

The door opened and a young woman came in acknowledged by all. She ordered a coffee and came to sit near my table chatting to the cleaner.

"We have an early holiday maker," the cleaner told the young woman.

"Hi, where are you from?" the lady asked.

"I actually live here in Spain but further down the coast, I just came here for some peace and quiet," I said.

"I'm Jean," the young lady said, "this is Mary," she pointed to the cleaner.

Behind the bar the owner appeared introducing himself as George and the assistant disappeared.

"Where are you staying?" Jean asked.

"She's staying in Tony's place," George replied before I could respond.

"So what do you think of it here?" Jean asked.

"This is my first day so I hope to explore more. It is certainly scenic and peaceful," I replied. "Can you recommend any good walks or places to see?"

Suggestions flowed over my head until George pulled out a tourist map then marked out some routes for me.

"How do you know Tony?" Mary asked.

"I don't know Tony yet. His brother Bob brought me here to stay for the week."

"Was he with Mahalia?" Jean asked.

"No, they went to see her family on holiday then Bob came back for work but Mahalia stayed on so she's still away."

"Is Bob staying with you then?" Mary asked suspiciously.

"Not at all, he dropped me off then will pick me up next weekend. He did some work renovating my house that's how I know him."

"Ok well if you need any help with anything come here to ask. People are friendly although some of the houses are closed for the winter," Jean told her.

I enjoyed my coffee, chatted a bit more but could not join in with the local conversations so said goodbye asking if it was safe to walk about by myself. They assured me of my safety so I set off further along the road to see where it led to. As I left I heard Mary say that I looked familiar but she could not remember why. Feeling relieved not to be recognised I walked seeing more isolated dwellings scattered in the distance, then returned to the beach to sit and contemplate until I felt hungry. Pulling out a sandwich from my bag, I munched happily drinking water. Lying on my towel I snoozed feeling relaxed until a dog came along to sniff my face. Startled I awoke.

An anxious looking lady came rushing along calling the dog back. Introducing herself as Pauline, the lady apologised for the dog's behaviour and threw sticks for the dog to chase. Pauline told me that Bob had asked her to make contact with her to check whether I needed any help or advice. I told Pauline not to worry, everything seemed to be fine.

"It's so quiet here and peaceful," I said admiring the coastline.

"Not for much longer I'm afraid. You came just before it all kicks off."

"Do you live here all year?"

"Yes, I heard you live near Bob."

"Yes, it's always fairly busy but especially during the tourist season. This is a pleasant change. What do you find to do here?"

"Well, I'm an artist so I paint. We are not too isolated there is a town down the coast with all the amenities including a supermarket etc. I can take you if you want. There's also a thriving social scene hereabouts with various opportunities. It's a question of taste to find something that suits you. Personally, I find the time flies."

"Ok I am just thinking about my potential future activities when I go back. If you are going into town again may I accompany you to see what it's like."

"Sure, I will pick you up. Give me your mobile number and I'll call. It's not a big place but adequate to supply all your needs."

"Ok thank you," I said exchanging numbers.

At first I found the quiet a bit disarming. People waved to me when I went out or greeted me on passing. After a while I relaxed and relished the serenity of the place. For once in my life I had no obligations, commitments or responsibilities. I enjoyed planning leisurely days walking, sunbathing with occasional swims. Although I usually took a book to read, I rarely opened it being almost hypnotised watching the sea and light formations. It was pleasant to feel that I had the area more or less to myself. Perhaps in season it became busy but I felt relieved not to have to make conversation and felt inclined to remain there for longer.

On Thursday Pauline took me to the local market in a little town further along the coast. It was compact but flourishing. While Pauline did her business, I strolled along fascinated by the buzz and studying the stalls with interest. I had stopped taking my mobile phone everywhere but enjoyed taking photos on this occasion. Prices were reasonable so I bought some fruit and a tee shirt. My phone buzzed while out and I discovered a message from my friend Lynne in England. It seemed that Lynne had accumulated 10 days leave from work to use before the end of March and wanted to visit me. Overjoyed I replied immediately inviting her over. It would be something to look forward to.

Bob texted to say he would be arriving Friday after work and asked if I wanted anything bringing. I asked him to check if there was any post at my place and asked what he would like to eat. He replied saying they would dine out his treat. The cleaning lady worked while I was at the market so everything felt fresh and clean on my return. At the market I found a small mini market where I stocked up on milk, yoghurts and a few extras feeling uncertain what Bob may like. The market provided some good vegetables but I refrained from buying too much if I had to leave after the weekend. I made the second bed up with clean sheets feeling sad that my holiday break was nearing its end. The villa, the place and simplicity of life there had grown on me.

On Friday afternoon as the day was drawing to a close, I showered and put a dress on being uncertain where we would dine. Wearing makeup with freshly shampooed hair, I felt almost girlie and ready for anything. Spraying perfume to complete the look I awaited Bob's arrival sitting on the porch reading a book. Bob arrived at dusk, dumped some post in my lap and headed off for a shower. Among the post was a summons to Court for Arthur's trial. It would coincide with

Lynne's visit and could take several days. The location was not local as it was being held in the nearest city to the former Cult centre. This would mean booking accommodation at the time as it would not be suitable to keep driving there and back. I decided to ask Bob or Chris the best route to take.

Emerging from the house looking smart and fresh, Bob stopped taking in my crestfallen expression.

"Are you not pleased to see me?" Bob asked anxiously.

"Oh I am it's not that, here look at this," I said handing over my letter.

"I see, well you knew it would be inevitable,"

"Yes, I suppose so but it's not convenient and I don't want more publicity."

"You could ask to give evidence concealed behind a screen then."

"Do they do that?"

"I'm sure they would but it seems like you will have to stay there for a while."

"Yes, but there's time to figure it all out. My friend Lynne is planning to visit me for ten days in March, so it will probably take place while she's here."

"Well she can support you in your time of need."

"She's using up her remaining leave from work."

"Ok let's file this away for now and go out for dinner, I'm starving."

"Where are we going?" I asked putting the letter away.

"Up in the hills, I bet you haven't been there."

"No I haven't."

"It's rustic, traditional and the food is delicious. I haven't been for a while, my brother goes regularly."

"I hope you thanked him for letting me stay."

"What do you think of it here?"

"At first it was too quiet but now I am hooked. It's really got to me. I don't want to leave."

"Good, it's not always this quiet though. When the season starts it gets lively."

"So everyone tells me, part of its charm is the quiet for me, it's very relaxing."

"Do you feel better now?"

"I do thank you, the letter just unnerved me."

"Forget about the letter deal with it when you get back. The night is young, let's enjoy ourselves and have fun."

Bob drove along a winding path along an isolated route until cleverly concealed he parked alongside a hidden restaurant illuminated by coloured lights. It looked like something from a fairy tale. I caught my breath with surprise and pleasure. Bob was greeted warmly by the proprietor and they exchanged an animated conversation in Spanish. Welcoming us to a table on the veranda which had a candle centre piece, the waiter handed us menus and departed returning with a bottle of water and two drinks of wine which were on the house. Bob told the waiter he was driving so would not drink any more. We ordered and chatted while the food was being prepared.

"Everything is fresh here with local ingredients. It's all healthy and good quality."

"Sounds wonderful, this place is a hidden gem," I said admiringly.

"Yes, it's a well-kept secret amongst the locals."

"Have you heard from Mahalia?"

"She seems to be enjoying her new job."

"Is she coming back? Doesn't she miss you?"

"She's not planning to come back as far as I know. I suppose she may miss me but she has all her family and friends around her."

"Do you miss her?" I asked with the wine loosening my tongue.

"Sometimes it gets a bit lonely but not often. I have been too busy to notice. There's so much work with little time to fit everything else in so the answer is mainly no."

I lowered my eyes to avoid revealing my emotions. Bob observed me so I could not meet his eyes. Other guests arrived and some background Spanish music played discreetly, so I was able to look around distracted. The starter arrived with side dishes. Bob explained what they all were while I enjoyed discovering the flavours.

"What about you Rosie? Do you get lonely?" Bob asked tentatively.

"I have been on my own for so long now, I don't really think about it. Going out during the day suits me, I rarely go out at night so this is a big deal for me. Thank you."

"Don't avoid the subject."

"Are you talking about relationships?" I asked surprised.

"Of course we are both adults."

"Well I don't expect to get much attention these days at my age. Besides I don't do casual relationships, I need to care for the person I'm with to make it meaningful. There are many easy women around on the lookout but that's not for me."

"Good, I am glad to hear it. What type of man do you go for? Would Chris be your type?"

"Not at all but he is a decent man and a good friend. He has helped me so much."

"So you don't mind he has a new partner?"

"Of course not, I introduced them. I hope they will both stay happy."

"Do you want a new partner?"

"Goodness, I haven't even thought about it. Why are you asking?"

"I want to get to know you better."

Rosie blushed and focused on her meal wondering how to respond while her heart was beating fast.

"I don't know how to respond as in my mind you are spoken for."

"Every time I see you there are other people around. When we talk I feel we bond well. My time with Mahalia was a convenience thing, not a big love affair. We used each other to service our needs. She needed accommodation and I was flattered that such a pretty girl liked me. It was never going to be permanent."

Before I could reply the next course arrived. Feeling flustered inside I could barely eat or concentrate. I wondered whether Bob was offering me an invitation or perhaps the wine was affecting my brain cells. Either way I found Bob incredibly attractive and sensual. He smiled at my obvious confusion and discussed the food to help me calm down. The meal, the location and setting were romantic.

"This must have incredible views in the day time," I said.

"Oh it does, we can go for a drive up here sometime."

"When do we have to go back?"

"We have all weekend and possibly one day more if you want but then I must return."

"What a magical place and such a special week, thank you so much for bringing me here," I sighed.

Bob topped up my wine glass while he drank water and I felt tipsy but ecstatic to be there with him. We chatted and had a dance on the inner dance floor to some Spanish music. Holding me tight and twirling me around the floor, I laughed with my eyes sparkling. A classical guitarist appeared to entertain the audience and they listened spellbound applauding enthusiastically after each piece.

"Worth coming then?" Bob asked.

"I feel like we are in a movie. This is probably the best night in my life."

"Surely not, what about when you got married?"

"Oh please, this whole evening is pure magic. Have you been married?"

"Yes a long time ago, you know I have a daughter."

"Of course, I think the wine has addled my brain cells. So having been married once you know that it is not always easy. Only in the movies or novels do all the couples live happily ever after."

"Why do you think I am still single?" Bob joked.

"Well you are a very attractive man so I am sure it's not from lack of attention."

"Do you find me attractive then Rosie?"

"Too attractive for my own good," I said smiling. "I am not used to drinking so please excuse me if I speak out of turn."

Before Bob could speak the waiter brought coffee and little decorated chocolates. I felt sleepy and tried to fight the temptation to sit back and snooze. Watching me Bob urged me to drink up before they left. Time had flown since their arrival and I allowed Bob to lead me to the car. I thanked the proprietor and chef before leaving praising their skills and great ambience. In the car I leaned back while Bob drove slowly around the winding roads back home. On arrival I was asleep and snoring gently. Amused Bob helped me out, leaned me bodily over his shoulder and escorted me into the bedroom, lay me on the bed, removed my shoes then covered me over to sleep. He used the bathroom, checked I hadn't moved then took himself off to the back bedroom to sleep pleased with the successful evening.

Next morning I woke up with a hangover to find Bob preparing breakfast encouraging me to eat up. Bob sent me to shower then after breakfast took me for a drive exploring the little villages hidden in the hills and beyond. It was fun exploring the scenic charms of the unexpected locations. We had a light lunch in a remote farmhouse then headed for the coast where we lazed and swam during the afternoon. When it became cooler we strolled along the beach before heading home.

"What a lovely day it's been Bob, thank you so much for taking me," I sighed.

"What's the sigh for then?"

"It's a shame we have to go back tomorrow."

"We can come again if you want."

"It's going to be so busy back home full of people everywhere."

"We need those people to secure income so that we fortunate ones can live here all year round."

"I know but …"

"It could be worse, imagine if you have to go back to England."

"Oh don't remind me."

"What's happening to your place there?"

"It's been let out to a couple of students one is related to my in laws."

"Don't you worry that students may not look after it?"

"My kids will keep an eye on it. Besides it's earning its keep and I don't want to be there."

"So are you staying here now?"

"Well after all the marvellous work you put in, it would be a shame not to."

"Can you put that on my website?"

"Maybe but you don't need to drum up work."

"It doesn't hurt to spread the word or the compliments."

"Ok I think you do first class work."

"That's not all I'm good at," Bob said leering.

"Behave yourself!" I said with my heart fluttering secretly.

"Let me know if you want to find out, I aim to please."

I tutted and blushed self-consciously which made Bob laugh delightedly. Back home we sat on loungers outside watching the sunset before heading in to have a simple supper using up supplies from the fridge. We cleared the kitchen wiping things down then I went to pack my belongings saying I would change the bed in the morning.

"Should we put the bedding and towels on in the washing machine before we go?" I asked.

"Leave them in the laundry basket next to the machine for the cleaner to do next visit. If we put them in and she doesn't come until later in the week, they will need doing again."

"Ok then. When will your brother come?"

"Next school hols I guess, probably for the Easter break."

"Will you come down to see him?"

"Maybe if I get time, why do you want to come back?"

I shrugged saying: "Of course but I have Lynne visiting and the trial to fit in."

"Who is Lynne?"

"My closest friend, she has been nursing her mother recently that's why she hasn't been yet. We went to school together and were inseparable."

"Is she married?"

"No, she was engaged but broke it off."

"What does she do for a living?"

"She teaches primary kids and special needs."

"Well she will be good company for you."

"Let's just enjoy our last evening and forget about the rest. Can we find a good movie to watch?"

Bob knew how to work the technology to get Netflix so we settled on the sofa together watching a thriller. When it finished they both felt tired and were falling asleep so went to bed separately.

"The sea air knocked me out, goodnight Rosie, you will have to wait to sample my prowess another time."

"Goodnight," I replied yawning.

Next morning after toast and coffee they packed up, Bob checked all the house was secure then they drove slowly home stopping off for drinks and snacks along the way. As they travelled the landscape became busier being more developed. By the time I was dropped off at home I felt disappointed to leave Bob. He studied my expression then smiled, patted my shoulder, told me to behave myself then waved goodbye. I went into the laundry room emptying my bag there then had a long glass of chilled orange juice. Feeling lonely and vulnerable I sat by the pool without putting the lights on. Nobody called or texted me.

While I had ample time to please myself regarding my activities life was quiet. Naturally, the day after Lynne arrived I was summoned to Court for a few days. I booked a cheap hotel for the two of us online and told Lynne to go exploring. However, Lynne had never been to court and wanted to see what it was like as a spectator. The first day I had to report lunch time but there was a break then I was not called during the afternoon so sat waiting outside for nothing. It was boring and I decided to take a book to read the next day. Lynne went sightseeing. I was finally called in and sworn in English to tell the truth then I sat down and awaited questioning by both sides.

Asked to give an account of my initial meeting with Arthur by her lawyer, I dutifully obliged. His lawyer cross examined my report by asking her sharp questions like:

- Did you approach Arthur first?
- Why did you sit on that bench?
- Who spoke first?
- What was said?
- Did I always speak to strangers?
- Why did I accompany him to his vehicle?
- Why didn't I try to escape?
- How did I escape?

I explained that Arthur had approached my bench wearing a cast on his leg and using a walking stick. He sat down at the other end of my bench.

"What did you say?" the lawyer interrupted.

"I didn't say anything, I was busy thinking."

"What were you thinking about?" he asked.

"Probably what to have for my evening meal as I was getting hungry."

"So how did you get talking?" the lawyer snapped impatiently.

"Arthur dropped his walking stick in my direction so I bent down to pick it up for him."

"Did he thank you?"

"I think so. He asked me if I was a local."

"What did you say."

"I said I lived here."

"He asked where I was from in England."

"Did you tell him."

"No, I did not want to engage in conversation with him so I prepared to go when he asked me if I would be kind enough to escort him to his vehicle."

"You agreed then."

"I asked him how he would manage if nobody was around to help him."

"Did you not suspect that his cast was false?" the lawyer asked.

"If somebody approached you wearing a full leg cast using a walking stick would you suspect they were false?" I asked pointedly.

Ignoring my remark the lawyer told me to continue.

"Arthur said he struggled but it would be much easier if he could link me. I felt reluctant and asked how he could drive. He said the vehicle had been adapted for him. It was parked along the kerb a bit lower down so I accompanied him deciding to go home afterwards."

"Then what happened?"

"Arthur opened the door of the vehicle and asked me to move some stuff onto the floor from the seat for him. As I leaned over he pressed something over my face and everything went black. It smelled like chlorophyll."

THE LIFE OF ROSIE

"Are you sure you didn't encourage Arthur?"

I looked at the lawyer with contempt saying: "I may be a single lady but I am not looking for a mate. I restrained myself from adding "especially not Arthur." The questions and drilling continued requiring a detailed description of the activities and set up at the commune. Complying with all the repetitive questions worded slightly differently to try to catch her out, I refused to disclose how I escaped eventually. Even when my escape was detailed I told the court:

"I owe my freedom to the help of a few good people and I will not disclose their identities in case there are any fanatics left who may look for them."

The court told me that I should answer but I steadfastly refused until finally said: "I have answered your questions to the best of my ability. My escape will remain confidential. That's all I am going to say."

The court was adjourned and I had to return the next day in case there was any follow up. Some media reporters were waiting outside the court so my lawyer led me out of a side entrance into his car where he drove me away to meet Lynne. I felt exhausted and longed for it to end. My lawyer expected to finish my appearance the next day but advised me not to leave the country before the trial was over. It could last a few months as evidence was being gathered from former members and present witnesses. The media were having a field day as it was the quiet season.

Chris, Bob, Frances rang me then in the evening my children rang. I spoke to my grandchildren and told everyone it was very tiring but I was coping. They all thanked Lynne for being around. Lynne was enjoying herself and was even chatted up on the beach. They ate out and found bars with live music in the evening. Next day I was released before the lunch break so they went back home where Lynne enjoyed my pool and comfortable living. As a treat they ordered takeaway food with wine. I invited Chris with Wendy, plus Bob to join us. Chris brought a guy called Trevor with who was visiting him. Lynne got on well with them all and they drank, sang, wined and dined with enthusiasm.

When they eventually left Lynne was excited saying I was having such an enjoyable dream life.

"It's not always like this," I told her, "most of the time I live alone and often it's too hot for comfort."

"I like the heat," Lynne said, "back home we don't get enough of it."

"Well you can always stay here as long as your mum is ok."

"She's settling into this sheltered accommodation. At least I know the place is supervised. I think she's made friends with some of the residents. At least she knew someone from her school days there. I was surprised they recognised each other as to me they both look like old ladies."

"Have you rung her?"

"Yes, she said she was playing bingo so I was interrupting her."

"Oh well it sounds promising."

"Yes it's got a hairdresser, laundry room, a chiropodist attends and there is a doctor on call for the residents if required."

"Shall we clear up tomorrow properly when we've thrown the waste away?"

"No, you go to bed I'll do it," Lynne told me. "It's the least I can do, I'm too excited to settle yet."

"Who has excited you?" I asked pausing.

"Well truthfully I liked Bob and Trevor, but the other couple were fun too."

"Ok so I suddenly feel tired so goodnight for now and thanks for doing that."

"Sweet dreams."

I went to bed hoping that Lynne hadn't fallen for Bob but unable to stake a claim. He had been attentive to both women equally and even brought along his guitar to accompany the singing. Thankfully the neighbours had not complained as they kept the noise down. It had been a successful evening and I felt shattered as I drifted off to sleep.

Lynne wanted to do all the touristy things visitors enjoyed while on holiday. I dutifully escorted her around showing her the popular places. They encountered Frances at a bar with the expat brigade. Frances handed Lynne a leaflet showing activities during Lynne's stay inviting her to join them.

"There's a karaoke evening tonight if you are interested," Frances told Lynne adding "You will be most welcome to come."

Lynne asked me if they could go. Normally Lynne would not be seen anywhere near such an event. I did not want to go so asked whether Frances would take Lynne.

"I know it's not your thing Rosie. Never mind, I will be delighted to take you Lynne. I will call for you around 8.30 pm then. We can have a few bevvies first to loosen up," Frances said.

Lynne thanked Frances profusely.

"What's got into you?" I asked Lynne. "Has the sun affected you?"

"Ah Rosie I am on holiday and so everything is new. I don't want to be conventional, here I want to try every experience."

"Well, be careful you don't overdo it or get taken advantage of."

"Rosie my dear, you have all this year round, let me enjoy myself. I wish I could stay."

"Ok but most of that crowd are older than us and get boozed up."

"I'm a fully grown woman, I can handle myself. What will you do instead?"

"Eat, chill, maybe watch something or read."

"See, so let me live a little while I have the chance."

Lynne dressed up while I watched indifferently. Frances called for Lynne and they left in full conversation. I decided to wait up for Lynne to return. On holiday Lynne seemed to be a different person probably because she'd been cooped up taking care of her mother for so long. Hoping Lynne would enjoy herself, I was nodding off on the sofa when Lynne returned well after midnight. Immediately, I could see Lynne was excited.

"Well?" I asked.

"It was great Rosie, you should try it sometime. After the karaoke session we moved to a bar where we saw Chris with Wendy and Trevor."

"Was Bob there too?"

"No"

"So Trevor is still around."

"Oh more than that, Trevor is looking to buy a place to run a bed and breakfast. He has seen a few and is considering purchasing. We sat with them and he filled us in with all his plans."

"Did Frances contribute to the ideas?"

"Oh she left me with Chris and went to join some friends at another table. Trevor told her that he would take me home so she left with them."

"So Trevor brought you back?"

"Yes, Chris and Wendy left one way, Trevor accompanied me back here. We got on so well, he's an interesting guy."

"Is he single?"

"Yes, never been married. He's been busy building a career in England."

"Doing what?"

"An accountant but he's fed up with all that and wants to try a new venture…"

"Has he done hospitality before?"

"I don't think so but he also wants to stay here."

"You seem quite smitten by him."

Lynne blushed and grinned saying: "He's most definitely my type."

"So will you see him again?"

"He's invited me to go with him to inspect the short list of properties tomorrow."

"My goodness, how will you manage to sleep tonight?"

"I don't know but perhaps the wine will knock me out when I lie down."

"Did you drink a lot?" I asked studying my grinning friend.

"I don't know," Lynne replied dreamily.

"Well you better get some sleep now while you can, it's already tomorrow."

"Ok then goodnight," Lynne said sauntering towards her room.

"Goodnight," I replied going to my room.

During the rest of Lynne's visit she spent as much time with Trevor as she could. When it was time to depart for home Lynne was upset and told me she would return. Thanking me for my hospitality, Lynne felt in love with Trevor and heartbroken to be leaving him. Trevor drove Lynne to the airport and seemed equally smitten.

THE LIFE OF ROSIE

I hadn't heard from Bob since my return which felt odd. I asked Chris about him and discovered he was working away on a building project. Wondering why he had not called after work, I decided not to make contact either even though I was dying to speak to him again. Since my return I missed the tranquillity and solitude of Muranos. Home seemed too large, it was comfortable and would be easily rented out. An idea was forming as the season approached, perhaps I could rent out my Spanish house and take a rental somewhere in Bob's brother's area. It was too busy at home and would just get more crowded and hotter as time progressed. Although I enjoyed the Spanish lifestyle, I would not have chosen such a popular tourist spot to buy in. My husband had probably loved the cheap booze and cabaret lifestyle.

With Bob remaining unobtainable I asked Chris for advice. First I asked him how to get to the area. I wondered if he could help me find somewhere small to rent in the Muranos area for the summer.

"Isn't that where Bob's brother has a place?" Chris asked.

"Yes."

"So why not ask him?"

"Because he's not here and you are."

"I can plan the route for you, the satnav will take you. Why do you want to go there?"

"Because it is peaceful and spacious."

"How do you know? Have you been?"

"Yes, that's where I went secretly to get away from all the media attention."

"I gather Bob took you there then left you. Ok so what about your house?"

"If I can find somewhere there, I will rent my place out for the season."

"What about your family? They may want to use it."

"Well they will have to book in advance. I will need income to run it."

"Don't you want to go back to the UK?"

"No, my place is rented there anyway."

"You are full of surprises. I heard it's very quiet in Muranos."

"That's why I like it. At first I needed to adjust but coming back here overpowers me now."

"Won't you be lonely there?"

"I made a few friends and acquaintances. Who knows? I can always return."

"Let's look online then."

They left the situation for the time being while I considered my options. On the way home I remembered Pauline, the dog owner who had driven me to the nearby town. We had spent some time together so I rang her to catch up.

"Hi Pauline how are you doing?" I asked cheerfully.

"Is that you Rosie? How are you?"

"To be honest I am having withdrawal symptoms. I had just got used to the peace and quiet there. Here seems very busy and noisy."

"Well you chose to live there."

"Not really, my late husband purchased the property here. I would have gone for somewhere a bit quieter. He lived here with my replacement although they never married."

"I'm sure you will get used to it again soon."

"Well actually Pauline, I was thinking of renting out my house for the season. It's in good nick now and should prove popular. So I was wondering if you knew anywhere in your area that I could perhaps rent. It needn't be fancy or large, one bedroom would do. What do you think?"

"Oh I don't know, I will take a look around and make enquiries for you. There are some hotels scattered but I suppose you like the area you stayed in. It will not remain as quiet as before once the season gets underway."

"Sure but compared to here it will be. How's life in general there?"

Pauline filled me in on the latest news then ended the conversation telling me to leave it with her and she would enquire. Although Pauline had a one bedroomed apartment, she had a small room where she kept the dog apparatus and storage so it was not suitable to accommodate me. At a pinch I could sleep on her sofa but I needed a place long term. Before making any firm decisions I decided to return to Muranos to check out the accommodation situation first hand. I texted my children telling them to book in any time allocation for the summer months before I rented. Finally, I sent Bob a text asking if he could recommend any rental accommodation around Muranos, then set off.

As I headed to Muranos, Bob returned surprised to hear of my departure. Chris informed me that Bob was back and Mahalia had returned. On hearing the news I felt dismayed and assumed Mahalia and Bob had reunited. Mahalia had returned briefly to collect her belongings and inform Bob that she would be staying at home permanently. They had a farewell meal and Bob accompanied Mahalia to the airport. This caused a delay in his response to me. He texted me saying he would look into it and ask his brother if his place was available. Bob had work piling up so was unable to get away for a week. When he managed to drive down to Muranos in the early hours of Saturday morning, I had gone on a day trip with Pauline so we missed each other.

I spent one night on Pauline's sofa then booked myself in a small place down the front. In the café the day after the trip I was handed an envelope with the keys to Bob's brother's place with an invoice for monthly payments if I wanted to stay. It seemed reasonable and I felt excited but wanted to finalise my arrangements first. I rang Bob and left a message saying I would be returning to rent my house for the season first. Thanking Bob for the offer, I advised him that I would be happy to take up the rental once I got sorted. However, when I returned home Bob was working away again so I made plans, contacted my children with the rental agent details, then texted Bob to say I would be sending the first monthly payment as requested. Tempted to invite Bob to visit I hesitated thinking Mahalia may not like it. Reluctant to invite the couple round, I decided to leave it and see what happened. I packed carefully and put my confidential paperwork and special belongings into the bank.

Driving myself to Muranos felt like coming home. This time I dropped my luggage and shopping supplies into the house, filling up the fridge then rushed outside to go into the sea to cool off. It felt invigorating and I splashed, paddled, lay on my back basking in the scenery and feel of the place. Although there were more people about most were fairly distant so it still seemed delightfully quiet. I felt happy and seriously considered buying a property somewhere there. Perhaps I could sell the English house as I did not want to return there. The Spanish place would provide good income for rentals and the children enjoyed using it. They could not afford to replace it. Muranos was probably too quiet and isolated for young families.

I linked up with Pauline and made friends at the café with many locals even improving my Spanish. Before long I felt like a local especially when I saw pale skinned tourists visiting. Some of the owners of the various houses returned as they used them as holiday homes. The atmosphere became cosmopolitan with representatives from Europe, America, Canada and even New Zealand. People came and went so it was always interesting to people watch. An Australian guy called Lee bought a villa and had regular visitors. Some evenings people would gather along the beach to play music,

THE LIFE OF ROSIE

drink and even barbeque. Spiritually, I felt I had found my haven.

Determined to relax and enjoy myself my plans were interrupted by a call from my daughter.

"Hi mum, how are you?"

"I'm fine thanks how are the family?"

"We are all ok. Nathan is taking the kids on a Center Parcs activity holiday with his parents for half term so he suggested I visit you to check on how you are faring after your ordeal," Sadie said excitedly.

"I'm doing fine now so when were you thinking of coming?"

"If it's ok I can leave next Friday."

"Well you know I'm not in the house at present, it's been rented out."

"Yes you said so where are you exactly?"

"I'm in a village called Muranos about two hours further down the coast. It's very quiet here and picturesque."

"Ok so how do I get there?"

"The best thing would be to hire a car at the airport with sat nav and drive straight here. I will cover the expense for you."

"Ok I'll see what I can do and get back to you. Do you want me to bring anything?"

"Yes please, bring some English cheeses including Cheddar and Stilton."

"Fine anything else?"

"If I think of anything I will text you. Let me know the details. Don't expect much in the way of entertainment, I told you it's quiet here. I like the peace and tranquillity."

"Sounds wonderful, I can't wait to come. This is just what I need and so unexpected."

They chatted some more then hung up. I was startled by the news, pleased to see Sadie but wondering how she would find this new location. Once the details were confirmed I would go to town to stock up on shopping. Alone I lived modestly with simple meals. I told Pauline about my daughter's impending visit. Pauline made suggestions about potential outings and things to do if it was too quiet. We agreed to go to the market together. Apart from the local friends and acquaintances I had made, Pauline seemed to be my closest friend in the area. We shared confidences, life stories and had grown close. Both waited for Sadie's safe arrival. When Sadie pulled in front of the house late afternoon, I was thrilled to see her.

Sadie admired the view and brought her case with presents into the house. They were just unpacking and setting out preparations for dinner when there was a knock on the door. Surprised Sadie opened the door to find Bob holding flowers and a bottle of wine.

"Who is it?" I called from the kitchen.

Bob and Sadie were equally surprised to see each other. I was amazed so stood paralysed.

"I should have let you know I was coming," Bob said, "Sorry I didn't know you had your daughter staying."

"Sadie arrived just before you. How are you? Come in," I said awkwardly.

Taking the flowers and wine I thanked Bob and led the way into the kitchen setting an extra place at the table.

"I hope I am not disturbing you," Bob said sheepishly.

"Not at all, you are always welcome," I said adding: "Where's Mahalia? Isn't she with you?"

"She went back home for good now," Bob said.

"Chris said Mahalia returned," I challenged Bob.

"She came back to pack the rest of her belongings then returned. We had a farewell dinner party with all her friends. It seems she was offered her dream job and reunited with her old flame so I doubt that we will see her again in the near future."

"Oh I thought you had been reunited," I said.

"Didn't Chris tell you that? He was at the party," Bob asked.

"No, I haven't spoken to him for a while."

"Who is Mahalia?" Sadie asked sensing tension.

"Mahalia lived with me until recently. We went to visit her family home in the Philippines at Christmas and she decided to stay."

"Are you heartbroken?" I asked.

"Not at all, we had a good friendship but a mutual understanding that this was always a temporary relationship. I wish her well because she is a very talented girl," Bob said.

"What does she do?" Sadie asked.

"What can't she do? She does arts and crafts, has great people skills and can turn her hand at most repairs," Bob said. "Something smells good, I hope you have made enough."

"I always make too much so am glad to share it. How long are you staying?" I asked Bob, bringing a casserole to the table.

"Well actually this is just a fleeting visit to see how you are faring plus to advise you that my brother is bringing his family over in May for about ten days," Bob said.

I suddenly had an idea so asked Bob whether his brother would perhaps be interested in staying in my Spanish place for a change. The rent would be the same as I was paying now.

"Perhaps his family would enjoy the pool and all the amenities there," I suggested. "It's still Spain but would be a change for them."

"I have no idea but I can ask. It would be more convenient for me to see them," Bob said enthusiastically. "Are you sure?"

"Yes, so when do you have to return?"

"Tomorrow, I am in the middle of a project then I have another working away," he said.

"You are a busy man," Sadie remarked.

"Always, I need extra pairs of hands. I always keep my word and try to get things finished on time," he replied.

"To a very high standard," I said: "What a shame you can't stay longer to have a rest. We could have gone on adventures."

"Well I will have to come again then," Bob said earnestly.

I blushed and busied myself with the food turning to get something from the fridge. Sadie looked smug when I returned. Bob was enjoying his meal with chunks of local bread. After dinner when all was cleared away, I suggested going for a coastal walk in the cool evening air. Sadie discreetly excused herself saying she had to call England. Bob and I walked side by side self-consciously. Trying to resist the urge to fling her arms around Bob, I felt unable to converse naturally.

"You didn't get in touch," Bob said.

"Neither did you."

"Didn't you want to make contact?"

"Yes but I didn't because I thought you were back with Mahalia and it wouldn't be right."

"I meant to but I was too busy working and by the time I finished and eaten, I was exhausted. My thought was to get this project finished asap then I could come over here for a break. Perhaps we could go out together but as you can see, I got it wrong again."

"I didn't know Sadie was coming she only decided last week because her husband is taking the kids on an adventure break for half term with his parents. Nathan suggested Sadie came here to check on me."

"And how are you doing?"

"Coming here relaxes me. I like it so much I am thinking of checking out property prices around here for the future."

"Would you sell your villa? It would fetch a good price now it's modernised."

"No, I am considering selling my English house instead. I don't want to go back there to live."

"Ah a woman of property. I dabble a bit in the property market so I could keep an eye out for you."

"Thanks that would be great. Nothing is settled yet but here suits me. At the villa I felt withdrawal symptoms and it seemed very busy and noisy. Had I bought a place in Spain originally, I would have chosen somewhere quieter. Now the busy season is upon us, it will be worse plus hot."

"I'll ask my brother if he fancies a change then. You are offering a more desirable residence than he has plus the pool. His kids would love it there. They are at an age where they need amusements etc."

"What about you? Do you have any plans?"

"To get through my workload then take a break."

"Where would you go?"

"I'll decide when the time comes. Would you be interested in coming with me?"

I blushed and tingled inside at the prospect saying: "Well there's no harm in asking, let's wait and see."

We both laughed and walked on slowly chatting about people and places we knew, proposed developments and food.

"That was a delicious meal you made, I'm glad you are a good cook."

"Thank you."

"I'm not a bad cook myself when I get the opportunity."

"My kitchen is yours to use any time," I told him.

"I may take you up on that madam. Let's go back to keep Sadie company."

We walked back without holding hands but I felt elated. After a nightcap Bob slept in the box room, while Sadie caught up with her family in the spare room. I found it hard to sleep knowing Bob was so close. I wondered if anything would have happened if I had been alone in the house. It took me hours to calm down and fall asleep. During the night I heard somebody use the bathroom but it did not disturb me. In the morning I was disappointed to find a note on the kitchen table from Bob saying: "Thanks for putting me up. Keep in touch. Enjoy your break Sadie." His car was gone and he had not disturbed Sadie either.

"You like him don't you mum," Sadie said during breakfast.

"He's a decent man," I replied.

"Well he must like you too to come all this way."

"It's his brother's place so he probably came to check all was ok plus to tell me about his brother's proposed visit here."

"So he couldn't have done that by text or phone call?" Sadie said slyly.

"He could hardly check the place over if he wasn't here."

"I think he came to check you over."

"Well I did have a bad experience and it was Bob who brought me here to escape from the media attention."

"So it's a shame I played gooseberry huh,"

"Don't be silly, there's been nothing between us."

"Yet"

"Sadie he's been living with a younger attractive woman since I've known him. I didn't realise that she has gone home for good."

"So now you know?"

"Now he's there and I'm here. He also said he's going to be working away."

So show me around, let me see what the attraction is for you. Do you want to live here instead of at the villa? Explain to me about your intentions as you already have two properties."

I took Sadie around the bay, to the café and around the neighbourhood. It was a calm pleasant day with the sea sparkling in the sunshine. Sadie agreed it was scenic and peaceful but asked where the shops were and what facilities were available. When I explained that I loved the quiet and tranquillity, Sadie was dubious about how that would be enough long term. As my family were grown and I had the distinction of being able to please myself regarding my activities, I tried to reassure Sadie that this was what I needed at this stage of my life.

"We will go to the market in the nearest town which has a small shopping area. This is a traditional area, unspoilt and I like it. Families, friends and a slower pace of life suit it. People take time to drink coffee, chat, it's not suitable for families that need arcades and amusements or techno water sports. To me that's a relief, at the villa it gets busy along the coast plus too hot. Here you can just take a dip and admire the beautiful sunsets."

"My goodness mother, you sound like a different person."

"Maybe I am, perhaps it is getting old, but I never chose the villa location. After my experience I appreciate the simple things in life now. Before I took everything for granted assuming it would continue indefinitely. Now I value space and peace."

"Ok I get it but can you afford to rent when you own two properties?"

"The villa belongs to Martin and yourself as well so I will not sell it. However, I think we can sell the English house to raise funds so that I can buy something in this area."

"We have rented the English place and deposited the income in a separate account."

"Yes, I know that. However, I can't see myself living there again. If you want to use it for rental purposes perhaps I can find some other solution to raise funds to live here."

"Think about it carefully, remember you are here in summer now when everything is picture perfect. How will it be in winter when everything closes down?"

"Truthfully, there's not much to close down. Some of the holiday homes will close but when I first came there was hardly anyone about so I fell in love with it then."

"What if something develops with Bob? How would he work here?"

"Let's not jump to any conclusions. I just take one day at a time."

"Don't you get lonely? Isn't it too isolated?"

"Pauline is nearby and I have made contacts with some locals. I didn't have a big social life at the villa."

"That's because you didn't mix with Frances and her social crowd."

"Oh please, boozing, cabaret, karaoke and drag nights have never been my scene!"

"Yes, but you went hiking and joined other things plus volunteered."

"I'm sure that if I stay here I can find similar things to join, I haven't investigated that side yet."

"There's not much here although I admit it is picturesque."

"There's more than meets the eye, Bob took me for a meal in the mountains here at a beautiful authentic restaurant. I must enquire how to get there and treat you to a meal there. It's a magical experience."

"Perhaps the magic was being with Bob!"

"Behave yourself," I said smiling. "What shall we have for lunch?"

"How about we go to that fancy restaurant you told me about?"

"Well I am not sure when it opens but we can check because I picked up a card at the time."

Back home they rang to discover it opened late afternoon so they booked a table then lazed around on the beach before showering and changing. They decided that Sadie would drive as the satnav in her car was the best. I advised her to go slowly as the route was winding and twisting as they climbed upwards with the restaurant hidden from view until the last moment. When they arrived Sadie was enchanted and the young waiter seemed smitten by her so was very attentive. Everything was tempting and delicious. We opted for a special trial menu tasting a variety of offers. I explained about the fairy lights and music on the night I came. Sadie said she needed to bring Nathan as it was so romantic.

We returned home feeling full and sleepy, it had been a wonderful meal. They shared a bottle of wine then went to bed. Next day was market day so they set off with Sadie looking for small gifts to take home. The ambience was friendly with fresh produce, delicious food aromas, enormous fruit and vegetables, plus plenty of bric a brac plus clothing offerings. On the way back we stopped at the local café for something to eat and drink where we were welcomed with people asking if they had found any bargains.

"Everybody is so friendly here," Sadie said.

"Yes, once you are accepted they are very welcoming and helpful."

"It's beginning to grow on me why you like it here."

"Be careful it's addictive."

On Sadie's last day they lazed around on the beach taking chairs, cheese sandwiches, cold drinks, fruit and sunhats. The idea was to bathe and shade in stages without having to go back home. It was very convenient to reach the house so there was no pressure or travelling. Lying back Sadie sighed asking me if she really needed to go home. I had enjoyed my daughter's company and was sad to lose her. Before Sadie left she told me that the place had a special quality that she appreciated, but perhaps the villa was more suitable for family holidays while the children were young. There was scope to go for walks and climb the hills if Martin's crowd came out. Hugging each other tightly before Sadie reluctantly set off for the airport, I felt sad to see her depart.

Texting Bob to say Sadie had departed and could he confirm the dates his brother and family were coming out, I received a reply from Bob saying his daughter was visiting him for a week or ten days. His brother was considering the accommodation swap with the family. Bob had sent photos of the villa which the family liked. He gave dates and promised to advise soonest when he received confirmation. I told Bob to say hi to his daughter then added that I would return to my villa if his brother wanted his house back for the holiday. I then told the rental company to reserve rentals for those dates but have the property ready for private family use. There would be a charge but it was part of the agreement that the property would be available for family use when notified in advance.

THE LIFE OF ROSIE

This meant that Bob would be unlikely to appear in the near future. When his brother arrived he would visit so either way, I would not see him for some time. His brother Tony would want to check on the property even if he decided to swap. I wondered if they looked alike or had similar temperaments. In most families each sibling had a different personality. For the first time I felt lonely and missed having somebody close. Telling myself not to be melancholy and appreciate the good fortune I had in being there did not lift my mood, so I had an early night and slept soundly.

A spirit of melancholy hung over me next day. Nobody called me. When I tried to contact others they were unavailable or away. My family were naturally busy with their own affairs. Deciding to look for some voluntary work or activity to keep active, I felt lethargic unable to motivate myself to move. I decided to return to my house when Bob's brother returned. Perhaps a return to a familiar bustling area may be conducive to action. All my close friends and family were far away. In Muranos I had Pauline to hang out with but no shared history. Pauline was visiting someone currently. In the villa I could contact Chris, Frances and other friends. Muranos was still enticing but being solitary made me long to share it. I felt a sense of failure ending up alone but was not inclined to seek a new partner.

Years of care had left me feeling liberated to make my own choices, be independent and to decide on my actions. Company was pleasant when desirable but other people had their own tastes, expectations and desires. I did not feel inclined to cater or carry anyone else. My family were loved and accustomed to sharing activities together all participating. Friends were not dependable as seen by Sandra who took advantage of me, then Lynne who spent most of her time and energy pursuing Trevor. Perhaps I was too compliant and was seen as a soft touch for a cheap vacation. Equally annoying was the fact that I seemed to have lost my way and needed to find my future direction.

THE LIFE OF ROSIE

Deciding to make a list of likes and dislikes I was heading to my laptop when I received a text from Bob telling me that his brother Tony wanted to take me up on my offer to swap properties for this coming break. Dismayed I regretted my offer but could not refuse. It seemed Tony would arrange to visit me during the period to check out his house. We would both live rent free in each other's places for the duration. I went for a long walk hoping to exhaust my restless spirit and clear my head. Life was challenging and I could only blame myself for the current debacle. Sometimes I annoyed myself more than anybody else. Added to my dismay was the fact that I had no opportunity to see Bob or even Chris indefinitely.

My villa had summer bookings well in advance. Martin had booked in later on with Sadie before the school holidays ended. Perhaps I could stay in Muranos until then unless Tony had plans for the school holidays which seemed inevitable. Faced with uncertainty and emptiness ahead, I slumped down on a rock formation overlooking the bay. An old man was fishing nearby and waved to me to join him in some liquid refreshment. At first I tried to ignore him but he called to me and waved his hand in invitation. Reluctantly I rose and went to sit alongside his chair. He spoke to me in fluent rapid Spanish so I told him to slow down as my Spanish was slow. Laughing he poured me a drink and waved at the scenery telling me how beautiful life was.

From my rough translation with a few English and French words thrown into the declaration, the man told me that life was what we made it. We come into the world alone and depart the same way. Modern life was a struggle, it was difficult with ups and downs. Television and cinema gave people false hope and ideas. Stories in books made people expect their dreams to come true. It was all nonsense, people had to work to earn to achieve. Real life needed much effort. If you have your health and intelligence then most things were possible with hard work. Sometimes life was good but it did not last. People should not expect to succeed by sitting at home. The man poured me some more drink which tasted like a fruity liquor. It relaxed the tension in me and made me feel dreamy.

Seeing me relaxing the old man smiled and began to put his gear away. Saluting me and patting my shoulder, he folded his chair, collected his belongings and walked slowly away. I remained behind thinking about his words which had made a positive impact on me. Perhaps the drink had affected me but I felt content to sit gazing at the calm sea until the stone surface felt too hard on my bottom. Slowly I stood up, stretched and then sauntered back home watching the approaching sunset on the horizon. When I reached home I felt that the dialogue with the old man had been a kick up the backside to stop feeling sorry for myself and reinvent my lifestyle. Feeling more positive I decided to listen to the advice I had been given and reactivate myself in the morning. When I arose I started by doing an aerobic workout before showering and breakfast.

After breakfast I headed to the café to ask if there was anything I could volunteer for. Owner George told me enthusiastically to go immediately to help a lady called Maria who prepared and distributed meals to the needy. Her assistant had fallen and broken her leg so she urgently needed help. Handing me an old bicycle George gave me directions to find the Centre which was inside a housing development away from the coast. Dutifully I wobbled my way down a road until I got the hang of the bike. Propping it against the Centre wall I hoped it would remain there. Heading inside I found a middle aged lady distributing food into containers. Greeting me in Spanish, she knew why I was there, told me to wash my hands and handed me an apron.

I was instructed to pack a sandwich, apple, cake and drink carton into individual bags. Some alternative sandwiches were to be packed in different coloured bags. We worked silently concentrating. When all was ready with the food in containers, Maria loaded up an old milk float cart and indicated that I climb on board. We chugged slowly down the houses stopping to distribute the cooked meal and a sandwich bag. I carried the supplies and followed Maria around. Maria introduced me to everyone and chatted briefly. People were pleased to greet us and thanked us. At one house where the elderly lady was in bed, Maria tied a bib around her and told me to feed her the hot meal. The sandwich bag was placed by the bedside. Maria departed leaving me feeding the lady.

When Maria returned and we set off for the last few, I asked how people managed if they could not feed themselves. My Spanish was limited but Maria understood and told me that these people had help from the social care. Today there was a problem. Maria thanked me and asked if I could help prepare for the next day. Back at the Centre over coffee, Maria handed me a packet of boxes and showed me where to lay them out ready. We also wiped the kitchen down until it was spotless. Maria asked if I could return the next day at 7 am. Feeling suddenly exhausted I nodded and reclaimed the bicycle struggling to return to the café. It had been a rewarding but tiring experience. If I continued my Spanish would improve plus my fitness.

Back home I showered and had a siesta. Having only seen the coastal areas it had been a surprise to find a community tucked away inland. The Community Centre offered activities besides the Meals on Wheels. Twice a week there was a pensioners group who had entertainment and lunch laid on for a low charge. Some people paid for meals to be delivered for various reasons. There were a few bachelor farmers or lone dwellers who did not want to cook, a few new mothers, some people were recuperating from surgery, or even the elderly who could not go out anymore. This kept Maria and her limited staff busy so I was a welcome addition. Before I met any of the clients Maria ensured somebody introduced me first explaining that my Spanish was limited but I was learning. The client base was scattered within a radius of Muranos. It was picturesque inland too with fragrant smells from the herbs, crops and wild flowers.

I participated enthusiastically learning the names of my new friends quickly. It meant early starts and late finishes on lunch days but felt worthwhile. Sometimes I watched the entertainment as I was working and felt that the community spirit ensured everybody was taken care of. It was a small community but nobody was neglected and often people brought in treats to share. There was laughter, piano music and singing, crafts, flower arranging and games. Occasionally, school children visited from the local town or entertained. Each week there was something different or favourite sessions were repeated with variations. A mobile hairdresser called every fortnight for a low charge.

Before I realised the date, it became the week Tony and family were arriving to stay at my villa. Bob called to remind me and said he would be calling round one day to check all was well. I told him to text me in advance advising him that I worked helping Maria these days at the Centre. When Bob asked if I needed anything bringing from home, I just asked him to remove any personal items lying around. My intention was to clean Tony's place to perfection before his visit. This meant a complete overhaul plus laundry washed, dried and put away. The prospect of seeing Bob again excited me so I used extra face cream and body lotion in advance and got the mobile hairdresser to give me a trim. I also tried to eat healthily before he came.

On the day of the visit I returned after the lunch was served and cleared, to find a jeep in my car park space. I parked nearby and hoped I was not too hot and sweaty. Combing my hair in the car mirror I went inside to find Bob and Tony at the kitchen table with the remains of a meal. They were discussing some plans. Bob rose to greet me I'll have them then noticed his hands were sticky with water melon juice. While I instinctively wanted to race to hug Bob, I hung back suddenly feeling shy. Bob had told me Tony was an architect. Tony rose to greet me, he was a similar height to Bob but had more pointed features and a lean frame. There was a slight resemblance but Bob had captured the family good looks.

"Thank you for letting me stay here," I told Tony relieved to focus on him.

"Is everything ok? Do you have any problems?" Tony asked her.

"It's great, I have really fallen for this area. How about your family? Is the villa good for you?" she asked.

"It's wonderful, the kids love the pool and all the amenities around. It's costing me a fortune as they want to try everything they see," Tony said.

"How have you been Rosie?" Bob asked.

"Fine thanks, this volunteering is keeping me busy and I am meeting so many interesting people," she replied.

"Yes, there's more than the coast to discover here," Tony agreed.

"I had no idea when I came and I keep finding new places," I said enthusiastically.

"Tony is thinking of building an extension here," Bob said.

"Really? What do you have in mind?" I asked.

"I brought Bob to check out the feasibility and quote me," Tony told me leading me outside to show me his plan.

Bob followed close behind me. I suddenly felt hot. Excusing myself afterwards I went to have a shower and change into my swimming costume and beach wear.

"What are your plans Rosie? How long are you thinking of staying here?" Tony asked when I returned.

"I would like to avoid the summer heat and crowds around the villa if possible. It depends on when you choose to use your house. Ideally, I was thinking of looking for a small place in the area perhaps to buy," I said wistfully.

"Oh really, shall I keep an eye out for you? What's your budget?" Tony asked looking every inch a business man.

"Well I'm not sure. I want to keep the villa for our family who are joint owners but I may sell my English house because I don't want to return. It's rented at present and I hope to rent the villa all season except when my family need it," I told him.

"Would you rent initially?" Bob asked.

"Probably, I can't finalise anything yet so it's just a pipedream but the more I stay here, the more content I feel and less inclined to leave," I said.

"We feel the same," Tony agreed. "Your place is fine for a young family short term but it is too commercialised."

"Yes well I would not have chosen to live there but my late husband bought the place with his lady friend. My kids and I inherited it after they died," she said.

"What happened? You said they died," Tony asked.

"A drunk driver ran over them after a festival," I explained.

"So how old are your kids then? Are they here too?" asked Tony.

"They are both married with two children each but live in England. I have three grandsons and one granddaughter all of whom I adore. We are a close family and I miss the children, but we keep in touch and they visit during the holidays," I said showing Tony a family group photo I kept on the window sill.

"That reminds me Rosie, my wife sent you something," Tony said reaching for his rucksack pulling out a big box of chocolates and a bottle of wine.

"Thank you that is so kind, I didn't expect anything," I said blushing.

"Do you fancy a swim on the beach?" Bob asked.

"Good idea," I agreed.

"You two go ahead, I have some calls to make then I will join you," Tony said reaching for his mobile.

I walked alongside Bob conscious of his proximity.

THE LIFE OF ROSIE

"Did you miss me?" he asked.

"Yes," she replied.

"I missed you too."

"You didn't make much contact," I grumbled.

"Look who is talking!"

"Ok I guess you were busy working."

"I was working away trying to get everything completed quickly."

"Time goes fast when you are busy, I find that now."

"Perhaps we can get together soon," Bob suggested.

We opened our folding chairs and dropped our towels, water and sunscreen onto the chairs before walking to the sea. Bob ran in and submerged himself splashing Rosie who hesitated trying to enter in stages. She tried to run away from Bob shrieking but he pulled her in and held her in the water. All my resistance melted and I remained still. Bob pulled away letting me fall then swam quickly away. Irritated I swam sideways watching Bob's outline getting further away. When my energy was depleted I sat in the water shallows allowing the sea to wash over me gently. Bob came back beside me and was just about to say something when Tony came splashing into the sea. The two brothers swam off together. I returned to the chairs to dry off and relax.

After lazing on the beach for a while the men drank beer, showered and took me out for dinner to a place in the town I had not been before. They were driving back in the evening when the roads would be quieter. I felt disappointed to see Bob leaving again. He told me he would be back to build Tony's extension once he had caught up with his immediate workload. Newcomers would have to wait. Before they left with Tony driving Bob hugged me tightly and whispered that he would return as soon as he could. He relinquished me as Tony sorted the jeep out and I waved them off. It had been a

THE LIFE OF ROSIE

pleasant distraction from my daily routine and I felt sorry it had not lasted longer. I would wait for Bob's return and hoped the extension would take some time to build.

The Centre had a day trip out so I to escort the more vulnerable. It would be interesting to explore new places. Now that I knew everybody I felt comfortable with them all enjoying their gentle humour. Hearing repeated tales of past exploits and adventures from these elderly citizens who proudly told me that they had been young and daring in their day never failed to move her. Their faces lit up as they exaggerated their stories. Sometimes I had to shout my responses if they forgot to put their hearing aids on. Maria packed supplies to take although a meal was part of the arranged outing. First they visited an ancient monastery where they enjoyed Maria's picnic provisions. There were landscaped gardens and fields to view. I pushed a wheelchair around and breathed in the scented air enjoying the shady parts.

Next they were driven to a town I had not heard of with scenic views from high. It had a good shopping centre plus various amusements with bars playing music. There was a bull ring in the centre but it was closed while they were there. I was told to go exploring as somebody else would stay with the elderly. Feeling free and exhilarated I explored but decided I preferred my current location. It was a clean tidy town but old fashioned as if it had passed its heyday. Most of the people I saw moving around were older probably because the young ones were working or studying. After a round of soft drinks and cakes, everybody piled back on the bus to go home. A quick sing song started the journey then they fell quiet with some falling asleep.

Back at the Centre I helped unload passengers and belongings before driving home. As the main summer holidays were approaching I looked forward to seeing Martin and family who had reserved the villa for two weeks. So, when the phone rang I expected to hear about his plans. Instead I was shocked to hear that Maisie's mum had suffered a heart attack and was in hospital. It couldn't have happened at a worse time because Martin had to work away for a time. Maisie was at her mum's bedside and planned to move in with her when she was released. This meant that Martin couldn't bring the kids and there was nobody available to look after them.

"I'll have them," I volunteered as soon as she had enquired about Maisie's mother who was a kind widowed lady.

"Well I'll have told Sadie and Nathan to use my slot and perhaps travel over with all four kids, then you could take our two with you."

"Sure, I will go back to the villa to wait for them and stock up on provisions. Can you get the children on the same flight?"

"I will check after this conversation."

"Let me know soonest."

"Are you staying at this other place now?"

"For the time being as it's cooler."

"Sadie said it's beautiful but very quiet. Do you think the kids will like it?"

"Of course they will there's nothing to dislike. We will have fun."

"I don't know when I can come over to collect them yet."

"Don't worry, they can spend all the summer holiday with me if you want."

"Not likely, we want to spend time with them too."

"Ok but tell them grandma is waiting with open arms."

"Thanks mum."

"Don't worry, I will find lots of adventures for them. Tell them to bring their favourite toys and beach stuff with them as I don't have ---much here."

"Fine, I'll text you when I book the flight. Thanks mum, I love you."

"Love you too, send my best wishes to Maisie's mum."

They hung up and I thought about the forthcoming visit. Abby and Mark were good kids and always enjoyed visits with Grandma Rosie. I would take them to the Centre and local market. They could perhaps explore the area, enjoy the beach and perhaps find other children locally. I would ask at the café. This meant returning to the villa to stock up before Sadie returned with her family, so I would see Isaac and Zak again. All my four grandchildren would be coming over. What a thrill it was for me to contemplate. I felt like I had won the lottery. Before they arrived I had bought treats and stocked up. It was impossible to settle until they came safe and sound.

Trying to hug all four children at once they laughed and all spoke at once trying to tell me all their tales. Nathan brought the luggage in while Sadie carried their extra bags. Each child had a small wheelie case so while they allocated rooms, I poured cool drinks. Before long the children had changed and plunged into the pool splashing and laughing. Sadie changed for a quick dip to cool off. Nathan joined her shortly afterwards. It was mid afternoon so not as hot as earlier so everyone enjoyed themselves. Unpacking would wait so I decided we would talk around dinner. Meanwhile I marvelled how much the children had grown, how pale Sadie looked. The sound of laugher and happy voices thrilled me.

Apparently Maisie's mother was still in hospital but was going to be moved to a rehabilitation centre. During dinner Nathan asked whether I would prefer them to keep Isaac and Zak for the two weeks. I declined saying I planned to take them to Muranos early next morning.

"What will they do there?" Sadie asked her. "I know it's beautiful but there's not much for the kids."

"What's Muranos?" asked Abby.

"It's where I live these days. We will have adventures of a different kind from here," I promised.

"Are we coming?" asked Zak.

"If your parents want you to. Enjoy yourselves here first then perhaps you can come for a part of your stay," I suggested.

"Is it far?" Nathan asked.

"About two hours but an easy drive," I said.

"It's scenic but quiet," Sadie told them.

"What will we do there?" Mark asked.

At night Sadie and Nathan took my double bedroom, the kids slept in the second bedroom. I used the box/office room. After breakfast next morning I drove off with Isaac and Zak. The others said they would visit soon. They stopped on the way for a cool drink and bathroom. As we drove into Muranos the sun glistened golden across the bay. It looked like a postcard and the kids were impressed. While they explored the house the kids were disappointed to find the swimming pool smaller than the one at my villa.

"But look how close we are to the sea. We can go for a dip soon if you want. However, promise me that you will not go off to the sea on your own," I told them.

They changed and raced down to the sea where they splashed around swimming and playing for a while before drying off then heading home to eat. Everyone was tired so had an early night. Next morning I woke the children up early telling them they were going to start their first adventure by packing food bags for people who needed them. Uncertain whether that could be classed as an adventure, the children complied and accompanied me to the Centre where they were warmly welcomed and indulged with cookies and sweets. Dutifully they helped to prepare the food bags then adored the old milk float vehicle for distribution. Everywhere people were pleased to meet the children and offered them treats or jokes.

Back at the Centre while I helped to clear away, I told the children the next day would be lunch plus activities and entertainment so they would meet some interesting characters.

"Are there any kids?" Isaac asked.

"No so you will be special guests but don't be sad there's loads going on," I told them.

"Like what?" asked Zak.

"Piano playing, chess, flower arranging maybe or paper crafts like moving puppets, maybe music, we will have to wait and see," I promised.

"Is that for kids too?" Zak asked.

"Sure if you fancy trying something new. Lots of people know how to do stuff so they can teach you then you can show off when the others come."

"What will you do?" Isaac asked.

"Well I will help serve and clear away, stack the dishwasher etc. Many of these people have interesting stories and experiences. Some may look old but they have lived full lives. You may even pick up some Spanish as they don't all speak English."

"We can teach them English and they can teach us Spanish," Zak said enthusiastically.

Silently I blessed them for being so positive and accepting. Initially I thought old people may not appeal to children but they would gain valuable experience by participating. If they disliked it I would have to withdraw for the duration of their stay but instinctively felt they would enjoy getting involved and for the attendees it would be a welcome bonus liaising with the children. Next day after distributing the food, the children were the centre of attention. Isaac went to learn how to play the piano. Zak joined the men to study chess and Parchís, a popular game in Spain among adults and seniors which used dice. Other members offered to teach them how to make things, play card tricks or grow vegetables and flowers. In fact the children were so excited they asked me if they could go every day.

After the Centre we headed to the beach with a ball and drinks. They had a lazy afternoon and were content to sit to watch the sunset after dinner. I asked them if they liked Muranos, both nodded. Next day was market day in the nearby town so I asked whether they wanted to drive there with me or go in the Centre bus. Both opted for the Centre bus. It headed out early so we climbed on board with the food distribution carried out by Maria's friend. Already the market was buzzing with people viewing offers of everything from enormous fruit and vegetables to clothing and artefacts. After wandering around for a while I took them to a familiar café where I greeted people I knew who offered to find children companions for the visitors to play with. Phone numbers were exchanged to make arrangements.

When we returned home we found a familiar van outside the house. It seemed that Bob had arrived to start building the extension. He was outside the back drilling when we entered. He had met all the family before and had brought some treats with him for them. We all greeted him, I felt shy and embarrassed because I did not look smart or groomed. Bob laughed and hugged us all. Mark asked Bob about his tasks so patiently he explained simply.

"Perhaps Mark will go into property development one day," Bob said.

"What's that?"

Again Bob explained while Isaac and I prepared a meal.

"Will you show me how?" Zak was heard asking. "It sounds ace."

While they were eating dinner Bob got a phone call from Tony which he took outside. He came back in distraught saying there was a family emergency so he had to leave immediately.

"What's happened?" Rosie asked concerned.

"My mother's been rushed to hospital so I have to go to England. I'll leave all my building stuff here, perhaps you can lock up anything small. When I get back I will start the job but I have no idea how long I'll be."

"I'm so sorry, I hope your mother will recover soon. Is Tony with her?"

"For now but he lives in Southgate while mum lives in Yorkshire so it is not ideal."

"Do you know what's wrong with your mum?"

"We're waiting for a diagnosis but it doesn't sound good. Sorry to rush off but I need to get back for my passport and to pack a few things. I probably won't be in touch regularly but you can text me if you want," Bob said approaching his van.

"Don't worry, drive safely you must be tired. Let me know if I can do anything for you from here," I said.

The children joined me solemnly watching Bob's departure. Sadly I felt perhaps I was not destined to be with Bob. I also felt anxious about his mother's condition. Feeling inadequate because I could not help him, I cleared the table while the kids spoke to their parents on their evening call. Each evening Maisie and Martin called to check on their children. I assured them that the children were having fun. They had made friends with some local children and were picking up some Spanish. Either I or the other parents supervised them. Both children were tanned and active leading an outdoor life swimming, playing football etc.

Before their holiday ended Sadie and Nathan visited Muranos for an overnight stay bringing Abby and Mark. They asked whether they should take the boys back to England with them. Both boys did not want to go back and told their parents who were trying to make arrangements for the summer holidays. I told them to leave the boys with me as they were no trouble. Perhaps Martin and Maisie could take a break and come over to collect them later on when Maisie's mum was stable. Whilst Martin liked the scenery and location of the house, he enquired where the shops and facilities were. I took them to the café and next town where they ate out and invited them to join the boys volunteering at the Community Centre next morning.

"We came for a break to see you, not to work," grumbled Nathan.

"Uncle Nathan it's fun, you will like it," Isaac told him enthusiastically.

"But you have to get up really early," Zak advised.

"Early on holiday," protested Mark.

"It's worth it and we can chill afterwards. It's market day so we can go there and do the beach or whatever suits you later," I offered.

"How long does this volunteering take?" Sadie asked.

"Only a few hours but we go early to prepare everything before it gets too hot," I said.

"And what exactly do we have to do if we go?" asked Nathan.

"I think you can do the distribution run, you may be able to drive the milk float," I suggested.

"Milk float!" Nathan said surprised.

"Wait and see, it will be fun," I promised.

"What about me then?" asked Sadie.

"You can prep the food orders with me, pack it up ready to go," I said adding: "Many hands make light work so we will finish faster if we all help."

"What do the boys do then?"

"They are very good especially with the clients, wait and see. It's an experience," I said heading out to sit in the shade near the pool with a drink.

Early next morning despite a reluctant start we all headed off to the Community Centre and assigned tasks. The kids packed the food bags, Sadie and I made sandwiches in containers, Nathan packed the milk float and checked to make sure it was roadworthy. Music played in the background as Nathan set off with the boys and a regular member to distribute the food. Meanwhile Sadie, myself and volunteers set the tables for lunch and prepared all the essentials ready for serving. We stopped for a refreshment break as the boys returned. Isaac and Zak rushed to show their cousins the piano, card games, chess set, musical instruments and Centre amenities.

After helping to serve and chat to the clients which proved entertaining as several had a good sense of humour, we helped clear away, load the dishwasher then Nathan played guitar and did a duet with one of the regulars. Isaac played his party piece on the piano, Abby was shown some elementary flower arrangements. Mark and Zak played a card game. When they departed everybody waved to them thanking them for spending part of their holiday time looking after them. Several expressed a few words in English.

"That was more fun than I thought," Sadie said looking pleased.

"Yes, it was better than expected. That old milk float is a museum piece," Nathan said.

"But it got you there and back," I said.

"Just about," Nathan agreed smiling.

We spent the afternoon on the beach returning to the house for afternoon tea. The kids splashed and played games in the pool. Martin rang to enquire about the kids. Maisie's mum was fading so she was staying nearby. He hoped to be able to fly out to collect the boys before too long if they did not want to return with Nathan.

"How about I fly back with them when it suits you?" I offered surprising myself.

"Can you do that?" Martin asked surprised.

"Of course I can, let me know in advance before they return to school. Perhaps I can visit Maisie's mum. I will need to stay somewhere preferably at my house," I said.

"That's fine because it is summer holidays so the tenants have gone home."

"Well get someone in to clean and tidy it right through before I return then."

"Thanks mum, I will talk to Maisie later and see what she thinks. It would be helpful as there's nobody here to supervise them or collect them from day centres."

"They are fine here with me. At present they are in the pool with their cousins."

"Ok so leave them. Did they all go to the Centre today?"

"Yes and were very helpful. Everyone had fun."

"That's good so take care mum, love to everyone, got to go now.," Martin said hanging up.

Maisie's mother died peacefully in her sleep. There were funeral arrangements to make plus the house clearance. I was asked to break the news gently to the boys who adored both of their grandmas.

After their evening meal I told the boys that their other grandma had been very poorly. She could not get better so had gone to heaven.

"Did she die?" Isaac asked.

"Yes, so she is not poorly anymore and will be with grandpa in heaven," I said.

"So we won't see her again?" Zak asked wondering whether to cry.

"Perhaps you will one day when it's your turn to go there," I suggested wanting to cry myself as I had always enjoyed being with my departed in law.

"That's sad for us but I am glad for her," Isaac said seriously.

"Yes," Zak agreed uncertainly.

Martin offered to collect the children after the funeral when Maisie had recovered enough to sort out her late mother's property and assets. It would take her some time to grieve and collect herself as she was very upset, so it made sense for the children to spend more time with me. Whilst the parents missed their children greatly, the boys enjoyed playing with their new friends outside. They still helped at the Centre and were constantly enthralled by new stories or abilities the residents showed them, particularly card tricks. Instead of life in Muranos being too quiet, the boys loved it and looked healthily fit and tanned. They were too busy to be disobedient and were always willing to help with everything so we made a successful team. Abby and Mark were envious that they could not stay with them.

Towards the end of the school holidays I made arrangements to fly back to England with the boys. Martin would meet us at the airport. We returned to my villa to collect winter clothes. It was being rented out so we could not stay but spent the night in a local bed and breakfast place towards the airport. The villa seemed to be in good condition but the surrounding area was too crowded for us. We were used to the luxury of space and tranquillity in Muranos. At the airport we had to wait and toured the shops. The flight was uneventful but the air seemed cooler as they approached our destination. Fortunately, it was a mild summer day so although it was not as warm as Spain, it was pleasant. When we cleared Customs, Martin was waiting for us exclaiming how fit his boys looked.

THE LIFE OF ROSIE

We went to Martin's house where Maisie had a meal ready. She hugged her boys saying how much she had missed them, how they had grown, admiring their tan and rejoicing at their arrival. I received a warm emotional hug from Maisie and tried to express my condolences but Maisie waved me away. Understanding that Maisie was not able to deal with sympathy yet, I changed the subject and asked how life was faring in the UK. On the BBC World News bulletins I heard negative input so queried how the cost of living was affecting people. Although a non-political family, the subject kept the conversation going throughout the meal. When we had finished I asked to be taken to my house in order to give the family some privacy.

Entering my English house again I felt like a tourist. It was familiar but felt different somehow. Everywhere was clean and tidy. I recognised the furnishings and fittings but felt as if it belonged to someone else. It did not feel like my family home anymore. Feeling it was too quiet I checked supplies and decided to go to the local supermarket to get some provisions planning to stock up on some favourites to take back to Spain. Although I had no return date in mind, I felt that I needed to decide during this trip about my future. It made no sense to rent out the English house and the villa whilst paying rent in Muranos. Putting the decision on hold, I enjoyed my shopping trip treating myself to some instore clothing and a coffee before returning.

In the evening I contacted all my friends and former colleagues to enquire whether they wanted to meet up for a drink reunion while I was there. I asked which date and place would be suitable to catch up. Bob was still in England somewhere so I texted him to say I had just arrived. While waiting for replies I fell asleep watching television. Waking up in the dark I went to bed without checking my phone and slept deeply. In the morning I felt uncertain where I was. It was a dry dull day so I dressed warmly compared to the locals and wondered what to do. I felt inclined to check my cupboards and wardrobes to see if I could clear unwanted stock. Sadie called to check all was going well. I felt unsettled as if I needed time to adjust to my native land.

Sadie invited me to dinner saying Nathan would pick me up. Apparently the kids wanted to see me. I went out to buy some wine and flowers for Sadie, plus some treats for the kids to take with. Over dinner we caught up with family news. Nathan asked how long I planned to stay.

"I don't know, it feels so strange to be back. It takes some getting used to," I replied.

"Is it the fact that the sun doesn't shine here every day you mean?" Sadie asked.

"No, it's not bad weather wise. I just feel I don't belong here anymore. Perhaps the Spanish climate suits me now. At present I am wondering whether to sell my house here and buy something suitable in Spain," I replied.

"You can rent it out here. If you do it up at bit more you can get a good income," Sadie told me.

"But then I can't replace it with something to my taste," I told her.

"What about the Spanish villa?" asked Nathan.

"That's looking good these days but I would prefer to live somewhere quieter," I said.

"Like Muranos?" asked Sadie.

"Maybe, I feel at home there now," I replied.

"Are you planning to keep renting there?"

"No, that would be foolish but if I rent out the villa, I need somewhere to live plus finances to buy. As I feel unwilling to live here again, perhaps selling this place would be the ideal solution."

"Is that definite?" Nathan asked.

"Not yet, I need to think carefully and get quotes from estate agents for the valuation," I said.

"Does Martin know your plans?"

"Not yet because I am still uncertain."

"We can rent out your house here until you decide," Nathan offered.

"I have only been here a short time so let me consider the matter," I said.

"What are you going to do here?"

"Well I've contacted all my friends and former colleagues so hopefully I can set up a few reunions," I told them.

"Take your time to adjust and perhaps you will like being here again," Sadie suggested.

"Sure and I get to see all my beautiful grandchildren," I said smiling at Abby and Mark playing in the garden.

Bob sent me a text saying his mother had died. Immediately I sent a message of condolence and asked about the funeral arrangements. I did not get a reply so could neither attend nor send any flowers. The next time I heard from Bob was to say that he was flying back to Spain the next morning. I replied saying I was still in England. Sending him repeated condolences, I said perhaps we could catch up when I returned to Spain. There was no reply but I heard from most of my friends including Lynne who was finishing her teaching career. She planned to move to Spain to open a bed and breakfast place with Trevor further inland from my villa.

I carefully arranged reunion meetings with various groups and enjoyed catching up. Life was hectic for all but I did not feel I was missing anything by living abroad. Everyone complained about the constant price increases. Some people had aged while others remained the same. Everybody had a story to tell with various ups and downs. It was good to see everyone again but I felt that I had not missed out on anything special. A few had health related problems either themselves or close relatives. Work wise people had endured the pandemic and got used to working from home. The return to the office had not always been welcomed. Wages were not keeping pace with rising prices all round. Mortgages were worrying for people who had no fixed amounts.

I felt kinship but a sense of estrangement. Once I had shopped and caught up with people, I decided to return to my villa in Spain so contacted the management company to tell them to halt further bookings. They had some future bookings and told me to call in to see them on my return. I knew I had to decide whether to rent or remain in my villa. Being in England made me hesitant to go out at night or to walk about in secluded places. In Spain I felt safe day or night. I called three estate agents to quote for my house asking whether any work was needed to get a good price. Sale and rental quotations obtained, I flew back to Spain feeling a sense of relief to walk out into warm sunshine. I took an airport bus then a taxi to get home as nobody was expecting me.

At first I spent a couple of days adjusting to the climate change lazing around the pool and catching up on my tan. I suddenly felt exhausted so after stocking up on groceries I kept to myself. Feeling better on the third day I texted Bob to say I had returned. He replied saying he was spending time with his daughter and would be travelling around. There was no mention of any return dates. Next I rang Chris but got no answer so sent him a text to say I was back. He answered late afternoon saying he would see me at their pub that evening. Lynne was in another inland area with Trevor renovating their future bed and breakfast place. Feeling reluctant to go to the pub alone, I decided to call on Frances.

When I rang her bell nobody answered. Before giving up I decided to leave the present I had brought Frances from England around the back of the house where I found a depressed Frances sitting in the shade with one leg in plaster.

"Frances what happened to you?" I asked shocked.

"I broke my leg," Frances replied. "Did you just ring the bell?"

"Yes, how did that happen?"

"I got tiddly and fell over my bag."

"Oh dear, how long have you been like this?"

"A couple of days ago and I am stuck here now."

"Do you want a drink or something to eat? How can I help you?"

"It's fine I have ordered some home help three times a day. Tell me about England, when did you get back?"

"I came back on Monday but needed a couple of days to recover, I felt exhausted. Here's a small present," I said handing over a big box of chocolates and some perfume.

"How lovely of you," Frances said happily opening the chocolates and offering me.

"It's just a token of my appreciation."

"These are my favourites and I like this perfume too, reminds me of my youth," Frances said spraying liberally.

"So are you stuck here or can you go out?"

"I have a wheelchair but nobody to push it."

"I can push it for you."

"I can't use a Zimmer frame or mobility scooter yet because I can't put any weight on my bad leg yet. There are some crutches but it's too much effort and pain."

"Well Chris said he would see me at the pub later on, how about we go together?"

"I can't drink while I am on medication."

"So you can have soft drinks like blackcurrant with lemonade. Everyone would be glad to see you and sympathise."

"I'm not sure."

"It will do you good to get out. I'll come by to help you dress and do your hair if you want. We will go slowly and not stay too late. Help me out here, I don't feel comfortable going on my own."

"Ok if you help me. If it's too much we have to come back."

"Sure, so what's been going on here? Have you seen Bob since he lost his mother?"

"I saw him with a young woman before the accident but from a distance, not to talk to. He'd not been back long."

"Perhaps it was his daughter?"

"Maybe I don't know. I only met the married one once and it wasn't her."

"He sent me a text saying he was spending time with his daughter travelling."

"So what about England, did you like it?"

"It was familiar but time does not stand still and I felt like a stranger at first. I enjoyed meeting all my friends and family, going shopping but then I had enough."

"Didn't you want to stay there and be near your family?"

"Not really, they lead busy lives. Everyone is worried about price rises for everything, they are all busy rushing around."

"How was the weather?"

"Mixed but not too cold. It feels good to be back in the sunshine again."

"I suppose you have become used to good weather every day now. Will you stay here or go back to the other place?"

"I am staying here for now until the booked rentals are finished. While I will honour the bookings, I don't want to make any more until I decide what to do."

"With what?"

"My future, I have the house in England which I am thinking of selling although it rents out. This place here is for my family too but is too big for me really. I felt at home in Muranos, but it is stupid to pay rent to someone else. There I helped at the Community Centre and it was really good fun."

"I'm sure you could find something like that around here if you look. Did you buy stuff in England?" Frances asked munching chocolates with enjoyment.

"Some clothes and cosmetics. Now tell me the gossip about here," I said.

We chatted comfortably until the home help arrived to make lunch for Frances. I arranged to return later to help Frances get ready. Then I took a slow stroll down the promenade wearing a sunhat and sunglasses admiring the blue sky and sea. Spain felt more like home than England now. After leaving Frances, I headed down to the beach for a paddle in the sea. Feeling the heat I plunged into the water enjoying swimming. It definitely felt good to be back.

Later I paddled back along the beach then went home for a siesta. After a light meal I called for Frances and helped her get ready to go out. I pushed the wheelchair along the side of the house and headed off to our local bar we called a pub. Chris and Wendy were already seated talking to a few people. I waved and pushed Frances over. They all made a fuss of Frances who saw some of her friends in the opposite corner so asked me to park her there.

Chris stood up to take a drinks order and asked me to help him carry the drinks back. I followed him to the bar.

"So how was old Blighty then?" he asked while they waited to be served.

"Not as good as here," I replied smiling.

"Did you miss the sunshine then?"

"The weather wasn't too bad for England, but I was ready to return."

"I've got something to tell you."

"Oooh go on then."

"I'm thinking of getting married again."

"To Wendy I assume."

"Yes, what do you think?"

"Well it seems a bit soon. Why bother since you are living together anyway?"

"We are getting along well. I like being married, it also has a sense of security and togetherness."

"You haven't known each other very long."

"Long enough. Of course Wendy can never replace my first wife in my heart, but I think we can be happy together."

"But living together is not enough?"

"I want a long term relationship and am prepared to work at it."

"Have you proposed to her?"

"Not yet."

"Well when you do make sure to do a romantic gesture."

"Like what?"

"Like in the movies and best story books. How about a fortune cookie or something."

"Aren't we a bit old for that?"

"You are never too old to be romantic. She will probably swoon with delight."

"Where will I get a fortune cookie?"

"Oh honestly, that was only just a suggestion. Do your own gesture or make one inside a muffin or something."

"Do you think Wendy will say yes?"

"Why shouldn't she? You are well heeled, successful, have a full head of hair and teeth. Your daughter is independent so you are quite a catch."

"Well you didn't think so."

"I am not looking to be attached. Besides I value your friendship and I hope you do likewise."

"Of course that's why I am discussing this with you."

"Personally, I did not have a happy marriage so am not looking to try again. You were happily married for a long time so I suppose you enjoyed the status. Do as your heart feels fit."

"Ok thanks for your opinion. I will let you know the outcome."

I sat and chatted about my English trip, fads, fashions and gossip for a while. Frances sent someone over to tell me that she would be accompanying her friends to a club. They would take her home so I need not wait for her. Thanking them I waved to Frances as she was wheeled out then walked slowly home enjoying the calm evening air. Restless at home I poured myself a few drinks to calm down before going to sleep. Even at this age, people were pairing off hoping for happy endings. Lynne with Trevor, Chris with Wendy. Asking myself if that was suitable for my future, I could not decide but doubted I would be successful. Only Bob had excited me and we could not get together despite several attempts. Perhaps it was not meant to be I thought, then went to bed.

Next day I awoke feeling energetic and sociable so I had a quick swim then showered and dressed before walking along the promenade hoping to meet somebody I knew. Before going out I called on Frances but got no reply. There was a friend staying with Frances who was helping her and taking her out to appointments and commitments so it was not surprising. I ambled along the promenade not encountering any familiar faces. Finding myself near the bench where I first met Chris, I sat down but nobody approached me. The only reaction I received was from a baby in a trolley parked opposite the bench while two women had a brief encounter. I played peekaboo with the baby who chuckled.

Normally I was prone to strangers exchanging conversations with me especially in England at bus stops, on trains or shopping, even if it was only a remark about the weather. On this occasion I would have been satisfied with a simple remark like "it's turned out nice again" but nobody bothered. I felt invisible and wondered why people only made contact when a person was busy or distracted. If I did not want to be disturbed it happened continuously. When I felt amiable and ready to socialise nothing materialised. Perhaps I needed to get out more to make new friends. Feeling low I headed back home stopping for lunch and a cold drink in town. While waiting for my meal I received a text message from Martin telling me that Stephen his best friend had lost his father to cancer.

Stephen's mother Jane, had been a close friend as our sons were constant companions. Immediately I texted Jane my sincere condolences and invited her to come to Spain for a visit when she had sorted things out. We had not been able to meet in England as she was nursing her sick husband. Saying a change of scenery would be good for her, I said Jane could stay indefinitely and how welcome her company would be. Apologising for being unable to attend the funeral or comfort Jane, I said I would be available to talk at any time. If Jane took up my offer in the future, I would try to help my friend heal and make a new life for herself. Being away from England meant that I had missed out on family and friends events. Jane was easy going with a pleasant undemanding personality so I hoped to see her.

When Jane rang me to check if my offer was still available, I was delighted telling Jane to book. I would meet my friend at the airport and told her not to book a return flight. Telling Jane to bring summer clothes and text flight details, we were both excited about the visit. I would not put any pressure on Jane giving her time and space to adjust and relax. When Jane was ready I would take her out showing her the lifestyle and opportunities in life there. Tony enquired whether I wanted to return to his place in Muranos. I told him at present I needed to be at the villa but thanked him for the invitation. He replied saying he was considering selling it to move somewhere with more facilities suitable for his growing family. I asked about the selling price and said I would keep it in mind.

In England my family led busy lives. In Spain Chris and Wendy seemed to be keeping a low profile, Frances was being cared for so I had no commitments or obligations. There were voluntary groups covering meals on wheels, Food Banks, helping people with shopping or lifts. I felt reluctant to commit myself so looked for activities to enjoy like walking, art, exercise classes where I met lively younger friends. If anybody asked me to help worthy causes I agreed when I could. Once I thought I saw Bob in the distance with a young woman, but he was too far away and crossed over the main road before I could check. If he was back he had not made contact with me so I abandoned hope of seeing him again. Life was less complicated when emotions were held in check.

Jane arrived pale, slender and ready to enjoy the climate. She brought me a tin of impressive homemade cookies in a variety of flavours. I thought they were bought professionally. It seemed Jane wanted to try to bake to start a fledgling business.

"I have always enjoyed baking and experimenting with flavours," Jane said. "Frank liked eating my goods but never encouraged me to share my skills. He was a conventional man who liked his home comforts and did not want my attention distracted."

"You must miss him," I said sympathetically.

"To be truthful it is a relief. He declined swiftly and needed constant attention. It was awful to watch and very tiring. I put him in a hospice eventually which eased my burden, but it was a struggle getting him there. Now he's gone I can discover myself again as a person."

"What about the children, how do they feel?"

"Stephen has his own family to care for, he was upset but is coping."

"How about your daughter?"

"Sammy is leading an active life in York with her family. At first I thought she would be upset as she used to be a daddy's girl when she was young. After seeing her dad suffer she also feels relieved now. She told me to make the most of the life I have left while I can. We are both on the same page now."

"How funny life is. Our boys are best friends, we are both grandmas now and ready for new adventures," I said smiling.

"Of course, let's see what we can do!"

"Would you like to get married again?"

"No chance, I've done my bit. How about you?"

"These days I can't commit to anything, I just want an easy existence. There is only one man who turns me on but it hasn't worked out."

"Really, is he from here?"

"He lives here but is from England originally."

"Single?"

"Divorced with two grown up daughters."

"How did you meet him?"

"He did some work on my place."

"Does he like you too?"

"Hard to say, perhaps he just charms all his lady customers in order to get repeat business," I said laughing. "However I am not looking for romance."

"Snap. Who needs men anyway? Let's discover what we can achieve without them."

"Hi five," I said.

Jane asked me if she could do a big baking session in my kitchen. When I agreed Jane asked me to show her around the area featuring all the bakeries plus bars and centres popular with the expats.

"What do you have in mind?" I asked watching Jane pack her dazzling tin assorted biscuit selection.

"Well initially I would like to hold baking demonstrations to arouse interest with a view eventually to holding baking classes. If the response is good I hope to be able to sell some of my products to existing bakeries once I can set up with facilities."

"That's very ambitious but if you work hard you should be able to achieve it," I said encouragingly.

"Yes, with your help everything is possible."

"I don't bake anymore."

"Ah you can assist me, together we can make it."

Jane printed off flyers of her stunning biscuit tin showing off its variety of flavours. She then encouraged me to take her to all the local bakers and organisations she could think of. Speaking to the shop owners and managers of entertainment centres, Jane asked whether they would be interested in holding a bakery demonstration event. She would bake and the audience would get to eat the contents with a drink. It could be held at any convenient time and if successful perhaps could run for a few weeks. A few places were interested and Jane was invited to bake similar contents for sale in their shops. I suggested informing the local news bulletin once arrangements were made. Feeling pleased with their initial interest they headed for the supermarket to buy provisions.

It seemed that Jane made a basic dough then produced and decorated oblong biscuits in varied formats. Some had raisins in with white icing, some had chocolate partial filling with chocolate icing, there was a cocoanut topping sitting on jam, the plain ones had almond toppings. There seemed to be rainbow toppings and a multitude of fillings. Jane taught me techniques. I had not planned to get involved but began to enjoy it. The house smelled delicious and there was the temptation to indulge but Jane was strict. These production runs were for promotion and samples to engage customers who would buy the ranges. A pink iced range with pink and yellow filling caught my attention so Jane allowed me to have a few. We baked batches then booked a cookery demonstration at the local café frequented by the expats.

I produced suitable flyers which we circulated around town. We baked and bought suitable cardboard boxes with cellophane covers to hold the products.

"This has given me a new lease of life," Jane said enthusiastically. "I have always wanted to try something like this."

"Well you have been working hard, do you know how much to sell them for?"

"I will ask the bakers when I take samples round."

"I never expected to do anything like this," I said smiling.

"Oh I couldn't do it without you Rosie, you give me the confidence."

"I don't see how."

"Well you are so practical."

Armed with samples we toured the bakers again and some of the bars and cafes to plug our event. Jane received orders from a few bakers to produce individual ranges of her offering. The tin selection would be good for special occasions. Armed with notebook and pen I wrote everything down. One baker offered Jane the use of his facilities if she wanted to work with him exclusively. Flushed with interest Jane thanked him and told him she would think about it.

"This just proves that where there's a will, there's a way," Jane told me.

"Well you seem to be creating interest."

"Yes, I reckon we can make a business with this. We can offer other English delicacies too and develop a range."

"What's next then?" I asked her.

"Perhaps lemon meringue."

On the day we arrived early to set everything up. We were well prepared and had plenty of samples to distribute. A sizeable crowd turned up, paid the entrance fee then settled down amicably. Jane introduced herself explaining that she had recently arrived to visit me and loved baking. I also introduced myself as a local on skivvy duty which made the audience smile.

"I want to share my skills with you and am thinking of running a few classes if anyone is interested. Today we are baking cookies and I want to show you how you can produce a whole batch of varieties from one basic dough mixture. So let's begin."

I kept Jane supplied with everything to hand that she needed. The audience watched with interest as Jane simplified her technique. In the background I assisted discreetly, removing and washing used equipment, keeping Jane supplied. Whilst the baking was taking place, Jane and I distributed samples that had been baked earlier while drinks were laid out on a table. At the end of the session Jane invited potential orders of

THE LIFE OF ROSIE

full tins or partial cookie orders. I left Jane to write down an order list while I packed up our equipment and took it to the car. Therefore I missed an order from Bob's daughter Katie who asked for a full tin to be delivered to her father the following week with a note saying: "Lots of love from Katie."

"What did she look like?" I asked annoyed to have missed her.

"I'm not sure, young woman, long fair hair, pleasant."

"Damn, I would have liked to have met her."

"Why?"

"It's her father that I liked at one time."

"So what happened? She said she's going away so won't be here next week. This was a surprise for her dad who has been a bit low lately."

"Did she say anything else?"

"She just gave me his name and address."

"I just can't get it together with that man so I have given up."

"You can deliver the biscuits if you want."

"No, he knows where I live and hasn't made contact so I am not chasing him."

" Well she did say he's been a bit low lately."

"Probably because his mother died recently. Never mind, you did well to get so many orders."

"Yes, I will pay you for the energy I use."

"Will you do another?"

"Yes, next week is lemon meringue and a simple cheese cake."

"Well it was fun, I enjoyed it."

"I did too, it had a great atmosphere, people were interested."

"Let's chill around the pool to recover."

Opening a bottle of white fizzy imitation champagne, they sipped, and relaxed.

Jane kept baking and sent me off to deliver the orders. When I reached Bob's place he was out probably working, so I left the parcel round the back then texted him to say he had a surprise waiting for him. I also said I hoped he was ok and that I was a good listener if he wanted to talk. Back home the house and neighbourhood smelled of fresh baking. It was tantalising especially when the kitchen surfaces were covered with cookies. Jane had taken some phone calls for extra orders and was already planning the next demonstration session.

"If you keep this up we will both blow our diets," I grumbled.

"Life is to be enjoyed not starved," Jane replied.

"You are slim enough but I don't want to put on weight."

"Don't eat any then, move out of the way while I sort these out."

When all the batches were done we both made the delivery rounds then sat along the promenade people watching. Sharing the house with Jane meant delicious smells emanating constantly. Sometimes I helped her but went out when she needed space to experiment or I needed to escape. One evening she ran out of some supplies so I offered to go to the supermarket to replenish. There were a few things I wanted on the shopping list so I was pushing my trolley around when I noticed Bob in the distance. Pleased to see him I rushed forward and tapped him on the shoulder saying:

"Hi Bob, good to see you. How are you doing?"

As he turned around I saw a sad defeated look on his face. He had lost his spring, humour and joie de vivre. He just nodded absently.

I wanted to hug him but knew I mustn't.

"I'm so sorry for your loss Bob, it must be terrible. Do you have time to have a coffee my treat?"

Bob shrugged looking defeated so I took charge telling him to meet at the checkout when he finished his shopping which he seemed to be doing aimlessly. I was nearly finished so told him I would not be long then hurried off for the remaining few items. Fortunately, I was familiar with the layout so I arrived at the checkout first then sat waiting for Bob. We took our shopping to our cars then went to the supermarket café at the side where I ordered for us both. Neither of us wanted to eat.

"Did you like the cookies your daughter left you?" I asked Bob.

"They were good," Bob said with a ghost of a smile.

"My friend Jane made them, she is staying with me and keeps baking, full of ideas."

"Did you drop them off?" he asked me.

"I did the deliveries while she carried on baking after getting orders from her demonstration. She's doing another one this week."

"Sorry I should have thanked you."

"That's not necessary. Tell me what's wrong, I can see you are not happy."

"My mother died and I was not there beside her. In fact I don't remember the last time I saw her. There she was at the end of her life with me blithely carrying on miles away."

"But she knew you loved her."

"Did she? How did she when I was never around."

"Of course she knew because you were her son. I bet she was proud of your success and new life."

"I didn't even know she was ill, Tony never told me. He was the dutiful son always there."

"She probably told Tony not to tell you."

"She wanted grandchildren so adored my girls and even stayed friends with their mother. I let her down by not going to university, having a broken marriage and destroying our family."

"Stop this nonsense with ridiculous recriminations. I am sure that was not the case. Every normal mother cares eternally about her offspring and only wants the best for them. If your marriage was unhappy then your mother wanted you to find a route to heal the pain. She must have enjoyed seeing your girls when they visited and followed your trail via communication from you or Tony. Did you send her birthday cards and Mother's Day?"

"Of course, Christmas too. I should have gone over."

"Did you intend to go?"

"No, I don't like the climate now."

"So she accepted that. Did you invite her over here?"

"Yes she came once and loved it. I wanted her to move in but she wanted to stay among her friends and family at home."

"So you see you gave her the opportunity, she knew you are living well and that you loved her so there's no need for recriminations now. She wouldn't want you to suffer now she's gone."

"I should have been there for her," Bob said tears filling his eyes.

I held his hand massaging it through my fingers saying: "It's okay to cry and feel sad that she's gone, let it all out. You have to let her go and rest in peace. She would want you to have a good life and find happiness again. Just do the best you can and remember her advice and experiences with you. That way she will live on in your heart and memory. She will want you to go forward."

Bob held his hands over his face and cried silently for some time. I handed him some tissues and waited patiently feeling bad for him. Giving Bob time to recover I passed him his drink to finish then escorted him to his car. Hugging him tightly for a few minutes, I told Bob to call me if he needed company or assistance then went home not knowing whether I would see him again or not. A few days later a bunch of flowers was delivered to me with a note from Bob saying, "thank you for being a good friend." Jane was impressed.

I left a message on Bob's phone to thank him. He called back to ask if I fancied a trip down to Muranos to help sort the place out. It seemed Tony wanted to buy a new house somewhere with more interests for his young family to enjoy. Bob was going down to clear personal stuff and get the place ready for sale. The idea excited me, I couldn't wait to go back. I told Jane that she would have to manage alone for the weekend. The idea crossed my mind about buying Tony's place but I would need to sell the English house first to get funds. It was being rented for now.

"Look at you all excited like a teenager!" Jane exclaimed.

"I love that place," I sighed.

"I don't think it's just the place," Jane remarked.

"If I had been planning to buy a house in Spain, I would have gone somewhere like that. I thought about buying the place myself but it means selling the English house and that would be final."

"Really? Are you not planning to return to England one day?"

"I prefer the climate here and have got used to this lifestyle. When I went back I felt strange there."

"So are you having a romantic liaison this weekend then?"

"Don't push it, probably not knowing my luck."

"Doesn't he fancy you then?"

"I haven't had the chance to find out. Nothing ever works out when we get together."

"What do you mean?"

"The phrase "a spanner in the works" seems to be applicable."

"Oh well, I shall wait and see with bated breath then."

"Chance is a fine thing."

I had a few days to prepare so had my hair trimmed and blown professionally, treated myself to a massage and checked my wardrobe taking my best underwear. When Bob pulled up to collect me, Jane came out to be introduced and asked if he enjoyed the cookies his daughter bought him. He shook hands and told Jane she had done an excellent job saying he would recommend her to his customers. Obviously charmed, Jane beamed at him and waved them on their way. We settled down comfortably playing Golden Oldies on the radio during the journey. I felt happy and excited to be returning to Muranos again. I was also considering selling the English property. We didn't stop for a drink so arrived during siesta time. Bob was surprised to see a black car parked outside the property.

"I wasn't expecting anyone to be here," he told me as they collected their belongings.

As he reached for his key the door opened and a fair haired lady came out to hug Bob tightly. I stood back shocked. Bob remained motionless before pulling away exclaiming:

"Lisa what are you doing here? Rosie this is Tony's wife Lisa," Bob said.

"Rosie as in the owner of the lovely villa we stayed in during the holidays?" Lisa asked delighted.

"That's right," I told her holding her hand.

"Well it's your fault we are moving. The kids loved it so much it made us realise that they need more action to use up their energy," Lisa said.

"Why didn't you let me know you were coming? I could have collected you at the airport?" Bob asked.

"It was a last minute decision. Tony told me you would be coming over to sort things but I realised that I needed to see what we had left here in case there was anything personal," Lisa explained.

"So you don't trust me," Bob said.

I told Lisa how much I had enjoyed staying there and had accompanied Bob to lend a hand to check I had not left anything behind as I had left unexpectedly.

"Are you interested in buying the place?" Lisa asked frankly.

"To do so I need to sell my English home which is rented at present. The villa belongs to my family as well. They use it for holidays."

"It is gorgeous."

"Thank you, Bob did an excellent makeover. We inherited the villa from my former husband when he died. I would have bought somewhere more like here but that's probably because I am older now so prefer the serenity."

"Well Lisa since you are here make yourself useful and brew up while we unload the van. I brought boxes and packing materials. Come on Rosie let's get cracking."

"Yes sir," I said saluting following him out while Lisa put the kettle on.

While unloading Bob said wryly to me: "I don't know how you do it."

"Do what?"

"Always manage to save your virtue when I am around. You'd think by this age it would be easier."

I gasped with indignation while Bob loaded up with flat boxes and went inside.

Instead of a takeaway Bob drove us to a place in the next town for a simple meal. It was tasty and inexpensive so we all relaxed enjoying the background Spanish music. On the way back I asked Bob to drop me off so that I could stroll back along the promenade.

"I'm sure you two have family affairs to discuss," I told them sweetly.

Bob looked annoyed that he had to drive back. I left them to it and sauntered along admiring the onset of sunset along the coast. Breathing the sea air I felt as if I had come home. Muranos had lost none of its magic spell. As I drew along the coast I sat on a bench admiring the view and looking forward to the morning. It had always been my special time to enjoy the scenery before the daily routines kicked in and people emerged. When it grew dark I returned to the house to find Lisa and Bob discussing something so I yawned and headed for the guest room suddenly feeling tired and disappointed.

Next morning during breakfast Lisa pulled me aside saying that she apologised for interfering with their plans.

"Why? Did Bob say anything?" I asked her surprised.

"I didn't realise he was seeing anyone."

"We're not dating yet, just good friends," I said blushing.

"He's been through a rough time I'm glad you are here for him. Do you want me to disappear?" Lisa asked anxiously.

"Don't be silly, of course not."

"What's all that whispering about? Where's my breakfast? Two women in the kitchen and nothing on the table. How many women does it take to ..?" Bob called.

"All right sir, breakfast is on its way. You had better earn your keep in return," Lisa teased. "Go and sit down Rosie, what would you like?"

"Just some toast and coffee if possible," I said offering to help.

"Go and sit then we can plan our moves," Lisa said pushing me away.

We went methodically room by room eliminating anything that was surplus to essential requirements. The house would be advertised furnished as seen. It was clean and tidy so needed minimal clearance. Summer clothes, a few books and toys plus beach equipment were packed into boxes. I found a few of my belongings tucked away. We left the bathroom and kitchen wear as we would be using them. Lisa planned to fly back the next day so Bob offered to drive her but she needed to return the hire car to the airport. Unfortunately, Bob had a job waiting for him so we were unable to stay any longer so we would all depart at the same time. I asked for a break to explore the local area and greet the staff at the café, so went off happily. The trip had not gone to plan but I had enjoyed it. The temptation was to buy the house myself but I was not sure I could afford it.

After breakfast next morning we packed up and went our separate ways. I had enjoyed meeting Lisa and felt I had made a new friend. During the journey Bob asked me what my plans were.

"I don't have plans," I replied.

"Will you rent the villa out?" Bob asked.

"I don't know, it belongs to the family who will probably use it during school holidays. Besides where would I stay?"

"You could stay with me if you like."

Shocked I blushed saying: "Thank you but that would not be right."

"Why not?"

"Well it's very kind of you but there's something missing."

"Like what?"

"We are not in a relationship."

"We could give it a try if you want to. Do you?"

"Gosh, I don't know what to say. Are you propositioning me?"

"For a lady who lives alone you are always surrounded by people and circumstances. It's difficult to get close to you."

"Women are supposed to be wooed and pursued."

"Within reason. Are you into all that romantic stuff?"

"It's not something I am used to."

"Well I bought you flowers. What did you do?"

"I made you meals occasionally and Jane made biscuits for your daughter."

"So what do you think about giving it a go?"

"I want to but am afraid."

"Afraid of me?"

"The situation, I haven't been in a relationship for a long time, I'm so out of practice."

"Practice makes perfect and it will be fun finding out."

"You had a young girl until recently, I'm full of lived in bits and less appealing."

"We are both older and experienced in life. It should be easier and more comfortable because we don't have to prove anything or impress anyone. Hopefully, we can just be ourselves and take each day as it comes. I work long hours as you know so you can do whatever you please."

"I feel nervous so let me think about it. It's not that I don't want you, I am afraid you will be disappointed with me."

Bob pulled over into a lay by taking both my hands in his looking into my eyes.

"The only disappointment I have is not being able to grow close to you. It never seems to work out. I can't offer you anything fancy but maybe we can both enjoy quality times together with the time we have."

My eyes filled with tears and I swallowed. Silently Bob resumed the journey. When I could speak again I asked him what his plans were for the future.

"Well everybody has been using my place as a storage area so I intend to clearly label boxes and put everything in a lockup. There's stuff Mahalia left, my daughter left stuff in her room, now there's Tony's. If you come we can shift everything and you can arrange it to suit yourself. As long as you leave enough space for us to relax, I am not fussy about design although I favour open plan minimalism. At present you would not think so. My daughter's room is being used for storage."

"What about your daughters? What would they think about me?"

"They want their dad to be happy. It's none of their business, they lead their own lives."

"Do you keep in regular contact with them?"

"On WhatsApp mainly."

"Is Katie who ordered the biscuits the one who works for the UN?"

"Yes, you just missed her. She's quite Bohemian off duty."

"What's the married one called?"

"Emily, she's married to Pieter and lives in Holland. They are expecting their first child in the Autumn so I will become a grandfather."

"Wow congratulations!"

"Yes, it will be exciting for me."

"Won't they be surprised to find me following on from Mahalia?"

"Because she was younger you mean? We were never serious, it was an easy going relationship mainly of convenience. She is with her first love now, they were together from school before they broke up. I filled the gap and restored her confidence again. We were never meant to last so don't worry about her."

"Thank you for telling me. Can we take this slowly and ease into it naturally? I feel like a nervous teenager again."

"Sure, I promise not to take advantage of your good nature. Do you need more flowers, chocolates or perfume perhaps? I'm so out of practice at this too."

They both laughed and eased the tension that had been built. Before dropping me off outside my villa, Bob pulled me towards him and kissed me passionately, then followed me out to hand over my luggage. He winked at my startled expression then drove off. Jane was out but the house smelled of recent baking. With wobbly legs I went inside with my pulse racing. My lips felt burning as if stung. I felt invigorated and alive. Already I felt impatient to see Bob again. He left me without making any contact for a further week to give me space which only made me feel extra keen. I could not bear to discuss the situation with Jane or anyone else but that was all I thought about.

"You are very distracted lately, did something happen?" Jane asked.

"I'm trying to think about my future," I told her.

"About the villa you mean? Did you want to buy the one in Muranos?"

"No, I'm not sure what to do. The English house is rented for now but I don't want to live in it. If I want to buy somewhere else I need to sell it. The villa rents well but I have to fit in with the family requirements and live somewhere else if I rent it."

"Do you want me to move out? I can look for a rental somewhere too."

"What are your plans? You also have your place back home."

"Well seeing that my baking success is growing here, I think I would like to sell up and move here. I can also train further at home and get equipment together to bring over."

"Wow Jane that's a big step. I will help you if I can."

"Thank you, I have been thinking about it too. We can develop it together if you are interested. Meanwhile I value your assistance, it gives me confidence."

"Well let me know when you decide. It has been great living with you."

"Likewise, we make a good team. Do I detect you have some interesting plans lined up?"

"What do you mean?" I asked blushing.

"It's okay, tell me when you are ready. I'm on your side."

Once Jane had decided to move to Spain she booked a flight home, took contact details with several bakers, suppliers and café/bar outlets. She booked a taxi to the airport and refused to allow me to accompany her. Instead she neatly packed her summer and beach wear for me to store, washed her bedding, cleaned her room and set off early in the morning. I waved her off before returning to bed. The house felt strangely empty without Jane. We had been comfortable together and tolerant of any mishaps or differences of opinion. Whilst Jane had been there the house always smelt good. Sadly I walked around feeling the place looked too tidy.

On the same day Bob sent me a text asking if I would be free at lunch time at my place. I replied I would. Bob said he would bring lunch and perhaps they could have a swim beforehand. There was something he wanted to discuss with her. Feeling pleased I showered and put on my best swimwear. Bob turned up in his working clothes holding a bag of food and a bunch of simple wild flowers. I laughed with pleasure to see him and took both bags off him. We put the food in the fridge, then showered with Bob offering to wash me all over. Giggling we plunged into the pool which glistened in the sunshine. The outside gate to the back of the house was locked so we were out of sight as the pool was not overlooked.

As we swam around the pool Bob lunged up and grabbed me unexpectedly. I squealed and wriggled before relaxing in his arms. It felt surreal yet natural, I succumbed to Bob's embrace. He lifted me onto him in a closed embrace where we floated and bobbed about the pool in unison. I swooned with delight as we two became a couple. Emerging from the pool on wobbly legs, we shampooed and washed each other in the shower in loving embraces. Bob put out the lunch while I set the table and brought cold drinks. Feeling elated I asked Bob what he wanted to talk to me about.

"Phew woman, I won't be fit for work at this rate," Bob said teasing me.

"Is this your lunch break then?" I asked.

"Yes, shame I have to go back later. However, I wanted to ask you about Tony's place."

"What about it?"

"I know you like it. Why don't you buy it at a discount?"

"I don't have money to buy it."

"How many properties do you own?"

"Well my house in England is fully paid up but is rented at present."

"Is it in good condition?"

"It's ok, pretty standard three bed property. I lived there when I was married."

"Do you know what it's worth?"

"Not currently no. If it was modernised to your standards it would be worth more but it is in good repair and plainly decorated, very serviceable, convenient area for shops, schools, transport etc."

"Would you consider selling it?"

"Perhaps, I have thought about it because I don't want to live there anymore."

"What about this villa?"

"My late husband bought this and lived here with his girlfriend. It was probably left for the kids but I inherited it on their behalf. We all use it so as I am his former wife, it is not really mine to sell. It does fetch a good rental now that you have done such a good job. If I had planned to buy a place in Spain, I would not have come here. Now I am used to it and the way of life."

"Ok so if you decided to sell the English place would you be interested in Tony's place?"

"I love it there but it would not be good for you there."

"Why not?"

"It's too isolated, how would you earn a living?"

"Word of mouth, advertising, the surrounding area is full of dwellings and hidden villages etc. I have my van and equipment so I can work anywhere. Maybe I could work less and do other things."

"Like what for instance?"

"Never mind, I can't tell you all my secrets on our first date!"

"You haven't left much to the imagination!" I giggled.

"Watch it you siren unless you are looking for trouble," Bob said rising.

"Stop it, haven't you got work waiting?"

"There's still time for a brief siesta, let's go," Bob said leading her by the hand to the bedroom where they both lay down and napped.

When I awoke Bob had departed leaving his imprint on the bed. At first I thought I had imagined the whole scene but felt euphoric. I waited to find out what would happen next. One evening I met Bob for a drink in our local bar. He asked me what my plans were.

"I don't have any plans," I told him.

"So what are you going to do?"

"Must I do something?"

"Of course, lazing around in small doses is ok, but if you don't keep your mind and body active you will lose your fitness and age quickly."

"I didn't realise that I was supposed to keep busy all the time."

"You were active in Muranos, the Centre and café admired your efforts."

"Really? I enjoyed doing that."

"Exactly, so why don't you do something similar here then?"

"The fact is that this place does not motivate me. It will sound snobbish but I don't feel at home in this environment. Everything is geared towards the typical tourists with whom I don't feel a connection."

"Muranos suited you better then because ..?"

"I like the serenity, the coastline is like an embrace. Also it never gets too busy or crowded. There's the local town and market for ambience but the peace and vibe feels like home to me."

"So why not go back there and start over?"

"Are you trying to get rid of me?"

"Not at all, I can come over at weekends. You can stay at Tony's place and perhaps he can stay at yours if it suits both families when he wants to visit."

"Why should I pay rent when I own a place here?"

"You could make a reciprocal arrangement or buy Tony's place in instalments. I can help you with the purchase price because I have inherited some money now."

"So are you suggesting I rent this place out then move to Muranos?"

"If you want to or perhaps we could go travelling at the weekends to see if you favour anywhere else."

"I thought you worked at weekends too."

"I don't have to, it's enough during the week. Perhaps I may work less because I have enough to live on and own a few properties that I rent out. In fact I have shares in Tony's place. We could come to an arrangement."

"Really? Well my family plus Tony would have to come to an accord. It sounds very tempting. This villa is smart and ideal for holidays but it has never felt like home because I didn't choose it."

"Maybe this is the time to start new lives while we are able."

"I think the air is better in Muranos too, the hills seem to shelter it from the extreme heat most of the time."

"If you return there I expect you to be active. Find something that interests you. Jane had her baking, my daughter travels, do some sport or something creative."

"Yes sir."

"There must be something you can do, volunteer again, swim, walk, paint, write, anything. If you are stimulated it doesn't feel like work or a burden. Don't give up yet."

"It's true what you say. I will think about it."

"If you want I can drive you down there with all your stuff in the van."

"First we need to sort out the occupancy for this place with Tony and my kids."

"Fair enough, what about the letting agency?"

"They can take over providing the others liaise with them about availability dates."

"How does this conversation make you feel?"

"More inspired, I think staying here makes me lacklustre. Going there seems inspirational. As long as we keep in touch I can cope."

"Of course we will get together, I waited a long time for you. Look I am not into all that romantic stuff but I am not wasting what we have. Let's take it slowly and see how we go. Even when we are not together I will be faithful and preparing to join you as soon as. Perhaps I may find opportunities in that area."

"It all sounds promising," I replied feeling excited.

"I see a glint in your eyes now so let's go back to your place," Bob said standing up.

I liaised with the family and Tony before contacting the rental agency. The family and Tony agreed to inform the agency when they would be using the villa and would pay a token charge for maintenance only. This enabled me to clear my belongings and drive down with Bob the next weekend. It was a bright day with clear skies and I caught my breath at the view when we arrived. Everything remained as we had left it. We dumped the bags then rushed to the sea to splash, swim and enjoy ourselves. In the evening we ate out planning to shop for provisions the next day. At a convenience store we bought some basics for breakfast and drinks. To me it felt magical being there with Bob, I felt like a teenager again when he held me in his arms.

THE LIFE OF ROSIE

When Bob departed I decided to go round to the Community Centre to tell them I was back. It was mid-morning when I arrived surprised to find the Centre strangely quiet with an unfamiliar lady behind the counter. Wishing her good morning, I asked where Maria was. The lady speaking Spanish said Maria's daughter was expecting a baby so she had gone to stay with her. I asked in Spanish why the Centre was so quiet. It seemed the clients had gone on an organised trip. Without introducing herself the lady asked what I wanted. Taken aback I suddenly experienced a senior moment with a lapse in my Spanish vocabulary so struggled to communicate.

What I tried to explain was that I had been helping at the Centre until recently. Now that I had returned I wanted to help again. Impatiently the lady dismissed me saying that it was not necessary. They had volunteers and I needed to be vetted, or at least she mentioned documentation. Looking around for an interpreter I failed to recognise anybody and decided to return early the next day hoping to do the Milk Round again with the meals on wheels. Both women failed to communicate. Obviously, the lady in charge seemed to think I was a tourist who had stumbled into the Centre when it was virtually closed. Disappointed and disliking the unfriendly attitude I went back to the café to complain to owner George over coffee.

"Ah well, Maria's about to become a grandmother so she's staying with her daughter to help," George said.

"What about Alberto who did the Milk Round?" I asked.

"Ah he had some business to take care of so went to stay with his son in Barcelona to get his assistance. It's some family matter."

"So what about the regulars? Will I know anyone?"

"Probably, Berta is not a bad sort when you get to know her."

"Is she the woman in charge?"

"Yes, she's taking her responsibility seriously and as the new temporary manager wants to make a good impression."

"She was rude to me."

"Berta doesn't speak English or mix with tourists much so probably couldn't understand you."

"How come I never met her there before?"

"Because she is Maria's cousin who lives in another village in the mountains."

"So, I need an interpreter to explain to her about my previous duties."

"Call in here on your way to see if anyone can go with you. Otherwise leave it for a while and find something else to do."

"Well I will give it a try as I enjoyed it previously. When do you think Maria will return?"

"How long is a piece of string? Excuse me, I must serve my customers."

Early next morning I set my alarm and set off to the café. George found a driver who was delivering goods to the Centre who agreed to explain to Berta about my previous experience volunteering there. Berta was not pleased to see me, refused to let me handle the meals and assigned me to menial tasks cleaning and washing dishes. I watched others handle the Milk Round and prepare the food parcels. Whenever I started to do preparatory tasks Berta interfered and stopped me. There was no compatibility between us. When some of the regulars came to play games and chat, they were pleased to see me and at lunch time I was heralded. This antagonised Berta so I realised that the situation was not feasible until Maria returned.

After visiting some of my former delivery regulars and touring around the area, I went home sadly missing the former ambience and fun. Aimlessly walking along the beach I decided next morning to take a folding table and chair onto the beach with paints and try to capture the scenic location. I packed a sandwich, bottle of water, along with paints, brushes and donned a large brimmed sunhat. The bay curved around in golden sunshine with the sea placid like a lake. In places there was a glow. I concentrated absorbed in my effort. During the morning people came over to me to see what I was doing. There seemed to be an interest in art so I thought about inviting other painters to join me. Perhaps we could start an art group.

I enjoyed painting so much that I decided to vary the view to produce another two beach paintings. The initial painting looked left so I faced the central vision, a third would be looking right. If the three paintings blended I would be able to pitch them together in one location. A few other resident artists asked to join me bringing their own equipment. We sat in a row sharing snacks and concentrating. Visitors stopped to view our efforts. George offered to sell any finished paintings on display in his café if suitable. This was an incentive to produce our best efforts. Our small group made new friends and enjoyed our activity. We discussed themes and various locations to follow on.

In the midst of my artistic endeavours I returned home to find Bob. He had made contacts in the area and solicited various work endeavours including some renovation maintenance at the Community Centre. By word of mouth plus simple marketing, Bob had some projects to fill. I explained about Berta plus the art group. While I was pleased to see Bob I asked him about the usual work he had.

"Delegation my dear, I have a team you know," he told me.

"Can they manage without you?" I asked.

"I should hope so, we've been together for years."

"Is there enough work to keep you afloat here?"

"Well let's wait and see. I am confident once I do good work here word will spread."

"Oh well, let's hope the Muranos magic weaves its spell on you too."

"It already has you minx, now show me how pleased you are to see me."

My Spanish villa was being rented again by the management company. When they wanted to use it, my family and Tony had to liaise with them. The English house was also rented. Bob proposed that we shared the running expenses of the Muranos house. Tony was looking for a new property to buy. When he found something Bob would invest with him in return for possession of the current home. Apparently, both brothers had been left an inheritance from their mother. Whilst all my rental income was deposited directly into my bank accounts, I had a modest living allowance enabling me to lead a simple life. This fitted in well with the low key lifestyle I enjoyed at Muranos. Bob was out most days and enjoyed fishing or bird watching in his spare time.

We ate fresh food, drank cold water and juices, swam, strolled along the beach and enjoyed quiet times together watching the sunset or reading. For me it was idyllic. When Bob had to return to check his business interests, I missed him and waited for his return. A yoga group took place further along the coast which I joined. The art group expanded to include craft making activities plus whoever wanted to sit alongside them. I still volunteered at the Centre a couple of times a week. On one occasion I was delighted to find Maria showing off her new granddaughter Annalisa who was like a little doll. Her daughter Mira was staying with Maria while her husband was working away. Sometimes I helped out at the café if George was short staffed.

By infiltrating into the community my Spanish improved and my world shrank to the immediate environment. England and the villa seemed another life time ago. When my family came over I told them to visit in Muranos where I kept the children happy arranging for interesting activities. Gradually, I lost

THE LIFE OF ROSIE

contact with my friends and colleagues. My focus was on Bob with whom I was so attuned that we could communicate without words. He found work opportunities around the area, word of mouth led to various tasks. Bob promoted his second in command into a partnership deal so that he did not need to return. Once his house was streamlined he rented it. Working around the Muranos area he reduced his hours and enjoyed a few hobbies. Fishing, watching wildlife, even playing games occasionally with the old men kept Bob content.

This was the happiest time in my life. I hoped it would continue until we grew old. Nothing was missing and even though I adored my grandchildren's visits, I appreciated the peace and quiet of my regular routines when they had gone. Bob was working in a remote village when a man approached him asking him questions about his work, his background and told him that in order to work in the area he needed to pay insurance. Sensing underlying tension Bob calmly asked for an explanation. The man told him that it was protection money. Bob replied that he was just completing his present task and would not be returning to the area so there was no need to get involved. In a menacing manner the man approached Bob saying that he had to pay his respects. Standing up against the man Bob was prepared to fight but the man looked into his eyes then backed off.

I sensed something was troubling Bob when he came home so questioned him. At first Bob said nothing but then confessed he had been astonished to find a local Mafia in the remote village. Urging caution and avoidance I told Bob not to go there again. They put it behind them as an unpleasant experience. A car drew up at the house with a man asking for Bob. It seemed there was an extension required at a mountain villa retreat. Would Bob be interested as the money was good. Bob took the details and said he would have to check his schedule and get back. Hesitating the driver told Bob to call soon or else another contractor would get the opportunity. Bob had a bad feeling about the caller and stalled. I said he should not get involved and suggested he go back to his original business for a while. Bob refused and carried on his routine until one day he did not return home.

At first I thought he had done overtime or gone for a drink with someone. When Bob did not materialise overnight I was worried. I went to the local police station to explain my concern. By now I knew the local police who were regulars around the café and town. They told me that Bob had accidentally stumbled into a 'no go' area controlled by a bad family who ran a protection racket. Everyone knew about them but there was no evidence to arrest them. If Bob had somehow offended them, they would seek revenge. All they could do would be to go over there to see if Bob was around. If they had him it was unlikely that the police would gain access to him, but they agreed to make enquiries and would get back to me. They looked nervous at the prospect but two of them set off in a police car.

A text message came from Bob's phone saying he had taken on an unexpected emergency job in a remote location so he probably wouldn't be in touch for a while. She shouldn't worry and ended telling me not to forget to feed the cat. As they did not have a cat I knew something was wrong. The text was sent from the local town and nothing further came. When I tried to call Bob the phone was switched off. Telling the police that the message hinted all was not well because they did not have a cat meant the police were aware of the situation. They advised me to wait to see if anything further developed. Nobody claimed to have seen Bob in the "no go" area so they could not do more unless time moved on with Bob still missing.

I felt under surveillance at times as if I was being watched but could not see anybody. Perhaps there was a hidden camera somewhere. I tried to stay among people and closed the shutters at night or when I was indoors. By trying to stay outside as much as possible and keeping my mobile charged, I struggled by myself as a week passed with no sign or news of Bob. Tony was due to fly out with his family for half term holiday staying at my villa. I decided to speak to him when he arrived. Tempted to go to the villa I hesitated being unwilling to divulge my other dwelling to anyone watching. Instead I used the café phone to call Tony telling him there was a situation and he should only speak generally on the line.

Tony drove down to see me. I motioned him to be silent and we walked along the beach casually as if on a visit. Once they were away from the house I explained about Bob's missing situation. Tony was alarmed and wanted to go straight to the police station. I told him I had been and they knew but could not trace Bob at present. They were aware of the situation. Tony asked me to take him to the "no go" area so we could snoop around. I told him I had tried that to no avail. Nobody claimed to have seen Bob plus everywhere was shuttered and closed off. Wherever Bob was working he would not be seen. I hoped he was working and not in trouble. Tony assured me that Bob knew how to handle himself, he had done boxing in his youth. We were both worried.

I persuaded Tony to go back to the villa and we devised some code phrases to communicate. Somehow knowing that Tony and the police knew about Bob reassured me that I had done my utmost to bring his disappearance to their attention. Intuitively, I felt that Bob was alive and doing something secretive. My hope was that he would be able to return home when he finished. Being without him felt like half a life. While Bob was missing I had no appetite and my concentration was lost. I constantly worried about his welfare. To try to calm down I went to yoga. In the café and at the Centre everybody kept on the lookout and were sympathetic as Bob was popular.

A few weeks passed with me despairing. I was losing hope of seeing Bob again. Life seemed empty without him. Trying to keep myself busy I took a more active role in the Community Centre now Maria was in charge again. The art group merging with crafts had become close friends. One afternoon I came home to find Bob sitting outside snoozing in the recliner chair facing the sea. Rushing forward I restrained myself from waking him and sat next to him waiting for him to wake up. I had a cold beer waiting for him. Bob slept on until the light began to fade so I went inside to prepare a meal for us. I didn't want to leave Bob outside all night or wake him so put a lightweight cover over him. Feeling hungry I ate and lay on the sofa waiting but dozed.

During the night Bob entered the house and took me in his arms before carrying me into bed where he held me tight. I thought I was dreaming and could not ask him anything. Falling asleep again I woke up alone. Bob left a note on the kitchen table saying he had to sort out some work assignments and he would see me later. Frustrated that I was unable to question Bob, I had to wait impatiently. I went into town to buy some steak to make a good meal that evening. Feeling uplifted that Bob was back again looking wholesome if tired, I felt life would be better now we were together again. At the Centre I smiled and hummed telling everyone Bob returned but we had not had chance to talk yet. Everyone was pleased for me and looked forward to seeing Bob again.

When Bob came home he showered and changed then sat down to enjoy his meal.

"Don't ask me where I have been or anything connected to it because I can't tell you," he said.

"What do you mean? Was it Mafia related?"

"Not at all. It's top secret so I can't say anything."

"But I have been so worried, I thought I would not see you again. Tony was too, I went to the police .."

"Sorry, I was unable to communicate because the area was out of bounds."

"Are you ok? Did they treat you well?"

"Yes, I am fine now. I tried to work fast so that I could finish and come back. It's good to be home."

"But .." I stuttered.

THE LIFE OF ROSIE

"Come here and show me how much you missed me," Bob said holding his arms out.

Bob refused to say anything further about his experience or whether he had finished for good, so they rebuilt their relationship with me being acutely aware that he could disappear again at any time. I didn't want to be clingy or possessive but was afraid he would leave me. To compensate Bob told me about all his planned activities to stop me worrying about him. He spoke to Tony regularly and mixed with the community gaining enough work to keep him employed sufficiently without pressure. At his original business all was going well with his new partner motivated so there was no need to go back there. Bob's place rented well because of its convenient location and minimalist content.

The aftermath of Bob's disappearance then reappearance made me question the meaning of life.

"Did you see the film Alfie?" I asked him one evening.

"That's an old one, I think so."

"In it the lead actress said: 'What's it all about Alfie? Is it just for the moment we live?' What do you think?"

"Well at present we can only live in the moment. Apart from our memories we can't go back in time. We can try to predict the future but it's only a guess."

"Yes but we live each day as if it will be forever yet time passes so swiftly and we can be gone in an instant."

"Humans are programmed to continue living as if it will be forever. What's your point?"

I sighed saying: "We are here for a short time so whatever we achieve or are capable of doing disappears when we do."

"Not necessarily, we can leave something behind or pass on skills to the next generation. Everything we do purposefully has meaning to someone."

"Our children do not inherit our abilities."

"They follow their own paths but their upbringing has significant influence upon their outcome."

"Our children have found their direction and will remember us."

"Obviously, so what is your point?"

"I'm wondering what I am doing with my life and whether it is enough or even worthwhile."

"I think you are worthwhile, you help others at the Centre, sorted an art group, been a good single mother and independent woman. You are not lazy and keep fit. How much more do you want?"

"In the great scheme of things it is very little."

"It is more than many achieve. You persevere and dedicate yourself to doing your best, helping others when you can and causing minimum harm."

"Whatever a person does it passes on to others who are finding their way. We take nothing with us. So, what is all the effort for?"

"It's to lead you along the best path you can manage, to be a positive influence and to be compassionate and helpful to others less fortunate."

"Wow you sound like a preacher."

"All true religion is a spiritual guide, the concepts are sound. It cannot be held responsible for the corruptions indoctrinated by some of the followers greedy for power and influence. When applied well it helps people to lead more meaningful lives."

"Are you a believer?"

"I do not practice faith but I was brought up to believe. Not everything can be understood by mankind. However arrogant or intellectual scientists may be, they only see what they can understand. Our origins and history are largely speculation with scanty records."

"Do you think that we are doing ok living together?"

"I'm not complaining, I find it suits me. How about you?"

"I really enjoy being with you. When you weren't here I felt like only half a person. Do you think we are doing enough?"

"Enough for what? We are trying our best to live decent purposeful lives. There's no competition or nothing to prove. As long as we can pay our way and sustain ourselves we can manage."

"I'm so afraid you will go away one day and leave me behind."

"Is that what this is all about. Come here," Bob said reaching for me. "Let's just take each day as it comes and try our best."

I came home one Autumn afternoon from the Centre to find a couple sitting on our patio eating and drinking. The door to the house was open behind them.

"Excuse me," I said walking over annoyed: "this is private property. How did you get in?"

"Who are you?" the woman asked me.

"I live here so I can ask you the same question," I replied.

"Are you renting this place?" the man asked.

"No I live here so you had better explain yourselves."

"This is not your property," the woman replied.

"If you don't explain yourselves I am calling the police," I threatened.

"This is my father's place," the woman told her just as they heard a baby crying.

"Are you Bob's daughter?" I asked startled.

The man responded as the woman rushed off into my bedroom.

"Who are you?" he asked.

"I am Bob's partner, we live here together. Does he know you are here?" I asked.

"No, we thought we would surprise him to introduce him to his new grandson."

"How did you get in?"

"Tony gave us his spare key ages ago and since Bob was here, we came straight over."

"Didn't you know about me?" I asked.

"No, Bob is a private person and Tony didn't mention you either."

"How long have you known my father?" the woman asked returning to the room carrying the baby wrapped in a blanket.

"We've known each other longer than we have been together," I said.

"He was with Mahalia the last time we saw him," the woman said.

"Yes, she went back home and is with her first love now."

"So how did you meet my father?"

"A friend recommended him to do some reconstruction at my villa. We became friends initially, then after time got together after Mahalia left of course."

"So where is your villa?" the man asked.

"It's in Benidorm. Perhaps we should introduce ourselves, I am Rosie."

"My wife is Emily, I am Pieter and that little chap is Jan."

"He looks very cute, congratulations."

"Thank you," said Pieter proudly.

"If you had let us know you were coming, we would have bought provisions and made accommodation. We will have to go to the supermarket and prepare rooms."

"I put our things in the main bedroom," Emily said proprietary.

"Well I'm sorry but that's where Bob and I sleep. I can make up the other two rooms for you. I had better ring Bob and tell him to come home. One of you should come shopping to stock up. We don't have baby things or large quantities."

Pieter went to move their luggage from the main bedroom saying something in Dutch to Emily who hugged the baby and looked disapproving at me. I told her politely but firmly:

"Why are you looking at me that way? You have barged into my home and tried to take over. There was no warning or preparation. Your father is working and not expecting you. I am not someone he has picked up for a casual relationship. We are a well connected team. I don't know why he didn't tell you about me, but my family have met Bob and like him."

Pieter tried to soothe the two women diplomatically and motioned Emily back to the patio.

"Please excuse my wife, her hormones are still not adjusted yet. She meant no offence, I think she thought her father was sad and lonely without Mahalia. We mean well. I will go shopping with you when you are ready."

I rang Bob leaving a message telling him to come home as soon as possible as unexpected guests had arrived. Telling Emily I was going to the supermarket for provisions, Pieter consulted his wife about supplies. Emily looked through the cupboards and fridge then told him in Dutch what to buy. Throughout Emily's inspection I simmered inside resisting the temptation to comment, Emily had not impressed me. I only hoped his other daughter Katie would be more cordial. Emily looked disapprovingly at me as I left with Pieter. I hoped Bob would get the message and return before them so he could talk to his sulky daughter.

"How long are you staying?" I asked Pieter.

"About ten days if that is ok."

"I am sure Bob will be delighted. If you want private family time I can go back to Benidorm."

"Don't do that on our account. Why are you in Muranos if you have a place in Benidorm?"

"I inherited that villa from my late husband who was killed in a car crash there. It is a smart villa with a big pool but I would not have chosen that location. Muranos suits me because it is quiet and peaceful. From the moment I saw it I fell in love with the place."

"What about your villa?"

"It's rented out. In fact Tony and family have stayed there. My English home is also rented."

"Will you go back there?"

"Only on a visit to see my family but not to live."

"Do you have children?"

"I have a son and daughter with four beautiful grandchildren, two each. We have arrived now."

As they collected shopping bags and a trolley, Pieter asked if I was serious with Bob.

"Most definitely, we have an ongoing love story. Without him I feel incomplete. You can see for yourself."

"Well I'm sorry for our intrusion. Emily is not normally unfriendly, she was probably being over protective of her father. As the youngest daughter she was always a daddy's girl. Katie is more independent and liberal."

"Look I don't want to cause any tension in the family. If there's a strain I will move out for the duration of your visit. I volunteer at the Communal Centre and run an art group so I am well known here now. I'm sure somebody would put me up."

Pieter apologised profusely saying he would speak to his wife when they got back. After that they focused on shopping discussing what to buy. I liked Pieter he seemed genuine and kind. He pushed the trolley and I consulted him before putting in the contents. When we returned home we found a proud Bob cradling his grandson. Emily was in the kitchen cooking an omelette with peppers, tomatoes, cheese and some onion. I felt pleased to have restocked supplies. Bob spoke to Pieter and told Emily to bring some cold beers. In the kitchen I unpacked the shopping and tried to stay out of Emily's way. The two women did not speak until the omelette was ready accompanied by a salad and a few new potatoes. I would have made chips with them but was not consulted.

"Well grandpa, how was your day?" I asked Bob sitting down.

"It had a happy ending, did you see this boy Rosie? Isn't he wonderful?" Bob replied beaming.

"Well it was a shock to find strangers on the patio when I came home with the door open. We got off to a bad start as we were all suspicious of each other," I told him.

"You should have told me you were coming. I could have met you at the airport," Bob said ignoring me.

Conversation during the meal centred around the new arrivals and family talk. Emily went to change the baby and feed him. I went to see if the bedding in the guest room was clean. Luckily the twin beds were made up ready.

"Where will the baby sleep?" I asked Emily.

"We brought a carrycot with spare bedding," Emily replied.

"Oh that's good, we bought nappies and baby wipes plus a new baby towel." I said trying to be helpful.

"Right, I did come equipped but it's good to have extra."

"Ok so I will leave you to it. Let me know if you need anything. I've brought you clean towels and a bin for the dirty nappies with some plastic bags."

Emily did not reply so I returned to the living room saying to the men:

"I already told Pieter that if you want to have private family time I will move out for the duration of the visit."

Bob looked startled asking why I would even think that.

"It's just that Emily does not seem pleased to see me and I don't want to cause tension in the family."

Pieter said that Emily's hormones were not back to normal yet, he would speak to her later. Bob told Pieter that Rosie was his soul mate and this was her home too. Emily should understand that and relax. He told me that Emily was probably tired from travelling and not to take it personally. After that Bob went to admire his grandson again. Pieter went to sort out the unpacking in the guest room. I cleared the table and kitchen, then had a shower and went to bed feeling apprehensive and drained. I did not know if the visit would improve after a good sleep. Bob came in later smelling of beer, hugged me then started snoring.

In the morning while preparing breakfast Emily apologised stiffly to me. We both scrutinised each other and politely agreed to start over. There was an uneasiness between us. Usually I bonded with most people I met. At the Centre I was popular and conversed with strangers easily. It was rare for me to find somebody disagreeable. I decided to exit as much as possible to avoid our guests. Bob could entertain them and accompany them as much as he liked. Pieter was pleasant, the baby was adorable but the friction with Emily seemed difficult to accommodate. Meals, visits and activities would be Bob's domain.

THE LIFE OF ROSIE

Bob told me that Emily was suffering from postnatal depression so Pieter thought that bringing her to visit him in scenic sunny surroundings may help to cure her. Emily expected to have her precious daddy to herself. This explained her irritability and dislike to me who was viewed as competition for Bob's favour. I told Bob that Emily should seek medical advice. Bob said he would take some time off and escort his daughter around. Pieter was willing to look after the baby so if I did not mind, Bob would try to help Emily to recover. I agreed to be accommodating.

The next day while Bob set off early to sort out his working arrangements in order to take time off to spend with Emily. I told Emily about the yoga class on the beach. When I invited Emily to accompany me, I noticed a flash of interest.

"What about the baby?" Emily asked sullenly.

"I'm sure the baby will enjoy some male bonding with daddy," I told her.

Pieter came along hearing the end of the conversation and volunteered to take his son a stroll along the coast. They would meet mummy when she was finished then they could all go out for lunch. To my surprise Emily went to get changed and we set off down the coast.

"It feels good to be free," Emily said.

"You must always find time for yourself," I remarked.

"Easier said than done, babies are very demanding."

"Sure they are but they grow so quickly, make the most of the time he sleeps."

"How did you manage with two?"

"Well there was a gap between them so I was just getting one out of nappies by the time the next one came along. I didn't want any more though and my husband wasn't accommodating like Pieter. He was useless."

"Did your children turn out well?"

"Yes, I am very proud of them. They have lovely families, good careers and modern homes. Best of all I have four beautiful grandchildren, two each."

"It will be years before I get to that stage. I don't know if I am suited to motherhood."

"Well nobody knows in the beginning but after a while it becomes routine and you know what to expect."

"I prefer to go back to work and let someone else manage the child care."

"If you do that you will miss so much. As baby grows you won't be there when he sits up, crawls, stands or even walks."

"At present I am too exhausted to even care. All I seem to do is feed, change nappies and wash him. He has no concept of day or night and seems to have colic so cries a lot."

"Why don't you use this break to rest and relax. You go out with your father and leave the baby with Pieter and myself. We can take him for walks in the fresh air and do the nurturing between us. In fact, you can go off with Pieter if you want and I can mind the baby. I have experience so he will be safe with me."

"Why would you do that?"

"Because it would be my pleasure. All my babies are grown and I probably won't get to play with your baby again for a long time."

"Well I think you are mad but if you want to we can try. You had better take good care of him. Just because I dislike doing it doesn't mean he is not precious. I don't want another one."

"Of course he's precious and I will take good care of him. You may change your mind later on. I think your baby looks like his father."

"Yes, everyone says that."

"Well if you have another it may take after you. We are here now. Have you done yoga before?"

"I go to classes regularly. This may be a different version but it should be interesting doing it on the beach in such lovely surroundings."

"Muranos is special, I'm glad you agree."

We spread our mats alongside each other and followed the instructor. Pieter pushed the baby very slowly along the coast. He felt relieved that his wife had gone off with me hoping it would lead to a breakthrough in relations. Since the birth Emily had been irritable, constantly tired and lethargic, expecting him to do everything for her. She did not take into account that he had responsibilities at work to consider. He had hired some home help for Emily who had gone back to work even though she was feeling tired and pressurised. Perhaps this break for limited duration might give them both the chance to recuperate. He felt I seemed to be a decent person with a positive outlook. Pieter hoped I could influence his wife.

I encouraged our visitors and Bob to go out exploring the area to enjoy a holiday while I looked after the baby. It was a long time since I engaged with a baby but it all came back to me as I took over feeds and dirty nappy changes. As I was relaxed and competent baby Jan was no trouble. He barely whimpered for attention but I sensed his needs and took over automatically. In my arms Jan remained calm and quiet. When Emily took over Jan cried and screamed vigorously. Everybody noticed and Emily was not pleased. Calling her aside I told her:

"Babies can't speak to tell you what's wrong but they can sense your mood and temperament. If you are stressed, angry or upset, that filters through to the baby and frightens him. Before picking Jan up try taking a deep breath to calm yourself and count to ten. Try to think happy thoughts and be relaxed with him then he won't cry."

Emily looked thunderous.

"Your baby is precious, you made him and he needs you to protect him. If you are uneasy he is afraid because he can't understand. So many women long for a baby, you are so fortunate to have such a beautiful boy. I will miss him terribly when you go."

"Do you want me to leave him here?" Emily asked.

"How can you even think that? What about Pieter and Jan's grandparents? I understand that modern life can be stressful but you should enjoy your holiday now, then savour each stage of Jan's development. It will pass very quickly. Be gentle with him and patient to earn his trust and allow your love story to develop with familiarisation."

"I don't want to be a mother."

"It's too late now, you are a mother so do your best. It is your new project for a few years. Jan needs you so chill out now and calm down. He will grow up fast, enjoy this stage where all he does is drink milk and sleep. Once he is active he will be all over the place."

Emily sniffed but looked thoughtful and left all the baby care to Pieter and myself. Grandpa Bob joined in when he was allowed. Apart from occasional glances, Emily took no notice of him. I worried what would happen at departure time. Pieter said he would seek medical help for Emily and asked if we could look after Jan while he took Emily to a Spanish therapist. Feeling protective of Jan and caring deeply for him, I invited Pieter to leave the baby with me for as long as he wanted. I had bonded completely with the baby and dreaded losing him. The couple drove away for two days and nights. Pieter came back alone leaving Emily at a centre. A devoted father Pieter was obviously upset at Emily's lack of interest in their child.

Pieter had to return to Holland due to a work crisis so left Emily in the care centre in Spain. Baby Jan remained with us. I took him along to the Centre where everybody fussed around him and to the art group where he enjoyed the sea air. Jan was no trouble and people enjoyed seeing him. When he was awake he smiled. One morning just before I was about to leave the house the phone rang.

"Hello," I answered.

"Hi is that Rosie?" a cheerful voice asked.

"Rosie speaking, who is that?"

"Hi this is Bob's daughter Katie. Thank you for making my dad happy."

"Oh hello Katie, do you know about me?"

"Of course I do, I talk to dad regularly."

"Emily claimed not to know about me."

"Well she's not well at present as you know. She knew but has always been very clingy to dad."

"She was hostile to me when she came."

"You have to make allowances because she's having some kind of breakdown. Do you know how she is?"

"Pieter had to fly back to Holland for work so he left Emily recovering in a care centre. We haven't been able to visit yet because they told us to leave her at present."

"How's my nephew?"

"He's thriving here and really coming along. We are enjoying having him because he is no trouble at all."

"Well thank you for your care. I can't wait to see him. Actually I am ringing to tell you that I have booked a flight over and will be arriving this evening."

"Do you want picking up?"

"No, I'll hire a car. Don't go to any trouble I will give you a hand with everything."

"Are you sure you will be ok? Can I get you anything special to eat?"

"I'm a vegetarian and don't eat much so no worries. When I land I will call you from the airport before I set off."

"Fine, I look forward to meeting you Katie. Bob will be thrilled."

"See you later Rose."

After the call I hurried to check the bedding in the guest room and put out clean towels. The contrast between the two sisters was vast. Katie sounded warm, bubbly and enthusiastic. Hopefully, Katie would get along well with me. When Bob found out Katie was coming he was delighted. He said he would pick up some of Katie's favourite things on his way home. I took out my cook books and picked a vegetarian meal to make when I returned later and planned to buy some extra juices. Already I sensed a kindred spirit visiting us. Perhaps Katies would have a positive influence on her sister. Pieter rang me before I left to check on Jan. He was pleased Katie was coming and hoped she would be able to visit Emily. I dutifully rang the care centre to enquire about Emily and was told she was comfortable. They said Emily was making slow progress but it would take time.

Katie arrived mid evening with one suitcase and a bag full of presents for Jan. She hugged Bob and myself equally and was enchanted by the baby who was sleeping.

"How adorable, what a little doll, I can't wait to see him awake," Katie gushed.

In appearance both sisters differed. I could see a prettier version of Bob in Katie but with dark hair. Emily looked nothing like Bob so perhaps favoured her mother. Katie said she would sleep in the small bedroom but I gave her the twin bedded guest room so she could spread out and be comfortable. Katie and I bonded instantly. We felt as if they had always known each other. Bob asked Katie what her plans were. Next day Katie would ring the care centre and insist on seeing Emily. It would be better for her to visit alone the first time to assess how Emily was. At present it seemed Emily had told Katie that she didn't want to see Pieter because he was too nice.

"How can anyone be too nice? Pieter is a lovely guy," I protested.

"Emily is not herself just now, she said she is sick of everything. Her mind is unbalanced," Katie said.

"She's taking no interest in the baby." Bob said.

"She did not plan on motherhood and wants to get back to work," Katie said.

"Jan is a beautiful baby, he's no trouble. However, when Emily picks him up he screams. I think he senses her feelings and is afraid of her," I said.

"It seems Emily is not into her marriage or anything other than her career at present." Katie told them.

"This breakdown is serious, I hope she recovers for her family's sake," Bob said.

"It's sad but I'm sure with help Emily can get better. She has always been a bit of a control freak. For the baby's sake I hope she can be more flexible otherwise she will have to hire help with her son," Katie said.

I immediately felt protective of the baby and offered to care for him.

"You can't deny Pieter fatherhood, let's see what happens," Bob told her.

To change the subject, which was upsetting, I asked Katie about her role in the United Nations which sounded exciting. Katie was just about to reply when Jan awoke and gave a little cry. Immediately I picked him up and handed him to beaming aunty Katie. Handing Katie his bottle of milk, I watched her coo and sing to her nephew. Bob brought out some drinks and snacks before putting out a clean nappy with baby care products ready to change him. What a contrast Katie was to her sister. I felt I had gained a new friend. Katie asked me about my family while she admired her nephew. I found some photos to show her later. While she was looking through my photos Sadie rang for a chat.

Next morning Katie went to visit Emily, Bob went to work and I took Jan to the Centre where everyone fussed over him. Katie returned in the evening saying Emily was claiming she was fed up with her marriage because Pieter was too nice, she didn't favour motherhood despite having a beautiful baby son, her lifestyle made her feel trapped and she wanted to start over. The care centre was trying to give her some relaxation medication which Emily refused to take. She asked Katie to take her away. Katie was due to go to Albania on an assignment then to Guatemala so had no permanent base to offer. Emily took no notice of anything Katie tried to say, so she return feeling frustrated. Bob looked worried, baby Jan comforted them both.

Deciding to try again Katie went back to see Emily to discover she had discharged herself and disappeared. When Katie rang Pieter to see if Emily had returned home, he had no knowledge as he was at work. He said he would go home to check and advise them. Katie called me into the kitchen to tell me some confidential information.

"I don't know whether to tell you this Rosie, don't tell dad or anyone else. Promise,"

I promised noticing the anxiety on Katie's face.

"Emily told me that Jan is not Pieter's biological son. Apparently Pieter had a vasectomy. She had an affair with a work colleague. Pieter knew and was happy to be the father to the baby."

"Goodness me, poor Pieter," I sighed. "He seemed very proud of Jan and attentive. He will make an excellent dad."

"Emily doesn't want to resume her married life with him."

"Did she say why?"

"He's too good for her. She wants to focus on her career."

"What does she do exactly?"

"Medical research scientist."

"Does that take precedence over raising a beautiful baby?"

"Apparently, unless she's fixated with her fling bloke."

"Have you met him?"

"No, it's the first I've heard but I don't catch up with Emily much."

"You are both very different types."

"Tell me about it!"

"Shouldn't Bob know about this?"

"No, my dad will want to tell Pieter and it's private business for them."

"Do you think Emily has flown home?"

"She could have done as she had her passport and cards."

"Her suitcase is still here with her clothes."

"That won't bother Emily, she has more at home."

Pieter rang to say Emily was not home but he thought she might have been as some of her wardrobe seemed emptier. He was uncertain if she had packed to go away. He asked to be kept informed when they knew anything. Katie assured him she would keep in touch and he promised to do the same. Bob came in at the end of the conversation so Katie explained that Emily had disappeared from the Centre. Bob immediately rang Emily repeatedly until she finally answered her phone to tell him she was fine, not to worry. Bob told her all the family were concerned about her. Emily told Bob she was going to make a new start and would be in touch then hung up and switched her mobile off. The number did not work again so she must have changed her mobile.

Every evening Pieter rang to enquire about Jan. He planned to return to collect his son perhaps during the weekend. I suggested that he leave Jan with them until he sorted out care arrangements for him over there. Whilst Pieter's mother offered to help with childcare, she worked part time. The baby was too young for nursery, Pieter had to work, it seemed Emily was not concerned and had not appeared. The best solution seemed to be with us temporarily. Saying it was not fair to them, Pieter said he would search for somebody reliable locally. I told him Jan was thriving for now with family who loved him and was no trouble.

Before Katie left I insisted that she informed Bob about his grandson's origin. Bob was shocked and upset at Emily's behaviour. Katie cried leaving Jan, hugged everyone then drove off promising to keep in regular contact. When Martin rang he said I sounded emotional. I explained that Bob's daughter had just departed and had been upset to leave the baby so it had made me sad. They chatted about life in general. I felt really disconnected and for once wanted to end the conversation. England and Holland felt remote compared to my present life. I was too attached to baby Jan and dreaded losing him, especially as he had started to smile when he saw me.

"Imagine how Pieter must feel," Bob said.

"He adores Jan and doesn't realise we know anything about his origin," I remarked.

"Yeah well let's keep it that way."

Pieter rang to say Emily wanted a divorce.

"On what grounds?" asked Bob angrily.

"I don't know, perhaps she's fed up with me. Honestly, I tried hard to please her," Pieter said sounding upset.

THE LIFE OF ROSIE

Bob tried to call Emily but to no avail. We had lost contact with her. Apparently, she was no longer working at the same office and had not left permission for her location to be revealed. If legal divorce proceedings went ahead, Emily would have to reveal her address in the documentation. Pieter was upset and stopped calling every night. Between both parents it seemed Jan would be remaining in Muranos for the foreseeable future. Bob loved to play with Jan when he came from work and often took him out pushing the carriage along the front, telling everybody he knew to admire his grandson. In the evening they lay Jan down on a blanket and watched him try to kick his little feet around.

Pieter informed them that Jan was registered on Emily's passport so he could not collect him. While Emily was isolating from her family and friends, Pieter was trying to contact her in various ways to tell her to collect Jan. When he finally made contact offering to collect the baby, Emily cruelly replied that Jan was not his so there was no need. Bob was furious at her response hearing Pieter's devastation. When Emily texted Bob to say she would collect Jan at the weekend telling him to get everything ready, Bob asked her what she intended to do about his care seeing that Emily and her mother worked. There was no reply. We both worried about Jan's welfare and felt reluctant to hand him over when the time came. We took Jan out on both weekend mornings.

Emily showed up early Sunday evening in a hire car. Bob sent me outside so he could speak privately to his daughter. I took Jan for a walk, the baby gurgled and smiled at me. There was a gentle breeze and the baby had a lovely golden glow. I sat on a bench feeding him. We were both Content and I wanted to cry at the prospect of leaving him. Unless Emily showed some care and had a firm plan of commitment for Jan's future, I could not hand him over. Although we had no grounds to keep the baby, I felt afraid he would suffer neglect with Emily. Pieter had stopped calling because he was too upset facing divorce proceedings and losing his child who was registered as his on the birth certificate.

When I returned to bathe and change Jan ready for bed, a sulky Emily was smoking on the balcony and Bob was preparing an evening meal. Obviously Emily was staying overnight. She did not greet me or check on Jan. When I invited Emily to bathe the baby, Emily shrugged without moving. Bob took the baby so I sat down opposite Emily avoiding the smoke asking her what she planned to do with Jan.

"It's none of your business," Emily replied.

"How can you say that when we have been taking care of him?" I asked blazing.

"I'll find someone to take him."

"What do you mean take him? When? Where? Explain yourself."

"If the family don't want him, he can go into care."

"Well we are family and we want him. Just leave him here and clear off. Arrange all the paperwork and we will adopt him and raise him here. You are not fit to be his mother."

"You are old people."

"Older and wiser so what? We have experience in raising children and if you took any notice of your son, you would see her is thriving here in this climate. Everybody here loves him."

"Did you discuss this with dad?"

"Your dad and I want Jan and enjoy taking care of him. Your dad pushes him around showing him off to all his cronies."

"If you take him it has to be forever."

"I realise that. What about Pieter? Why have you been so cruel to him? What did he do?"

"He's boring, always Mr Goody two shoes, everything correct and predictable. I can't stand him."

"Why did you marry him then?"

"I thought stability would be good but it was entrapment."

"Pieter is devastated by your behaviour. He adores the baby too."

"Yes well, if he wants to see him he'll have to come here then if you keep him."

"Don't you want to see the baby? Check how he's grown and thrived here."

"Babies all look the same."

"Jan doesn't he is beautiful."

"All that pain and what do you gain, a liability needing constant attention."

"Do you have no feelings at all for him?"

"I hope he has a good life with someone else."

"Unbelievable, you don't deserve him. So many people would love to have a baby. Jan is so good, he hardly ever cries and doesn't give us any trouble."

Emily looked at me with disdain then called Bob to join them to discuss keeping Jan. Bob studied Emily saying:

"I can't believe you are my daughter. What happened to you? Just leave the baby here, go back and arrange the adoption papers. Rosie and I will raise my grandson and I hope we do a better job than I managed with you. Just leave when you are ready and don't come back unless you come to your senses. I am ashamed of you and upset for poor Pieter who is a decent man. You don't deserve him. Go your own way and see how happy that makes you."

Bob stood up and went inside before he lost his temper. Emily started crying then went to the bedroom to collect her luggage before driving off. Rosie saw her go into the nursery to look at Jan who was sleeping peacefully. Without speaking to anyone Emily let herself out of the house and drove away. It was evening so they assumed Emily would head to the airport or stay overnight somewhere. She left bad vibes behind her. I hugged Bob silently for a while then said we would have to buy some more supplies and clothes for the baby who was growing quickly. Bob apologised for Emily's behaviour and sounded really upset. Katie rang then so I left him to explain the situation while I finished our meal.

After the phone call Bob went out to cool down. I rang Katie to ask her if she could get Emily to seek help. Katie told me that Emily had called her in tears saying Bob had shouted at her. Apparently Emily said she did not know how to care for a baby, she could barely manage to look after herself. Saying everyone was against her because she lacked any motherly instincts, Katie thought Emily was frightened. I said that Emily needed some help which she wouldn't get by shutting everyone off.

"I can't tell her anything because she dislikes me," I said.

"She blames you for taking her dad away from her. He was always protective of her being the youngest."

"Well pardon me for breathing!" I exclaimed.

"I tried talking to her about counselling but I don't know if she was listening."

"Pieter stopped calling us now. She was very destructive telling him the baby wasn't his, he is devasted facing divorce proceedings too."

"She is obviously having a break down. Perhaps I can take some leave when I find out where Emily settles then take her somewhere myself. Meanwhile you are both keeping the baby I believe."

"Yes, poor mite. We couldn't send him off with Emily in her deranged state. She only took a quick peak at him before she left and had no interaction with him."

"It's very good of you both, I'm sure a baby is not what you expected, he must interfere with your plans."

"No, he's a good baby, no trouble. Your father loves to show him off."

"Well this is a desperate situation. Keep in touch and I'll let you know if I hear anything."

"Same here, be careful wherever you go."

Life flowed in their usual routines until the next school holidays when Martin was bringing his family over for the first week with Sadie's family the second. Bob suggested they took a break and went over to the villa to spend family time together.

"But we won't all fit in the villa plus there's no baby stuff," I answered.

"Don't worry, I will get us fixed up with a place to stay. You can go to the villa every day. I need to go back to see my partner and catch up with a few things. It will be good to catch up with my old buddies and regulars," Bob told her enthusiastically.

"I thought your place was rented out."

"It is but I have another smaller place we can use, I'll make sure it is available for two weeks."

"With the baby here I have been neglecting my family," I said sadly.

"All the more reason to enjoy them while they are here. At least they are more welcoming than mine."

"Katie is friendly enough, I really bonded with her."

"Because you are both positive people. I ruined Emily spoiling her."

"Have you heard from her?"

"Not a thing but I feel sure she will turn up one day."

"You told her not to come back."

"That was because I was angry. Besides when do kids listen to their parents?"

"Most of the time."

"Well when Emily recovers from this postnatal depression she hopefully will revert to a decent human being again."

"Shall we go a day earlier to prepare the villa, do a shop etc.?"

"Good idea, we'll clean up here and lock everything away."

Tony decided to bring his family over for the school holiday so he took over the Muranos place while they were away. It worked out well for all the families. Katie was pleased. She was in Mongolia so couldn't join them so asked for photos exclaiming with pleasure how Jan was growing. He had a sloping baby seat which could rock and enjoyed watching people. A smiley happy baby he slobbered and moved his feet about when he was lively but still slept for hours. As he grew I bought new outfits from the market which had colourful supplies. Everyone knew Jan and chatted to him when they passed. He had become a popular member of the community.

We packed Bob's van and set off stopping midway to feed and change Jan. It seemed lively and busy when we arrived. The villa looked brighter and larger than I remembered. It was obvious that the cleaner had been with the beds made and everywhere was tidy. We decided to stock the fridge and cupboards with initial provisions so drove to the supermarket where we bought quantities of fruit, salads, bread, milk and general provisions for Martin and ourselves. After stocking the villa, Bob drove us to a small apartment in town where we would be staying. I opened the windows to let fresh air in while Bob unloaded the van. It was on the second floor which meant carrying the buggy up and down. Although a basic holiday apartment, it was adequate. I planned to spend most of the time around the villa.

Eating out in the evening at one of our favourite places, we were reunited with several friends who were out walking along the promenade. Before long we were surrounded. Everyone enquired about the baby. Proud grandpa Bob was delighted to show him off. After the meal we went along to the bar where the former regular crowd congregated. When the music started playing I took Jan to the ladies to wash and change him for bed. I wheeled the buggy up and down until he dozed off. Eventually, I returned to the apartment to put Jan in his new travelling cot then showered and went to bed myself feeling suddenly exhausted. When Bob returned I was sound asleep so he didn't wake me.

After breakfast next morning I wheeled Jan to the villa waiting for Martin to arrive. Bob went off to see his partner and do a few errands. He told me he would book somewhere for the evening meal for all the family, his treat. I should advise him the time and location then he would see me there. Kissing Jan and making him laugh, Bob pecked my cheek and set off happily. Walking to the villa felt familiar but strange as I had become accustomed to quiet tranquillity. This was a complete contrast. Cold drinks and juices awaited in the fridge. I put sunscreen on Jan and myself, plus hats and sat near the pool with Jan in the shade giving him water to drink. He seemed fascinated to watch the sun shimmer in the pool making the water sparkle.

Martin and family arrived noisily and happily. I rushed to greet them exclaiming with pleasure how much Isaac and Zak had grown. They seemed to be all long slim legs and arms. Hugging everybody I heard Jan crying, he must have woken up and not known where he was.

"What's that?" Martin asked puzzled.

"It sounds like a baby crying," Maisie said surprised.

I dashed off and returned carrying a red faced Jan who was rubbing his eyes.

"Everybody please meet Bob's grandson Jan. We are looking after him at present."

They all made a fuss so Jan leaned into me to hide. I told Jan who everybody was and played with him to make him laugh. He was uncertain initially but when the boys approached him, Jan was fascinated. They went into the dining area where the table was set. I parked Jan in his chair to watch then put a cold meal out with drinks and desserts.

"Wow this is a feast," proclaimed Zak who enjoyed his food.

They all began talking at once because I wanted to hear all about their lives. Automatically I sat Jan on my knee and fed him while he stared at them all. Bob rang to check they had arrived safely and told me he had booked dinner for them. He would see them at 7.30 pm at the restaurant unless I needed him earlier. I agreed to the rendezvous and told him to have fun. I sensed he had plenty to tell me but let it wait for a more suitable time. Maisie asked me how our union was faring.

"Honestly, Bob is my soul mate, he's the best man I ever met. We have a wonderful life together."

"Does his family like you?"

"Katie, his eldest daughter is delightful, she works for the United Nations so travels extensively. Jan's mother, Emily, is suffering from postnatal depression following the birth. She lives in Holland so cannot cope with the baby at present."

"Oh dear, is she married?" Maisie asked concerned.

"Her husband Pieter is a decent bloke but works full time. His mother works too, so there isn't anyone to take care of Jan who is too young for nursery. We offered because we have both fallen in love with him," I said looking down at Jan who was looking at me adoringly.

"Seems like the feeling is mutual," Martin said smiling.

"Bob's treating us all for dinner so we will meet him at 7.30 this evening at the restaurant."

"Where is he now?" Isaac asked.

"He's gone to see his business partner and run some errands. When I met him he lived here and had loads of work so he must have plenty of catching up to do."

"I remember him when he did the house renovation," Zak said.

"Are you still living in Muranos?" Isaack asked.

"Yes and loving it there."

"Are there things to do? Does it not get too quiet?" Martin asked.

"Not at all, the quieter the better. We have become part of the community now. It's hard fitting everything in."

"Do you still go to the Community Centre?" asked Zak. "It was fun there."

"Yes, they all make a fuss of Jan. I take him with and park him there."

We chatted while the boys changed and jumped into the pool. After lounging around during the hottest spell while Maisie unpacked, the family wanted to go for a walk along the promenade to the beach. We locked up and strolled along the front while the boys raced down to the beach chasing each other and splashing in the sea.

"Where do they get so much energy?" I asked.

"They're still young," Maisie replied. "Where are you staying?"

"Just in the centre on the second floor of a block of flats."

"Are you renting it?"

"Bob says he owns it," I replied.

"A man of property!" Maisie said enviously.

"He works hard for it."

"What's it like?" Maisie asked.

"Very basic but clean and we won't be in it much, just for sleeping. I want to spend time with you unless you want to be private," I said.

"Do you want us to find you space at the villa?" Martin asked.

"Not at all, you enjoy it. I won't monopolise your holiday I promise."

"Don't be silly, we want to share it with you and little cutie pie here," Maisie said tickling Jan's chin as he beamed at her.

We walked along then sat overlooking the sea while the boys swam and played on the beach. As the afternoon progressed more people came out to stroll. I left them to go back to the flat to shower and change saying I would call for them around seven. At the flat I showered Jan and put him down to sleep. After my shower I lay down on the bed next to Jan and dozed myself. I awoke groggily, changed Jan then fed him and dressed him in a Babygro for the evening. It was time to get ready so I chose a smart dress that Bob liked, applied makeup and perfume then pushed Jan to the villa to collect the family, taking a blanket for the baby for later.

"You look nice grandma," Isaac told her.

"Is Bob here?" Zak asked looking behind me.

"He will be waiting for us at the restaurant," I told him.

All the family were ready except Maisie who had been busy sorting everyone else first. We all walked slowly down to the centre towards the restaurant. On the way we saw Frances who came over to welcome me back. After a brief chat and a promise to drop by to explain everything, Frances left. We arrived at the restaurant about ten minutes late. Bob was waiting wearing a white open necked shirt which displayed his tan. I felt my heart flutter at the sight of him. Welcoming all her family and picking Jan up to play with him, Bob endeared himself to them all.

Maisie whispered to me: "He looks super fit, I can see why you fell for him."

I smiled, we all ordered drinks and studied the menu. Bob sat Jan on his knee until the food arrived when Jan sat back in his buggy with a view of them all. After a full bottle of milk Jan was dozing off so I slipped the blanket around him and put the buggy in the reclining position. Dinner was lively with animated conversation and tasty food. The boys asked Bob so many questions, Martin had to restrain them so he could eat his meal. Bob promised to tell them everything during the week. It was a successful evening and we hugged when we departed declining to go on for drinks in a bar. After the journey and sunshine, Martin's family were tired and went back to bed.

Bob told me all the details of his exciting day, extolled the virtues of Martin and family, chatting virtually nonstop until we got back. He carried the buggy with Jan inside upstairs and gently lifted the baby into the cot without waking him. Afterwards he led me to the bedroom where silently he undressed me and showed me how he had missed me. We slept soundly from the wine until Jan woke us after 7 am.

"He's hungry," I murmured.

"My turn," Bob said getting up to prepare his bottle nestling the crying baby next to me so I could change him.

It was too early to go to the villa so we idled over breakfast, pushed the buggy around town while we picked up a few extra items, then had a coffee. Jan was smothered in sunscreen and wore a floppy hat. He looked very cute and had a sunshade over his buggy. Even at this early hour the place was getting busy. We separated in town as Bob had plans. Armed with a big bag of baby provisions I walked over to the villa after ringing to check the family was around. They decided to go exploring the town and amusements so I tagged along then sat watching while the family entered some entertainment sites. Afterwards we headed to the beach. I left them to take Jan somewhere quieter for lunch and a change before returning to the villa where we sat by the pool with Jan in the shade.

The adults discussed the economy with constantly rising prices back home, global warming, strikes, world crises and situations constantly changing. They sympathised with Ukraine and watched China circulate Taiwan. Immigrant housing and illegal crossings were another topic. They thought that living in a warm climate probably saved money on heating and food bills. Sometimes they discussed family, friends and neighbours with updates on activities. In Spain the pavements and areas were cleaned regularly, at home litter was a problem, waste dumping and even graffiti in some areas. The National Health service was also in crisis and it was difficult to get an appointment to see a doctor. I paid monthly in Spain so did not have a problem if I required assistance.

While it was warm we relaxed and lazed comfortably together. Eating healthy simple meals suited us. Bob joined in regularly and I was careful not to overstay my welcome. Everyone played with Jan who adored attention from the boys. The week passed too quickly and everybody felt sad when it was time to leave. I only had overnight to prepare for Sadie's family who were due the next day. Promising to return during the big summer break, everyone hugged and kissed Jan. Bob drove them to the airport using his van with the boys in the back. In the villa I stripped the beds and towels doing laundry while the cleaner came to do the floors and rooms. We worked well together making everything pristine. It had been a lovely visit all round.

Next day I waited at the villa again having stocked up at the supermarket. Jan was used to sitting in his chair watching the pool. As the flight had been delayed it was late afternoon when Sadie and family arrived. Once again there were hugs all round and introductions made to meet Jan. The baby was getting used to viewing strangers now and eyed Abby and Mark with interest. Abby was very taken by Jan and sat him on her lap. Sadie wanted to help me to prepare a meal with desserts. Bob had been doing some work so came after showering to join us. Mark and Bob were engrossed in conversation about football and sport while the children sorted themselves out and played with Jan.

Sadie and I were always close so we went around the shops together and left the men and boys planning a game of football, Abby took Jan for a walk with instructions to keep him shaded. During the week their arrangements were informal

THE LIFE OF ROSIE

with pool, beach, amusements, long walks to explore the area, picnics and family games. All arrangements were flexible and comfortable. We all caught up at dinner to go around the table talking about our activities. It flowed so smoothly that we were all caught unawares when it was time to leave. I had no plans to return to the UK, so felt emotional to part from them.

"When will I see you again?" I asked near to tears.

"In the summer holidays, don't worry grandma, we'll see you soon," Abby told her.

We hugged and waved from the taxi to the airport. Feeling emotional I went inside to have an alcoholic couple of drinks before stripping the beds and clearing up. The cleaner was booked for the next day but I did the laundry then sat with Jan near the pool waiting for Bob to come. It had been wonderful to see all my family again. How I loved my grandkids and was proud of my children's achievements. Everybody bonded well, my son and daughter in law were perfect partners. I felt sad to see them go. Life in England was expensive and tough these days. The weather was unreliable. By the time Bob arrived I was tipsy so he took care of Jan and decided to stay in the villa overnight. Next morning we left early eating breakfast out before the cleaner arrived. A new family was due later on.

"Shall we go home now back to Muranos?" Bob asked.

"Has Tony gone?"

"Yes they went two days ago."

"You didn't get to see him this time."

"I did they came up here one day to see me."

"Oh I should have joined you."

"No, I explained your family were here visiting so they understood."

"How are they all?"

"They look well and are still thinking of finding a place over here but perhaps making a permanent move."

"Can they do that?"

"Tony says he can work from anywhere."

"What about his family? The kids need school and doesn't his wife work?"

"I'm sure they can sort things out if they find a place."

"Wow it's been an eventful couple of weeks, I feel tired now."

"Yes, me too. It's been fun but I get your point about Muranos now, it will be good to get back to peace and quiet again."

"I suppose we need to shop again for provisions. Let's get the basics in and I will go to the supermarket tomorrow," I suggested.

Stopping en route to a popular cheap supermarket we stocked up before returning home where we found a bottle of wine on the table, a vase of flowers and some chocolates with a note from Tony wishing them well.

"How thoughtful," I said sniffing the flowers.

Jan demanded attention so I washed him, changed him then fed him before laying him on the floor to kick about. As he had slept during the journey, he needed activity to get tired again. He had a unit above his head full of dangling toys that he liked to mess with and watch. I noticed that the baby kept looking around probably wondering where all the people had gone. Bob played with him to make him tired. I heard gurgling and laughter from them both while I unpacked the shopping. Later all three of us went to bed at the same time feeling exhausted. In the morning I wondered where I was when I awoke just before Jan. Bob made some business calls then set off early.

Returning to the Centre with some sweets to distribute, I left Jan with the regulars while I helped in the kitchen. Later when I was approaching home pushing Jan, I noticed two women sitting on our balcony. My heart sank, I had hoped to get back to rest.

"Not again," I told Jan. "Why do people think they can just use our patio?"

Jan frowned in sympathy. Drawing closer I realised that one of the women looked like Emily but could not be sure from the back. The other lady was unfamiliar. Undecided whether to go home or sit for a while to see if they would leave, I sat down on a bench watching while Jan drank some water. The women remained immobile so sighing, I pushed Jan home going around the back to the patio. I stopped to face the women waiting for an explanation. Emily sat still looking at Jan in his buggy. Jan made moves to be picked up. The unknown lady stood up and bent over the buggy saying: "Hello gorgeous boy, you must be Jan. How handsome you are."

I picked Jan up and moved him away.

"Who are you?" I asked.

"Oh sorry, I am Bob's wife Larisa, Jan's grandma," she said introducing herself.

"I'm Rosie. You didn't tell us you were coming."

"It was a last minute thing, we're here to discuss the baby's future," Larisa said.

"In that case you need to wait until Bob returns. Can I get you a drink?"

I opened the house and poured cold drinks. Larisa asked for cold water. Bob was startled when I called him to tell him Larisa and Emily had arrived at the house. He swore saying he could not get there for another hour or so as he was at a critical point. I told him to come soonest and faced the prospect of having to deal with the two women on my own. Studying them on the patio with Jan, I felt huge, plain and very ordinary. Larisa was slim, groomed to perfection, glamorous and appeared sophisticated. Mahalia had been young, fit, slim and pretty. After a full morning at the Centre, I needed a shower and rest. Instead I prepared Jan's bottle.

"Oh let me give him that please," Larisa said holding out her hand.

Before I could reply, Larisa had lifted Jan out of his buggy and sat him on her knee. I hoped Jan had a wet nappy to spoil Larisa's outfit. Jan looked around for me but settled down with his bottle. Excusing myself to shower and change, I put on some makeup and a clean outfit. Reluctant to prepare an evening meal, I decided to wait until Bob came home. I did not know what plans the women had but would not ask them anything until he returned. Hoping they were not planning to stay with us, I felt anxious about losing Jan. Emily avoided eye contact and seemed content to watch her mother handle the baby. I was shocked to discover that Bob may still be married to Larisa having thought they divorced a long time ago. Larisa spoke to me when I emerged looking fresh and clean.

"I believe you saw Katie recently."

"That's right," I agreed.

"How is she?" Larisa asked.

"She looked good, very bubbly and positive. We got on well."

"Katie is a live wire, I'm glad she's ok. She's always travelling so I don't get to see her much but we keep in touch."

Emily stayed silent while Larisa held Jan and continued her conversation with me.

"Have you known Bob long?" she asked.

"Long enough to care for him."

"He's a good man, we met when we were both too young," Larisa said blithely.

I wished Bob would return as I felt uncertain about the situation. Using Jan as an excuse I took him from Larisa saying he needed changing deciding to bathe him at the same time. Larisa followed to watch so we both headed to the bathroom where I laid out his towel, clean nappy and sleep suit with baby lotion and wipes. Larisa seemed to be monitoring my activities. As I washed Jan on his bath chair, Larisa splashed water over him to make him chuckle. Larisa insisted on drying him and dressing him asking whether she needed to put any lotion on him. She brushed his hair with the soft baby brush and carried him lovingly back to the patio where she held him in her arms.

The implications seemed to be that Larisa had come to take over Jan's care. As a stranger, I had no connection to the boy but had come to love him so she felt deeply perturbed. I would not ask anything until Bob arrived tempting though it was. My impression was that Larisa had a new husband and perhaps family. If Emily had come back to take her son, I could not prevent it but the thought frightened me. There was an uneasy atmosphere as we all waited for Bob. When he finally arrived hot and sweaty, he went straight in the shower before greeting them. I took Jan off Larisa to put him to bed. The visitors waited for Bob on the patio. Deciding to leave them to talk privately, I remained in Jan's bedroom where I could hear the conversation through the open window.

Bob asked them why they had come unannounced.

"To take the baby back," Larisa replied.

"Back where?" Bob said sounding irritated.

"With us to England where he belongs," she replied.

"Says who?" Bob snapped.

"With his mother and family," Larissa replied calmly.

"I haven't seen Emily behave like a mother yet, she hasn't even held the baby," Bob said annoyed.

Emily remained silent.

"The baby will have better opportunities at home," Larisa continued.

"What do you mean?" he asked.

"Well for a start I can provide him with a good education and opportunities."

"For goodness sake Larisa, Jan is just a baby, he is years away from being educated."

"Well what can you give him out here in the wilds?" Larisa sounded annoyed.

"Love and attention, fresh air and a healthy climate."

"If you don't mind me saying, you and your partner are a bit long in the tooth to take on a young active child."

"And you are not? What is the age difference between us Larisa? Have you forgotten?" Bob sounded angry.

"Ah but you see I can hire help."

"So you think some stranger will care more for the child than his own flesh and blood?"

"I am his grandmother too."

"This baby is not a toy that you can play with when you feel like then hand over when he needs attention or it is inconvenient."

"You have no right to keep him."

"Nor do you so don't try to take him."

"Emily is his mother so she has every right."

"Emily has shown us that she couldn't wait to get him off her hands. I have no reason to believe that she has changed in that respect."

"She was scared as she had no experience with babies. I will teach her and help her."

"Don't make me laugh Larisa, you are too vain and self-centred to care for a baby."

"I brought our girls up remember, you were hardly around."

"Excuse me for making a living to support you in the style you wanted to be accustomed to. Katie turned out ok but Emily is a disappointment."

"Perhaps because you spoilt Emily more. She was your baby girl, you indulged her too much."

"What happened to you Emily?" asked Bob. "You had a good husband who loved you, a modern home, the perfect baby son. Why have you thrown it all away?"

Emily replied: "I felt trapped and imprisoned."

"Nobody forced you to do anything. Pieter is a decent bloke, he would make an ideal father and husband. That wasn't enough for you so you betrayed him and had an affair. Where is this sleaze ball who impregnated you? Is he still around?"

"That's over now," Larisa answered.

"I'm not speaking to you. Pieter wanted to raise Jan as his own so he would have forgiven you."

"I don't want Pieter or any contact," Emily sobbed.

"Well I don't want my grandson going to a callous, uncaring environment. Larisa you lead a superficial lifestyle and are more interested in appearances and whatever fad is in vogue. This boy will stay here for now until he is ready for educating then we will see. Before I hand him over to anyone else, I want to see motherly love and caring. Check him out now, he's growing well, healthy and content. We live a simple lifestyle here with a healthy diet. You can visit whenever you want but you are not taking him with you."

"We will see about that. I will get legal advice and I suggest you do the same. You will not win," Larisa threatened.

"This is not a battle Larisa, the future of this little boy lies in his welfare. We have witnesses to reflect the callous disregard shown by his mother. I can also bring most of the local population as witnesses to the care we bestow on him. Here he is loved and adored. You want to take him to a cold climate in foreign surroundings then abandon him to some stranger to look after him. How is that a good idea?"

"What if we take him and you can bring him over for holidays?" Larisa asked.

"If you want to see him the door is open here but don't try to take him."

"Emily has the right," Larisa said sulkily.

"She has forfeited that right. I have something in writing she left me with. So now get out of here. Only come back when you can behave decently to the baby who deserves so much better than your empty offer."

"Are you throwing us out?" Larisa asked sounding surprised.

"You came here uninvited, your presence is creating bad vibes so leave before I lose my temper."

"Where can we stay?"

"That's your problem, Rosie call them a taxi," Bob called.

"She's your latest fling then, a bit older than you are used to," sneered Larisa. "At least Mahalia was young and pretty."

"Mahalia is going to get married to her first love soon. You nasty bitch Larisa, Rosie is worth more than you a thousand times. How dare you criticize her. Now get out before I throw you both out."

Bob opened the front door and the two women stood outside with their bags waiting for the taxi. Slamming the door behind them, Bob stood in the hallway blazing with anger. I emerged from Jan's bedroom feeling safe that he would not be abducted and waited in the doorway in case they returned. The taxi arrived, so when we heard the car door slam, we both felt relieved and went to have a stiff drink.

"Do not let Jan out of your sight in case they try to kidnap him. Vary your routine and stay alert if you see any strangers," Bob advised her.

"You should also be cautious. Emily has the right to take him."

"No she doesn't, don't start me off. I will not allow this child to grow up under Larisa's influence."

"She is an attractive woman."

"It's all artificial, she looks a wreck without all her cosmetics."

"She's groomed and glamorous but seems a cold personality."

"You have no idea, she used me and pushed me to be successful, then when I was not available to fit in with her schemes and ambitions, she threw me over for somebody who was more affluent and biddable."

"How awful, I'm sorry, you must have suffered. At least Katie has turned out well."

"Katie was always independent and could amuse herself for hours. She was no bother. Emily was clingy and whingy so I tried to give her more attention."

"That obviously didn't help."

Bob sighed and poured another whisky.

Jan slept soundly throughout the night. I lowered his blind in case anyone tried to break in. When he awoke for his early morning feed around 6.30 am, I nurtured and cuddled him until he relaxed again in my warmth. Bob checked the security around the place before leaving. He also drove Jan and myself to the café to await the Centre truck to collect us when they picked up their order for the day. I had packed extra clothing, nappies and filled the baby bag in case I had to run away with Jan. At the Centre I entrusted a couple of local friends to maintain close contact with Jan while I assisted in the kitchen. When I explained briefly about the situation they kept Jan next to them vigilantly.

Bob said he would make enquiries about obtaining legal custody of Jan if I agreed.

"Do you think that would be possible?" I asked.

"We can try."

"Perhaps they will think we are too old."

"Larisa is hardly much younger."

"It's Emily who holds the key."

"Yes well I have never seen her handle the baby even once. I have a written statement handing him over plus witnesses to say she's has shown no interest."

"She could say she's changed her mind."

"Why should she when she obviously hasn't?"

"Why do they want to take Jan suddenly?"

"Perhaps it's suddenly cool in Larisa's group to be a grandparent."

"But who would look after him?" I asked anxiously.

"They would pay someone."

"That's terrible when he is happy here and thriving."

"Do you think we should get married?" Bob suddenly asked.

"What do you mean?" I asked startled.

"Well if we are married it shows stability."

"Is Larisa married?"

"Yes to her rich bloke."

"I think we are fine as we are. Are you suggesting a marriage of convenience?"

"No, but if they ask how long we have been together it's not that long."

"If Jan was not involved would you have proposed?"

"Probably not."

"Well then there's your answer. I know we are mature but that kind of proposal sucks. Before I would even consider it, you need to try much harder. Your idea of a proposal leaves much to be desired as my headmistress used to say," I said getting up and going to attend to Jan in a huff.

Nothing further was said during the week. On Friday night Bob asked me if I fancied a Chinese takeaway for a change. I agreed and thought no more about it. When I bathed Jan and put him to bed, Bob suggested we took a stroll along the beach in the moonlight and perhaps had a paddle.

"We can't leave the baby," I said worried.

Bob called their neighbour Denise who was nearby to ask if she could just babysit for a short while so he could take me for a moonlight paddle. Denise agreed and came to sit on the porch telling us to take our time. It was a lovely evening so we strolled off. Holding hands we walked to the sea then paddled along for a while. Bob held me tight and embraced me with a passionate kiss. Surprised I said I felt like a teenager again. Instead of letting go, Bob hugged me to him swaying sideways.

"Have you been drinking?" I asked him.

"Shush woman, I'm trying to be romantic."

We sat on the sand watching the waves turn silvery in the moonlight before strolling back to the house where Denise had gone inside. Bob led me along the road on the front of the house. I entered to check on Jan who was sleeping with his arms outstretched on either side of his head. Bob thanked Denise who departed. When I went into the living room I noticed the patio was brightly lit. As I entered I found it decorated with flowers, candles and banners with champagne on ice.

"What's all this?" I gasped.

Bob got down on one knee handing me a box and asked me to marry him. Overwhelmed with emotion I was unable to respond. Tears came to my eyes.

"Will you hurry up woman and say yes, my knees are killing me," Bob complained.

Tutting I nodded telling Bob not to spoil it. The ring fitted and I glowed with joy. At the meal were fortune cookies, mine was a marriage proposal. Bob's said happiness lay in the future. We ate mindlessly holding hands across the table then drank the champagne. Aimlessly wrapping up everything, we went to bed happy. When Jan woke them early morning, Bob got up to take charge of him.

"Last night was amazing, the most wonderful night of my life," I told him stretching.

"I wanted to take you somewhere romantic or for a meal but we have Jan so it was a bit tricky."

"It was perfect just the way it was, I loved it and had no idea you were planning it."

"You told me to try harder."

"Well you exceeded."

They kissed while Jan banged his spoon at them so they kissed him too, one on each cheek. The baby gurgled and laughed with pleasure.

"Let's have a happy family future," Bob said.

"Here, here," I agreed, "Somebody needs his nappy changing. Who is a stinky boy?"

Jan laughed happily while Bob told me it was my turn.

We discussed what type of wedding to have. Neither of us wanted any fuss so we decided to have a quiet civil marriage ceremony. While Bob sorted out the paperwork we decided to get married quietly then tell the family afterwards.

"They don't need to spend money on the fare and presents, let's just keep it simple," I suggested.

"We will need witnesses so I will get my partner Dennis to stand in for me. Who do you want?"

"We have to go back to the villa for the ceremony or somewhere there so I will see," I said.

"Jan can accompany us."

"It's a family affair."

"I've already made enquiries about custody for him during the service."

While we were making preparations for the simple ceremony, Pieter turned up to see us. He told Bob he was coming but didn't need meeting at the airport. On arrival he went straight to Jan to embrace him. Jan was propped up sitting in his buggy and slobbering. Pieter was enthralled by him and brought him toys. I invited Pieter to accompany us as a witness to our wedding while he was there. Pieter said he was honoured. At the wedding Pieter and Dennis, Bob's partner were the witnesses. I wore a simple chiffon dress bought from the market with pretty sandals, Bob wore a white short sleeved shirt and chinos. Baby Jan wore his best outfit. After the ceremony when Dennis threw confetti, we all went for a meal and a few beers.

As a wedding gift we spent the wedding night in a smart hotel down the coast in private seclusion. Pieter looked after Jan for us. After breakfast the next day we returned home back to the normal routine. Before we left we rang our respective children to advise them that the wedding had taken place. Explaining that we had not wanted any fuss. We had done it that way to save the families expense and time off work, we would celebrate next visit. Dennis had taken a few wedding photos which we sent on. Kate, Martin and Sadie were thrilled for us.

Emily ignored the phone call and text message. A few close friends sent congratulations and teased us. I replied: "What do you expect at my age?" They said Bob looked attractive and asked if he had any brothers.

Back home Pieter gave Bob a copy of Jan's birth certificate and various paperwork that Emily had left behind. They were now divorced although Pieter was upset he could not raise Jan. The birth certificate named Pieter as Jan's father but Emily said she would deny it. He also had to work full time to support himself. I told Pieter to enjoy Jan while he was staying and invited him to come over any time.

Bob explained that he was investigating potential custody for Jan. I explained that Larisa and Emily came to visit to try to take Jan away.

"Larisa would be a poor choice as she is not in a happy relationship," Pieter said.

"What do you mean?" I asked.

"Well her husband sees Larisa as an ornament to display. He is older than her and career driven. They argue and fight regularly. It is a marriage of convenience, but Larisa has to know her place so can't go too far. She dare not risk being cut off from her expensive allowance."

"She wanted to take Jan away saying she would teach Emily how to look after him," I told him.

"What would her husband reckon to Jan being with them?" Bob asked.

"Highly unlikely I imagine, he does not want any appendages or responsibilities," Pieter replied. "Has Emily shown any interest in Jan?"

"None whatsoever," Bob relied.

"I'm worried about Jan's care and safety if either of them obtain custody," I said.

"Will you be able to manage him long term?" Pieter asked.

"Yes, we can and will, I have to convince the authorities. Emily gave me a written statement handing him over to our care," Bob said.

"We will be older than the other parents but we have experience and love for the little boy. He will not be neglected or handed over to strangers," I remarked.

Pieter handled Jan lovingly and nursed him to sleep in his arms.

"If you can work from home over here, you are welcome to join us," Bob offered.

Pieter sighed and said he would see what he could do in the future. At this stage he resented Emily's behaviour and his only concern was Jan. He put Jan to sleep in his cot then went to drink beer with Bob. I left them together and took a shower plus caught up with the laundry and housework. Later Bob told me that Pieter would seek opportunities to find work over here in order to be near Jan who was legally registered as his son.

There had been no news from Larisa or Emily until Bob received a phone call from Larisa saying she wanted to open a bank account for Jan to make monthly payments for his upkeep and future. Bob gave her the name of his bank telling her to open a new account there. She also told him that Emily had applied to emigrate to Canada and was waiting to hear. As her passport would need to be renewed beforehand, Emily would not put Jan on the new one. This meant that Pieter could put Jan onto his passport in due course. If Pieter could stay in Spain then Jan would have a legally acceptable future there too. Bob had not heard back legally regarding custody so everything was open for now. Meanwhile Jan could sit and was moving his legs about.

Since Brexit UK nationals who plan to live in Spain for more than 3 months must register as a resident and on the Padrón at their town hall. For periods longer than 90 days, a long-stay visa and a residence permit is required. This means a person needs to become a resident to stay long-term in Spain. If someone is not keen on changing their nationality, they can apply for an "EU long-term residence permit" (permiso de residencia de larga duración) after 5 uninterrupted years in Spain or any EU state. As a non-EU citizen, a residence permit in Spain valid for 3 years can be obtained as long as the property purchased is valued at over €500,000.

In calculating the proof of income for non-lucrative residency, an annual income of 400% of IPREM is required. The IPREM for 2023 is €600 per month. Therefore, as an individual, a regular guaranteed monthly income of €2,400 is required, or a yearly income of €28,800. To apply for a Spanish visa some requirements such as a proof of sufficient financial funds, a clean criminal record, and an overall good health certificate are required. As a highly skilled worker, the European Blue Card, which is equivalent to the Green Card in the United States may be issued. All this information was compiled by Pieter as although he was Dutch, he was uncertain whether Emily's nationality would figure in the application so checked the British side too.

In Holland Pieter taught high school computer studies which would give him suitable hours for vacations and terms times. He made enquiries back home to rent his house and get back to Spain urgently to be with Jan. He returned during school end of term break and was pushing Jan in his buggy talking to him, when a young woman stopped him to ask where he was taking Rosie's child.

"Does she know you are out with him?" the woman asked him blocking his way.

"Of course, I am the boy's father," Pieter said startled.

"You are Jan's father? Where is his mother then?" she asked.

"We are divorced now so I can't say. Who are you?" Pieter asked.

"Oh, I'm Carla. It's just that we look out for each other around here so I had to make sure you were legit."

"Thank you for your concern, it's good to know my boy is in safe hands. I'm Pieter," he said shaking hands.

Jan gurgled at Carla who kissed his cheek and tickled his tummy. With formalities over Carla accompanied Pieter part of the way chatting. It seemed that Carla was a university lecturer on vacation visiting her parents in Muranos. Her mother was English and her father Spanish. Pieter explained his situation saying he was seeking employment to stay in Spain to raise Jan.

"How's your English? I mean you speak fluently but how about writing and reading?"

"I studied part of my degree in England, which is where I met my ex-wife, so I am ok."

"Why don't you apply to the International School then, they may need someone next term?"

"Really, where is it? Can you tell me the name and address?"

"I will find all the details and text them over to you. Give me your mobile number."

Carla and Pieter exchanged numbers then stood chatting for a while until Jan got restless. They parted so Pieter could feed and change Jan. Each felt pleased by the new connection. At home Pieter told me how pleased he was to find that the locals looked out for each other. I knew Carla and her family and said that they may prove helpful in finding some work for Pieter. When Pieter received the details he wrote a formal application. Carla told Pieter to call the headmistress directly. Apparently Carla knew the head well and had advised her to expect Pieter's call. He called immediately excusing himself for disturbing the head during her vacation. After a brief chat the head invited Pieter to visit her for an informal chat.

Flushed and groomed Pieter went to meet the head sitting in the shade in her impressive landscaped garden. Taking his Curriculum Vitae and paperwork in a folder, Pieter explained his previous experience, his desire to stay in Spain to raise his son and current situation. Although nothing was definite at this stage, the head felt there could be a potential vacancy nearer term when people planned their future. In turn, the head explained about the school policies and academic aspirations saying they catered for an international private clientele. It had a friendly ethos with many wealthy influential families sending their offspring there. Shaking hands before leaving the head with some paperwork, Pieter had enjoyed the meeting and thanked her for her time apologising for disturbing her vacation.

Carla called him to enquire how he fared. They arranged to meet to discuss the situation. Pieter wanted to treat Carla to a meal or drink to thank her for her help. I watched as a friendship began between the couple. Carla's parents were friendly people who were regulars at the café because it was local to their house. In Muranos the locals knew each other and met regularly. It was too soon to think about romance but I felt that Pieter would fare better with Carla if it happened. Bob told me not to interfere. While Pieter was in Spain he desperately searched for work and managed to help out at a pub for a few nights. All too soon Pieter had to go back. Each time he was heartbroken to leave Jan who slobbered all over him. Bob told Pieter not to sell his property until he was certain he could stay in Spain.

Pieter returned home to continue his enquiries. Carla managed to get him a temporary position at the International school. Depending upon his performance, results and flexibility to expand his role, Pieter had a chance of being hired permanently. It was a trial role. He left his Dutch employer offering to do part time work online if required. Initially, Pieter stayed with us, but as it was a long drive to work he looked for somewhere to stay locally. Carla found him somewhere and their friendship continued. Weekends and some evenings Pieter came to stay with Jan who seemed attached to him. Bob told me to encourage the relationship because he felt Pieter would take over Jan's care in the future.

"Why do you think that?" I asked.

"Emily made Pieter have a vasectomy so this is his only chance to raise a child."

"At present, he could marry again."

"Yes but he's not fertile unless he can get it reversed."

"Well let's see how his friendship fares with Carla. She's been helping him."

"She's a high earner too, career woman, so there would be two good incomes."

"We want what's best for Jan," I protested.

"Of course we do, but so far only Pieter has stepped forward to take action."

"Don't we count then?"

"Of course but at our age we are in the grandparent class," Bob told her.

"Speak for yourself, I'm still a young chicken," I snapped.

"In your dreams!" Bob told me walking off.

Life continued in a routine with Pieter becoming a regular visitor taking care of Jan who was approaching his first birthday. An active boy, Jan could crawl, sit and roll but had not mastered standing up yet. We decided to hold a birthday party for him at the café with the local bakery providing a special cake and some fancies. George said the café would provide the sandwiches and snacks as their birthday present. I invited the Centre who wanted to make their own separate birthday party. The art and crafts group all contributed presents and cards. Everyone adored Jan who smiled happily at them all however silly they behaved.

Katie flew over specially to embrace her nephew accompanied by her male boss.

"This is a first," Bob said.

"Do you think she is serious?" I asked.

"Let's wait and see, I think he is older than her."

"How much?"

"I'm not sure but let's play it low key. Katie doesn't tend to stick to boyfriends long."

Another surprise came with the arrival of Larisa who wanted to celebrate her grandson's first birthday. She hugged him fondly and played with him for a long time. Jan giggled, gurgled and slobbered delightedly. One of his presents was a walker frame with a seat so his little legs slotted in and away he ran all over the house. Everything had to be lifted off the floor away from little hands that put all his finds into his mouth. Pieter and Larisa were amiable. Carla came along too and Pieter introduced them. Later Larisa told Bob she approved of Carla who she thought would be more suitable for Pieter. When asked for news about Emily who was the only one not to acknowledge Jan's birthday, Larisa shrugged saying she thought Emily had emigrated to Canada by now.

"Doesn't she keep in touch with you?" I asked surprised.

"She has abandoned us all. I have no idea where she is," Larisa replied looking upset.

"Why Canada?" asked Bob.

"It's far away enough, they speak English and she saw a documentary about it. As far as I recall she liked the scenery. Maybe because Prince Harry started off there Emily thought it was the cool place to be. Who knows? That girl is very secretive."

"Does she have someone else there?" Pieter asked.

"I don't think she knows anyone there but I can't tell. Emily has always been beguiling so she will attract some poor man. She picked a good husband, then had an affair with a work colleague because of his intellect. Incidentally, he broke off with her when she became pregnant because he felt it wasn't fair to you Pieter," Larisa revealed.

"So he doesn't know?" Pieter asked shocked.

"Not a clue," Larisa answered. "Emily gets bored easily and has no patience to work things out. If she latches on to another man it will be because he offers her wealth or fame or something she values."

"Does she not think about the baby she left behind?" I asked.

"Probably not very often. Maybe one day when she matures she may develop a conscience. At present she is only self-centred and intends to cut all ties with her past. I think she wants to reinvent herself," Larisa said.

"Does she contact you?" Bob asked Katie.

"No, only on my birthday or rare occasions," she replied.

Katie had introduced her boss, Gerry, an amiable man mid-thirties, who hovered discreetly around the edges of the party to give them privacy. Nobody had mentioned him because the timing was wrong. Larisa asked Katie if she was dating him but received an enigmatic smile before they were interrupted. I offered him refreshments and exchanged a few comments with him. Being uncertain about his appearance, everyone was being circumspect whilst observing him from afar. Gerry knew he was under surveillance so tried to withstand the scrutiny politely. For the cake entry Katie joined Gerry and they sang happy birthday together. Jan was held by Pieter to blow the candle out oozing slobber juice but enjoyed his cake which adorned his face. He sat clapping hands.

Another party awaited the next morning at the centre with balloons, banners, toys and a welcoming crowd of regulars who made a big fuss of Jan, their favourite baby. Jan loved the attention babbling away in baby talk with excitement. He knew it was a special occasion and raced around the Centre on his walker. When he tired he sat on the floor and for the first time tried to pull himself up holding onto a chair but couldn't quite manage it. Everyone cheered so Jan felt pleased with his efforts but then rubbed his eyes so went in the buggy after eating then fell asleep. Everyone continued the party and enjoyed themselves while the star attendee dozed. It was a warm day. Katie took Gerry a walk around the area explaining about the Centre's work. Larisa and Bob also went for a walk while I worked in the kitchen preparing lunch.

Martin contacted me to say that my English house needed roof repairs. There were tenants living there who said a few other repairs would be needed too. When I told Bob, he suggested we went over to fix it.

"But someone's living in it now," I told him.

"Do you want to live there again?" Bob asked.

"No."

"So let's go over, I'll do it up then we can sell it for a good price," Bob suggested.

"Why should we sell it? We could never afford another one there."

"We still have my place and a terrace I rent out."

"I can't just throw the tenants out, they must have a contract."

"Tell them to move out while renovation work is carried out or ask if they want to buy it."

I rang Martin to ask the tenants whether they would be interested in buying the property. As I wanted to carry out renovation work there, Martin should ascertain whether they would move out. Bob offered them a stay in one of his properties in a different area. Martin enquired and they did not want to move because it was convenient for work. Apparently, they were renting for six months and had barely reached month four. If they refused to move Bob told Martin to inform them that work would be carried out while they lived there. It may resemble a building site he advised. The tenants said they would endure the work so Pieter took Jan to live with him, while we headed to London.

Before visiting my house I spent time with Bob visiting his places of interest and meeting his friends and family. We had a pleasant time with everyone welcoming me. By the time we went to find my house via Martin's, we had been entertained wherever we went. Martin had moved the children into one bedroom in order to offer us a room to stay. Bob visited the property using my key. The tenants were out at work but knew he would be visiting. While Bob inspected the premises, I walked around marvelling at how familiar everything was but also how alien it felt. I no longer felt a connection to it and would not miss it when it was sold. It had been a struggle living there raising the family alone with ever increasing prices and bills.

Bob made plans to extend and fit a new kitchen and bathroom, sort the roof, modernise the interior and estimated several weeks work. He waited behind to meet the tenants while measuring up and ordering materials for his work. One of his contractors Wes, lived in the vicinity so came over to discuss the project and agreed to work with Bob like in the old days. When the tenants came Bob discussed the scale of work. As the tenant was dismayed, Bob asked if he had somewhere he could stay. When his partner arrived they discussed the situation again. Bob asked whether they would consider taking cash for the duration of their existing contract or whether he could pay them rent for the interim. They both worked full time and said rents locally were beyond their means.

In the end Bob suggested they move into his terraced place in Middlesex which was in a good area. The male tenant could work from home while his partner would have to find something new. Bob offered a list of contacts who could help her find work. They asked about the rental cost there. To reassure them Bob drove them over and bought them a meal at his local where he introduced them to the pub manager. As they liked the area and the house suited their needs, it was a case of thinking about moving. Reluctant to put any pressure on them, Bob left them back at my place to consider their options. Wes ordered materials for the renovation which were delivered and stored. It added impetus to the tenants as they realised what was in store so they accepted Bob's offer but had to give notice at work.

I took Bob around to meet my friends, neighbours and remaining bits of family. All were surprised that I had married again and welcomed Bob into our group. The general consensus was that I had done well to nab a fit guy at my age. With much teasing and banter, Bob enjoyed the attention and had fun. Even the guys in the group got along with him. The women were jealous that I found a guy who could build and do all the works. Before work started Bob was invited to join the male outings. Once work got underway it reminded me of the show "Homes under the Hammer" as I watched my house get gutted. There was very little I wanted to keep apart from family photos and mementos. Telling Bob I did not want a grey interior which seemed to be in vogue, otherwise I gave them free reign. The house should be light, bright and spacious I told them.

Meanwhile I caught up with all my grandchildren. Martin and Sadie led busy lives, the children were growing up more independent with good social lives, so I helped when I could. The kids had homework assignments, social engagements, sports activities so regularly needed lifts. Their parents were rushing around trying to keep up with everything. When I made dinner or helped out in the house, they appreciated it. Midweek Bob and I hosted a family meal out. Whoever was available attended and they voted the menu for the following week. Anybody who was unable to attend was offered a takeaway or fish and chips. It gave them chance to catch up. One week Katie and Gerry turned up and were introduced to the family. They all bonded as Katie was always vivacious.

"They must be dating all this time," Bob remarked.

"Well he seems to be lasting the course so far," I replied.

"He's a lucky man, I hope he appreciates her."

"Of course he must, Katie is special."

Larisa heard they were in the UK so invited them over for a meal. As Katie had told them that Larisa's marriage was not happy, Bob excused them saying he had a deadline to meet so couldn't spare the time at present. She told him to make it over before he left. Apparently, Larisa did not work and enjoyed her high standard of living which made putting up with an unhappy marriage worthwhile. I could not have done that. Bob told me that I was fortunate to have such a wonderful husband so I did not have to. I smacked Bob and tutted. Our time in England seemed to fly by.

While Bob worked I shopped and explored the area to see what had changed. My clothes needed updating because the sun bleached them with frequent washing and the colours faded eventually. All the supermarkets carried inexpensive clothing ranges so I stocked up for all occasions. My underwear, beachwear and even sportswear were replenished. Finding opportunities for special occasion wear, I treated myself acquiring an extra suitcase. I also bought Bob new clothing despite his protests. Somebody suggested we both undergo a full medical check-up whilst here. There was a leaflet going round offering a full examination for a set amount. Deciding they would be overhauled before leaving, I booked us in.

In the evenings we regularly rang Pieter to check on Jan who was now living in Carla's place because it was more spacious and suitable. Apparently, Jan was contented and did not seem to be missing his grandparents. Carla adored Jan so was enjoying spoiling him whilst Pieter tried to maintain some discipline. Bob was amused and told me he had been right.

"What do you mean?" I asked.

"I told you Pieter and Carla would get together," Bob said smugly.

"Maybe but he's not got a permanent posting yet."

"Carla will fix it, she went to university with the head there."

"Let's hope he fares well then."

"We may have a wedding to go to eventually," Bob smiled.

"Will they take custody of our boy then?"

"Of course and we will be grandparents. By the way Mahalia had her second son recently, I forgot to tell you."

"How do you know?"

"I got a text and congratulated her."

"Should we send a present?"

"Already dealt with."

"Time whizzes by, my grandkids have grown so much, they all have long slim arms and legs now."

"They will fill out eventually like their grandma."

"Hey cheeky, watch it," I said rising to chase Bob.

When the house was completed it looked totally different contemporary and desirable. Everything was fresh and minimal with bifold doors leading to the garden. I wanted to live in it myself. It would fetch a good sale price or rental and already there were many enquiries of interest. All the neighbours admired it. The garden was landscaped with a patio at the back. Before it went on the market I wanted to stay in it briefly to check everything out. We had our medical scheduled so hired some rental furniture for a week. It was almost time to head back to Muranos. After we received our medical results, we would book a flight. Bob revisited his friends and contemporaries while I stayed local showing everyone my new look house. They were all envious that I had such a talented husband.

During the medical examination I went first with Bob being seen simultaneously by different personnel. Results would be given in a few days when everything had been checked thoroughly. As we ate healthily and enjoyed an outdoor active lifestyle we both expected to receive a clean bill of health. When I was called in again to repeat a couple of tests I asked whether I should be worried. They assured me that they were double checking the results to ensure accuracy. At my results consultation the doctor would go through everything with me. Bob was not called back. Martin and Sadie asked if I needed them to accompany me but I declined.

I was diagnosed with skin cancer which frightened me. As it was in its early stages it could be dealt with and hopefully cured. The doctor told me that at one time a cancer diagnosis was something close to a death sentence. That is less true these days. As our understanding of the wide variety of cancers grows, the spectrum of treatment options widens, so a cancer diagnosis is no longer regarded as a death sentence. There is now a great deal of realistic hope for a long and healthy prognosis. Skin cancer when treated early has a 99.9% five year relative survival rate. This is because while skin cancer is quite common, it is also very easy to remove surgically. Since it occurs on the surface of the skin, it is easy to detect. Early detection means early treatment, which means a high survivability rate. I was given literature to read and a choice of treatment to surgically remove it.

As the National Health Service was in disarray with strike actions and long waiting lists, I could not be treated immediately. Even if I chose to go privately, I would need to remain in the UK until I was cleared. This meant that I could not fly back to Spain. Bob needed to return because he had commitments with his partner and contracts. He offered to cancel but I insisted he went ahead saying Martin and Sadie would support me. Although I felt frightened and nervous, I said I would stay in my house with the rented furniture for the duration. If I needed any care, Sadie would take me. Bob was reluctant to depart before my surgery so he booked me in privately and postponed his departure.

THE LIFE OF ROSIE

It was decided that my treatment would be curettage and electrocautery which is a similar technique to surgical excision, but it's only suitable in cases where the cancer is quite small. The surgeon used a small spoon-shaped or circular blade to scrape off the cancer before cauterising the skin to remove any remaining cancer cells and seal the wound. Afterwards the procedure may need to be repeated 2 or 3 times to ensure the cancer is completely removed. Cream would be applied to the affected area for several weeks. I submitted myself to be treated trying to be brave even though I felt frightened. Trying to be a good patient was not easy. In future I vowed to wear sunscreen and wide hats outside. I usually wore sunglasses. Although I had not sunbathed profusely, being outdoors a great deal in the warm climate had caused my condition.

Warning my family to be cautious in warm climates was the beginning. My English friends rallied round to support and visit me. At home I felt lonely without Bob. I didn't want to remain longer than necessary but was not ready to sell the house in case it was needed again. Bob rang every day and I even spoke to Jan who was staying with Pieter. Everyone was waiting for me to return. I remained indoors most of the time feeling reluctant to go outside except for brief shopping trips locally. My confidence had shattered and I felt afraid that I must look scarred or ugly. Reassurances that I looked okay did not register and I even felt afraid to go back to Spain. Sadie accompanied me for medical appointments. I was not signed off completely for some time as I needed a follow up check-up.

By the time I was able to travel back to Spain I felt overwhelmed by the heat, lacked confidence to circulate and remained indoors or in the shade. At first I was uncertain whether Bob would still find me attractive but he showed me how much he cared. Everybody gave me space to adjust and welcomed me back when I appeared. I sought volunteer work to help people suffering from cancer or other ailments. It meant travelling to locations but I went weekly to assist in any way possible. My time at the Centre was reduced to one or two days, but I still painted in the crafts group which had moved further down the coast. Yoga also helped me to relax so I wore a headband to shade my face. Muranos suited me because of the tranquillity. Bob worked less but kept active and busy with hobbies. We suited each other because we harmonized when they were together.

Carla and Pieter were living together and raising Jan who was a happy toddler. He loved visiting his grandparents because we always spoilt him. Eventually, marriage was planned but they had to sort out paperwork regarding Pieter's status plus obtain a secure employment contract for him. Meanwhile Larisa kept sending monthly payments for Jan. Emily did not contact anyone. Katie phoned regularly and visited sporadically. She seemed to still be with her boss, Gerry but never mentioned whether it was serious. Bob liked Gerry but thought perhaps he was a bit too old for Katie. I thought that if Gerry made Katie happy, that was all that mattered. Telling Bob that after Mahalia, people had thought me too old for him. Bob just tutted and said I was a mature vintage. The community they lived in had grown slightly. Everybody looked out for each other and accepted special occasions or different beliefs. It was an ideal situation for me as I was gradually reverting to my former self in a more cautious way.

Life continued comfortably as Autumn moved in. The temperature was pleasant in Muranos. Back home all my grandchildren were now in high school. I felt proud of all their achievements and texted them regularly. Sadie was making some home improvements, Martin had built an extension to his house. The tourist season was slowing but not ending. Muranos was not on the usual tourist trail so visitors tended to find it accidentally after visiting the neighbouring market town. I did not tend to mingle with the tourists unless they needed assistance. My Spanish had improved marginally and I planned to take lessons when a new course started. Everybody expected English to be spoken so foreigners did not make enough effort to learn Spanish.

THE LIFE OF ROSIE

Pietro brought Jan over to see them regularly, a cute toddler who was enjoying nursery life, he had bonded well with Carla too. To all appearances they seemed to be a typical family when in fact there were no blood ties between them. They were trying to get their paperwork sorted so that Carla would be Jan's adopted mother. Larisa kept in touch but did not visit. There was no news about Emily. Mahalia sent photos of her two boys beaming with pride. Since my cancer scare I checked my diet and took vitamins. Bob went fishing and played cards in between work which he had slackened off. He was out more than in but found time to swim or go for walks with me. Instead of a pub drink we went to the café which was our social hub.

I imagined that life would continue along a steady path into old age. As a couple we had no frictions or arguments, Bob and I were comfortable together and did not try to control or interfere with each other's interests. Therefore when Bob collapsed and died unexpectedly with no previous health issues, I was devastated. He had been walking along the promenade with his fishing rod when he suddenly keeled over and collapsed onto the ground. It was several minutes before anyone noticed and went over to investigate. An ambulance was called but Bob was pronounced dead on arrival. Somebody was sent to the Centre to inform me. The whole community were shocked and distressed. For a long time I felt numb and could not absorb the information.

Martin flew over to arrange the funeral and take care of me. Food arrived, my washing was done plus shopping appeared. I did not eat or move much. Everyone tried to help me. Even Larisa offered to go over to stay with me. Sadie came for the funeral which passed me by in a daze. Bob had left a will leaving the bulk of his estate to me with adequate financial support to Katie and something for Emily on the proviso she got her act together and re-joined the human race. It would certainly cause some controversy should Emily appear again to claim her inheritance.

THE LIFE OF ROSIE

When Martin and Sadie had to return home, Katie stayed for a while with me. We did not talk much and Katie took me out for walks, made sure I ate something. Life for me seemed frozen with disbelief and sorrow. There seemed only emptiness. I had no interest in moving forward or taking care of my appearance. Tony offered his support and sent his wife to stay with me when Katie had to leave. When I understood that everyone was afraid I would commit suicide if left alone, I told them all that I would slowly come to terms with the situation and they should let me get on with it. After thanking them all for their support, I asked to be left alone to learn to cope.

Little Jan broke through my despair. Instinctively, Jan climbed upon my knee and threw his arms around me, burrowing into my chest. He remained still and quiet with me for some time until we both dozed. When Carla went to check on Jan, she found us both sleeping harmoniously in a deep cuddle. Afterwards when we awoke we drank and had cake. It was the first time I had looked like myself. Somehow Jan had broken my stupor. I asked Carla why we couldn't have lived happily ever after like in the stories. Carla said life was a journey on a learning curve. Sometimes you went up on the winning side but often there were bumps along the way and you fell down.

"But Bob was not old, he kept fit and active," I protested.

"It was a quick way to go, he was not diagnosed with a blood clot," Carla said.

"He never went for medical attention except during the pandemic for vaccines."

"At least he did not suffer from old age and decay."

"Yes, but he should have enjoyed more years."
"We don't decide when the end comes so we have to make the most of every day."

"I don't know what to do without him," I sighed.

"He wouldn't want you to give up."

"I know but I seem to have lost myself along with him," I said crying.

"Perhaps you just need to take small steps at a time. Take walks, read, make sure you eat. When you feel up to it you may want to help others who are also suffering distress or traumas. Some people are housebound due to physical complaints, perhaps they would appreciate some company or assistance. Try simple ways to get through your days. Instead of mourning constantly, look around and try to help others get through their journeys. By giving you will surely get back the strength to continue."

After Carla left I reflected on her words and tried to summon up the energy and enthusiasm to think about my future. I received sympathy cards from all Bob's friends and neighbours back at the villa who were shocked. Bob's former partner Dennis now took over the whole business and offered me his assistance at any time. I told him to inherit Bob's tools and equipment if he wanted them as I could not use them. He suggested I kept them in reserve saying he would take them if he needed them. I now had Bob's property plus my family villa in a popular tourist area but had no desire to return there. Muranos was suitable to hide in. All through the winter I kept a low profile. My family and friends rang regularly to check I was managing.

Every day I missed Bob and imagined his invisible presence in the house. Sometimes I dreamt he was still around. Once he wagged his finger at me indicating that I should get out. I no longer dyed my hair and ate sparingly, so I aged. Looking at my reflection in the mirror I saw an old lady looking back at me. As Spring approached and Jan's birthday, I went to the hairdresser for a makeover. I also bought some new outfits as my old clothes were too big and faded from continual washing.

THE LIFE OF ROSIE

Buying lots of fruit, salads and vegetables, I tried to eat healthy and drink plenty of water. In time I looked almost a shadow of my former self before deciding belatedly to take Carla's advice. There would be people worse off than me so I decided to find them and offer my assistance. It was the only way forward that I could make.

The end

Printed in Great Britain
by Amazon